Nicotine

Also by Nell Zink

The Wallcreeper

Mislaid

Private Novelist

Nicotine

NELL ZINK

4th ESTATE • *London*

4th Estate
An imprint of HarperCollins*Publishers*
1 London Bridge Street
London SE1 9GF
www.4thEstate.co.uk

First published in Great Britain in 2016 by 4th Estate

First published in the United States by Ecco,
an imprint of HarperCollins*Publishers*, in 2016

1

A catalogue record for this book is
available from the British Library

ISBN 978-0-00-817917-5 (hardback)
ISBN 978-0-00-817919-9 (trade paperback)

Designed by Shannon Nicole Plunkett

Printed and bound in Great Britain by
Clays Ltd, St Ives plc

Nicotine

A thirteen-year-old girl stands in a landscape made almost entirely of garbage, screaming at a common domestic sow. The skyline of the port city of Cartagena, Colombia, stands overcast in the background, shrouded in cloud that melts to the Pacific.

The sow shakes its jowls. Instead of entering its pen made of tamarisk boughs, it turns to face the girl. She swats it on the nose with a metal bar. The sow squeals, a glottal shriek. A second, larger sow approaches, gnashing its yellow fangs with loud clicks as it snuffles over the surface of the trash. It raises its head to look at the girl, who urinates where she stands. She doubles over and screams. The pee washes stripes in the dark grime on her legs.

A middle-aged American in a white shirt and khaki pants, carrying binoculars on a strap around his neck, rounds a pile of empty detergent bottles. He takes a heavy branch from the fence. He drives both sows into the pen while the girl lopes away. He calls after her, "*¡Momento, momento! Quédate, maja. ¿Cómo te llamas?*" He walks toward her.

"*Amalia,*" the girl says.

"*Ven conmigo. Te doy de comer,*" the man says, holding out his hand.

She drops the metal bar and follows him as if she had nothing to her name in the world except this one stiff, coarse, bloodstained smock. And in fact she owns absolutely nothing but that one formerly white smock, and she never returns to the dump.

TWO DECADES LATER, TWO HOURS into the year 2005.

A cigarette fights intense humidity in utter darkness. Its dim firefly of tobacco flies upward and brightens with an intake of breath. It falls and comes close to dying.

The invisible smoker lounges naked on a heap of animal skins. She is twelve, brown-skinned, black-eyed, with long, dense dark hair. Her hairline is very low, hardly more than an inch from her eyebrows, and her nose hooks like the numeral six. Her legs are short, her waist thick, her breasts small and high.

Five tall, pale men silently walk a narrow trail broken through week-old snow. They wear mukluks and nothing else. Behind them, the steam of a burning Christmas tree rises from the chimney of a house. A two-story farmhouse, red paint peeling off clapboard, hunkering below the cliffs of the Palisades just south of Nyack, New York. The night is moonlit but overcast.

The first man in line carries a kerosene torch in a bamboo holder. He is seventy-one, the oldest person present, with white hair and a white beard. The torch trails a greasy plume of black smoke. He holds it so as to spare the others, and the wind carries the smoke away. The men's boots scrape on the snow, a regular noise like caterpillars eating leaves.

The group approaches a dark mound—a sweat lodge on a wooden platform, a simple hut, built of willow and covered with deerskins.

The white-haired man plants his torch in the snow. It illuminates a blue one-piece ski suit and furry mukluks at waist level a few feet away, lying on the crust of ice on top of the snow. Frowning, he raises a flap. The smoker extinguishes her cigarette on the rim of a three-legged iron cauldron and drops it inside, between two hot stones.

"Is that the koala?" a younger man says, peering into the lodge. He looks very much like the old man, tall and trim and muscular, with the same full beard, his hair still black.

The old man, father to him and the girl, yanks four deerskins off the willow frame, exposing a quarter of it, and says, "I'm disappointed in you, Penny."

"Stop it!" she says. "You're making me cold!"

"You should be in bed."

"I couldn't sleep. You won't let me smoke in the house, and it's freezing out."

He turns to the group. "I'm really sorry, everybody. Now I have to air out the lodge, and it's going to take time to get back up to temperature. Maybe an hour?" He speaks to the girl again. "Get your butt in the house," he says. "Now."

Penny slithers out over the ice to grab her ski suit, puts it on, and zips it up. She wriggles into her mukluks, brushing powdered snow off the furry shafts. She runs back down the slope a hundred yards to the house. Four men follow her: her two half-brothers and two of her father's friends. There is light in the downstairs windows. Some of the others are still awake, talking in the kitchen.

From the front door she goes straight upstairs to bed, stripping off her ski suit by the dim glow of a night-light. She lies down under a narrow polyester comforter. The flannel sheets are a faded dark red. She turns to face the wall and lies still for ten minutes.

She sits up, too unsettled to sleep. She thinks of going downstairs to ask for some water from her mother. Naked and barefoot, she ventures into the hall.

Through a bedroom door at the head of the stairs she hears a couple having sex. She opens the door and flips on the light switch. She sees the dark-haired man—her half-brother Matt—still naked, collapsed on his girlfriend, and says, "What happened to fasting before sweat lodge? No food, no sex, no alcohol."

Matt says to his girlfriend, "I swear to you, I'm going to kill that fucking brat."

"I swear I'll kill that fucking brat," Penny singsongs, mocking him.

He withdraws and steps off the bed. He lunges at his much younger half-sister.

He is right to assume she is inured to nudity. But his penis at that moment is like nothing she has ever seen. His anger, likewise. She senses a connection between the two, something exclusive to him that is not good or pleasant. She loses her sense of precociousness. She is still clutching the doorknob when he picks her up under one arm. He carries her back to her room while she kicks at his legs. He throws back the covers and drops her into bed.

A silent tussle follows, typical for siblings, but not quite right. More like a father tickling his child, but still not right: a naked man in his midthirties using force to hold an adolescent down in bed. She raises her foot to kick him in the stomach and accidentally brushes his penis with her calf. She shrieks in the shrill, spontaneous monotone of a child ten years younger, so close to Matt that it reverberates in his ears like tinnitus.

Reflexively placing one hand over her mouth and nose, he says, "For Christ's sake." She makes a fist and punches him in the chest. For him, the sensation is that of being struck by an errant ping-pong ball. Then he becomes aware that his penis, still tacky from sex, is tugging on the skin of her thigh, stuck to it. He releases her, with a certain dramatic self-awareness, both his arms flying upward, as though a latch had been sprung.

He stands. She turns over to face downward and sobs, contracting and expanding her body in an inchworm-like way that reminds him of laughter or orgasm. He covers her with the sheet and comforter and says, "Come on now, be quiet, you crazy kid. Calm down."

As he steps into the hall and closes the door he sees her mother, Amalia, rounding the corner from the stairwell. "Hey, Matt!" she says. "What happened?" She is brown and sturdy, three years younger than her stepson.

"Penny had a nightmare that made her scream. She scared the shit out of us. She's all right. Good night." He returns to his girlfriend, closing the door.

Penny's face is flushed. Her eyes are red; her cheeks, streaked with tears. "Did you have a bad dream?" Amalia asks, sitting beside her.

"Matt tried to rape me," she says, flipping over and sitting up into the light to display her tearstained face.

"Oh my god. That is a bad dream! You scared everybody in the whole house!"

Penny shakes her head and falls back on the pillows. Amalia kisses her cheek, buries her face in her daughter's thick hair, and wrinkles her nose. "What's that smell? You smoke cigarettes? Be honest."

"Yeah."

"Why you steal my cigarettes? Why don't you ask me?"

Penny is silent. Somewhere inside her head, where logic matters, she rebels against the absurdity of asking permission to do something forbidden. Outwardly, in her face and eyes, she shows only remorse.

WHEN AMALIA IS GONE, PENNY rises and puts on her ski suit. She sneaks out the front door and walks uphill through the snow to the barbecue pit where the old man, now dressed in blue coveralls with a Peruvian-style ski cap on his head, is reheating the stones for the sweat lodge.

"Daddy," she says.

"Come here, baby. I'm sorry I got so PO'd." He tries to put his arm around her. She shrinks away. He tries to look at her face. She hides it. "Tell me. What's wrong?"

"Matt tried to rape me."

"And? Did he succeed?"

"No."

"Well, then obviously he didn't try."

"Daddy!"

"Imagine you're trying to cut a baby mouse in half with scissors. Come on. Visualize."

She sniffles, visualizing, and says, "No way."

"That's right. Something stops you. If you ever got as far as trying, that mouse would be in two pieces. And that's how I know Matt didn't try anything. Now turn off your little narrative self-righteousness machine and tell me what happened."

"Matt dragged me in my room—"

"Where was Naomi through all this? Go back to the beginning. I want this blow by blow. I want to hear the details that don't matter, as if you were describing a dream that didn't make any sense."

Penny nods. "Okay. Naomi and Matt were in their room making a lot of noise, so I opened the door to ask them to be quiet—"

He throws his head back and laughs.

"What's funny?"

"You didn't ask them through the door? You know sex is a private thing, and you know it's polite to make noises while you're having sex. At least you ought to know it at your age, and I think you do know it. I think you opened that door because you wanted to piss them off."

"That doesn't give him the right—"

"To do what? What did he do?"

"Okay, he got mad and put me to bed, but it was weird."

"Now you're playing dumb, pretending to be a little kid. It's my fault for not treating you like an adult after you smoked up my sweat lodge. And Matt's fault, too, for not treating you like an adult after you stopped him making love to Naomi. Do you seriously believe it wasn't just as strange for him?"

Penny is silent, embarrassed. She turns away to kick at a concave bank of melting snow, stained orange by the reeking kerosene torch.

"You can't have it both ways. You're not a kid anymore, and nobody should treat you that way. Not even yourself. We are equals here. You take responsibility and apologize, and I'll talk to Matt. Deal?"

"I hate Naomi," Penny says, looking at her boots.

"It's not our job to like her," Norm says. "It's Matt who needs to love, honor, and respect her. We are all individuals."

"What don't you like about her?"

"Let's see," he says, pushing a rock deeper into the embers with a length of kindling. "She wants like hell to marry my senior son."

"What's wrong with that?"

"She is constantly bowing and scraping to please him, and she sucks up to me and your mother. She's a bore. She's going to lose him. Now, I'm Jewish enough to wish he would settle down already with some nice girl and give me some grandchildren. Wouldn't that be nice? Little nephews and nieces everywhere?"

"Babies are cute," Penny says.

"Now, if there's one thing I hope you figure out in life, it's how to learn from other people's mistakes instead of having to make them all yourself. Right now you have a chance to learn from Naomi. There's no point in loving people, if it makes you act phony. Because then you can't even say 'I love you'!"

"She says it all the time."

"She says 'love' and 'you' all right, but where's the 'I'? It's gone! Missing in action!"

Penny picks up a stick of her own and pokes the embers to make them glow. She smiles at her father and he smiles back.

"I," he says firmly, hugging himself with his hands on his upper arms. "Love," he adds, standing tall, spreading his arms high, looking at the sky. "You!" he concludes, leaning down to hug her close. He sways. Revolving, they trample the snow.

"Now me," Penny says, and imitates the ritual, swaying so hard her father loses his balance and almost stumbles into the fire.

"And so to bed," he says. "Next chance I get, I'll tell Matt you're a grown-up with all the attendant dignities and he can't push you around for any reason, no matter how much you act like a jerk. From now on, he negotiates. Deal?"

"Deal," Penny says.

MATT, IN A CRUMMY MOOD, trudges up to the sweat lodge to keep his annual ritual sweating appointment. It is nearly 4:00 A.M., and he would rather be asleep.

His father confronts him. "Did you lay hands on Penny?"

It is a striking picture. Lit by dim orange flames a little way off, the two men resemble two antagonistic big cats—one young and naked, an image of power; the other now sweet-looking, in thickly insulated coveralls and a goofy hat.

Matt rolls his eyes. "News travels fast," he says, taking off his mukluks. "And no, I did not touch her. I was a little antsy coming off some cocaine and she barges in our room, okay."

"You will not touch her. She's twelve years old, and she's my daughter."

"Jesus, Norm. Shut up." Matt dives into the lodge. He arranges a few sheepskins in a row and lies down heavily.

Norm strips to join him. "When are you going to marry Naomi?" he asks as he crawls through the entry. Reaching a wolf pelt, he rolls over and sits upright.

"That girl loves me blindly, like a dog. She doesn't even know me."

"Nobody ever really knows anybody, but some women would make excellent mothers."

"I don't need a mother. Give me some steam. I'm cold."

Norm dribbles water from a ladle over the stones in the cauldron. "Talk to me," he says. "Tell me why you won't start a family."

"Because I'm happy," Matt says. "I have a fulfilling career, and I'm financially and emotionally independent."

"I think you miss out, not having a community of any kind."

"And I think you miss out, depending on community for your sense of self. Those clients, man. You're out there milking the most vulnerable people in the world, so don't tell me it's your community."

Norm says softly, "I help heal souls when bodies can no longer be healed."

"When they won't be needing the money anyway. I'm not here to take life lessons from you. I have my own life. I make an honest living, and I'm proud of what I do."

"Design garbage trucks."

"Designing prototype mobile waste compactors that are changing people's lives. While you're telling them life is fine the way it is—that it's fine they're dying, because they rode the cosmic snake. Teaching them resignation. You know why I don't need a community? Because garbage trucks are necessary. I don't have to sell anybody on garbage trucks. And don't tell me your drug dealing paid for my education. I could pay off anybody's student loans ten times over with what I've made with creativity and working my ass off. So don't tell me I design garbage trucks. I am literally saving people's lives, increasing landfill capacity so we don't have to burn that shit and fill the air with dioxins until everybody gets terminal cancer and has to come to you for a trip to Brazil and ride the cosmic snake. Or would you rather we dump that shit in the ocean?"

Norm dribbles more water over the stones, and visibility in the tent drops to near zero. The steam hides his look of profound distress. Matt, stretched flat on his back, suddenly snores. He is sleeping.

The other men—including Norm's younger son, Patrick—return as well and take places on the furs around Matt, careful not to wake him. They sit cross-legged, and Norm leads them on a spirit journey.

APRIL 2016. ELEVEN MORE YEARS have passed.

A hospital towers above a river that flows through a large city in northern New Jersey. Its facade is white, with long, curving ribbons of blue reflective glass. The architecture echoes the forms of the river below, but not its colors, which are pale green with black banks.

Penny sits in an armchair upholstered in black plastic, surrounded by dull beige walls. She wears red ballerinas, shiny black leggings, and a white cotton sweater that is falling off her left shoulder. No makeup at all, but clear skin and thick, dark lashes. Her bra strap is showing, a half-inch strip of black satin. Her hair hangs to her elbows. Sometimes she looks out over the river. The arms of the chair creak when she shifts her weight.

She reads aloud to her father, who sits propped up in a hospital bed. Hardwood veneer clothes his headboard in a warm color like champagne. Steel spigots, labeled OXYGEN and SUCTION, are set neatly into recesses in the wood. The book is Norman O. Brown's *Life Against Death*.

He laughs at a turn of phrase in the book. He coughs. Blood begins to flow from his mouth.

Still holding the book, she runs out of the room. She stands outside the door, looking both ways. There are many people in the hallway, but she doesn't know who is responsible. "Help!" she says.

A nurse abandons her cart stacked with medication in paper cups. Another nurse abandons her desk behind a counter. They run past Penny and into the room.

While Penny walks unsteadily to a waiting area with potted plants, the nurses place a dark blue towel under her father's chin. The bright, glassy blood turns his beard pink and the towel almost black.

He coughs, his mouth full of blood, and says, "No. No."

"Tell us what we should do, Mr. Baker," a nurse says. "Remember your advance directive. A transfusion now would set you back two weeks."

He shakes his head and croaks, "I don't want to die."

The nurses stand upright, touching the bed rails. "Whole blood and platelets," the first nurse says. The other nurse rushes out the door.

Blood runs from his mouth. He breathes noisily through his nose. The color of his face changes from beige to gray. He inclines his head to the left to let blood flow to the pillow, breathing with great effort. His hands, hidden under blood-soaked blue towels, never move. His bare arms are spotted with subcutaneous pools of purple.

He has some kind of acquired hemophilia, and his bone marrow is not keeping up.

Penny, light-headed, sits on a sofa in the waiting area. She calls her mother and says fearfully, "Dad's going to die."

"Bring him home," Amalia says firmly. "Let him die here at home."

A SOCIAL WORKER ON THE hospital staff, a handsome, curly-haired woman in a navy blue blouse, invites Penny into her office. "You look exhausted," she tells her.

"It's been busy," Penny says. She pulls her legs up under her on the sofa, discarding her shoes askew on the floor. The pose makes her body seem child-size. Her hair shades her eyes and covers her bare shoulder.

She does not see herself as adequate to the task at hand. She knows dying is natural and universal and that anyone can do it.

That everyone *will* do it. Not a challenge, but child's play. Having subtracted her doubts and fears, she is left with nothing. Her gaze is empty as a pigeon's.

"From here on out we're going to hospice care," the social worker says. "No more interventions. We keep him comfortable. He'll have another event like he did this morning, and bleed out. It's a gentle way to go. Most likely he'll bleed from the rectum in his sleep."

"We already talked about it."

"His wife told me she wants to care for him at home. Is she your mother?"

"Yeah."

"Does she work?"

"She's an HR manager at an investment bank in the city. I'm between assignments, so I'm completely free."

"You have any siblings?"

"I have two brothers. One lives on this South Pacific island. But the other one is in Fort Lee, and he's his own boss, so he can swing by Morristown during the day to help me out. Then Mom will be there at night."

The social worker touches her on the knee. "You want to take responsibility. You're a good daughter. But my task here is to make a judgment call. You say your mother is a professional and your brother in Fort Lee has his own company. Those sound like busy people to me. Your father needs attention and care twenty-four seven, and you need to get your rest. If he starts bleeding, he's going to need somebody with steady hands to administer a sedative. Of course it could be a professional. Would that be an option for you, financially?"

"I would need to ask Dad. I can ask Mom when she gets out of her meeting."

"Okay," the social worker says. "From the way this sounds, given your father's condition, I'm going to work on a referral to inpatient hospice."

"But what about taking him home?"

"If you can line up the caregivers. But for now, to be on the safe side, I'm going to knock on some residential hospice doors. What religion is he?"

"Shamanist."

"I mean the one he was baptized in."

"Jewish."

"Hmm," the social worker says. "They have a long waiting list."

ANOTHER DAY PASSES.

"I want to die with my boots on, like Ambrose Bierce," Norm tells Penny, his voice thin and dry. He is still lying in the same position in the same hospital bed. His hands, also in the same positions, are now adorned with tiny translucent pipes and green plastic valves. His hair, beard, and the sheets are all the same shade of white. His eyes are gray flecked with red.

"He went to Mexico to join Pancho Villa, and you can't even sit up," she says, standing at the foot of the bed. She reaches down and strokes his pink left foot. Friction with bedding has made the outer skin peel away. His toenails are striated, thick and brown as hooves.

"I waited too long," he says.

"You were bleeding out the day before yesterday, and you made them give you a transfusion," she reminds him. "Maybe if I stayed put, and held your hand, you could do it?"

She feels how sharp her tone is. She wants to be gentle. She wants to feel close to him. But she is trapped in an emotional paradox: his condition means they have nothing in common. Every time they speak of his dying, they become more alien to one another.

"I need to say good-bye to Matt and Patrick. That's what's stopping me. Have you talked to either of them?"

"I know Mom did," she says. "I follow them on social media. That's how I know they're alive." (The intrusiveness of ringing phones is something only older people arrogate to themselves. The younger generation is more considerate. Norm knows this. It's why he doesn't call Matt or Patrick.) "I could set up your phone to read their feeds aloud, if you want."

"No thanks," he says. "But get them to come see me in the hospice, okay?"

"Mom wants you to come home. She wants to do home hospice."

He shakes his head. "I saw what it did to you when I started bleeding out. I don't want you anywhere near me when it all goes down."

His reference to her fear makes her afraid. The strength and courage they desire—and lack, both of them—are the strength and courage never to see each other again. Fear is something they have in common. The fear breaks the emotional paradox. Her soft heart floods briefly with love, and she says, "Dad."

"Go home. I need to rest up. They're going to move me soon. But first give me a sip of water."

She picks up a plastic cup full of ice cubes and holds the straw to his lips. He says, "Ugh. I'm nauseated," and she puts it back down. He closes his eyes and his face goes slack. The dark color of his eyelids, matching the purplish circles under his eyes, makes them seem to recede, like eyes on stalks being retracted into a shell.

She thinks for a moment that he looks already dead that way. She anticipates that when he dies, all her shaky bravado will crumble. She will let out her suppressed love in a fury of crying, and everyone around her, even strangers, will understand and respect her desolation. She envisions herself a mourner in a long line of out-of-control female mourners, going back to the Greek tragedies.

"I'm heading out, Dad," she says.

He opens his eyes again and says, "Wait. There's a favor I want to ask you for tomorrow."

"Sure."

"I want you to bring my laptop from home. There's some dictation software on there that I never use. Maybe I can get it trained and dictate some things. My confessions."

"I would love that," she says brightly. "I have so many questions, especially about before I was born. Stuff like Matt and Patrick's mom. I know everything there is to know about your Philip Roth childhood and Mom's crazy-ass village, but I don't even know her name!"

"What I need is a time capsule. There's so much I want to tell you. But when you're an old lady. After the others are gone, like in that poem—'When you are old and gray and full of sleep, and nodding by the fire, take down this book—' "

Penny's throat constricts.

"You'll be all that's left. You and your children. You're twenty years younger than the boys and your mother, and you're going to live for seventy years after I die. The eggs of your children are already right there, inside of you. I can almost see them. It's like knowing my own descendants who can see into the future. I'll never be prouder of anything than I am of you. I was so lucky to get you."

Penny stands there with tears in her eyes, too upset to speak.

"Hey!" Norm says. "Don't cry, koala girl. Everybody dies."

Her voice is an elfin squeak. "I love you so much, Dad."

NORM GROANS AS A GIGANTIC ambulance driver and his slightly smaller assistant move him from a high, heavy gurney into his new bed at the Anglican hospice in North Bergen.

The room is spacious. It has an upholstered bench where family members can sleep, two armchairs, and four straight-backed chairs around a big table. The morning sun comes drilling through the windows bright as an atom bomb. The bed is wide, of heavy construction, like something manufactured to the highest specifications. The vase on the table holds a bouquet of birds-of-paradise—green, orange, and blue. The card from Amalia says, "Love you, darling!"

After the emergency medical technicians leave, Penny sits down in one of the armchairs. She sets the laptop case at her feet with her bag. At Norm's request she lowers the blinds. Sitting in an armchair facing him, she plays with the controls for the bed, resting her feet on it and letting the bed pull her into a slump.

He smiles and says, "Leave it like this for a while. I like this position."

"How are you doing?"

"Not perfect. I have this god-awful crick in my neck. Maybe it was the ambulance ride. I felt like I was going to get bounced right out of that thing." He moves his head from side to side and sighs.

She offers to do acupressure. She positions her hands and finds a certain spot between two cervical vertebrae.

"That's the spot," he says.

Three minutes later, he says it's not helping. When she releases her hold, she is dismayed to see that the pressure has caused a dark bruise. She asks, "You want to do the dictation software thing?"

"Not right now. I had a busy morning. You could read to me a little. Maybe I'll fall asleep, and then I'll see you tomorrow when I'm awake. Don't forget to take the laptop when you go."

"Nobody's going to steal it."

"What makes you think that? You see any expensive equipment in this place?"

"There's towels and a pillow," she says after opening a few closet doors. "Want a pillow?"

"Sure, I'll take it."

She folds the pillow and arranges it artfully to support his head. "How's that?"

"It's helping," he says. "I guess it's just muscle strain."

Over the course of the next hour, she leaves, taking the laptop, and he moves his head. The pillow falls down.

He sleeps through the fall of the pillow. He wakes up with a terrible crick in his neck.

EARLY EVENING. A FIFTYISH, BLOND-HAIRED woman in a blue lab coat knocks twice on Norm's open door and enters his room. He is wide awake, staring at the blank TV screen.

She introduces herself as the deputy director of the hospice. She says that there are important decisions to be made about his care. Of course family members can be involved, but they aren't indispensable.

Norm says he feels qualified to decide on his own. She produces a form on bright green paper. She runs down a long list of ways he might procrastinate, from defibrillation to antibiotics, all of which he rejects. She shows him where to sign, and he inscribes legible initials.

She concludes by asking—somewhat unexpectedly, in his view—"And what do *you* want?"

"After all that? I want for it to be 1951, and for you to be a root beer float."

"It's a serious question. Think carefully."

"How about 1968 and a smack overdose? I just don't want to be an old man dying in a hospice. But I guess that's what I'm stuck with."

The doctor is silent. She blinks.

"As you might imagine, I'm in bad shape physically," he adds. "I'm weak. The discomfort keeps me from concentrating, so I'm bored out of my mind. And it's driving my daughter crazy. I hate for her to see me like this, but I can't make her go away."

"She loves you very much."

"She adores me. It's heartbreaking."

The doctor nods and smiles. Cautiously she asks, "Are you religious?" He doesn't respond. She asks, "Have you tried prayer?"

"To whom? I don't imagine God is in charge of this. This seems more like a case for the other guy."

"Mr. Baker—"

"God is life. I'm not one of those people who thinks death is part of life. I think it's pretty darn obviously the opposite of life, to be perfectly frank. That's why I have trouble getting psyched up for it."

"That doesn't mean help won't come to you if you ask. Ask, and it shall be given. You have to open your mouth and *ask*."

"I'm an enlightened person." Seeing her trace of a smile, he adds, "Not like a Zen Buddhist! Enlightened as in the Enlightenment. Rational. Open-minded. I don't believe in God, but I do believe in religion. Ritual and tradition go a long way toward resigning you to a lousy prognosis. I spent half my life studying shamanism, and I've been asking every spirit I know for help, believe me. But until they get off their butts and help me out, maybe you could scare up some kind of painkiller for this crick in my neck."

"We have a volunteer massage therapist on staff who's very good."

"Is it tantric massage? That might really help."

"I beg of you, Mr. Baker, please take your situation seriously. Tell me what form you want your care to take."

"Ma'am, I am not catching your drift. I have no idea what it is you want to hear!"

She lacks legal authorization to tell him what she wants to hear—that he would like to be knocked out cold, and dead in a week—or that this moment, the one he drowned in morbid lightheartedness, now already past (she dares not harp on her theme), was the moment when he could have asked to sleep soundly through his last days on earth.

The request would have been honored. But general anesthesia isn't a menu item, because the hospice is run like one of those brothels that are nominally strip clubs. The license affords no protection to the dancers, who must turn tricks as furtively and nervously as hospice staff dispensing painless deaths.

And Norm does not want to die. Not yet. He wants to say good-bye to his sons. He craves the good-byes. Knowing all that he knows, he thinks it is worth greeting death with open eyes and intact senses if it means he can see his sons one more time. He is an emotional man. He can't turn it off.

"I'm dying, and I'm terribly depressed about it," he insists, trying to reassure the doctor that his feelings do justice to his surroundings. "I'll be grateful for anything you can do for me." He sees that she is still disappointed. He frowns and faces forward again. "Is *Jeopardy* on yet?"

At his request, she turns on the TV. Alex Trebek descends from his orbiting satellite into the box, bearing images of certainty and fair play.

Norm relaxes. The doctor places the remote, with its built-in speaker, in his curled right hand and leaves the room.

THE NEXT MORNING AT TEN-THIRTY, Penny arrives at the hospice in Norm's Mercedes S-Class, not forgetting the laptop.

He says he is in too much pain to do anything but train the dictation software. She says she is a fast typist and could take dictation while he speaks. He laughs and says that would take a stenotype machine. He reads a list of words aloud to the computer. She suggests recording an oral history on audio or video. She says her phone has voice recognition software that works without training. He asks to be left alone.

He feels too poorly, he says, to speak anymore at all, because the pain in his neck and shoulder is spreading. "It's like a crick in my neck that reaches all the way around my rib cage and into my back," he tells her. "Like being twisted too far."

Penny fetches a nurse, who tells her to tell him to try to sleep. He agrees to try. She goes to the common room to drink coffee and read the hospice literature. When she comes back, he is awake. He asks to hear Mahler's Fifth Symphony.

EARLY IN THE MORNING, TWO days later.

Another doctor stands at Norm's feet, a sixtyish woman with elegant platinum jewelry. A laminated plastic tag identifies her as the hospice director. She wears a peach lab coat over taupe gabardine slacks and carries a clipboard.

"How are we doing?" she asks.

"Not so good," Norm says. "My neck hurts like hell."

"On a scale from one to ten, with ten being unbearable pain, where would you place this pain?"

"Eight and a half."

"Have you been letting the staff change your position?"

"Unfortunately I can't lie any other way but this way," he says. "Because of my neck."

She flips pensively through the papers on her clipboard and says, "I'm going to be open with you. There are some notes in your file that make me concerned you might be a drug seeker."

"I'm a seeker, all right, but I never took a recreational drug in my life!"

"What I'm hearing now is a drug seeker's request for opiates."

"Where'd you get that? I don't even believe in opiates."

"There has been concern on the staff, I don't know how to say this"—she shakes her head, as though doubting the notes on her clipboard in her own handwriting—"about a Satanic drug cult of some kind that you were involved with in Brazil?"

"What did they do, Google me? I thought this was a hospice, not the NSA!"

"Palliative care means treating the whole person," she parries smoothly. "With all his quirks."

"So give me some palliative care! I don't know what's wrong with my neck, but that massage your volunteer gave me sure didn't help. I remember some of my clients used to be on something called Dilaudid. Supposed to have euphoria as a side effect. You guys have that?"

She shakes her head. "We rely exclusively on modern therapies to keep our patients comfortable."

"Well, I'm not 'comfortable.' I'm in hell. Of course I feel right at home, as the founder of a Satanic drug cult."

"Mr. Baker, if you would prefer not to receive care in a Christian institution—"

He rolls his eyes. "Can't you tell I'm joking?"

The doctor folds her arms. "Being comfortable means not being in agony. It means not dying the way people used to die. Screaming. It means being able to function mentally."

"Well, thanks so much for the timely definition, now that I'm stuck here on my ass until I die."

"Mr. Baker, I would ask you to remain civil."

"All right. Civilize me. You're the renowned specialist in palliative medicine. Do something about my fucking neck."

For a moment, the director twirls her pen. She wriggles pensively, as though thinking with her intestines. Finally she says, "It could be muscle cramping. Some patients respond to a muscle relaxant."

"Then why doesn't somebody try it already?" Norm begs.

PENNY SPENDS AN UNPRODUCTIVE DAY with Norm, not working on his memoirs.

That evening, she returns to Morristown in a state of agitation and restlessness. The gate opens when it senses the car's transponder.

The house is H-shaped, very large; the exterior, white stucco with high, black-shuttered windows. The black perimeter fence encompasses one and three-quarter acres.

When she comes into the kitchen through the side door, Amalia is drinking beer and soliloquizing to Norm on the phone. She says, eyes on Penny, "Got to go, *cariño*. Your baby's home. Love you. Bye." She hugs her daughter and says, "I know, honey."

"You should come see him," Penny says. "He's not getting the right painkillers."

Amalia shakes her head. "On Sunday I will definitely come," she says. "Work is so crazy. We're up to our necks in a merger. It would be so much easier. I could see him every day, if he would be here at home."

"But what about the bleed-out? And taking care of him? I don't know, Mom."

"If he says he will do it, I will find a way. I will help you. Can you talk to him? Make him come home?"

THE NEXT MORNING, NORM HAS a new symptom. "Ih er eenh," he tells Penny. "Ah unh unh ee ah unh-ur unh."

"Slow down. I can't tell what you're saying."

"Anh uh eh ih ee. Ah ehr. Oh. Eh ee oh."

"Are you in pain?"

"Eh!"

Penny marches to the nurses' station, tears in her eyes. "My father's still in pain," she tells the nurse sitting there. "And now he can't fucking *talk*."

"I'll ask you to use civilized language," the nurse says, looking up from her cell phone. "Terminal distress and agitation are normal. If he doesn't fall asleep in a few minutes, I can send for the chaplain."

"He's upset because he's in pain and they won't give him any painkillers! All he got was a muscle relaxant!"

A doctor sits filling out a form at a desk behind the nurse. He looks up and says, "I could ask him whether he'd like a sedative."

"That's an idea," Penny says. "He told me once he used to take Valium on boat rides, after he was on this ferry on the Amazon that burned and he got this fear of ships. He said Valium set him right up!" She almost laughs herself at the ridiculousness of Norm's phobia, so she is surprised when the doctor says something even sillier: that Valium could damage his liver.

"Damage his *liver*? Who *cares*? He's dying!"

"It could hasten death," the doctor says. "We don't assist anyone here to die more quickly. It's God who decides how and when that will happen. We simply allow nature to take its course."

"We didn't come here to let God and nature decide. We can get them for free by walking out the door."

"What you need to understand is, your father is not dying. Not yet. His lungs sound normal. No crackles. His kidneys are functioning. He's at a very early stage. But if he's having more psychological distress than he can tolerate, I could consider starting him on twilight sedation. It's state of the art in end-of-life care."

"First you have to get him off those muscle relaxants so he can communicate! He wasn't distressed before, just in pain."

"I'll go see him now, and I'll ask him if he wants sedation, and we'll think about alternatives. I promise." The doctor gives Penny his hand. "You should go home and relax. Take a day off and get some rest."

"What if he dies today?"

"Not a chance," he assures her.

FOUR DAYS PASS. PENNY SITS by Norm, giving him ice cubes to eat. He coughs. He runs the ice cubes around his mouth with his tongue, but he can't swallow the liquid water. It runs into his beard, which is cut very short.

"He's not thirsty anymore," a nurse explains.

"Wah," he protests.

"He's asking for water," Penny insists.

"It's a habit," the nurse explains again. "He's on twilight sedation. He doesn't know what he's saying. He's used to asking for water. It's a habit like anything else."

"Wah," Norm says.

"YOU CAN DO ORAL CARE yourself," a friendly orderly tells Penny two days later. She shows her how to dip a rough rectangular sponge on a lollipop stick in water and offer it to him.

Norm sucks it hard. His spit forms a sticky web around the green sponge. The inside of his mouth is yellow, crusted with dried snot. The orderly shows Penny how to swab his teeth and tongue gently so that the crust still obscures his soft palate completely, obstructing his windpipe.

“Can’t you get that stuff out so he can breathe?” Penny asks.

The orderly shakes her head. “It’s not our policy to perform suction. That would only prolong his life.”

Penny runs a swab around the back of Norm’s throat and twirls it. The substance collects on the swab like cotton candy. She throws it away and tries another swab. A plate of dried mucus flakes off his throat like a loose poker chip. She hauls it out with the swab. Nothing disgusts her. She is gentle and caring. He moans his word “Wah.” The inside of his mouth is almost clean. It is red, gray, and gold. His golden molars shine. She feels a sense of achievement.

She wets a swab and inserts it in his mouth. His teeth clamp down on it and he sucks the water.

“It’s a reflex,” the orderly says.

After three more wet swabs, Penny marches down to the nurses’ station.

“I’m taking my dad home,” she says to the random doctor who is sitting behind the desk, doing paperwork. “I don’t care if it’s against medical advice.”

“It’s normal for patients to say they want to go home,” she says. “It’s a universal metaphor for being at peace in God’s love.”

“Do you even believe in God? You sound like the hospice manual.”

“I believe there’s a higher power.”

A room door opens and a very old man with thick, strong limbs lurches into the hallway, wearing a hospital gown made of paper. He elbows the nurse who pursues him. Penny follows them as far as the glass double doors to the garden. The old man stands next to the birdbath, scanning the parking lot for his car, while the nurse remonstrates with him. He has no keys or clothes. The weather is chilly. A security guard brings a wheelchair, and three staff members accompany him back to his room.

Penny returns to the nurses' station and says to the doctor, "If there is a higher power, how come it lets people get as weak as my dad and leaves their capacity to feel pain?"

"If he had pain, we'd know it."

"That's not true," Penny says. "He's a stoic."

"We don't know what he's feeling," the doctor says. "When people are very sick, their cognition is altered. We don't hasten the end of life. Every human being has a right to self-awareness, especially at the end, when we're making our peace with God. You might want to talk with our chaplain."

She turns away, defeated.

She goes out the front door and follows the concrete walk past the handicapped parking spots until she is off hospice property. She smokes a cigarette by the road. Butts line the gutter. A passing driver slows and raises his eyebrows. She turns back to face the hospice.

PENNY'S DISTRESS AND AGITATION ARE profound.

Norm built the world she once lived in, calling its entities into being word by word. But his word, which once was law, has surrendered to higher laws. He is so weak that a fly, landing on his nose, would be a higher law. He couldn't swat it away. He and Penny share a world not their own.

When his eyes seek hers, bright with the need to die and hopeful that she will help, she feels love, like a serrated knife, carving out her heart and giving it to her father.

FOUR DAYS LATER, AMALIA COMES to visit, bringing Norm's pet cat in a travel carrier.

The cat, a neutered male named Schubert, is small and black

with orange eyes, very pretty. He presses his body against the back wall of the carrier. "Look who I brought!" Amalia says, swinging the carrier up onto the bed and knocking it against Norm's hip. "He's sleeping," she whispers to Penny.

"He could be awake. His eyes are stuck shut."

Amalia leans closer and sees that Norm's upper and lower lashes are gummed together with dried mucus. "Oh my god! I should have come earlier! I was just so busy." She places the cat carrier on the floor at her feet and asks, "Did you talk to Patrick?"

"No. Was I supposed to?"

"He said he called you. He can't make it, but he knows Norm will understand. He's hanging a major show of photographs in Jakarta."

Norm says, "Wah."

Amalia seizes both his hands in hers. "I'm here, honey," she says. "Go back to sleep. I love you!"

Norm rolls his right hand from side to side.

"I haven't seen him move his hands in weeks," Penny exclaims.

"Oh, your kitty misses you, too," Amalia tells him. She pulls Schubert from his carrier on the floor and seats him on the bed-spread facing Norm. Holding his forelegs tight against his rib cage, she shoves him toward Norm's hand for petting.

Very slowly, Norm raises both hands and closes them around the cat's throat as though to strangle him. His thumbs press hard on Schubert's trachea.

The cat snarls and scratches him deeply on top of his right forearm.

"Fuck," Penny says, moved by her father's display of physical effort and will.

"Oh my god," Amalia says, moved by the blood that streams from his torn flesh. Norm does not wince or make a sound. His hands drop to the blanket. His right forearm gapes like a split pomegranate, and he seems to fall asleep. Schubert escapes and hides under the bed.

Penny is entirely sure—100 percent certain—that he was trying to communicate to Amalia that she should strangle him. That he does not trust her, Penny, to carry out such a wish, but that he wouldn't put it past her mother.

"Here, kitty, kitty, kitty," Amalia says, on her knees on the floor. "I should never have put this poor kitty in the car. Now he thinks he's at the vet!"

THE NEXT MORNING, NORM'S WOUND is badly infected. A spike of sepsis reaches to his shoulder. Under a thick wad of bandaging, his arm continues to bleed.

"Blood poisoning a-going to kill him now," an orderly tells Penny. "This man got no immune system." He smoothes a fresh sheet with his hand while two nurses support Norm, who has been rolled over onto his side. His skin, soft as silk and drained of muscle and fat, lies draped over his skeleton like a shroud.

Soon after, the assistant deputy hospice director surprises Penny by inviting her to sit down in the foyer between the baby grand piano and the flickering gas hearth. "I spoke with your mother," she says, "and we're discharging him to home hospice this afternoon. He's had no events requiring intervention. His vital signs are good."

"You are kidding me," Penny says.

"We admitted him expecting a bleed-out. His platelets are minimal, but there simply hasn't been sufficient trauma. He hasn't been eating or getting up. At this stage we anticipate death from kidney failure, assuming he doesn't start drinking again. I would strongly advise against intubation or intravenous fluids."

"Right, right," Penny says. "No painkillers because they hasten death, and no fluids because they prolong life."

The assistant deputy hospice director places a hand on Penny's shoulder. "This must be hard on you."

"It's harder on him!"

"It gets easier. He's going to die fairly quickly of systemic sepsis, with that arm."

Norm's advance directive—an end game far too much like Final Jeopardy for comfort—rejects antibiotics.

Penny bites her lip and says nothing.

SHE SITS WITH A SOCIAL worker in a cramped office behind the reception desk and discusses the equipment and assistance she will need in Morristown.

She will take delivery of an adjustable bed just like the bed in the hospice. Twice a day, a nurse's aide will help her change Norm's diaper. She will learn to administer the "e-kit" in emergencies.

Penny agrees to everything, and the social worker makes a phone call. She asks Penny whether anyone is at home, because the bed is already on the truck.

Penny retrieves her bag and the laptop from Norm's room—he is sound asleep—and drives to Morristown to wait for the bed.

She clears space in his library, the only room on the ground floor that lacks carpeting. The end tables are small, easy to move to another room. She sees the books that will surround him during his last days: Norman O. Brown, Georges Bataille, Jack London, Lévi-Strauss, Castañeda, Teilhard de Chardin, William James. And his own works: *Shamanism: Modern Social and Cognitive Aspects. The Cosmic Snake of Healing. Disengaging Death: From Cancer to Dancer.* If he could express an opinion, would he say he cares about books? She doesn't know.

Late that afternoon, an ambulance arrives, staffed by two burly EMTs. Norm rides his gleaming silver-and-red catafalque into the front hall, wheezing but not groaning as it lurches up the steps. The men heave Norm into the low, heavy bed and cover his body with an oversize sheet. Schubert curls up on his stomach. Penny prepares a cup of ice cubes and some swabs, in case he opens his mouth. He seems inert. A home health aide arrives to train her. He shows her how to put ointment on his bedsores with rubber gloves and use a hypodermic needle.

THAT EVENING AFTER WORK, AMALIA rushes to his side and kneels by the bed. “Darling, darling,” she says, kissing him. “I am so glad you could come home.” To Penny, she adds, “He doesn’t answer.”

“He’s on morphine and Haldol.”

“I wish we could talk.”

“No, you don’t! I’m so grateful they finally knocked him out.”

“Stop that. He’s just tired. He can hear you.”

AROUND 4:00 A.M., NORM HOWLS. He howls again. He bellows loudly that he wants to go home. Penny finds him asleep, bleeding lightly from the nose, with his left arm over the bed railing. Amalia sits by him until seven o’clock. Then she heads out to work.

Penny spends most of the day perusing social media in the kitchen, drinking coffee with Baileys, smoking Marlboros. She helps the aide with Norm’s hygiene and rubs his feet with urea cream.

NOT LONG AFTER—ONLY FIVE days—Matt drives to Morristown to say good-bye.

For days Norm has done nothing but breathe. Things happen to him, but his own activities are twofold: sonorous intake of breath and stuttered expulsion. Inhalation is shrill. It sounds painful. The home health aide says it isn’t painful.

Matt’s hair is still full and black, longish and wavy, something of an art-director mane. His beard, clipped short, is graying. He appears very large and solid, but slim, in a black merino sweater and charcoal gray slacks.

At first he stands at the foot of the bed, hands clasped below his belt buckle. He sits down on a chair by the head of the bed and reaches over the rails to place his hand on Norm's forehead.

Matt's face freezes at the sight of Norm's open mouth. It is a red hole through which his tongue pokes yellow, caked in a giraffe-skin-like pattern of dried mucus. "Jesus, Dad," he says. "You look atrocious."

Norm breathes.

"We always spoke our minds, so there's nothing left to say," Matt says. He waits. He takes Norm's left hand. "Good-bye, Dad," he says. "I love you."

He lowers his forehead to the bed railing and remains motionless, dry-eyed, for two minutes. He stands and leaves without speaking to Amalia or Penny.

Penny sits by Norm until deep in the night.

A WEEK LATER, WITHOUT ANOTHER peep of complaint, Norm stops dying.

Penny is holding his hand. There is no sound. At one moment he is dying audibly, each breath quick, forced, harsh, through whistle-like apertures in the material blocking his windpipe. The next moment he is still.

She glances at the window and sees gratefully that it is open. She becomes aware that humans have souls. These are slender birds like swifts, invisible and made of moist living breath. When a person dies, this bird urgently requires free passage to the sky.

In essence, if Norm hadn't smelled so horrible that she'd had to open a window in summer and let in the humidity, his soul would have been trapped in his library forever, unable to join the other souls.

She doesn't believe in the soul thing at all. She just knows it all of a sudden.

She places his left hand on his chest. She sits and stares at the rotting body in its leaky diaper for a quarter of an hour. She leaves the room and closes the door.

Seeing a flower arrangement on the side table in the front hall, she removes a few flowers. She goes back to the library and lays them on Norm's chest. They help, she thinks. Flowers really help. The dead thing looks a lot better with flowers on it.

She makes herself two espressos in a row, using the ultrafast pod machine, and calls Amalia at work.

"Don't do anything," Amalia says. "I'll be right there. Call that nurse and tell him not to come anymore. Tell the hospice agency to pick up that nasty bed."

PENNY DRIVES OUT TO BUY groceries with altered perceptions. She breezes through a stop sign and almost misses her turnoff. In the store, the very ugliest white people seem beautiful to her, their red noses and inflamed pimples alive with oxygen-saturated hemoglobin. At the deli counter she gets in line for pastrami, but lasts only a few seconds, fazed by cold cuts embalmed in nitrite solution and mummified ham. She pushes her cart to the cereal aisle and buys a box of Post Raisin Bran.

She drives back to her parents' house. She carries the box to the dining room table, where she rapidly spoons cereal into her mouth, savoring the blend of crispy vegetable matter and purest white cane sugar. She enjoys the feel of her own firm gums and smooth teeth.

Amalia comes home from work early—around five—because of the special occasion.

Halfway through the box of Raisin Bran, Penny puts down her spoon and says to her mother, "They could have let Dad sleep through all that. Everybody knows people are animals, only smarter. It's wrong to torture any animal, even for its own good. *Especially* then. But instead of giving him real drugs, they kept wanting him to be alert, so he could make his peace with God. I always thought religious people were massively annoying. Now I know they're *evil*." She shovels in a big spoonful of cereal.

Subconsciously—as a secret even from herself—she suspects that Norm wanted to stay awake to see his sons again. Though she doesn't believe it consciously, the suspicion hurts her, because of its extreme sadness. She wipes her eyes, not knowing why.

"Oh, Penny," Amalia says, hugging her. "You're so like him. Thank you so much for using your free time to care for him. That says so much about you—good, positive things. You're such a caring healer, exactly like your father."

"He never healed anything," Penny says. "He helped people pass the time and forget. And that is *sainthood*. Dad was a fucking *saint*."

THAT NIGHT, TRYING TO FALL asleep, she reviews her father's suffering. If she had tied him to a tree in the yard and left him there, would he have been any thirstier, any more uncomfortable than he was in the hospice? Would he have slept any less, or lasted so many weeks?

She remembers what he said about dying with his boots on. If he had gone to Mexico like Ambrose Bierce to die fighting for what's right, and been captured by *narcotráficos* and hung up by his feet, wrapped in duct tape and plastic sheeting—

She stops the thought right there.

It starts again, with chain saws.

She feels trapped in an abyss of human depravity from which there is no escape but death. Which is actually pretty ludicrous when you're twenty-three, in perfect health with no responsibilities, lying in a four-poster bed in your own room in a mansion, and for all you know you just inherited a boatload of money!

She thinks of everyone else's relaxed attitude toward Norm's death—sick as a dog, eighty-two years old, no biggie—and their near-universal failure to watch him die. She suspects the two may be linked. She had felt herself defiantly alone among heartless sociopaths, but maybe she was alone among sane, sensible people. Her hands go to her face and genitals as she imagines the Mexican torturers.

Around two o'clock, she gets up and sneaks past Amalia into the master bathroom.

There she finds an amber-colored, twist-top pill bottle of Valium, nearly full, dispensed before she was born, so brittle it cracks when she opens it. She holds one in her hand for a long time. She imagines the comfort it might have brought to Norm and cries. She takes it to bed with her, holding it to her heart like a beloved plush toy.

Norm's death is a runaway train. She boarded of her own free will. She waits for a curve, a bridge, a breakdown to stop it.

A DRIVER AND HIS SON arrive to pick up the adjustable bed, because other dying people need it right away. Penny's conversation with them is awkward. She refuses to let them in the house.

In the library, Norm still occupies the bed they want, his body now uncovered to the waist, flowers on the floor. His infected right arm, looking ready to burst, protrudes straight as a long balloon, fifteen degrees above the horizontal. The other arm lies heavy. Amalia, taking her leave, holds its dead white hand. Penny's altercation with the deliverymen is cut short when the hearse arrives.

The men who see to the disposal of Norm's body surprise Penny. Somehow she expects a doctor to pronounce him dead. But these are clearly undertakers, with long woolen coats and black hats. "What are they?" she asks Amalia. "Are they Amish? Are they Jews?"

"Norm wanted them," Amalia says. "They do an old-fashioned burial, inside of twenty-four hours. That was his wish, to rejoin the earth ASAP."

"Sounds like Dad."

"They will bury him their way, and we will honor his spirit our way. Forget the body. He's gone. Don't cry for the body."

The impassive men yank off the catheter without opening the diaper. Brown urine drips on the sheets. They roll the body—floppy again except for that infected arm—first into a black zippered bag, then onto a frail gurney with rusty chrome and tiny wheels. It gets stuck crossing the front hall. Too heavy. The wheels get no traction on the runner and sink behind four insurmountable bow waves. Amalia and Penny anchor the carpet with their weight so the men can back up. They steer around it and bounce tump-tump-tump down the front stairs. Amalia tips them with cash in an envelope. They drive away in their forty-year-old hearse.

Penny goes out into the backyard and sits down under a tree.

Making excuses for her daughter, Amalia overtips the deliverymen still waiting to take away the bed. They take it away. She double-bags the sack of urine the color of kidneys and carries it out to the metal garbage cans by the street. She mops the library floor and dumps the water in a basement toilet no one ever uses.

Penny comes back inside. She airs and dusts the library and carries the end tables back in.

AT DUSK THE TWO WOMEN meet again at the kitchen table, where they smoke cigarettes.

In the wreaths of ectoplasm Penny exhales, she can see her soul.

She wills her body to be equally wraithlike. Not sodden, not heavy, not dead, but filled with crackling, electric life, like a stale Marlboro on fire.

Turning off the lights, Amalia opens the French doors to the courtyard. They say little—two small women in a huge house, dwarfed by its vastness, its oversize, overstuffed furnishings, its large trees, its chaotic megacity, its largely empty universe.

ON SUNDAY, AMALIA DRIVES PENNY to the Morristown train station, where she catches New Jersey Transit into Manhattan. From Penn Station, she continues on the subway to the Upper West Side.

Her apartment is on the ninth floor of a modern building. There are many tall buildings like it on every side, most built in the nineteen-fifties. The street outside slopes to the black river. Pale green trees are visible in the park. The mosaic in the long, narrow lobby shows abstract fish and seashells suspended in blue waves.

The building is rent-controlled, with a very stable population. The apartment—Norm's old bachelor pad—has been the family's Manhattan pied-à-terre for many years. It even housed Amalia during her college years.

The doorman, not an immigrant but a local man whose father and grandfather were doormen at the same address, wears a too-large suit with a matching cap, like a limo driver. Penny says hello and picks up her mail. She has not been home since Norm's first weekend in the hospice. She drops the thick bundle of junk mail and bills into her tote and steps into the elevator with an elderly woman.

On the third floor, as her neighbor is leaving the elevator, Penny tells her that her father has died.

"I knew him only in passing, but my condolences," the woman says. "I'm sure he was a dear soul."

Penny laughs awkwardly and says, "Yes."

"Never stop smiling," the neighbor advises her. "Laughter is the best medicine."

The apartment is a small one-bedroom with a balcony off the

kitchen where Penny keeps her bicycle. The mahogany-stained bedroom suite remains from Norm's days as a grad student at Columbia: a low desk and dresser, a high wardrobe, and a twin bed with a tall headboard upholstered in brown vinyl with gold buttons. The kitchen table and chairs are chrome, vinyl, and yellow Formica. A framed Ph.D. degree in psychology hangs on the wall. The fridge whirs softly in harvest gold. The cabinets are avocado.

She sits down at the table to sort the mail. One envelope lacks a stamp. Inside it is a letter from the landlord, instructing her to vacate the apartment by the end of the following month due to the termination of the lease of Mr. Norman Baker, occasioned by his death *the day before*.

She calls Amalia.

"I can't believe it!" she cries into the phone. "How in the world did they know?"

"Oh my god," Amalia says. "I told no one. I was too grieving. But Facebook maybe? I updated my status to single. Maybe I am friends with somebody in your building?"

A brief silence, then Penny says, "They would have found out anyway because I told the neighbor. But you're not single. You're widowed! People are going to think you broke up with him because he was too old for you or something. You have to call and tell people he's dead. Nobody's going to notice an announcement on Facebook. It's going to get crowded out by other stuff."

"He was too old for me, *nena*. He died of old age. I'm forty-three, maybe younger. He was so old he didn't even have Facebook. How else can I tell people he's gone? I have to invite them to the funeral. I can't call them all. Oh my god, that would take forever."

The two women stop conversing and tap their phones until Amalia's Facebook page appears.

"Oh, so many consoling words," Amalia says. "People are very sympathetic."

"Yes, they love you," Penny says.

They scroll for a moment in silence.

Seeing condolence messages from coworkers, Amalia remarks to Penny that she hopes to retire young so she doesn't end up like Norm. "He worked until he fell down dead. I want to retire at fifty, fifty-five, tops. Maybe I won't live so long. I never saw old Kogi people."

"How would that work moneywise?" Penny asks. The question feels heartless, even to her, but she feels no connection between her heart and her mouth. "Do you plan to sell the house, or the clinic?"

The clinic is a sprawling international-style bungalow in an upscale residential section of Manaus, nicknamed (by Matt and Patrick) "the Last Resort." Norm's terminally ill clients were able to stay there in comfort, convenient to hospitals and air transport, while authentic shamans from the interior treated them using traditional rituals and herbal compounds.

"Norm sold the clinic ten years ago. We pay rent to the new owner. We needed money for taxes. So much interest and penalties. You know the IRS. You can run, but you can't hide! Unless you're a criminal. Then it's easy."

Instead of laughing at the joke, Penny says, "Oh. I thought I might inherit something."

"Our money is tied up," Amalia says. "But you can take anything of Norm's that you need."

"What do you mean? His orthotics? His didgeridoo? He didn't have a lot of stuff I can use."

"No, only real estate," Amalia admits.

"What real estate?"

"Oh, different real estate. You know."

Penny thinks of the summer place in the Palisades and hopes there are no plans to sell it. She hopes it stays in the family forever.

She isn't worried about money. She just wants a job and a place to stay so she doesn't end up worrying about money.

She doesn't feel guilty for thinking about money. It's the foundation of material existence, at least until the revolution comes and sweeps it away. Until then, we need to find our place in the money ecosystem, our niche in the money chain. You can't understand the modern world if you can't imagine selling what you love best. You're under no obligation to take part, but you have to understand it. That's what Norm taught her. It's why she majored in business.

THE MEMORIAL SERVICE TAKES PLACE thirteen days later, on a Saturday in May at the summer place, commencing at 7:00 P.M.—a potluck and drum circle.

Matt brings Patrick, who is tired out after a twenty-two-hour flight to JFK and a night of drinking in Manhattan with an old girlfriend. He picks him up at Newark Penn Station. They listen to traffic and weather on the radio, and Patrick dozes off.

They are among the first to arrive. Matt parks on top of the Palisades, in a field on the other side of the road, near the mailbox. They walk a quarter mile down to the house on hairpin turns.

The gravel driveway is narrow and not well maintained. When other mourners drive past, Matt and Patrick hold still with their bodies pressed against the basalt.

There is a breeze on the ridge, but down in the woods the hot, still air lets mosquitoes hover. The two men twitch at odd moments, reaching down to slap arms, legs, and their own faces as they talk.

Patrick asks Matt how Amalia is holding up.

"Like you'd expect," he says. "Doing fine."

"And Penny?"

"Poor kid's a mess. She spent a month obsessing over Dad. I wouldn't have lasted five minutes. He looked like a zombie."

"Well, he was dying."

"He wanted to be alone. You know how a cat will just creep away and die by itself? You were right not to come. I'm sorry now I bothered him."

Patrick wonders whether Matt is looking for a hug. It seems unlikely. He continues shuffling along next to his brother, hands in his jeans pockets.

He is slightly shorter, lithe and weedy, more graceful in the way he moves, and all in all even handsomer, in a way that's hard to put your finger on immediately; he looks kind. His eyes look concerned and sensitive. He can get any girl he wants, a power he exploits to make desirable women pursue him for five or ten years at a time. At age forty-four, a professional art photographer on a tropical island, he has slept with only nine women, and he has never been alone. His career likewise has never hit a snag. Patrick is all sweetness and decency. But not sweet and decent enough to hug Matt.

"I miss Dad," Matt says. "I really do."

Patrick turns away, puckering his lips, as though tasting something sour.

NORM'S ACOLYTES ARRIVE FROM ALL over—medical students, fans of holistic medicine, fellow practitioners, patients whose illnesses relented, aspiring shamans, veterans and benefactors of the Last Resort. They leave their cars at odd angles, blocking each other's escape. No one will leave until they all leave.

The women carry big pots and bowls of food. The men carry coolers and drums: congas, bongos, tabla, djembe. The dress code is garment-dyed linen in earth tones, tooled leather, and jewelry made of rock. Thin-skinned, thin-haired, physically vulnerable people are one main cohort: Norm's former clients. Another is colleagues and friends, old-school hippies—rude, furious, elderly sensualists channeling Falstaff with all their might while their wives read Isabel Allende. A third is college students: self-styled sixties throwbacks who greet each other with palms pressed together, whispering shyly, "Namaste."

There is consensus among the hippies that Penny is an "old soul."

Many have known her since she was a baby playing on the floor of the clinic, back when Amalia was in college and Norm lived full-time in Manaus with a babysitter. Then came his financial breakthrough, the triumphant return to America and his wife, her career, the Morristown house, the good suburban schools for their daughter. The utter estrangement from his sons—but that makes sense to the disciples, knowing their history. They see Penny as the bearer of unique potential.

Though in fairness they see many people, including nearly all their friends, that way. There is tacit agreement among Norm's followers that they make the world a better place by living in it. They don't change it. They redeem it, through the searching way they live their lives. The cult is populated by realist aesthetes. A cult of personality for those cultivating personalities. Expecting nothing more from life than self-actualization, accepting nothing less. Willing to settle for others' self-actualization if their own turns balky.

Initially it was realist aesthetes in a hurry due to piss-poor diagnostic outlooks. Lately it's realist aesthetes with time on their hands, drawn to the shine in the eyes of the survivors. Captivated by their intensity after Norm (with unspoken apologies to Epicurus) persuaded them death could be ignored.

Most have been to Manaus to see the cosmic anaconda.

Penny wears a shapeless white cotton shift. Also a Cambodian anklet with little jingle bells on it—something meant to help parents locate toddlers, but she likes it. She ties small, white freshwater snail shells into her hair, so that they click when she moves her head. She starts dancing the minute the drumming begins. She is tipsy, it should be said, on cachaça from Norm's stash in the cellar, formerly used to create alcoholic mists for purposes of shamanic healing. Her half-brothers remain on the periphery, talking. For nearly twenty minutes no one else dances.

Because she has special meaning for Norm's devotees, they like to watch her dance. They hope one day she will follow in his footsteps, as his sons show no sign of doing. (Mourners overhear them discussing the Yankees.) They find her entirely Indio, as though the shaman had managed, in impregnating Amalia, to suppress his own ethnicity—a feat that ought not to be past a shaman, it seems to them.

The older drummers play African polyrhythms. As they tire out, the beat gets fatter and heavier. The students join Penny in dancing, some chanting Norm's name. At twilight the old hippies' wives approach the margins of the service, wearing red hats and carrying big, white drums. The beat becomes bombastic, all skittishness gone.

When the sun goes down, the mood shifts from trance to fury. Everyone is stomping. The West African–style drummers reassert themselves. The sound becomes frenzied. A woman with a strong voice keens a pentatonic song with the text "Norman, find your home, fly free."

Around eleven, Penny gets thirsty and seeks to exit the mob of dancers. A girl student takes her hand and tugs her sideways. All the dancers find hands to hold, and the dance, which had centered on her until then, becomes a spiral with dancers moving clockwise toward the hub, passing under a bridge made by a man and a woman Penny has never seen, and returning counterclockwise to the margins: a Shaker folk dance.

As soon as this free interchange of positions in the circle arises—this democratization of the memorial service—her brothers, chatting casually about nothing in particular as they have been for hours, leave the yard for the house.

Penny misses them immediately. When she reaches the outermost circle, she drops the hands of the boy and girl beside her to go after them. She finds them in the kitchen.

"Who in hell *are* all these people?" she says by way of a conversational opener.

"You should check your eyeliner," Matt says. "It's smeared to hell and gone, and your hair is full of random debris."

"Leave her alone," Patrick says. "Come here, kid sister. Give me a hug. I, for one, would like to say that I really admire what you did for Dad, staying with him like that. You're a *mensch*."

"Thanks," Penny replies, thinking that too many years on a Francophone island have left Patrick speaking his father's English.

"I hear it was hard for you."

"Oh yeah. Seriously fucked-up."

There is silence in the kitchen under the storm of people drumming and chanting "Norman! Fly free!" outside.

"What a bunch of drug-heads," Matt remarks. "They probably think we're going to break out the psychedelics any minute, like at the Finger Commune. We should tell them there's acid in the tiramisu." He pokes an aluminum roasting pan full of tiramisu with its wooden spoon. "One hit of acid, and whoever eats the most tiramisu has the best chance of getting it."

"That tiramisu is *mine*," Penny says. "Tell them it's in the oatmeal or whatever this shit is." She nods at a large glass bowl filled with a grayish substance.

Smiling, arms folded, Matt walks out to the drum circle. The music quiets. Young strangers appear in the kitchen to fill their plates, shyly, with heaps of cold buckwheat kasha.

Soon the strangers are festooned around the yard and even the house, where they lie on rag rugs and Colonial-style furniture, looking fixedly at the spines of books, waiting and hoping. Penny sits down next to Patrick on a braided rug to eat her tiramisu. "Aren't they insane?" she asks.

"Definitely."

Swaying to the music as she eats, she closes her eyes and says, "I really love this place. I love the river."

"I remember Mom being here. I mean our mom, not yours."

"What was she like?"

He shakes his head. "I can't really talk about her. It's painful. I just wanted to say that I remember her here. Right here, on this very rug." He pats the rug. "Playing cards with us. Maybe Uno."

Finished, she puts her bowl and spoon aside and lies down flat on her back. "Then tell me a story about Dad. Something with Colombia in it."

"You know I'm a photographer. I don't tell stories."

"Well, it's his funeral, and nobody's talking about him."

"That would be bad luck. He's gone. We don't know what he's doing now."

"Flying around," she says. "I saw it."

"You saw his soul?"

She nods.

"Damn, Penny. You're very special."

"Special. Great word."

"I mean it. You were always a cool kid."

A cloud dims the sun in her mind. Always a cool kid? He was twenty when she was born, and living in the Philippines. They hardly know each other. He can only be thinking of the last time he saw her, in this same house, eleven years ago. She doesn't remember whether he ever saw her before that. "Let's not talk," she says. "I like the music. You want something to drink?"

"No, thanks."

Penny takes her bowl and spoon to the kitchen and fixes herself a hot toddy (cachaça, lemon, hot water). She rejoins Patrick on the rug and they sit in silence. She no longer tries to feel close. Visitors who glimpse them assume they are deep in intimate familial communion.

Patrick takes out his phone and shows her photos of the beach near his house, his neighbors' children, and their pets.

MATT STANDS IN THE DOORWAY of what had been Norm and Amalia's bedroom upstairs and says, "May I come in?"

"Please," Amalia says. She is sitting up in bed, wearing a thick bathrobe over a flimsy nightgown. A Marlboro smolders in an ashtray. She stubs it out.

He closes the door and says, "We need to talk."

"Sit by me," she says, patting the bed.

"No. You're a fire hazard."

She laughs.

"You're going to burn this house down. That's what we need to talk about. Your notions of maintenance."

"Ha-ha. Everybody says I look great, for an old lady."

He rolls his eyes and says, "Well, I've been noticing that you've been letting the house go to shit. Not just this place. Even the Morristown house."

"What?"

"It's my fault for not hiring a yard service after Dad got sick. You can't just let grass go to seed like that. Grass is supposed to be short. Those tall stems get like nylon fishing line. You can't get through it with a regular mower. They'll snag it up. You're going to need a harvesting combine to mow that lawn, if you wait even one more day."

"The lawn?"

"Not just the lawn. The whole place needs a paint job. And the garage. If anybody could see it from the road, you'd be in violation of the covenant. But you don't even get the yew trees trimmed, so thank God"—his sarcasm has a vicious edge and an anger that thoroughly dwarf his topic—"it's our secret."

"We have so few secrets anymore," Amalia says wistfully, trying to be playful.

"I just wanted to tell you," he concludes.

"Can I ask you something?"

"Sure."

"Are you happy? Are you seeing anyone? I care about you a lot."

"Can't you concentrate on one subject for even one minute? Yes, for your information, I get in. Maybe not at this party. Dad should have specialized in treating a disease that strikes the young and beautiful—chlamydia, maybe. Something curable, like pregnancy."

"So you don't have a girlfriend."

"Amalia. I can tell you're working up a crying jag, so before you start—before you launch into your tantrum—allow me to inform you that I am not lonely. I'm rich enough to buy and sell these girls I 'date,' yet somehow they never think to ask me for a dime. Do not worry about me. Worry about starving children."

"You're exaggerating."

"I'm a businessman. That's why I can't look at our house in Morristown without thinking of the equity you're throwing away every day you don't get that lawn mowed!"

"And I can't look at you without thinking of the love you throw away—"

"Jesus fuck. Shut up! I'm sorry your husband died, but leave me out of it!"

"He was your father."

He pauses. He opens his mouth and closes it. He turns, stomps out of the room, and closes the door behind him.

"Leave me out of it, too," she calls to him through the door.

She sniffles, listening to the nails on his boot heels click as he stumbles down the stairs.

PENNY LIES FOR A LONG time on the rug—even after Patrick gets up and goes in search of a beer. Seeing Matt approaching, she rises and returns to the drum circle. Now it is reduced to its stubborn kernel, Norm's closest living associates. The older men play complex patterns softly. The older women crouch, shuffle, smile.

The sky begins to grow light. At the circle's eccentric center, by the fire, Penny dances. Her body rocks, feet almost still, shells clacking as her hair sways. She feels entirely significant, as though she could be no one else and nowhere else—like nothing else matters, like a pilgrim in Jerusalem. Songbirds arc through the clearing, and sparks and ash hang in the air, discoloring her dress, burning holes. She looks at her feet. In the gray soil that bears her weight, mixed with spent embers and churned by the stomping, she can see Norm's dead face.

When the sun breaks the horizon, she breaks down, the way she imagined. She screams her premeditated grief. It is Norm's howl of desire to go home. A long roar. But it is not cathartic. Instead of going out of her, the howl goes in—a long shard of something broken, straight into her broken heart.

She stops dancing. She goes upstairs, undresses, and falls asleep in lukewarm bathwater. Amalia finds her there and puts her to bed.

THE FOLLOWING EVENING, WHEN THE guests have all left, Amalia explains her position to her child and stepchildren. "By the laws of the State of New Jersey, your father's property goes to me. I think it's the fair way. You are young, hard workers. I'm an old lady. Time for me to think about the future."

Matt and Patrick—both older than Amalia—shift their weight on the hard padded benches that line the kitchen. "I don't think that's accurate," Matt says. "Though I certainly wouldn't pressure you to sell the house right when the market is taking off. By law, you get twenty-five percent up to two hundred thousand, and fifty percent thereafter."

"I don't begrudge you one dime," Patrick says. "You were there for Dad all those years. Come on! I was in New Caledonia! I'm still there. I'm doing fine. I can wait to inherit whatever there is to inherit, *whenever*."

"Beginning with this beautiful place," Amalia says. "We all have free use of it, of course! But it will be nice if it stays together. I could never support seeing it cut up."

"You couldn't pay me enough to subdivide this property or let it leave the family," Patrick says.

"Since I'm unemployed and just got evicted," Penny ventures, "maybe I could stay here?"

"It was the boys' mother's house," Amalia says. "I can't give it to you."

"I don't want to run off with it," Penny says. "Just sleep here."

"What's wrong with Morristown?" Amalia asks. "You could help me take care of the house. Mow the lawn."

"I'm out of college. I don't want to move home. Please?"

"What about the house in Jersey City?" Matt says.

Patrick and Amalia look at him critically.

"What house?" Penny asks.

"Grandma and Grandpa's house, where Dad grew up," Matt says. "We could finally unload it. Penny could stay there for a while and hold the fort."

"I never heard of it," Penny says.

"You can't do that to her," Patrick says. "It's not habitable. The roof burned, and the basement stood full of water for twenty years. The whole place is rotten. It's probably condemned, or already gone."

"That was just Norm talking out his ass," Matt says. "I drove past it twice in the last week. There's people living there."

"It's an empty shell," Patrick says.

"What house are they talking about?" Penny asks Amalia.

"A falling-down house in a big slum," she says. "Where Norm's parents die in a fire because his father is smoking in bed." She gazes absently at the knotty pine paneling on the opposite wall.

"They died in a fire?"

"Of the smoke. It didn't hurt them. They were very old. But it's real painful for Norm. All the years he won't talk about it, won't do anything about that house. Like it never happened."

Penny lets that sink in. For a moment she sees her dead grandparents still in their bed, like mummies in a museum, frozen there by

Norm's denial. With relief she recalls that the house is inhabited, at least according to Matt. She says, "Okay. But how can I live there, if other people live there already?"

"They're living there illegally," he says. "You get rid of them."

"Oh, so now she's your gentrification shock troops," Patrick says. "You blow my mind."

"She's a warm body. You can't make an eviction stick without putting facts on the ground."

Patrick looks unhappy; Penny, merely confused.

"Whatever, blah, blah," Amalia says. "That house is a ghetto. Probably you looked at the wrong address."

Matt says, "Listen up, Amalia. I don't mind giving you a life interest in the place in Morristown, and I don't mind time-sharing our weekend getaway here with the three of you. But Grandma and Grandpa's place isn't Home Sweet Home for any of us. It's free money. And I think it's an ideal project for Penny while she's unemployed. We could pay her some kind of per diem off the top, minus prorated rent, after we sell."

"I don't know," Penny says to Matt. "If it's so ghetto, is it safe? What if it's a crack house?"

"What did they teach you at school—raising Labrador puppies for fun and profit? What do you say when someone tries to sell you drugs? 'No, thank you, sir, I don't need any drugs today.' Then you walk away and call the professional gentrifiers in riot gear."

Amalia says, "What do you think, Penny?"

"I guess I could look at it." She takes out her phone. "What's the address?"

"She'll never even find that house," Patrick says, "because ten to one it's fallen down."

"What do you know about real estate?" Matt says. "You live in a house made of palm fronds."

"Location, location, location," Patrick replies.

WHEN THE FESTIVITIES ARE OVER, Penny goes home to Morningside Heights.

She lies on her back in her father's old bed, trying to sleep. There is so much to think about, but she can only think of one thing: him.

She turns on her side. Her breathing echoes in the springs of the mattress, reminding her of his last days of life. His labored wheezing in the weeks when he could do nothing else. Each breath more difficult than the one before, while she waited in desperation for his heart to fail.

She turns on the light and sits up against his headboard. She drinks from his water glass. She sees herself surrounded by his furniture.

She smokes a cigarette. She lies flat again. She tries to think about the unfairness of being evicted and under pressure to work for the family instead of moving on with her life, but instead she thinks of Norm's death for two solid hours before she falls asleep.

PENNY MARCHES FROM THE GROVE Street PATH station in Jersey City toward the home her grandfather set on fire. It is a sunny Tuesday afternoon in mid-June, and a long walk—more of a bus ride, but the weather is so nice, and she hates buses. The low laburnum hedges along the sidewalk are filled with wild bees. She hears a blue jay screech.

The neighborhood soon becomes alarmingly ugly. Clapboard row houses wear crooked aluminum siding in mildewed pastel shades. Concrete front stoops are faced on the sides with orange-hued fake brickwork. Flimsy aluminum railings imitate wrought iron. Blocks of cheap postwar construction alternate with blocks of prefab that could have been put up yesterday. She navigates an industrial block awash in broken glass, populated by delivery vans with flat tires. Low, flat-roofed garages crowd the sidewalk.

She turns into a cross street—a block of larger houses. They have roofed front porches, with wooden railings turned on lathes and coated in innumerable layers of paint. The paint, in chips, lies under the railings. The houses are high and tall, the sort of brick town houses people call brownstones, with big front windows and broken, crooked venetian blinds. The windows gape black, as though there's nothing inside.

The next block is better. On one side, small row houses, well kept and tidy. One even has several colorful wooden pinwheels jammed into the dirt in the window boxes, like flowers. The other side is brownstones that look lived-in.

The four-story, detached brick house on the next corner takes up three lots. It is shaped like an inverted L, with the front door in the long side. The porch wraps around the corner of the house, paralleling the sidewalk, with ten feet of crabgrass between them. The mansard roof is not entirely convincing. Penny's phone tells her that she has arrived.

She walks up on the porch. A watermelon cat—that's what Norm used to call tabbies—sleeps on sweaters, a parka, and advertising circulars in a cardboard box labeled FREE. In place of a doorbell, there is a contraption screwed to a board, with a label reading: 1. SELECT TUNE BY SETTING SWITCH: JAZZ. TONY. ANKA. ROB. SORRY. 2. PRESS HERE.

A symbol is spray-painted on the bricks to the right of the door: an eighteen-inch circle containing an *N* a foot tall, its first upstroke ending in an arrow pointing down. An anarchist lightning strike. International symbol of squatters. To the right of the *N*, seven small, regular letters are neatly printed in thick black graffiti marker: *i c o t i n e*.

Penny sits down on a Windsor chair next to the FREE box and offers the cat her fingertips. It purrs. She looks around the quiet midday streets, from which everyone seems to have gone to work, except for a few scattered cars. She hears a clanking sound.

She stands and walks the length of the porch.

On a fourth lot belonging to the property, around the corner to the left, past the short leg of the inverted L, a beat-up white Chrysler minivan is parked on the twin concrete strips in front of an open garage. A man stands in the shade inside the garage, staring at a bicycle frame clamped into a stand.

The man is cute enough to have coasted through high school on looks alone—an academically worthless but benign (not dangerous) high school in the semirural Passaic County community where his father, a one-armed carpenter, survives on public assistance in a trailer in the woods. His mother, who drives a forklift in a tri-modal logistics center in Delaware, feels that he lacks a male role model. That's why she sent him to live with his father when he was thirteen. Also because her husband thinks he's a sassy smart-aleck and tries to bait him into a shoving match whenever they meet up, which is (for ten years now) never.

Penny is about to receive a fateful first impression. She sways, her hands on the railing. Indecision swings her body backward and forward. She calls out, "Hello?"

The man pauses in his diagnosis of a hairline crack in a weld and walks out until he is even with the garage door. He looks her up and down. He is in his late twenties, clean-shaven, tall, with blond hair in a ponytail, blue eyes, brown eyebrows, broad shoulders, narrow hips, and bare feet. He wears a T-shirt made thin by washing, and low-slung, threadbare Lees. Penny observes that he is slim and muscular, with a graceful way of moving, plus this inquisitive yet self-assured dignity-type thing. And he's *working*. Alone on a weekday in the garage of a big house, his own boss, maintaining a human-powered vehicle. A living embodiment of masculine self-reliance.

She thinks a series of hastily jotted firecrackers and red heart shapes, mentally texting friends about her discovery.

He turns his head and spits tobacco juice into a bush.

She thinks again: redneck, but *CUTE!!!*

Turning back toward her, he says, "Hi there. Can I help you?"

She says, "My name is Penny. Do you live here?"

"Yes," he says.

"How long?" she asks.

"Since the beginning," he says. "I was the one who found this place. You want to check it out? Come inside and get the full tour?" He gestures toward the house.

For a moment she wonders why his first reaction is to offer her a tour. Does the house get tourists? —No, but there's no reason a stranger would show up on the doorstep unless she needed a place to stay. Right?

Penny is not sure she wants a tour right this second. She is dressed for mass transit and walking through a bad neighborhood. Now she wishes for clean hair, littler shoes, and something on her ass that is not pants. She's a short brown woman in athletic socks, carrying her purse in a plastic bag. To racists, a higher primate. To lefties, a Person of Color. To absolutely no one, the would-be heiress to the property, here to throw him out. Of course that has advantages. She slumps and squints to heighten her stealth. Maybe when she comes back dressed as herself, he won't know it's her?

Her feeling that she is playing a role and playing it badly—that were he to assess her as poor, pitiable, and false, he would not be wrong—makes her droop even more as she agrees to the tour. Nothing could be more to her sinister purpose than a tour. She'll be able to report back to Matt on the condition of the interior. She dislikes herself heartily.

The man says his name is Rob. He confounds her expectations by assuming she's smart.

"This house we call Nicotine is one of a group of properties administered by Community Housing Action as housing for political activists," he says. "CHA serves as an umbrella organization for housing co-ops located all over North Jersey. The requirement to live in them is that activism be your main occupation, but it's from all over the progressive spectrum. The houses all have themes. Some are pretty trivial—bicycle activists like me, tree tenders, you know, small-time BS—and some are big mainstream political issues like environmental stuff, disarmament, different health issues, AIDS and TB and whatever. This house has a slightly different genesis, because we don't actually share an issue—"

"Except nicotine, I guess. I saw you spitting tobacco juice."

"I noticed you didn't take it too hard."

"If you'd seen the stuff I've seen lately. Oh man! Also, I'm a smoker, not that I can afford it."

"Then welcome to Nicotine. Come on in."

He opens the front door to a hallway cluttered with winter boots. A narrow staircase mounts straight ahead. At the end of the hall, the barred transom of an overgrown and inaccessible back door filters greenish light through young trees that press against it from outside. To the left are carved wooden double doors, presumably leading to a living and dining area. The door to the right opens into a large, airy kitchen, with bay windows in two directions. He points the way there.

A chubby woman, older and taller than Penny, stands at the counter in basketball shoes, peeling carrots. She wears a tiered skirt made of orange canvas with an elastic waistband, and a faded pink T-shirt with an iron-on image of a wolf. To Penny her clothing is thoroughly ridiculous. Her ears poke out through her long black hair. She faces Rob and grins, pushing its greasy strands back behind her ears without putting down the peeler.

"Hey, Sorry," he says. "We have a visitor."

"My name is Penny," Penny says. "I like your house!"

Rob picks up a bright red coffee cup promoting the anticholesterol drug Lipitor and spits in it. Sorry winces and shakes her head. She discards her carrot and peeler and asks Penny whether she would like some Turkish coffee. Penny says yes, please, and Sorry requests that she and Rob take seats in the dining room, back across the hall and through the double doors.

"This room looks like you never use it," Penny says to him. They sit down at a long wooden table that could easily seat fourteen. The veneer bubbles upward as though it had been left out in the rain. What once was a cut-glass chandelier, now missing all its glass elements, hangs overhead, three mismatched bulbs in its six sockets. The wallpaper is greenish, marbled in silver that echoes the black marbling on the smoked-glass mirror over the empty fireplace. On the mantelpiece are two statues: the Blessed Virgin Mary in latex (a fund-raising dildo for a feminist collective in Chicago, Rob tells her) and a similarly pliant My Little Pony in yellow with dirty hair. On the wall is a curling black poster: TEST DEPT. Beyond a broad archway that leads around the corner of the house, the room is dedicated to storage, filled with cardboard boxes, plastic containers, newspapers and magazines, and bicycles.

On the table, a pack of American Spirit cigarettes—a British American Tobacco brand boasting all-natural poisonous alkaloids—lies next to a thirties-vintage tabletop lighter and matching ashtray.

Sorry joins them, carrying a hanging brass tray with the coffee cups, Turkish-style. She takes a cigarette and taps it on the table many times. She leans forward to light it, inhaling deeply. The stoner-like concentration with which she does this impresses Penny.

Like her housemate, she seems to assume their visitor is bright and curious. On exhaling, she says, "Here's why I live at Nicotine. I got fucked over in my first drug trial. It was an antihistamine-SSRI phase one interaction thing supposed to run a month and pay eight thousand dollars. They had to let me go after *four days*. They gave me the whole eight thousand, but I was never the same. The drug interaction caused what you might call the onset of mania."

"She was clinical," Rob says. "She was living at this feminist house,

Stayfree, and let's just say they're not heavy into command and control, so they didn't know how to deal with it. They called the cops. That was their creative way of getting her back into medical custody."

"First and last trial I ever did," Sorry says. "Never again."

"I never did a drug trial, but I heard about them," Penny says. "It's supposed to be easy money."

"Massively easy," Sorry says. "I left the ER and spent the night skulking around this vacant lot like I was in the partisan resistance. In the morning I took all my money out of the bank to go to Afghanistan. I know exactly what I was thinking, too. I was going to lead the revolution in Afghanistan. But thank *God,* I didn't have a visa, so I got stuck at the airport and ended up back in the hospital. I came *this close* to being deported to Jordan."

"Why Jordan?"

"That's where I'm a citizen. Anyway, they put me on lithium. And I took that shit, for a while. But I found out there's a less toxic substance that cools me down and lets me concentrate." She glances at Rob over her cigarette. "Though I *still* don't know how you can put wads of tobacco in your *mouth* and *spit.* Like constantly holding tobacco soup *in your mouth.*" She shakes her head. "Now cigarettes, you breathe in deep, you get your oxygen and everything you need, and when you breathe out you're excreting all the bad stuff, like your lungs are a kidney or a liver or something." She demonstrates.

Rob removes a cigarette from the pack on the table and begins shredding its contents with some baking soda into a Paxil cup.

"Maybe it's just what you're used to?" Penny suggests. "I don't much like the smell of stale smoke, but it doesn't bother me seeing him spit. Maybe because of the way I was brought up."

"How was that?" Rob asks.

"My family is pretty weird." Unconcerned about discretion—she can't imagine the conversation taking a turn that would lead her to say her family owns the house—but intent on seeming as interesting and good-natured as possible, she says, “First off, my mom is Kogi. This people from Colombia.”

“I’ve heard of them,” Rob says. “On the mountaintop, with the gourds. They keep the universe going.”

“Now they’re more into slash-and-burn cattle farming in national parks.”

“What’s their deal?” Sorry asks.

“They used to be the ultimate weirdo tribe,” Penny says. “Their whole lifestyle was chewing coca. That’s all they did. I mean munch it like goats, all day every day. Wandering around chewing coca leaves with builders’ lime until their molars were flat, smearing their spit on these gourds. But that was just the men, obviously. The women cooked and cleaned and got traded between totemic clans or something. That’s why my mom blew out of there.” Sorry laughs, and Penny adds, “It wasn’t so great for guys, either! To get shamans, they would raise little boys in caves, like the Irish bards. It happened to my great-uncle. Mom says when he got out, he was certifiable.”

“Like the Irish bards,” Rob says.

“So when she met my dad, he was working on building up this clinic for indigenous herbal therapies in Manaus, in Brazil, on the Amazon. Can I bum a cigarette?”

“Sure, help yourself,” Sorry says, offering her the pack. “So did he, like, heal people with coca?”

“No. With this jungle vine that makes you trip your brains out. It will heal absolutely anything, because it makes you puke like there’s no tomorrow. That’s how it works. You go in thinking you’re sick, but by the time you’re tripping and losing every ounce of fluid in your body, you realize you didn’t know the meaning of the word. Your immune system gets a jump start out of self-defense. It’s called ayahuasca.”

“I can’t tell whether you believe in it,” Rob says. “But the method sounds kind of Ayurvedic.”

"That's how traditional medicine *always* works," Penny says. "They purge you, or bleed you, or take your body temperature up to a hundred and six, or whatever. It's all like chemo, taking you down to zero for a reboot. Dad's specialty was cancer patients. So anyway, that's why I don't get grossed out over tobacco juice."

"So your parents shared an interest in traditional medicine," Sorry prompts her. "Or did your mom have cancer?"

"No, no," Penny says. "He met her in Cartagena. She made it from Kogi country all the way to the coast, and Dad found her taking care of these pigs at the dump. She was herding these fucking huge pigs that she was scared shitless of, and he made her an offer she couldn't refuse."

"Is the dump a tourist attraction?"

She stares quizzically at her own hand as she taps an ash into the ashtray and says, "You know, I have no idea what he was doing at the dump."

"Picking up chicks," Sorry suggests.

"She was thirteen! Almost the same age as my brother Patrick. He took her in because she was homeless and starving. Then she fell in love with him, and he made her wait five years. She always says it really pissed her off. She thought if they waited that long, she'd be too old to get married."

"Like Soon-Yi Previn."

"I guess. But she got with the modern life program really fast. First she went to high school in Nyack. Then she married Dad, and had me in Brazil, and then she went to Barnard, and now she's an HR exec in the city."

"She must be smart."

"She's just funny." Penny shrugs. "She doesn't talk enough, so she still sounds Colombian. You can practically hear her squeezing these weird-ass Kogi ideas through a filter of Spanish and English. About half the time she just says"—she lowers her voice to say the phrase in Amalia's rhythmic monotone—"'Oh my god, oh my god.' My dad was like not even from the same *planet*."

"Is he not alive?" Sorry asks.

"He died recently. He was really old, and really sick."

"I'm sorry," Sorry says.

Penny adds, "At her HR department everybody thinks she's this huge feminist, but it's only because she's still secretly so traditional, it weirds her out that men would apply for jobs. She's like, what are they doing cluttering up our workplace? Don't they have gourds to attend to?"

Sorry and Penny take long, amused drags off their cigarettes, and Rob tucks his chew into his mouth.

"Yeah, so, the idea behind this house," Sorry says. "You know how smokers, in this society, we're a step below meth-heads. I mean, say you shoot up heroin in the bathroom on an airplane. What happens to you?"

"Nothing?" Penny ventures.

"And if you smoke a cigarette?"

"Air marshals?"

"Summary execution!" Sorry says. "People walk around fucked-up on illegal drugs, on prescription drugs—on anything they want—and nobody cares. But smoke a cigarette, and you're on everybody's shit list."

"Preach," Rob says.

"You're a baby killer," Sorry says. "Same baby who's sucking on a nipple full of phthalates, eating antibiotic chicken, breathing PCBs, playing in dirt made of tetraethyl lead and drinking straight vodka while it rides a fucking *skateboard*—when that baby dies at age eighty-six instead of ninety, it's going to be because *you* lit a cigarette in a public park."

"I do kind of believe in that secondhand stuff, though," Rob says. "That's one reason I dip. It keeps the ill effects to myself."

"You're just closeted," Sorry says to him. "A closet smoker." She taps her cigarette on the ashtray and pushes down on the black knob that makes its surface twirl, dumping the ash in an invisible receptacle. "I'll never quit. It's this or lithium. One smoker in three dies as a result of smoking, one in ten of lung cancer. Those are way better odds than I'd have leading the revolution in Afghanistan."

Rob says, "Nicotine's kind of an outlier in CHA, because it's the catchall house, with activists working on all different fronts. But we do have this one thing in common that gets us ostracized at every single march and rally and everywhere we go. That's how we ended up banding together."

"They wouldn't even let me smoke at a NORML *smoke-in,*" Sorry says. "They said nicotine is a *nerve poison,* and they were drinking fucking *beer.*"

"It's activism that's poison," Rob says. "The police are out there beating the shit out of people, breaking ribs and hip joints like they did to Jazz at RNC—the Republican National Convention—and nobody minds if she walks in their march with a fucking *cane,* but they don't want her walking with a cigarette. And that's where I say somebody's consciousness is fucked-up."

"It's because they're good leftists," Penny says. "They want to blame perpetrators, not victims. And everybody is the smokers' victim. They'd triumph in the struggle and be living in the new Jerusalem, except we're killing them with our cancer sticks."

Rob and Sorry trade admiring glances, as though Penny had jumped through a hoop. She is thrilled to be sitting with them at their big table, reaping spontaneous approval for spontaneous utterances. She beams with joy. Rob is so cute—and Sorry so not in the running as competition—that she sees herself getting very close to him very quickly.

"I like you," Sorry says.

"If you don't mind my asking, how'd your name get to be Sorry?"

"It's Sarah," she explains. "'Sari' for short. But people in this country think I'm saying 'sorry.' I grew up in a settlement on the West Bank, so I spend half my life saying 'sorry.' It's a shortcut."

"You got any beer?"

"Want to see our bodega?" Rob replies.

He and Penny go on a beer run.

When she comments that the empty brick "brownstones" could be crack houses, he says they are empty because they were built on fill. Rather than install a drainpipe to carry the stream he buried, the developer 120 years ago dumped it full of dirt and trash. "The back halves are in ruins," he explains. "Every day they slide a little farther down into the creek."

"They could still be crack houses."

"I don't know. This is more of a heroin-type neighborhood."

They turn and walk for a few hundred yards parallel to a high chain-link fence separating them from an enormous asphalted schoolyard. The children have gone home, and the chain nets of the basketball court rattle in the wind. The afternoon is warm, but so dense with humid haze that the sun seems to have set already.

Rob holds the door of the bodega open for Penny. A small silver bell rings as it closes. They stand in front of a tall refrigerator, studying the selection. Rob chooses a bottle of eight-ball, and Penny buys a can of Foster's and three packs of American Spirits (an impulse buy, based on a sudden decision to quit Marlboros) because they cost five dollars less—each!—than they do across the river in New York City.

Back at the house, the conversation deteriorates into open flirting. Sorry goes upstairs. Penny gives Rob a slightly buzzed kiss on the cheek. He touches her arm with a kind of tenderness, but does not kiss back.

They make curry sauce with coconut shavings because it goes with carrots. When Sorry comes down to eat, they serve her in the dining room as though they were host and hostess and she the guest.

They say very little but look at each other often. Sorry finishes her plate and excuses herself.

Penny and Rob wash and dry the dishes. They do some nicotine, a bit drunkenly.

Around eight, before the last bus, he takes her hand and leads her to the stairwell. He returns her peck on the cheek. His hands wander the outlines of her body, briefly. He enfolds her in his arms like a long-lost friend. "You look like the sad-eyed lady of the lowlands," he says.

"I'm not sad." It's her first best honest answer.

He draws away to look in her eyes. Then, hesitantly, aiming carefully, he kisses her on the mouth. His lips rest on hers without moving for a full five seconds. His eyes close and he squints a bit, as though lost in thought. Then he pulls back, seeming to have considered and reconsidered and decided he shouldn't move too fast.

Penny decides it's sexy. It's like he thinks really kissing her would pose a risk, so he's slow to step on the slippery slope, take the bait, enter the trap. She feels spontaneous affection and trust, a sense of knowing him already forever. She notes that his genitals are pressed against her at waist level (he is a full twelve inches taller), and she wriggles, expecting a reaction—some kind of bulging—maybe a curl of something expanding in too-tight underwear?—some undeniable message that he likes her?

He hugs her affectionately while his crotch communicates indifference and boredom.

She considers kissing him in a more goal-oriented manner, maybe getting aggressive with her tongue. Then she remembers the tobacco in his mouth.

She kisses him on the neck, standing on tiptoe, and thanks him for a lovely afternoon.

"You should come by tomorrow when there are more people around," he suggests.

BACK IN MANHATTAN, SHE LIES on her back in bed, trying to sleep. She tries to think about Rob, but her pose reminds her of Norm. She turns on her side and then on her front.

Her breathing echoes in the springs of the mattress, reminding her of Norm. The week when he could do nothing but breathe, each breath more labored than the one before. Waiting for his heart to fail, his kidneys, his liver, anything. Holding the e-kit in reserve. What a mistake.

She remembers his thirst. The memory comes in the form of an invisible serrated machete cutting downward through her chest. Or maybe not invisible. Somehow black and white and dense.

She turns on the light and sits up against his headboard. She drinks from his water glass. She sees herself surrounded by his furniture. She lights one cigarette and then another, as though fumigating for ghosts.

She lies flat again and is haunted by Norm's last days for three solid hours before falling asleep.

THE NEXT DAY SHE DROPS by Nicotine around noon. There is no one around but Rob. He gives her the full tour. He is very proud of his house.

"When I found this place, it was a burned-out shell," he says. "Classic landlord BS, a so-called hot eviction. It must have got out of hand, because I can't imagine they wanted to lose a slate roof. But this place is solid. There was almost no damage, except to the plaster upstairs. And the basement was underwater, so obviously the boiler and the electric and the plumbing were fucked, but I pumped it out and got a loan from CHA to put a flat roof on it before the rain really did a number on the brickwork."

On the second floor, he opens the double doors—each landing has the same layout, with a large room to the left, behind a single set of double doors, and a smaller room opposite—and says, "This is where Sorry lives." The room is bright and pretty, with big windows. It continues around the corner of the house, through an archway like the one that connects the dining room to the storage area downstairs. An improvised wooden sofa, covered with attractive textiles, rests on cinder blocks. The walls are hand-lacquered in yellow with a red stenciled border. Silk scarves hang from the lamp shades. There is a very large, pale, moth-eaten Chinese rug.

"It's so big and nice," Penny remarks.

"That's because this house was never cut up into apartments. It has all the same rooms as when it was built."

They mount the stairs. The third floor is home to Anka (short for Anne Catherine) on the left and Tony on the right. He doesn't open their doors. He simply says Anka is a talented painter who works at an AIDS magazine, and Tony is a mystery—an older guy, maybe forty, who seems so normal and stable you have to wonder. "What's he doing here?" Rob asks, rhetorically. "Honestly, I don't know." Anka smokes only lightly, he says, and Tony smokes their housemate Jazz's organic homegrown by the ton, when he can get it.

"She grows her own tobacco? Is that legal?"

"You can have a few plants if you don't do anything creative," Rob says. "You hang up the leaves to dry for a month. Then you cut it up and smoke it or dip it, or make cigars like Tony does. That's about all. You can't sell it."

The last flight of stairs is narrow and steep, as if built to replace a ladder, and ends in a wooden lean-to on the roof. As they reach the top he points out bundles of tobacco leaves suspended from the ceiling like sheaves of grain, curing slowly in the still, moist heat.

The top-floor landing has two flimsy doors facing each other. Behind one of them, Rob inhabits a converted attic space with a small window and a skylight. It's indifferently finished, with mismatched pressboard paneling stapled to heavy beams and fiberglass insulation peeking through the gaps. Penny sees a futon, books, a fan, a space heater, and a straight-backed chair piled with clothes. He says this was the half of the house that wasn't damaged in the fire.

Opposite his room, a dented aluminum storm door opens onto the roof, which is painted silver and walled in on one side by the fake mansard that faces the street. It slopes slightly toward a vertical drop to the backyard. The roof belongs to Jazz, her plants, and the conservatory-slash-penthouse in which she dwells. In winter her glass-walled room is crowded with seedlings in plastic cups. Now the plants are lined up against walls, wherever their roots can get some shade, growing well in the open—three feet tall, with trumpet-like flowers. "Don't touch the leaves unless you want a rash," Rob advises Penny.

"It's nice up here," she says. The grid of rooftops stretching to the horizon echoes the sky's crisscrossed condensation trails. Intermittent trees poke up as puffy masses, echoing the natural clouds.

"Jazz was the first person to move in, when I was still doing gut rehab," Rob says. "She was sixteen. She saw nicotine as a civil rights issue. Her parents were growers. She's Kurdish American. You'll like her. Everybody likes her. She's getting back from Boston tonight."

Penny looks over the edge into the backyard—into the crook of the L—and sees a thicket filled with trash bags, tires, glass and plastic bottles, and the torn remains of a vinyl aboveground swimming pool. "Is that you guys' yard?" she asks.

"We haven't really gotten around to yard work yet," he says. On the way down, he pauses on the second-floor landing to indicate the door opposite Sorry's. "That's a really nice room, but I wouldn't advise you to request a viewing. That's where angels fear to tread."

"Did somebody die in there?"

"You wish."

"Now I'm curious."

He pushes the door open. The room has two high windows, both with the sashes raised and fine-meshed white screens. Obscuring their lower halves is a wall of rubber buckets, the kind stonemasons use for hydrochloric acid, minus their handles, and lined up on smoothly planed birch planks. “Four rows of thirteen buckets,” Rob says. “One for every week of the year.”

“I don’t want to know what’s in them,” Penny says.

“You definitely don’t,” he assures her.

“Where’d they come from?”

“We had this hard-core anarchist living here for a while. This prisoners’ rights guy with the Anarchist Black Cross, doing protests against the control units and diesel therapy and so on. He had done hard time and was—um—not fastidious. So when he heard rumors the police were going to run us out, he started saving ammunition. The police never came, and after about a year and a half he got in some kind of trouble, so one day he just comes home and grabs his stuff and leaves. Gone. And there was *nothing* we could do. We tried one time, me and Jazz. We shifted one bucket a quarter of an inch, and it was like the whole wall was going to come down on us. And we said, fuck it, forget it, who cares anyway? It doesn’t stink. It’s a work of art in perfect equilibrium, and somehow every one of those buckets is sealed. He must have used plumber’s toilet wax. So I figure, okay, bring it on. Evict our asses. Whoever occupies this house after we’re gone is going to be *very* unpleasantly surprised.”

“If I get rid of the buckets, can I have the room?” Penny asks.

Rob regards her. “*Nobody*,” he says slowly, “could ever get rid of those buckets. I don’t know what it would take. It would take direct intervention by God.”

“I’m clever and I’m strong,” Penny says. “And no bodily fluid has ever scared me.” She marches resolutely to the wall of buckets.

She touches one bucket lightly with three fingers, and it wobbles. The plank covering it sways forward and back. The plank below it sways back and forth. The whole thing starts to shimmy from right to left, and so on down to the bottom. She grasps a plank to calm it, and the entire construction reacts all wrong. It bucks interference, as though it had a consciousness. Somehow it gains kinetic energy even from the soft touch with which she releases her hold.

She rushes to the door, screeching, "Holy fuck!" She turns back to watch it.

"I told you so," Rob says solemnly. "Those are forever buckets."

He holds her in his arms and they watch the waves pass and repass through the low wall of buckets. They stand deep in awe, like the last to die in a disaster movie, the couple privileged or condemned to see with its own eyes the day of wrath—the asteroid, the tsunami, the retreat of a glacier—

When the wall stops vibrating, they retreat and close the door.

She sits on the sofa in the kitchen talking to Rob, glancing upward again and again, knowing it is directly above her.

ON FOOT, FROM THE BUS stop, late in the evening, Jazz returns. The house seems to stretch and open its eyes to meet her. Sorry descends the stairs with her arms held wide to embrace her.

Jazz (short for Jasmine) is a slim young person who never stands up straight. Her head is upright on her shoulders, but her spine flexes like an otter's with every gesture. She limps from her beatings at the hands of the police, but it's hard to tell. Her movements don't follow that kind of regular pattern. She gestures with unforeseeable grace. She rolls cigarettes with her left hand, using the right only to smooth each long, thin ovoid as she lights it. Her nose is crooked, as though broken in a fight or an accident, and her wrists bear old, deep scars from self-harm. Her clothing seems, to Penny, better than any clothing she has ever seen—a red-and-white tunic with a million fine details, pants of old combed cotton, loose and clingy, the couture of a peasant. Her eyes are large. She looks around smiling in a magnetic way.

Penny feels a burning desire to please her. She tells her about facing the monster. Jazz laughs hard enough to slap both hands down on her knees and lose a cigarette ash to the floor. She turns her head toward Sorry, showing Penny her lovely profile.

She tells them a little of what she learned on her trip to Boston—a visit to a women's poetry book collective—and says she is off to take a bath. This she will do, Rob tells Penny, for several hours, in an old galvanized tub on the roof under the stars, in rainwater warmed by admixture from an electric teakettle.

"What are your poems like?" Penny asks before she goes.

She turns and puts both hands on the table. Looking Penny in the eye, she says, "Take my arm, my sister. Follow me to where the shooting stars lie still. I saw them falling, he said, in cascades of living fire. There in the hillside village, they lay where they fell. The dead of Pompeii, cast in blue ice. I cradled a blue ice baby and its cold skin hurt my touch. A jet unzipped the sky, and through the rent yet more abortions fell. Fetuses of old women, young men, old men, and young women. Melting they formed a single sea, all personhood lost. We ran to the top of the city walls. Stop, we commanded heaven. Spare those who have not yet lived! Take us, the free! But that is freedom, heaven said—to fall." She pauses.

"Yikes," Penny says. "Wow."

"It's from my Kurdish Goth phase. Now I mostly write erotic poetry."

"It drives her lovers crazy," Rob says. "I think it's too explicit. It scares people off."

"Yeah, it doesn't always go down well with my exes," Jazz admits.

PENNY SPENDS THE NIGHT WITH Rob. They kiss chastely, they hug, they sleep. They draw closer together in their sleep than they did awake. She awakens at 4:00 A.M. needing to pee. She ignores the juice-jar chamber pot in his room and walks down three flights of creaking stairs to the toilet that shares a plastic curtain with the shower in a back corner of the kitchen. She thinks of the monster and looks up. Outside the first birds begin to sing.

She goes back to bed and lies next to Rob. She remembers the vivisection of Norm, his mute suffering, his misplaced courage. She burrows her wet face into Rob's chest and he clasps her tight. He says not one word, and neither does she. She entrusts herself to him. She doesn't fall asleep again. Still, she feels better. It's like being loved with unquestioning love.

SHE SPENDS THE DAY WITH Rob. He tinkers with a broken mountain bike frame in the garage. "It's not salvageable," he says. "I was going to turn it into part of a trailer, but I think it's already art."

"As in garbage?"

He unclamps it from the workbench and carries it to the gap between the garage and the house that gives access to the backyard. Half-swallowed by weeds, a pile of metal debris is rising. "Art as in art," he says, throwing it on the pile.

"What do you do with these bikes?"

"Fix them." He surveys the garage and the open space around it and spits. "But right now I'm out of frames. You want to go cruising?" He fetches a pry bar and a hacksaw from the garage. He beckons Penny to join him in the minivan.

They drive deeper into Jersey City, toward the Hackensack River. "Lampposts near the street," he tells her. "That's where people let a wheel get crushed by some car parking, and then they abandon the bike and it's *mine*."

Penny scans the curbs but doesn't see any bikes.

He stops before a bridge over a small tributary, and gets out to look down the revetment. "Bike," he says, pointing. He opens the back doors of the minivan and removes a neatly rolled towing strap. He gives Penny one end so that she can belay him—using a lamppost as a pulley—and he creeps down the slippery, overgrown riverbank to the bike. He loops the strap around it, and together they drag it back up the incline.

The spokes are grassy and the handlebars rusty, but the chrome-molybdenum frame and stainless steel derailleur still look good. "Not a dream bike," he says. "The dream is when you see a really good bike with the gel oozing out of the seat and realize some dweeb lost both keys to the U-lock and believes that bullshit about how he'll never get it open. Those puppies will bust with a two-pound hammer."

That evening, Penny prepares to spend another night with Rob by helping him kick back two forties. They go through seven cigarettes together. Once in bed, he kisses her on the cheek. They snuggle close. He lies on his back and pulls her up on top of him, sighing amiably. "I like feeling your weight," he says.

She feels happy and very turned on. She is determined to make the transition to being in love. Through tactical wriggling she determines once again that he is not aroused at all. His genitals seem liquid, like raw egg sloshing in a bowl.

She says, "Be honest. Are you gay?"

"What do you mean?"

"I feel like we definitely have a boy-girl thing, but I can't tell how you feel."

"I should tell you. I'm asexual. I'm not attracted to people in that way."

"*Asexual?* You are *so into me*!"

"Just not the way you think. I like you. I'm drawn to you. You're a good person."

Penny does not take "good person" as a compliment. Having been called "koala" half her life, she knows she has a *cara de buena persona*. She also knows that her body's bootylicious and he's held it for hours on end. She believes he is full of shit. "So you're not attracted to me," she sums up.

"Wrong. I'm fascinated by you, and I think we'll be close friends."

"You have potency issues," she says. "It's the nicotine and alcohol. I'm serious. You need to cut back."

"Listen to me. I don't respond to people in that way. Maybe you're not familiar with asexuality?"

"Oh yeah," she says. "That's it. I'm too Bible Belt to see that you're gender-queer."

"Hey. I can tell you're going through a difficult time, and I feel like I'm giving you support that you really need. I think it's the beginning of something good. Why are you putting sexual expectations on it?"

"Because I—" She hesitates and takes a deep breath. "Okay, maybe it is expectations. I have certain accustomed ways of going about certain things. Habits, maybe. And this is new to me. Because usually when I touch a guy's dick when he's in bed with me, it's not, like, *amorphous*."

"Thanks a lot."

"Give me a minute. I have to get my head around this." She ponders the issue for five seconds and says, "I don't believe you. I think you're impotent, and it's a medical problem. Erectile dysfunction or whatever."

"It wasn't a problem before you groped my crotch!"

"I can stop right now," Penny says.

"That would be respectful."

She slides out of bed and stoops to find her clothes. "I'm so in hell," she says. She can't feel blameless. She wanted to use him to discover a more shallow way of living. Memories of the dead were dragging her underground, and she wanted a life on the surface. The superficiality of skin on skin. So in all their hours of talking, the sum total of information she has shared with Rob about her father: nada. The man about whom she knows way too little knows nothing about her. But she would have fucked him, because she's that kind of shallow bitch—the kind who doesn't mind getting caught being that kind of shallow bitch. Who just found out she's been begging hugs off a neuter creature who pities her. Whee. And her embarrassment is nothing compared with her anger. She is (tacitly) angry enough to yell at him until he swears never to speak to her again. It feels like a setup designed to teach her a lesson.

"Come back here," he pleads. "I'll miss you."

"I thought you were straight. I'm going home."

"Please stay," he says, patting the futon. "We don't have to sleep together to sleep together."

Before she can find the words to say Fuck Off, there is a knock at the door.

She opens it to find Jazz standing in the lean-to, holding a cigarette and a glass of red wine. "I was just leaving," Penny says. "Sorry I got loud."

"I overheard your conversation, and I wanted to tell you to stop being so hard on yourself."

"You are kidding me."

Jazz's head wobbles tipsily, and she takes a drag off her cigarette with the side of her mouth. She says, "You shouldn't leave. You should never leave. You should stay here with this freak and *learn*. You're crushing hard on the Robster and thinking you want his dick, but it's not his dick you want. It's his *mind*. Get back in there and show the boy some respect, and you'll see—"

"Don't you think it's pretty fucking sexist, telling me to let him set the agenda?" She moves forward, toward the door.

Jazz raises the glass of wine and cigarette in her hand to eye level. She sidesteps to block Penny's escape. "Look at me," she says through the smoke. "Do I have a dick?"

"Honestly? I *don't know*."

Jazz flicks open her quilted dressing gown to reveal a deltaic butterfly-like arrangement of Wedgwood-blue silk and ivory lace. It looks pricey. "Check it out," she says, resting her left hand on

Penny's shoulder as she dandles her cigarette and wine in her right. "No dick. But I want you anyway, because I'm a sexual person. Not asexual like a certain vagina tease who leads women on because he likes the attention."

Confusion sets in. Penny sees a possible hell-hath-no-fury-like-a-woman-scorned angle, but Jazz does not seem to be looking for sympathy.

"You're hot," Jazz continues. "Like a woodland creature in heat to get fucked, and so smooth and brown no normal person can stand it, and this sexless bastard over here does not care, because he wants to be your friend. But I care. I want to get all up inside you and make you come until your teeth chatter. Go ahead. Grope my crotch."

Feminine beauty is not something Penny is used to seeing up close. Especially not beauty so reassuringly obscene. She had felt like a sailor on a life raft pelted by hail, and now Jazz is the mermaids, singing of life in caves under the sea. The obscenity is the neon sign flashing over the fairy-tale cave, telling her she's in the right place.

The standoff is brief. Her pride—as a curious person not entirely conservative—bids her extend her hand and tap the underwear. The slight touch turns the silk a darker blue. Jazz is very wet. When Penny's finger grazes her, she struggles to get her next breath.

"See?" she says. "We'll never be friends."

Penny touches the underwear again a little harder, in the interest of science. She puts her hand on Jazz's birdlike hip bone and looks into her eyes. She feels more or less as though a trapdoor had opened and dropped her into the Matrix. She sneaks a glance at Rob. He has picked up a back issue of *Popular Mechanics* from the floor and seems to be reading.

Later he enters Jazz's room to turn off the light (for privacy, because her rooftop greenhouse has no curtains). He sits in her armchair, watching the two women by the pinkish glow of mercury vapor streetlamps on atmospheric haze. He palpates his crotch once briefly and frowns.

THE NEXT DAY AROUND LUNCHTIME, over dry toast and tea, Sorry invites Penny to come along to the Friday potluck at Stayfree.

Penny says, "What, did you hear I'm a lesbian or something?"

"The whole neighborhood heard you're a lesbian!"

She imagines herself making loud sounds and can't be sure she didn't. "I was so fucking drunk," she says, apologetically.

"I was just busting your balls. We didn't hear a thing. When Rob came down this morning, he said you were with Jazz, and I put two and two together. He didn't look real ecstatic."

Penny frowns. "Well, it's not like he wanted—"

"What? Love, romance? He wants all those things. He's just not ready to pay the price."

"Well, if he doesn't want sex, he doesn't want sex. It would be really shitty to, like, rape him by humping his leg. And I was truly pretty drunk. And Jazz was so into it."

She frowns at the memory. The symmetry of sex with Jazz is still vivid. Breasts discovering the softness of breasts. Her clitoris grinding against Jazz's with inept abandon, pleased to find it equally indestructible. The silkiness of their faces. Their sweet little teeth.

Significant emotional asymmetry, however, had been introduced by her increasingly intense desire to involve Rob, who kept sitting there in the armchair. She remembers his staying for at least an hour, sometimes touching himself (he touched himself only once, but the movement caught her eye, and she naturally assumes it was part of a series), and that when she made eye contact, he got up and left. That's what she likes remembering best. Not the sexual ecstasies before and after. Just that Rob got up and left—that maybe, possibly, he was a little bit jealous?

"I take it you're not in love," Sorry says.

"Not with Jazz."

Sorry nods and lights a cigarette. "So you want to come to Stayfree?"

"And meet dykes? I don't know."

"There's no such thing as a feminist dyke. Not anymore. Stayfree is feminist men and women such as you and I."

"I don't know if I could eat much. But I could definitely stand to meet people. It's not like I know anybody around here." She tentatively touches the pack of cigarettes. She shakes her head.

"Go upstairs," Sorry suggests. "You can lie down in my room. I'll call you when it's time to get up."

Penny accepts the offer. As she relaxes, mounting the stairs, her head begins to throb.

Instead of the bed, she picks a spot on the rug in the sun. She curls up with her head on a pink-and-gold meditation pillow. Through the open window she can hear the clank of Rob's tinkering in the garage. After the minivan revs up and drives away, she sleeps.

AROUND FIVE, HER PHONE RINGS with the promised wake-up call. She returns to the kitchen, where Sorry assigns her to help with their potluck dish, a lentil salad, by shelling every walnut in a very large bag—fully five pounds of walnuts.

"Where'd you get so many walnuts?" Penny asks, putting down the nutcracker to shake her aching hand.

"I found them in the pantry. Probably from the trash at the co-op. It's a miracle they're not rancid. It would be a sad waste if they were. They did some study that if you eat a handful of nuts every day, it's as healthy as jogging. You can skip the exercise and eat the nuts."

"So shouldn't we be rationing them, to eat a handful a day?"

"Do I look to you like I believe in studies?" She taps an ash into a saucer next to the sink and returns to her task of grating carrots into a bowl. "Nuts are fat pills. I want them out of the house."

Laughing makes Penny shudder involuntarily. She works in pained silence. She doesn't have the appetite to try one of the nuts.

When Rob gets back from his outing, he comes into the kitchen.

“Hey, guys,” he says, clapping her on the shoulder. She sits up a bit to lengthen her contact with his hand, and he bends to kiss her neck. He shows them both a circular saw he found on a sidewalk in Hoboken. It lacks only a power cord.

“Great saw,” Penny says.

“I might build a gazebo out back,” he says.

They get him to taste the salad. He says it would be great if the walnuts weren’t rancid.

“Maybe we should have tasted them,” Penny says. “But there will be other stuff to eat. Are you coming along?”

“I don’t think so. People at Stayfree don’t really go for me. They think I’m a macho man.”

“That’s what I used to think, too. But haven’t they known you longer?”

“They never see me cuddling with a dude. I think that’s the problem.”

“They never see you cuddling with a woman who isn’t conventionally attractive,” Sorry says. “I’ve never seen you with a woman taller than you. Or older, or fat, or with short hair.”

Rob puts his arm around her and says, “I’m a tragic slave to my genetic program. I have no choice but to go with it. It’s like being born trans. I was born liking plain vanilla T&A.”

“Who you calling plain vanilla?” Penny protests.

“You should be more upset he called you T&A,” Sorry points out.

“I don’t see you herding any llamas in a bowler hat,” Rob says. “You’re a biz-ad major from Morristown.”

“I was raised in Brazil by animist drug freaks!”

Sorry says, “Ignore him. He’s jealous. You think she always tag-teams him like that? No way.”

“Thanks, Mom,” Rob says.

“You shouldn’t take it personally. He’s never had sex in his life.”

“Hey,” Rob says. “Cool it.”

"Well, have you?" Penny asks.

"Have I what?"

"Had sex."

"Of course I have. It's hard time pressure. If you say you don't want it, they take it as a challenge. Girls are like, 'Of course you didn't want my friend, she's a ska-ank!' Then they rape me. I'm hugging some girl and—*bam*—she's on her knees. They think it's going to be easy, like abusing a child."

Penny is shocked into silence, and Sorry says, "You're not any kind of child, Rob. Maybe you need to work on your communications skills—as in learn to say no—if all these women are taking it too far?"

"Now it's *my* fault," he says.

"Were you an abused child?" Penny asks softly.

"I just meant it's so weird they think they can physically dominate me. I mean, it's one thing holding down a five-year-old—"

"I get the picture," Penny says.

"You just don't like it when women make the first move," Sorry says. "You're a cis-het dude-bro on strike for better conditions."

"A blow job shouldn't be anybody's first move. I like being friends with women."

"You like worshipping size-queen starfuckers," Sorry says. She turns to Penny and adds, "He's in vicarious love with Jazz. He wants her more than anything in the world. Just not for himself."

"Jesus," Rob says, turning away.

"Are you a voyeur?" Penny says to him. "You get off living next to her?"

"I don't get off!"

"Maybe women go for your dick because your mouth is full of tobacco?"

"Ask him where Jazz sleeps when it's too hot or too cold or too loud in her greenhouse," Sorry says.

Rob leaves the kitchen and stomps upstairs.

"We just annoyed the living shit out of him while acquiring no actionable intelligence," Penny says to Sorry.

"You just don't want to hear it," Sorry says.

THEY BORROW HIS MINIVAN TO drive to Stayfree because it's raining. The house is on a dubious-looking block, with several abandoned houses on the same side of the street. The marshy vacant lot opposite is overgrown with high reeds. The facade is black, with the squatter lightning-bolt emblem in lavender.

Penny follows Sorry inside. The dark living room is lined with books and posters. The only white objects are the smartphone and cylindrical loudspeaker playing pop songs from the mantelpiece. Husky men stand around the sofas, eating. Shrill women fuss over the arrangement of food on the buffet. Sorry plunks down the salad. "Is this good?" No reaction. She proceeds to the kitchen to take a serving spoon from a drawer and returns, via the buffet table, to the front porch, where Penny is standing looking out at the street.

"We're the only girls here," Penny whispers. "I mean, as in—what am I trying to say? Am I being trans-phobic?"

"Hey, I miss women feminists, too. But I'm not willing to move back to Jordan to see them again."

Penny leans back, elbows on the railing, to look through the front window into the house. "I don't get your Jordan thing. Tell me. How are you Jordanian?"

"Most people in the West Bank have Jordanian passports," Sorry says. "Like sixty-five percent. They only started revoking their citizenship and making them stateless a few years ago. The king's trying to turn up the heat on Netanyahu."

"But you're Jewish, and super American—"

"My mom's from a really backward area of the Transjordan. She converted to marry a settler from Brooklyn. She thought Maale Nakam was the Paris of the Middle East. Now she's not allowed to leave it."

"Ouch," Penny says. "But can't you be American if your dad is?"

"He gave up his citizenship when he emigrated because he thought it would cancel his credit card debt. What can I say? At least I'm not stateless. But I had to get out of there. My whole family thinks I'm a radical feminist freak. And not for hanging out with trans anarchists. I mean like for thinking women should have the vote."

"I wish I was from one of those cultures. You know? Where you can be a feminist badass by riding your bike or playing soccer or whatever. I'd be like the Sudanese girl with cleats and a ponytail who speaks at the UN and people would be like, wow, let's give her NGO a lot of money. I'd have this NGO that teaches girls to interrupt boys when they talk."

"Global feminism," Sorry says. "Also known as back to square one." She leans close and adds sotto voce, "Don't mention sports around here. It's more taboo than dieting. Never let a transsexual think you might have a negative body image."

Penny laughs.

"Accept yourself," Sorry says. "Find your tribe and burn your bridges." She extracts an American Spirit from the breast pocket of her T-shirt and lights it.

Penny says, "Wait. If this is so totally not your crew—why are we here?"

"I used to live here. I love this house!" Her hand perches casually on the railing so the ash falls into an azalea. "All my friends moved out around the time I did, but the house lives on. And I love it. And now I'm going to stand right here and party on until our bowl is empty and we can take it home."

"Where'd they move to?"

"All different houses with projects that weren't explicitly feminist. We decided to take the fight to arenas where we wouldn't be fighting women all the time."

"Any of them here?"

"Yeah. One. She's a man. We don't fight, because we stopped talking."

"Is there an asexual house?"

"No. Why would they band together? They just want to be alone with their TVs and squee over Benedict Cumberbatch."

Penny nods. "I'm getting hungry. I'm going to go find something bland and stuff myself." She drops her bag at Sorry's feet and goes back inside the house.

She drifts along the buffet, looking at the food, sneaking glances at the people. Between the peach fuzz and the push-up bras, it reminds her of junior high. People seem uneasy and a little too excited about their new and unfamiliar bodies. She hears the sound of maternal instincts being vigorously applied to cats on the Internet. Another conversation, pitched deeper, revolves around grants available to emerging filmmakers. It all seems rather gender-polarized.

She searches in vain for her favorite feminine gender (tomboy).

To the extent that she can pull it off, her gender is babe. But at Stayfree her babe outfit (long hair, big shirt, leggings, flats) makes her feel like an interloper—like some rude woman-born-woman intent on boycotting femininity because she can take it for granted. The girly-girls on hand have spared no pains. They are as polished as knights in armor, bodies pierced, coiffed, tattooed, shoehorned into heels and dresses. The manly-men are gruff and earnest in word and deed. She's the only babe in sight. She lacks an audience. It's not her gender that's underrepresented. It's her species. Like a dog at a party for birds, or a hip-hopper at a party for Pagan bisexuals.

She is thinking too much. The air around her, thick with music and conversation, starts to thrum.

She takes a vegan brownie and sits down in an armchair, tucking her feet up under her without taking off her shoes. Her nerves are loud enough to block out the noise, and she thinks vivid thoughts: Sorry's mother trading her veil for a wig to keep house for an American. Her own mother, earning her keep from the day she was born. Norm's feminism—his not wanting her to be a girly-girl—that dovetails so neatly with Amalia's traditional culture, where women labor day and night. The workaholic-Disney-princess model of femininity that makes all the tomboys stay home with Sherlock. Is emergent filmmaking so very unlike chewing coca leaves and smearing it on a gourd? She finishes the brownie. It's good. Vegan brownie technology has moved on, she thinks.

She still has spoken to no one but Sorry. She returns to the buffet. Their salad is doing well—already nearly half gone. Maybe people are eating around the walnuts. She piles two plates high with pasta and pesto and takes them out to the porch.

They fall into girl talk. She entertains Sorry for half an hour with a succession of podgy and squirrelly local men on a GPS-enabled dating app.

IT IS SATURDAY. PENNY SITS at her mother's kitchen table in Morristown. She has a plan.

"I want to thank you for looking after that house," Amalia says. "I tried so hard to forget the whole thing. I didn't want to think about all the work it will take, and then to sell it for nothing. How bad is it? Is there much water damage?"

"I don't know where you guys got the idea that the roof is gone. The house is in terrific shape."

"You mean livable?"

"With a couple exceptions. The plumbing is an issue, and the heat, I don't know."

"Did you get an appraisal?"

"We'd be fools to put it on the market now. Jersey City is changing fast. There's high-rise condos going up, and art centers and stuff. Who knows where the prices will be in five years? And that's why I wanted to ask you something. Remember how Matt suggested that I could live there and fix it up? You know, keep it in shape with fresh paint, until the time is ripe to sell? Keep the yard nice?"

"You know I would prefer to settle the estate."

"But, Mom, there's a question of equity. It's *your* fault I lost the lease on Dad's apartment, and now I have nowhere to stay. You won't let me stay at the summer place, and you inherited a big empty house. Doesn't it make sense?"

"You could get a job, and rent yourself a place that's nice."

"I'm trying! But the job market's not easy. I don't want another internship."

Amalia sighs.

"The issue right now is, I need a place to stay by the end of next month."

"The summer place is not mine to give. I told you, it belongs to Matt and Patrick. It was their mother's."

"Who wants to be way out there anyway, when I can be close to the PATH train in Jersey City? The Palisades suck in cold weather. Two snowflakes, and I'm trapped. I couldn't get to work or anywhere else."

"Eh," Amalia says. "Maybe you're right. But if you move into Norm's childhood home, I'll never get you out. You'll be sentimental."

"I could get sentimental about anything with a roof on it, and this place definitely has a roof. I'm just being pragmatic. A pragmatic interim solution, so I don't become *homeless*."

"Oh my god, don't use words like that on your guilty old mother," Amalia says.

"You're not old. Dad was old."

"I could get you a job at the bank. We have a purchasing department, you know. You could have a good lifestyle. Don't move into that messed-up old house."

"Oh, please no, Mom. That would be too much. I don't want to be dependent on you for everything. I want to stand on my own feet. I just need a place to stand. Everybody would know it's nepotism. Word would get out, even if we didn't look like sisters. But we do."

Amalia puts her fingertips on her cheekbones and pushes her skin toward her ears. "Maybe I'll get a face-lift," she says. "Then we'll look alike."

"You don't even have any gray hair," Penny says. "I don't know what your problem is."

PENNY'S PLAN HITS A SNAG: all the bedrooms at Nicotine are taken. There is a long waiting list to move into Stayfree.

Sorry invites her housemates and Penny to eat lasagna on a Sunday night and brainstorm a resolution.

On Sunday afternoon, Penny helps her prepare the lasagna. She expresses surprise that it involves alternate layers of white sauce rather than ricotta. Sorry explains that her dad converted to Judaism from being Italian American. "Not his fault," she says. "These Hasidim accosted him on Fifth Avenue on Hanukkah. They thought he was an apostate. He was in default and on the rebound. Next thing you know, he's living in a settlement. Anyway, he says ricotta in lasagna is an abomination."

"So you're not actually Jewish."

"Jewish is a lifestyle. It's an attitude. What they used to call a religion. Anybody can be Jewish."

Penny laughs, because of course she's right.

At suppertime, Rob brings a six-pack and Jazz, a bottle of Chianti. Penny finally meets Anka and Tony. She has never seen either of them before. Anka works a full-time job and has friends at another house, and Tony sometimes vanishes for days. His housemates attribute these absences to women.

Sorry introduces them by pointing. "Anka," she says. "Tony. This is Penny. She's looking for a house."

Anka says, "Hi! Nice to meet you!" and waves.

She is in her midtwenties, the child of a research biologist and an American Red Cross executive, a graduate of Quaker day schools and Penn. She is an accomplished painter, using her talents to make portraits of acquaintances, which she gives away for free. She doesn't think of her painting as art because she majored in public health. She is lovely in the most conventional way—tall and blond—but so often troubled by serious thoughts having to do with her AIDS advocacy that she seems forbidding to people who don't know her. Consequently, she sees her boyfriend from high school when she goes home to celebrate national holidays. They have furiously passionate sex behind his wife's back. They know each other and the lay of the land so well, they've even done it in the baby's room while his wife was cooking. But Anka isn't easy, and she doesn't look it. No New York metropolitan–area single has ever persisted past the fifth date.

Tony—who says he's heard a lot about Penny, and shakes her hand—is a self-described "working stiff," currently unemployed and open to odd jobs of any kind, interested in staying off the grid. Never says why. Maybe (Rob tells Penny later) the problem is as simple as the threat of garnisheed wages for delinquent child support. He might be an escaped convict, or just violating probation. An undocumented immigrant with unusually good language skills? Nobody knows. And nobody cares, because he is laid-back, amusing, clean, and tidy. Tony is old, chubby, and balding by anarchist standards, but not by the standards of the New York metropolitan area.

As planned, the dinner-table conversation centers on Penny's residential options. Rob proposes DJD and Tranquility, two CHA houses devoted to alternative energy sources and the rights of indigenous peoples, respectively. Each is less than half a mile from Nicotine, inconvenient by public transport but amenable to biking, and not fully booked, for lack of suitable activists.

"Tranquility is vegan," Sorry points out.

"I can handle vegan food, except sometimes dessert," Penny says. "What's DJD stand for?"

"Donald Judd Daybed," Rob says. "There was this guy moved into the house, which at that point was called Pangaea, with this huge sofa called the Donald Judd Daybed, which is like a car shipping crate made of teak or some shit. It weighs more than a waterbed. It's like a house-within-a-house. So when he set it up on the third floor, the whole place started to list to one side. You couldn't close the inside doors. DJD is not brick like this place. It's wood frame. So they put it back on the ground floor, and when it got a scratch it came out that it's worth like a *hundred thousand dollars*."

"It's truly very comfortable," Tony says.

"Half the house wanted to break it up for firewood," he goes on. "The house theme is alternative energy, with pellet stoves and a heat pump, and they were always freaking out about the price of wood, and they were like, 'Free wood!' "

"Petty bourgeois ascetics," Jazz says.

"In the end they got mediators to come in from Movement for a New Society," Rob continues, nodding, "and they reached a consensus that it's 'super comfy.' And so overnight, the whole focus of the house changed from insulation and solar panels and everything like that to bundling up together with a lot of blankets on the DJD. They called it 'passive' something—passive recombinant thermal something—"

"And then Trine got pregnant," Sorry wraps up the story. The whole room (except for Penny) laughs. For several seconds Sorry,

Jazz, Anka, Tony, and Rob laugh. The laughter subsides to latent giggling.

"That was one sneaky bitch," Tony adds, giving his homemade cigar a few swift puffs. They laugh again.

"Trine was this woman nobody liked," Sorry explains. "I mean, nobody but *nobody* was fucking her. But somebody knocked her up. By accident! Like Leah in the Bible. I guess people were disoriented."

"Sorry, Tony my man, it *never* gets that dark in the city," Rob says. More laughter.

"What I don't get," Penny says, "is why they don't sell it and do something useful with the money. I mean, if it's really worth a hundred thousand dollars."

"So speaks a woman who never lived in a squat," Sorry replies. "Okay, they unload it. Who gets a share—the guy who brought it? The guy he lifted it from? Everybody who lived there when he did? The people who live there now? CHA? It's like what happens when squatters have a chance of getting title. The second and third generation is always like, '*Whatever-squat stays!*'"—she puts on a melodic whiny voice—"because they do the math and figure out that not paying rent is worth it. If a room would rent for five hundred, that's six thousand dollars you're saving every year. Stay in the house for twenty years, and it's a hundred and twenty thousand—way more than your share would be if you sold the house. And meanwhile there's inflation and attrition. The longer you wait, the more likely you're going to end up walking off with a million. Same thing goes with the DJD. People are biding their time."

"You would love the DJD," Jazz says. "I can see you now, curled up on it like a kitty-cat. It's so Penny. You'd never get up."

"Plus I'd fuck whoever came along, by accident."

"That's the sexual spell of the DJD. It has all the purity of minimalism, but it's a sofa—the most bourgeois item of furniture known to man—so it's like a biodynamic dungeon or a radioactive unicorn.

But listen. There's a massive environmental issue with that house. They're deep into conserving water. As in not letting it flow to the ocean. And not just in desert regions." She sees Penny's blank expression. "You know Belo Monte? A guy at DJD told me the Belo Monte Dam is a small price to pay for sustainable growth with zero emissions."

"Oh my god," Penny says, as though hearing that cannibalism is a small price to pay for trichinosis. "What about the other house?"

"Tranquility," Jazz says. "But I can't see you doing indigenous rights."

"What do you mean?" Rob protests. "Look at her Kogi amulets!"

"Penny is their worst nightmare. A modern woman. The great leveler. Entropy incarnate."

"It was my mom who blew out of indigeneity," Penny says. "Or indigence or whatever. I'd go back and spend my life doing coke and taking naps in a heartbeat! I like fricasseed guinea pig! I'd be an upper-class Kogi, obviously. Not one of the slaves."

"You can teach them the old ways," Tony suggests. "Then lead them to freedom."

"I think you should just interview at Tranquility and get it over with," Anka says, frowning at Tony and Jazz. "It's a nicer house. The room that's free has two closets and a parquet floor and a nice light fixture. They've been renovating the upstairs bathroom at DJD for like two solid years."

"Sold," Penny says.

THE FOLLOWING FRIDAY NIGHT, PENNY sits in the corner of a sofa in the common room at Tranquility. The other residents look at her with interest. She shares the sofa with Rufus, a middle-aged African American man, and a South Asian–looking man in his thirties named Barry wearing a Filipino dress shirt with eyelet lace and patch pockets. Two white college students, Jacob and Maureen, sit in armchairs, while an African American woman named Stevie occupies the rug.

"We hear you're Kogi from Colombia," Maureen says. Her right arm is decorated with a fresh, clear, deep black tattoo of a Kwakiutl orca totem. "That is so fascinating."

"Half-Kogi, I guess," Penny says. "Where are you guys from?"

"Louisville," Barry says. "My ancestors immigrated to Maryland in the seventies."

Maureen says, "Wilkes-Barre."

Jacob says, "I'm from around here."

Rufus nods in assent, indicating that he is also a local.

Stevie says nothing.

"Well, basically I'm from the Upper West Side via Morristown," Penny says. "And Morgantown. I went to WVU. It's my mom who's Kogi. She ran away from home and ended up meeting my dad, who was from New York."

"Just like me!" Stevie says. She has curly magenta hair and wears a forties-style bathing suit of plum-colored cotton gabardine with fishnet stockings and Chuck Taylors. She looks ageless and possibly about thirty-five. "My parents wanted me to finish high school and I was like fuck *you*. It's indoctrination. So I ran away. That's part of why I'm committed to indigenous peoples' right to self-determination. Nobody should have their way of life dictated to them."

"I joined the navy when I was seventeen," Rufus says. "That's when I started learning about oppression."

"Cool," Penny says approvingly. "I'm sure you know more about it than I do. I've never really had to follow orders, except in college, and at work, I guess. I mean, my parents weren't strict."

"It's stressful," Rufus says. "The navy is very traditional. Always doing things the way they always been done. I had to run away, too."

"What, are you AWOL? Do you get a lot of MPs coming around here?" Seeing that Rufus looks horrified, she adds, "Just kidding."

"Are there very many Kogi left?" Barry asks.

"No clue," Penny says. "But anyway, my dad was Jewish."

"That's a shame."

"Huh?"

"I mean, your mom could have married a Kogi."

"What do you mean? They're not an endangered species! Do you think my dad should have married a Jewish girl?"

"This interview is taking a strange turn," Rufus remarks.

"It's not a job interview," Penny says, turning to him. "I don't have to put on a fake personality. I get tired of hearing people say indigenous people should practice their folkways. White people don't have that responsibility, do they? They can innovate all they want, because it's their tradition to be modern, and I'm supposed to reclaim my ancestral mountaintop? Thanks a lot!"

Penny knows she is talking too much, but in the presence of five strangers she can't keep straight, she feels safe falling back on a familiar topic—herself—somewhat as when people dominate conversations in bars simply because they can't hear anybody.

"But it's genocide," Barry says. "Once indigenous peoples assimilate, they're gone."

"So if I convert to Islam to keep Boko Haram from killing me, I'm committing genocide."

"That's not what I meant."

"Sorting people into groups isn't what anybody needs. Not indigenous peoples, or anybody else."

Barry says, "It's an inevitable irony that you can't condemn genocide without using the perpetrators' racial categories. But that doesn't make it right to kill people because of their ethnic background."

"I didn't say I'm okay with genocide! I just meant that they call it a crime against humanity because it's subhuman, and I say fuck that. If somebody kills me, I don't want it to be beneath his dignity. I want it to be murder."

Maureen says, "I don't get what you're saying, but I think you might be a really interesting addition to the house. I like these kinds of discussions."

Jacob pipes up at last. "Do you sit down in the bathroom?" he asks. "Because that's my main concern with new indigenous groups in the house. Remember that Hindu guy who squatted on the toilet seat without taking off his shoes? And that girl who would only shit in plastic bags."

"But she was a runaway, and crazy," Rufus says. He turns to explain her to Penny. "It was sad. She would throw those bags out in the yard, and the cats would get in them. A kitten gets hungry enough, it will eat human feces—but I don't want to *know*. Don't confront me with that fact. Don't make me go out and clean up the yard and find all those little kittens with the bags ripped open and your shit on their faces!"

"Oh my god," Penny says, visibly moved. "How long did she live here?"

"Months," he says. "She was a street kid with nowhere to go. We couldn't throw her out until we found her a replacement abandominium."

"She had so many friends," Jacob says.

"She was tribal," Stevie says. "The tribe of underage sex workers from Garden City."

"So you guys are basically just suckers," Penny says. "Way too nice."

Shrugs all around. "We try to be friendly," Rufus says.

"Do you mind if I ask a question about the solidarity work you do as a house?" No one minds. They look flattered and expectant. She asks, "Do you support any groups engaged in armed struggle?"

"Do we *what*?" Barry asks.

"You ask if we building *bombs*?" Rufus says.

"I mean like the Karen in Burma or whatever. With your fund-raising. I'm basically against violence. I'm kind of a pacifist. Anything is better than hurting people."

"We're not in a position to raise money," Maureen says. Her housemates nod. "I mean, I give all the support I can to my favorite causes on social media. It's so many initiatives, I can't even keep track. I like Amnesty International, but I guess my favorite is UNICEF. They have this great program to make sure indigenous girls get food."

"I like UNICEF, too," Penny says. "I've actually done some fund-raising work for them." (She means while trick-or-treating in Morristown.)

"Maybe you can teach us something about fund-raising," Stevie chimes in. "I work with a collective that builds puppets for street theater, and it takes so much money. Just storing the puppets between conferences takes money."

"The puppets are great," Jacob says. "They're what made me into an activist. I saw them on YouTube."

"You can get more support with puppets than with anything else," Stevie says. "People go to a demo or see video and they see the police on one side and us on the other, and they see who's having all the fun. It gets them to join the revolution."

"The puppets are awesome," Barry agrees. The others nod.

Maureen says, "Lots of indigenous cultures do street theater with puppets. The Dogon. The Hopi." Again, they all nod.

"That sounds awesome," Penny says. "I love puppets."

She feels as though she were admitting a weakness for baby bunnies or chocolate sprinkles—not much of a confession, much less a commitment—but the resonance on the faces around her is so approving that her mind bends willingly. Why shouldn't loving puppets be a revolutionary act, in a world where so many people love drone warfare? Bunnies and chocolate sprinkles don't work as street theater—much too small—while values such as peace, love, and understanding are notoriously invisible. Puppets it is! Big ones! Why not. There are more inane things you could love.

Mustering these thoughts, she smiles in a way that comes close to the Mona Lisa. She feels that Tranquility is inhabited by hapless lunatics, but she'll be spending most of her time at Nicotine anyway, so who cares.

They ask her to leave the room for a moment. There is a swift consensus to take her in. They feel they have never met anyone quite so indigenous. They imagine both the Kogi and Jewish cultures as the sorts of patriarchies that produce women so strong they're actually matriarchies, if you take time to scratch the surface.

Her new room at Tranquility is on the third floor, with slanted ceilings and gabled windows. The oaken flooring displays an attractive herringbone pattern. She has nearly two hundred square feet of it.

Residents do not pay rent per se; they pay a co-op fee to cover food and utilities. Since much of the food comes from Dumpsters and the heat is off for the summer, the fee is currently very low—fifty-eight dollars and eighty cents per month.

BEFORE SHE HAS A CHANCE to hire movers at her mother's expense, Rob volunteers to move her things with his minivan. She can't say no, since arriving at Tranquility with professional movers would blow her cover big-time.

On the first Saturday in July, Rob drives into the city. Anka and Tony ride along to help out. With Penny's spare key to open the garage gate, he finds the loading area by the freight elevator in the basement of her building and lodges his vehicle between two pillars. The three ride up to meet her in Norm's old place.

Tony expresses his approval that there is so little furniture. He is somewhat less delighted after he tries budging it. "We could leave that big wardrobe," he remarks. "There's nothing saying we have to steal everything that isn't nailed down."

"What do you mean?" Penny asks.

"Is this not a sublet? This can't possibly be *your* furniture."

"They said I could have whatever I want," she says, more or less accurately.

Rob admires her bicycle—a light, fast ten-speed with a short wheelbase—and declares that it will be loaded last, being fragile. His admiration for the bike makes Penny proud. At the same time she is embarrassed by his uneasiness with the upscale nature of the building. Its very height and solidity seem to worry him. She feels glad he never sees the lobby or the doorman.

First Norm's massive bureau and desk descend and are loaded into the rear of the minivan, the desk tipped up on its side. Dismantling the bed takes time, but the headboard and mattress soon find space, surmounted by the kitchen table and chairs with their legs unscrewed. Rob fits in small things on the periphery—bags of clothes and little boxes of books Penny packed small enough to lift them herself. On top goes the bike, pedals removed, handlebars loosened and turned, as if it were going on a plane.

Anka and Tony spend a lot of time standing around, and Penny realizes they were expecting a walk-up. In reality there isn't much to do: load the elevator on floor nine, unload it on floor minus-one.

There is talk of returning for a second load until Rob measures Norm's wardrobe and pronounces it larger than his cargo space. "You'd have to rent a truck," he tells Penny.

She goes to see the doorman to ask about temporary storage. He remembers Norm with fondness. He opens the boiler room for her. The new heating system is much smaller than the old one, freeing up a great deal of space.

The air is suboptimal for wooden furniture—dank and hot. Penny assures herself and the doorman that the storage solution is only temporary. She knows it is not. She knows she will never rent a truck and drive into the city to pick up an immense wardrobe she doesn't need. Her room at Tranquility has a large closet, not a real walk-in, but with enough space inside to turn around and a shoe rack. By the time she moves again, the wardrobe will be warped. Still, they carry it—a massive piece of solid wood furniture—down and store it in the boiler room.

The thought of losing it bothers her, but she sees no alternative. She puts it out of her mind.

ANKA, ROB, AND TONY UNLOAD her things from the minivan to the sidewalk. She thanks them and asks them to stay for sandwiches. They say they should be getting home, but Rob agrees to accept five dollars toward gas and maintenance.

The Tranquility residents help carry everything upstairs, and their work is soon done. She serves them cold sandwiches with cruelty-free pastrami and sauerkraut from the Seventh-day Adventist grocery next to Bryant Park. They eat on the porch as night falls, running their fingertips over each slice of bread front and back to be sure the caraway seeds are not bugs.

Upstairs, she turns on the bright overhead light fixture and sits on the rug to survey her new abode.

Despite the fatiguing day, she feels supercharged with nervous energy. Her very own room, a house full of strangers, the heart of the CHA community—home to the people who interest her most in the world, Rob and Jazz—and all this furniture she associates very strongly with her father. She could exhaust herself emotionally just sitting and looking at it.

Her phone buzzes. A text from Matt, written in the style of an NYU student he occasionally "dates": Sis where u at. Drove by JC house. Looking good but no sis. What's the deal. They paying you rent???

She does not reply. Several minutes later the phone rings. It is Amalia.

"I am angry," Amalia begins. "Matt tells me you are renting Norm's house to *ocupas*! Why did you lie to me?"

"Nobody is renting out any house," Penny says. "We have occupiers because the house was in ruins, just like you said. You and Dad never fucking fixed it after it burned. They saved the house, and now they're living in it. They're terrific. I love them."

"Terrific," Amalia repeats.

"They're activists. They're wonderful people. I bet you could take them off your taxes as a charitable donation."

"Matt told me a very handsome man lives there. You want to tell me about it?"

"Tell you about what?"

"Are you in love again?" Momentarily cornered, Penny hesitates before replying. Her mother, sensing emotion, pounces. "Oh my god," she says. "You are keeping a lover, how is it called? A *kept man,* like a mistress, in my house."

"That is so not true!"

"You agreed as my agent to prepare that house for sale, and now you are defending a lover who won't pay rent. Buying yourself a boy toy for money. How much am I losing to your charitable donation? Three thousand dollars every month?"

"Don't be crude."

"Oh my god, how you talk to your own mother. I will have your brother take care of this problem. Do not go into my house again. Stay away from my house!"

"How is it your house? It's Dad's house. It's part of the estate. You only married him, and I'm his daughter. His own blood. I'm closer to owning that house than you are!"

"You have no brains," Amalia says.

Penny presses the red dot to end the call. She hyperventilates.

She calls the landline at Nicotine—a rotary phone on the wall in the kitchen—and Anka answers.

"I need to tell you something," she says. "I heard the worst rumor. I was talking to someone who works at a bank, and I was telling them about the house, and they said the owner died last month and the heirs want to sell it. Because of the redevelopment district or something."

Anka says, "You sound all excited and panicky, but what's the big deal? I thought Rob showed you the skeleton in our closet."

"You mean the bucket monster?"

"This house will never sell. I'd love to see them try. Let's engage a Realtor and have an open house this Sunday." She raises her voice. "There's something afoot in the real estate department, but we know the drill. Don't we?"

Tony's voice calls out from somewhere in the Nicotine kitchen: *"Ad nauseam!"*

"There's always somebody trying to collect rent from CHA squats. But you can't get blood from a proverbial stone, you know?"

"What if they just want to evict you and sell?"

"Two words. Bucket monster."

Penny relaxes. She tucks her phone under her chin and chats with Anka about their day while she rearranges her clothes in Norm's old bureau and sorts office supplies into his desk drawers. Suddenly she says, "I would so totally love a cigarette. What's the Tranquility house rule on smoking again? I think I have to cross the Pennsylvania line and air out my clothes before I come back."

"You forgot the part about washing your hair. Come on over! You can give us a hand with this beer Tony made."

WHEN PENNY ARRIVES AT THE house, Matt is there, seated at the kitchen table. The tea bag still rests in his steaming teacup, as though he has not been there long. "I see you crusty punks have met my little sister," he says in amiable tones.

Rob, Anka, Sorry, Jazz, and Tony turn to face Penny.

"Half-sister," she says.

"My independently wealthy little sister," Matt mocks. "So well-off, she'd never be tempted to fix up a rat-hole and put it on the market as a favor to her father's estate."

"Don't bend the truth," Penny says. "When I agreed to fix this place up, I thought it was empty. I changed my mind the minute I met you guys."

"Somehow word didn't get back to the other heirs," Matt says. "Your mother called me a few minutes ago, seeming dissatisfied, and I confess to having felt a certain disappointment myself, when I learned that you are spending all your time here casually fucking us over."

Penny is unable to think of anything to say. She looks at Anka, recipient of her most recent lie, expecting open contempt.

Anka smiles and says, "We could introduce him to our monster."

"Meeting this many parasites was enough for one day," Matt says.

"Pardon me, smart-ass, but I have beaucoup sweat equity in this place," Rob says.

"You've earned my undying gratitude. But now you all need to find loving homes."

"Why do you even care?" Penny begs. "You don't need the money!"

"That's right. I'm not poor, or even broke. I don't *need* my share of this house. I *want* it. I *desire* it." Seeming to have found her mute button, he adds, "You seem intent on exploiting it to serve aims of your own, or so I'm told by your mother. Sounds like the koala-face made a love connection. You want to tell me?"

Penny looks to the Nicotine inhabitants, expecting to see an anger that matches her shame. Instead they look expectantly from her to Matt. They seem intrigued.

Rob nods encouragement, and she asks meekly, "What if I somehow raised the money to buy out your share? Maybe CHA—"

"That won't be necessary," Jazz says, glaring at Penny. She takes a cigarette from the pack on the table. She lights it, gazing at Matt through a cloud of smoke, and explains, "He just said he's not in the game for the money."

He waves his hand and coughs. "*Nicotine house,*" he says, his voice low, slow, and sarcastic, imitating a longtime smoker's vocal fry. Turning in his seat and looking fixedly at Jazz, he says, "Please explain your presence here. You seem overqualified."

"These are my friends," Jazz replies.

"You're a sexy woman. Killer body."

"Interesting word choice. You don't look sixty-five."

"Correction. You're uncommonly attractive."

Jazz laughs at him.

Tony interrupts by asking Matt whether he is familiar with the legal doctrine of adverse possession.

"Fill me in," Matt says.

"It's that if you take somebody's property without their permission and they know it, and you know they know it, after some period of years it's finders keepers. So every time you tell us you knew there were squatters in here and didn't do a thing about it, you're giving us the house."

"In theory, that would be a real interesting theory," Matt says.

"Would you mind very much if we ask him to leave?" Sorry asks Penny. "I can't stand him."

Matt regards Sorry depreciatively. She is wearing a too-small striped tank top with PONY SLAYSTATION written on the front in glitter pen, crooked shorts, and her hair in pigtails. Her look: militantly antifashion.

All at once Penny feels stronger. She doesn't know whether she's in the right, but she knows it's right to defend people who don't know how to dress.

"I came over because I have plans with my friends," she tells Matt firmly. "I'm sorry, but you should go now, and we'll talk later. Call me tomorrow."

"She's asking you to leave," Rob says. "And so am I."

Anka, Jazz, Sorry, and Tony nod in agreement.

"I'd hate to undermine your social standing with these losers," Matt says to Penny, rising from his seat. His tea is still untouched. "Think about what I said," he adds, addressing Jazz.

"Nobody tells me what to think," she replies.

AFTER MATT LEAVES, THEY BEGIN decanting the home-brewed beer. It has a serious kick. Tony estimates thirty proof. "He's not my brother, I swear," Penny insists. "Half-brother at the outside."

"We can tell," Jazz says. "You're an Asian sex dumpling, and he's an aging Greek god."

"Ugh!" Penny cries out. "You don't know what you're saying!"

"That man has a hard-core Satanist vibe," Sorry opines. "Like he swore on a goat's carcass to be a sociopath."

"I think he wanted to kill Jazz and rape her dead body," Rob says.

"I would do it as a scene," Jazz says. "I thought he was hot."

"No, no, no, no!" Penny says, waving her hands in protest. "That is so wack. Didn't you hear him call you a parasite?"

"Who cares about that dickhead anyway," Rob says, having chugged his first beer.

"Actually it was *you* he said was a parasite," Anka says to Penny. "I wouldn't mind some kind of explanation."

Rob turns toward Penny and adds, "She's right. He's nobody and he never will be. But you, girlfriend! You could have been a little more open with us."

"I didn't think anybody from my family would just show up like that."

"And what about maybe being open with us, and letting us know what to expect?"

"That's rich, coming from you to her," Jazz says.

Anka says to Jazz, "Sexuality is private. But there needs to be openness on issues that affect the whole house."

"Don't gang up on her," Jazz says. "Look at her! She's as scared of him as you are. Don't worry, Penny. We don't blame you. He's old enough to be your dad."

"He's three years older than my mom."

Jazz asks how old Penny's dad was when he died, and she says, "About a million, but he got around."

"Very interesting family!" is Tony's remark.

"It's true," Penny says. "I never heard of any family more interesting than mine."

"Ooh, now she's throwing down the gauntlet," Sorry says. "Did I ever tell you about my mom's cousin from Jaffa who joined the SS but had to desert after this Nazi decided he was Jewish, and when he got back from Tashkent after the war my great-uncles got together and killed him?"

"Interesting Middle Eastern families don't count," Jazz says, "and an interesting Palestinian family would be one with no double agents."

"During the war my family left Long Island to work for Hughes Aircraft and saved enough money to buy a trailer in Santa Monica," Tony volunteers.

"Typical runaway teenage swineherd cover story," Jazz says. "You know they squatted that trailer because the Japanese owners were interned."

"I come from a long line of parasites," Tony says.

Rob says, "I get so tired of hearing we're parasites. It's capitalists are the parasites. Nobody cares if you're a rich asshole on a private island, but God forbid you should be poor with a decent house. Unless you inherit it. Then it's yours by divine right."

"We're not poor," Tony protests. "We're on strike! There's only one way to earn money in this economy, and that's scabbing. No offense," he adds to Anka, the only person at the table with a regular job. While everyone laughs, he lines up nine beer bottles next to each other and says it's a picket line.

Anka offers to tell a story, apropos employment, about her first day as one of three senior assistant editors of *HIV Action News*. She gathers her hair, ties it in an overhand knot on the back of her head to expose her face so they can hear and see her, and begins, "Yeah, so it's ten in the morning on my first day."

"Ten in the morning on the first day is not a story with a job," Tony says. "Give it three months."

"No, wait," Anka says. "This one hit the ground running. They were like, Anka, Anka, hi, come in, we're so glad you made it, we urgently need audio for this slide show, you enunciate so clearly. Please go down to the basement where it's quiet and read this script aloud into this MP3 player. And they give me this two-page printout and a recording device, okay? And it's about these little girls in Ethiopia. Their mother and father die of AIDS, and their mother's sister lets them sleep in a shed. She gives them food and water, but she's afraid to touch them, because the older one has, like, lesions. So it's the four-year-old feeding and cleaning the baby, who's like two, but can't walk yet. And the kicker. Ready? Every night it's the same thing. The four-year-old has to stay awake to fight off these cats that come in the shed to eat their scabs."

"No way," Sorry says.

"Yes way. When he said 'scabbing' it all came back to me. Every night these feral cats would come and bite off all their scabs, so their wounds never heal, because of course she's got KS and the baby's got herpes, like all over her body, so when they finally fall asleep from exhaustion the cats line up to lick their blood. This is like their primary source of nutrition."

"Jesus Christ," Rob says.

"And I seriously could *not* read this thing out loud without crying. I tried ten times! And I go upstairs and say, 'Sorry, can't do it.' And my boss goes and gets this color brochure to cheer me up, and there's a picture of the two girls, who are now like ten and twelve, wearing school uniforms because they're on free drugs from this organization we're publicizing, and they're looking all happy. And who are they posing with? Their same aunt, who's fostering them now for a hundred dollars a month!"

Everyone laughs.

"I know! It was my baptism of fire. So I go downstairs again and read it perfectly on the first take, in this calm, perfect voice, because instead of pity I feel this indescribable steely anger. This really weird anger, where you realize taking no prisoners means working with anybody and everybody who might help, never judging. That's the moment when I became a real activist."

Penny says, "Wow."

"I do not believe cats would do that," Sorry says. "Maybe it was a typo for *rats*?"

"There were no rats in this town," Anka says. "Because cats."

"Or *bats*?"

"Vampire bats are South America."

"Cats were in league with Satan way before bats," Penny assures Sorry. "I would know."

AMALIA WALKS FROM THE DINNER table to the central island in the kitchen of the house in Morristown. She slowly lowers a juice glass into the sink, rinses it with water, and sets it down without washing it. She stands still, her hand in the sink, looking at her own reflection in the kitchen window. With her left hand, clumsily, she reaches up to wipe her eyes. She sniffles.

She dries her hands on a dish towel and pulls a disposable tissue from a box. Still blowing her nose, she taps a photo of Matt on her cell phone screen. She waits until his voice mail comes on and hangs up, neither leaving a message nor texting him afterward. She sits down on one of two barstools and stares at her reflection for nearly a minute.

She walks to the couch in the living room, sits down next to Schubert the cat, and begins browsing the selection of video-on-demand channels. Without choosing a program, she turns it off. She pulls her knees in and lies on the couch sideways. She picks up her phone off the floor and texts Matt: I have to see you. ILY so much it hurts

Seconds later, the phone rings. Matt is behind the wheel of his Audi A5, stopped at a busy intersection on Tonnelle Avenue. The sedan is surrounded by large trucks whose engines idle as if they were full of rubble. The ambient noise makes him shout to be heard. He yells into the hands-free device clipped to the sunshade in front of him. "You're sick! Get help!"

"It's because of you I'm depressed," she says.

"There was never. Anything. Between us. Ever."

"Norm saw it," Amalia says.

"You're a crazy, melodramatic bitch," Matt says.

In Morristown, Amalia stands up from the couch and walks toward the refrigerator.

In Jersey City, the light changes, and Matt pulls into the intersection, to his left a double tractor trailer with an open load of scrap metal. The truck signals to turn right, and Matt realizes that a large fragment of waste steel from a die-cutting operation is hanging over the edge of the rear cargo bay, almost scraping his hood. He touches the brake pedal twice and hears tires screech behind him.

In the phone call, nothing happens, but neither hangs up.

Finally Amalia takes a pint of ice cream from the freezer and says, "Before he died, Norm asked me to take care of you. I think we both know what he meant. You're alone. You don't have anybody. All you do is work. I'm still young." She rummages through a drawer, looking for a certain teaspoon she likes.

"Women age seven years for every year a man ages," Matt shouts. "It's like dog years." The light goes yellow with his car still in the middle of the intersection. He has no choice but to turn left, which is the wrong direction for him. "In any case, I don't need to hear this," he says. "*Mom*. Bye now. I love you, *Mom*." He passes a Winnebago on the right and narrowly escapes being squeezed against a concrete barrier.

Amalia eats her pint of ice cream and watches two episodes of *Nurse Jackie*.

PENNY LIES FLAT ON HER back in bed, trying to sleep. Her pose reminds her of her father. She turns on her side and recalls his wish to dictate his memoirs. His anger when speech was taken away—his panic—and how stupidly, how idiotically, how much like a complete and total moron she failed to write the letters of the alphabet on a piece of cardboard and let him spell words by pointing.

The thoughts are like serrated knives in her heart, put there and twisted by the force that powers the universe: love. The same force that prompts her to turn again and lie facedown, fearful and motionless, paralyzed with grief. "I love you," she says aloud, naming it. Her words reverberate in the springs of the mattress, reminding her of Norm's last days. His labored breathing, the epoch when he could do nothing else. Breathing and nothing else, each breath more difficult than the one before, waiting in desperation for his heart to fail.

She turns on the light and sits up against his headboard. She drinks from his water glass. She sees herself surrounded by his furniture. She gets up, gets dressed, and goes out to the sidewalk for a cigarette.

Half an hour later, she goes back to bed. She thinks of his death for another hour and a half before she falls asleep.

ANKA KNEELS ON THE FLOOR at Nicotine, surrounded by large glass jars of water-soluble tempera. She reaches out with her dripping red brush and forms the letters *TTIP* on a sheet of pale blue poster board. She pauses.

“So what about tee-tip?” she asks Tony.

“Abdicates workers’ rights. Undermines environmental protections.”

Anka says she needs something shorter, and he suggests “TTIP SUX.”

“Present tense is a tactical error,” she says. “Makes it sound like we already lost.”

“What about ‘TTIP can be stopped’?” Penny asks. “Is that more empowering?”

“TTIP will fail?” Anka suggests.

“TTIP will attract Chinese investment in cheap American labor,” Rob says, meticulously pulling the paper off an American Spirit.

“That’s true,” Anka says. “But I don’t think so.” A lock of her hair falls forward, nearly brushing against the still wet *P* in *TTIP,* but she catches it in time. She sits back on her heels to tie her hair in a knot.

“TTIP, bad trip,” Penny suggests.

“I like it!” Anka says. “A trip is something you do voluntarily. Nobody makes you do it. And it can go *so* wrong.”

“It’s good,” Tony says.

Anka dips her brush in a jar of water until most of the red has dissolved. Then she immerses it in yellow tempera and adds BAD TRIP to the sign.

When the cardboard panels are ready—twelve of them—Rob attaches them to laths, using a hammer and carpet tacks. He, Tony, Anka, and Penny agree that they look nice.

“Are Sorry and Jazz coming?” Penny asks.

“I don’t know about Jazz, and Sorry’s already there,” Rob says. “Somebody has to sign in for the Blue Bloc.”

“ ‘Blue Bloc’?” Penny asks. “Like blue states?”

“Like smoke,” Rob says. “The reason we’re not allowed to march with anybody else. We might shorten their lives.”

“Is twelve signs enough?”

"Twelve is plenty," he says.

They eat breakfast—pancakes with defrosted strawberries scavenged from the trash behind a bar—and climb into Rob's minivan. Overloaded, it lurches from stop sign to stop sign and pitches forward and back after every pothole. Rob turns up the radio because it is playing the Peter Gabriel song "In Your Eyes." He sings along.

"This song's his pop star sign," Sorry says to Penny. "It was playing when he was born." They enter the Lincoln Tunnel, and Rob rolls down his window. "Fuck! Stop that! Jesus, Rob!"

"Diesel fumes and tire dust," he says. "This is what the nonsmokers are breathing while they scapegoat us."

"Close the window!" Anka demands.

He rolls it back up. The tunnel traffic slows almost to a halt. He scrounges a cup and a pack of cigarettes from a basket under his seat, clamping the cup between his knees. He pulls out a cigarette and peels and shreds it, looking up occasionally, still singing along with the radio. "Thousand churches," he sings. "Resolution."

"Can I get one of those?" Penny says. Anka takes the pack from Rob and passes a cigarette back to Penny. Sorry lends her a lighter to light it. "Sharing economy," she adds. She takes one more quick drag and passes the cigarette to Tony. He smokes it and passes it to Anka. She taps the ash into the ashtray, takes a drag, and returns it to Penny.

"I feel left out," Rob says.

"So conform, you dork!" Anka says. "Stop being Mr. Different and Special all the time!"

"Eating smokes is totally fucking disgusting," Penny says.

He continues to prepare his chew while driving the car with his knees. The tunnel is dark and the minivan's greasy windows make it appear an impressionist scene of a rainy night. Anka holds the cigarette to his lips. He inhales and says, "Whoa."

"What do you mean, 'whoa'?"

"Freebasing. Too pure."

Penny moves up from the right rear of the minivan to crouch between the two front seats. She takes the cigarette from Anka and inhales deeply. Rob turns to look at her.

"Where's your seat belt, young lady?"

She exhales. "I was going to shotgun you, but then I remembered we're in a traffic jam under the Hudson."

"Rear-ending somebody right now would bite," he agrees.

Tony suggests she kiss him instead of Rob. She shakes her head and frowns. Her resolve to doubt Rob's claims of asexuality makes her crush unshakable, plus Tony is, in her view, old and gross.

"You don't really want to get close to anybody," Tony says. "He's safe romance. Like safe sex without the sex."

"You're not my type," Penny says. "Too hardworking and ambitious. You remind me of the premed–computer science double majors at my college."

"Admit it! You're asexual!"

"At least Rob's a challenge," Penny says. "Where's the fun in hitting on you? You're too easy. When we get to the march, I could pay a hooker five bucks to come on to you, and you'd forget I exist."

"Penny, Penny," Tony says, shaking his head. "You have low self-esteem if you think a five-dollar hooker could get you off my mind."

"You are misunderstanding me in a big way," Penny says. "Low self-esteem would be if I got a crush on you for lusting after me."

"I love it when women fight over me," Rob says, tucking the chew into his mouth.

"If women didn't spoil this bastard for doing nothing at all," Tony says, "maybe he'd give them what they want."

"It's a market," Anka says. "The heterosexual economy that Rob dominates with his scarcity. You could learn a *lot* from him, Tony." To Penny she adds, "You ever read *The Gender of the Gift* by Marilyn Strathern?"

"No."

"I can't actually remember what it says, but you should definitely read it."

"I remember," Rob says. "You told me about it right after you finished it. It's about how capitalism and communism both say labor is value, and it can be alienated, because you're working for money to make a product to sell to people you never met. Except, the problem is, women are always doing this labor that you can't separate from them at all. Like birthday cakes and homemade socks and changing people's diaper nine thousand times. They do all this labor for free because you can't sell it. You can only sell *them*. The women."

"I'm not sure that's right," Anka says.

"We don't have slavery, obviously, but a good homemaker adds value to her partner and doesn't get paid, so same difference. She's like a natural resource to be exploited. Women are like nature."

"You make it sound like a sexist pile of crap," Anka says, shaking her head.

"Not at all," Rob says. "She was saying that Marxism isn't any better than capitalism, because they're both based on a world without friendship and love, where everything's for sale! A male world, basically. Money instead of nature. Welcome to New York." The minivan emerges into the gray light of the West Side. "So where are we going?"

"Bowery," Tony says. "We can park there and walk up to Union Square."

"Where there's no such thing as a free lunch," Rob continues. "Imagine if women started charging their kids for food. We'd all be up shit creek. Women have to give it away, or society collapses."

"Why would a feminist book be about that?" Anka protests.

"Why not?" Rob says. "This world look to you like the revolution has come and gone? I read there was just another Pew survey saying heterosexuals are ninety-seven percent of everybody."

"I bet it was self-identified, professed heterosexuals."

"Sure, yeah," Rob says, speeding up to beat a yellow light. "And they missed the other kind, the ones who don't know it yet." He shifts into fourth and catches the green wave. The minivan is bouncing and Penny goes to the rear bench seat to put on her seat belt. "Lots of those at Bible camp."

"Very funny," Anka says.

"If there were one sexual deviant in the entire US of A, you'd know it," Rob says. "Because it's click-bait. And no matter what his fetish was, people would say it's the tip of the iceberg. But nobody I ever met was the tip of any iceberg. You're all weird as fuck. I mean, I hope to hell there's only one of Jazz!" He pulls into the bus and taxi lane to pass a tow truck on the right. "Imagine two of her," he says. "But she cornered the market."

UP IN HER PENTHOUSE DRINKING maté, Jazz hears the doorbell play "In Your Eyes" by Peter Gabriel. She gathers her dressing gown close around her and puts out her cigar. The tune is interrupted and begins again. She puts woolen Kyrgyz boots on her bare feet and descends the three flights to the front door. She opens it and sees Matt—a strikingly beautiful man, dressed in a very perfect dark suit of ethereally soft wool with barely perceptible seams and a blue broadcloth shirt so fine it shimmers. He carries a bottle of Martel champagne, still dripping ice water from a cooler in his trunk, and a ten-inch square of focaccia with rosemary and caramelized grapes, wrapped in wax paper. "May I come in?"

"You may," Jazz says. "Is that breakfast?"

"Do you prefer coffee?" he asks. "We can go out." (He appends this suggestion in case she has company.)

"No. I've been awake for hours."

Hearing the "I," he knows she is alone. Leather boot heels clicking, he follows her through the front hall and up the stairs. The red quilting of her robe sways as she slinks through the house, her body dodging from side to side like a weasel's. On the third-floor landing, she turns and says, "There's nobody home. They're all at a demo against TTIP."

"And you?"

"I wasn't in the mood." She continues up the stairs.

In her room he sets down his gifts and says, "May I help you with your boots?"

She sits on the foot of her bed and raises one leg.

He pulls off a boot, and she raises the other leg. He pulls off a boot, unbuckles his belt, unzips his fly, and falls into a modified push-up, hovering above her on his hands and knees on the bed. Her legs are spread and she is smiling. He stands again briefly to take a condom from his pocket and unroll it over his penis. He lets his pants and underwear fall, without kicking them off (he is still wearing boots), and suggests she draw the curtains.

"No curtains," she says.

He looks out and sees, five roofs away, a woman watering potted plants with a green plastic watering can.

The landscape is a high desert, black and silver, touched with the red of rusting TV antennas and the white of satellite dishes. Storage sheds on the roofs poke up like the hollow hills of Cappadocia. He looks down at Jazz's face, and lowers his now blind, rubber-encased penis to her vagina. It is soaking wet. "Jesus," he says, sliding into the hot, wet space.

Jazz moves against him and begins to cry out. He looks up and sees the woman with the watering can. She is staring. He places his hand over Jazz's mouth and nose and thrusts into her violently. She squeaks—a muffled, wide-eyed, helpless gasp for air—and the woman with the watering can turns away. He grabs two handfuls of Jazz's hair and tugs her head down into the mattress. He fucks her for seventeen minutes, feeling himself hard and heavy as a stone. He lets himself fall, smothering her with his chest, embracing her tightly with his arms around her waist as he comes.

They lie still for a minute or two. He says, "Give me a kiss."

"Why?" Jazz asks. She pushes her hair out of her eyes.

He laughs and asks if she's thirsty. She nods, and he reaches to take the champagne bottle from the bedside table. He rests it next to her ear to open it, his weight on his elbows. The cork flies upward with a pop.

He drinks only a few sips before announcing that he needs to get back to work. Not seeing a wastepaper basket, he drops the condom on the wax paper wrapping of the focaccia and pulls up his pants.

Jazz follows him down as far as the landing on the second floor. She says aloud her long, anonymous e-mail address—a string of numbers at an anarchist domain—paying them both a compliment with her confidence that he will remember it.

ROB PARKS THE MINIVAN ON Bowery and the group disembarks. They walk uptown, holding their placards downward and facing in. They walk like jaded sophisticates, their mission not to change hearts and minds, but to pad out the small cohort of activist groups determined to be publicly identified with opposition to secret trade negotiations. The organizers expect at most eight hundred people. Around thirty will be agents provocateurs enjoying police protection, and another twenty will linger in the designated smoking area where Sorry now stands, finishing a cigarette.

She leans on a lamppost, at her feet a small portable fire extinguisher. The irregular polygon where smoking is permitted is outlined on the pavers in yellow duct tape. The smoking area is so far from the stage that the small crowd reaches nowhere near it. That makes it easier for the Blue Bloc minivan passengers to see Sorry as they walk up Broadway. She waves.

Rob waves back. They cross Fourteenth Street—looking both ways to see not oncoming traffic but distant mounted policemen on horses that stand foursquare and still, as though asleep—slowly raising their placards as they approach Sorry. She laughs approvingly at TTIP/BAD TRIP.

"It's nuts that we're so far away," Penny says.

"Yeah, we're pretty far back," Sorry says. "If you want to hear something, you can just head up front. You're not obligated to stay with us."

"No, I mean it's weird." Penny glances eastward to where demonstrators are gathering with large banners in black, red, and green. "It's like they're here against TTIP, and we're here for smokers' rights."

"That's how discrimination works," Rob says. "You exclude people because they have something meaningless in common, and pretty soon they're one big family."

"Plus I thought this was supposed to be a march."

"That's later," Rob says. "For people who want to get arrested." He turns and spits into a bush. "Not my thing."

"I've never had *any* interest in getting arrested," Sorry says, stubbing out her cigarette against the lamppost. "I'm allergic to institutions of that nature. Any place that locks you up." She tucks the tar-stained cigarette filter into a spring-loaded portable ashtray she takes from her pocket. She picks up a sign and faces front.

The sun breaks through the clouds, lighting up the banners and treetops. The weekend air seems fresh. An organizer's voice booms, but it is too far to hear well. "I'm going up front," Penny says. Holding her sign upright, she walks toward the distant loudspeakers, accompanied by Anka.

After they leave, several other smokers come to the lamppost to chat. Soon they, too, choose signs and walk toward the dais, accompanied by Sorry. Rob is left alone with Tony.

"She really digs you," Tony says. "I'm so fucking jealous, I might move out."

"That wouldn't stop her," he says. "And I don't know what you're worried about."

"She's different."

"True." Rob spits into a bush. "Why don't we talk about TTIP for a while? How much it sucks and all that."

"Who gives a shit about TTIP?" Tony says. "Everybody knows it's wrong. It's just a news item. Another bad omen in the sky."

Rob doesn't respond.

"Do you even know what TTIP stands for?"

"Transatlantic, trade, international, partnership?" Rob ventures.

"Nope," Tony says. "I don't know either, but that isn't it. Anyway, I'm more interested in knowing whether you plan to cut Penny loose anytime soon, so that maybe she notices I'm alive."

"No chance," Rob says.

"You're a female attention sinkhole," Tony says. "You lead them on. It's kind of shitty, especially for men within your gravitational field."

"What do you mean?" Rob says. "Would it be less shitty if I fucked them all?" He spits out his wad of tobacco on the asphalt and adds, not looking at Tony, "My political activities are a foregone conclusion. I'd like for my personal life to be different."

"You have it way too easy," Tony says. "If you want things to get interesting, gain twenty pounds and shave your head. That would put the suspense back in your life. You might even meet some women who don't follow you around begging for it."

Tony tries to relight his cigar with a cardboard match from an old yellow matchbook advertising a taxi service, but it has apparently been wet. He cannot get any match from the matchbook to light. "I'm going to catch up with those guys," he says, flinging the matchbook into a bush and tucking the cigar behind his ear.

"I'll come with you," Rob says. "It's not like I need to be in the smoking zone." He picks up the little red fire extinguisher and carries it like a schoolbook, cradled in one hand.

On their way forward they meet Anka and Sorry coming back

the other way. Tony joins them to return to the Blue Bloc, while Rob presses forward into the crowd, looking for Penny.

He finds her close to the stage. Setting the fire extinguisher down, he stands behind her and places his hands on her shoulders. He lowers his head to rest his cheek against her ear. She shivers with pleasure. A tall plainclothes cop in a button-down shirt and Mets cap touches his arm and says, "Weapons not allowed." His gaze indicates the fire extinguisher. Rob makes eye contact with Penny, and they return to the smoking section.

"How come there's no 'NORTL'?" Sorry is saying as they arrive. " 'National Organization for the Reform of Tobacco Laws.' "

"Because it would be superfluous," Tony says. "There's a huge industry devoted to making it easy to buy tobacco."

"At thirteen dollars a pack?" Sorry says. "If they want it to be easy, they're definitely fucking up. I have a medical need to keep my mania under control."

"By turning it into depression, thirteen dollars at a time," Tony replies.

Sorry laughs with the others. "I know. Financially, smoking is suicidal. But in every other way, it's the thing keeping me alive. I'm serious."

"Why don't you buy nicotine patches or gum?" Penny asks. "Wouldn't Medicaid cover it?"

"Because they're not indicated for manic-depressive disorder. They're for people trying to quit smoking."

"Not for people who think if they quit smoking they're going to die," Rob says.

"That sounds like some kind of paradox," Penny says.

The rally winds down. There is some discussion as to whether they should send Rob alone to get the minivan and pick them up, but they decide it's such a nice day that they should walk together back down to Bowery.

"Nice to know TTIP is dead and buried," Tony says.

"Did you see people there from any other CHA houses?" Penny asks.

"There's no anti-World-Trade-Organization house," Tony says.

"There aren't really any 'anti' houses," Rob says. "The houses are always *for* something. I mean, you can be against poverty, but you wouldn't go around saying it should be banned. That would be like the Trump campaign. On the left, you try to get the government to invest in your issue. Create sustainable growth via fairer redistribution of our tax dollars."

"If it weren't for cigarettes, you wouldn't be paying taxes at all," Penny says. "You're all pseudo-self-employed, right? And squatters, even if you are paying off a home improvement loan from CHA."

"CHA is probably bankrolled by the Koch brothers," Rob says. "You want to control the left, offer it cheap rent. We get to live for free, and what do they get? We stick to specific issues and work in a way that's potentially effective. Meaning we join the service economy, and the service we're providing is to be a sop to people's conscience. Make them think there's somebody out there fighting TTIP."

Penny looks at her sign. She says, "So are CHA houses ever bugged?"

"What for?" Rob says. "Informants are cheaper. Like you. Look at you. Just drift in on the wind, and you're living in Tranquility, with people there arguing that you don't need to pay rent. The Feds don't even have to give you a salary. You're grateful for a roof over your head. Maybe they told you there'll be a couple thousand dollars in it for you if you dig up something good."

"Like that dirty bomb you're building with the plutonium in the garage," Tony says. "That bomb is ineffective. I don't know why you keep building it."

"Being a fuckup gives me flexibility," Rob says.

"You're just typical white dudes," Penny says. "You can fuck up over and over and get away with it. Fuck up stuff a hundred times in a row, get it right once, and call it a learning curve. I *know* you people, man. I was a business major!"

"Anarchism is the poor man's B-school," Tony says.

"I mean it! CHA is like the dot-com boom. I had it as a case. It's like an overcapitalized start-up, having to adjust its goals upward to justify the faith placed in it by its investors. You know that saying 'Think Globally, Act Locally'? That's what start-ups do. You have to tell the VCs you're going to change the world, even when what you've got is an app that tells you when to refill the dog dish. To get liberal seed money for a free house for people like Stevie and Jacob, you have to say you're achieving way more than cheap rent."

(She has this critique ready at hand because something similar has been going through her head since she noticed she's heavily invested in Rob. She can't stop thinking he's both high potential and a liar. Undervalued businesses are dishonest, too, in their own way, right? If Rob didn't go around saying he's asexual, wouldn't she be standing in line behind dozens of competing emotional VCs? She's his only stakeholder. She could win big. That's her thinking.)

"I know what you mean," Rob says. "It's like facilitators, always telling you their nonviolent conflict resolution method would work in Syria because it worked at their community garden."

"But our ambitions really are trivial as all get-out," Sorry says. "Live one day at a time, and try to afford cigarettes by living in New Jersey."

"And bring down the WTO and put an end to globalization." Penny waves her sign in the air. A car honks its horn in support.

The others stand still and wave their signs, and several more cars honk.

THE NEXT DAY—MONDAY—A locksmith's panel truck pulls up in front of Nicotine and parks in the street. It is five minutes after 9:00 A.M. and the truck's loud idling awakens Sorry and Jazz.

Sorry looks out her window and yells, "Tony! Toe-neeee! Rob!"

Tony is not home—he is taking a walk, planning to tell everyone when he gets back that he went down to the union hall to ask about work as a welder—but Rob is in the kitchen, making moussaka with wilted broccoli, dubious mascarpone, and packaged prefab puff pastry he fished out of a Dumpster. He opens the front door.

"Is this the vacant house?" the locksmith inquires. "Where I was ordered to change the locks? This is not going to work." The locksmith is in his thirties, with a wedding ring, an orderly short haircut, and blue uniform coveralls bearing his name, Gene. He looks dissatisfied.

"There's obviously been a mistake," Rob says. "Maybe the wrong address."

"Just maybe. Because nobody told me I was going to be dealing with *squatters*."

"Who don't want you to change the locks."

"I didn't figure that." Gene returns his heavy toolbox to the truck and comes back up on the porch. "How long have you been here? This doesn't look fresh." He indicates the flaking lightning bolt squatter symbol and cobwebby individualized doorbells.

"Seven or eight years, maybe?"

"I'm not crazy about squatters, but what I really can't stand is slumlords who think they can waste my time," Gene says.

"You mean a skinny, bearded guy in an Audi A5? About forty-five?"

"I didn't see him. Just talked on the phone. He drives an Audi?"

Rob nods.

"Some people have fucking too much money," Gene says.

"You up for lunch? It'll be ready around eleven. Moussaka, if you're still in the neighborhood."

"Oh, that sounds so good. But I have to get over to Kearny." They shake hands.

JAZZ SLEEPS AGAIN UNTIL ROB calls her downstairs for lunch. After lunch she downloads an e-mail from Matt.

Doing his best to be charming, he draws on every rhetorical style ever demonstrated to him by anyone.

> Princess! Hope I'm getting your address right. Bae been on my mind so hard, I might be coming around 2CU real soon. But it won't be a surprise anymore, because my attempt to get keys of my own didn't work out. Do you people *ever* go to work? Three residents out of five at home on a Monday morning! Vive l'anarchie, or something. I should have your job. Do you even know what I do? I design discreet hydraulic compacting systems for waste disposal. I do some pretty work. You won't see it around JC (bc glam). But should you get up to Saddle River or down to Princeton one of these days, you'll see my stuff. Garbage disappears like it was never there. In that spirit I remain, yours ever faithfully, MB

Jazz deletes the mail, briefly. She restores it to her inbox.

ROB SENDS A TEXT MESSAGE to Penny: Leftover moussaka.

Around four o'clock in the afternoon, she arrives at the house. She brings a salad made of poached green asparagus, shallots, lemon, and blanched almonds. Jazz puts her arms around the bowl. "I love this salad so much, I want to make out with it," she says. She pulls the plastic wrap tight and sticks it in the fridge next to Rob's moussaka, which she says tastes to her like school cafeteria shepherd's pie, only moldy.

"Is Rob upstairs?"

"Out in the garage. But maybe we could talk a second."

"Sure," Penny says.

Jazz sets about making a pot of coffee. "So your half-brother Lucifer sent somebody around this morning to change the locks."

"That is so Matt."

"So now I'm confused. Is this his house, or yours, or what?"

Penny shakes her head and bites her lower lip. "I wish I knew! Seriously. It's a complicated patchwork-family thing."

"Right. Complicated because a man had two wives, not even at the same time, and three children. Baby, you need to lose your ethnocentrism if you want to keep living at Tranquility."

"All right! It's not complexity per se. It's that Matt's mother—well, also Patrick's mother—I have two half-brothers and they're both a lot older—I have no idea who she was. I never heard her name."

"That's actually pretty strange."

"I certainly never met her, or heard anything about her. I *think* she's dead, for the reason that we also have this summer cabin that I think must have been in her family. And now Mom inherited it, just like everything else. Dad was like forty years older than Mom, with two sons also older than her. So Matt and Patrick's mother, if she's not dead, she's in her seventies. So I think it's basically that Matt might be putting pressure on Mom to pay out a little bit of his inheritance. Which would also be my inheritance? But somehow I don't seem to have any say in what happens with it."

"Your dad didn't have a will?"

"If he did, I sure didn't see it."

"I think Matt killed his own mother by setting fire to this house, and that's why when he goes up near the attic where she died, his dick gets hard as granite."

"What?"

"Just thinking aloud."

"You *fucked Matt*?" Penny folds her arms tightly.

Jazz raises her shoulders and turns her head, picking up her coffee cup in both hands like a small child. She takes a sip. "He's intriguing! The innocent sex beast. Your brother wants it the way a guy can only want it if he's never getting it. *Really bad.* Desire like that turns me on."

"He's not my brother, and imagining he killed his mother in your room is perverted."

Jazz reaches for a cigarette, exposing a scarred wrist. "It's arousing to me. I try to discover what excites me first, and analyze it later."

"Bullshit," Penny says. "It's operant conditioning. You slept with him, and if he'd talked about his golf game, right now you'd be saying golf makes you hot. But knowing him, he didn't talk about anything. He just put his hands around your neck."

Penny glances downward, masking a vivid flashback to her father's final run-in with his cat. She can feel the incongruous serrated knife in her heart. It has nothing to do with the current conversation—she's pretty sure of that—just with the notion of hands on necks, which of course she brought up herself, so maybe it does have something to do with the conversation.

"He wants me," Jazz says.

"Is that why he sent somebody to change the locks?"

"Maybe he was going to give me the other key."

"This is *too* fucking romantic. You're turning me on."

"You're misunderstanding me," Jazz protests. "Sure, I fucked his hot, lonely desire. Poor Matt. He sent me a love letter. And now all I have to do is tell him I want to go on living in this house with my friends, and he'll find a way."

"To do what? Pay off the other heirs so you can keep living here? It's not his house! It could be Mom putting the pressure on him, I think because this house is the easiest way to raise cash. She's already accused me of doing what you want Matt to do—keep Nicotine a squat because I have a lover here."

"Maybe she'd be more indulgent of a man?"

"If she knew about you and Matt, she might come over here with some gasoline and light you on fire herself."

Jazz is silent. "Maybe I shouldn't always be plotting," she says at last. "I think with a family as complex as yours, I might be in over my head."

"I know I am," Penny says. "I'm too depressed to even look for work. And I can tell you why. My whole family is useless, and every night when I go to sleep the first thing I do is lie there breathing. Okay, that's normal, but when I do that—breathe—it reminds me of Dad. Because when he was dying, that's all he could do. Breathe. For *weeks*. I was such a fucking idiot not to walk away. No one could help him, and now I have PTSD complete with flashbacks. How am I supposed to go to sleep without breathing?"

"Maybe music would drown it out. Or you could masturbate."

"I tried all that. I still get Dad flashbacks. No, thanks. What I need is to not go to bed *alone*. To feel a living person—"

"Go back to Rob," Jazz says with conviction. "He doesn't *want* you, but that doesn't mean he doesn't like you. You rejected him for not wanting you, but you know what desire is worth. I mean, look at me and the prince of darkness!"

"Forget I said anything."

"Rob's different. Any other guy, to get that close, you'd have to be fucking. With him, there's not that barrier. You just get close. He won't resist it, if you don't. Trust me, there are worse things than a guy who can be friends."

"Just forget it."

"Then do what everybody else does when they can't handle sleeping alone—camp out on the DJD!"

PENNY TRIES JAZZ'S IDEA. FULL of leftover moussaka, tired from thinking and talking, she shows up at DJD after supper. Without consulting anyone, she curls up on the DJD. She reads an old cloth-bound hardback of *The Master and Margarita* that she finds glued to an end table with honey. (Her hypothesis: a previous guest used it to hide a honey spill.) All around her, the residents go about their business—talking, making tea, listening to music far away on upper floors. She is invisible. Each resident ignores her as though she were a couch surfer some other resident forgot to announce.

She falls asleep over the book. One moment she is reading, and the next she is waking up late in the evening, wondering where she is. From the kitchen she can see reddish light and hear voices—a vague, soft conversation that rises into laughter and back again. An unzipped sleeping bag covers her, no idea whose. She reaches out and feels the reassuring solidity of the DJD on all sides. A cat disengages itself from her hair. She realizes it has been serving her as a warm cap. "Mew," she says in greeting.

She pulls the cat down to chest level and presses it against her heart. Not sadly, but for pleasure. For the first time since Norm's death, the night brings her no grief and no terror.

The reason is obvious. It doesn't make her feel like a fool for missing it before—more like Eve driven from Eden. Of course she feels fine. It's like being small. She's back in Manaus, and the babysitter has tucked her in on her cot with the mosquito netting and is talking to friends over mocha in Portuguese, and her kitty Boni is in her arms.

She likes it. It works. No tension. No love. She nestles down into the mattress and soaks it up: the softness underneath her, the steady murmur of voices, the purring of the animal.

She wants a cigarette, but she doesn't want to stand out on the sidewalk to get it. She hugs the cat and falls asleep.

AT SIX IN THE MORNING, Jazz writes to Matt:

> That's such a coincidence, because I too am a hard worker who makes garbage disappear without a trace! To my knowledge I have no work on display in Saddle River or Princeton either one. Want to fuck someplace private? I have some ideas.

He replies within ten minutes with a room number on a high floor of a luxury hotel on the Paulus Hook waterfront, asking her to meet him there at five o'clock the same afternoon.

AT EIGHT O'CLOCK IN THE morning, with the cat squarely on top of her head, Penny awakens on the DJD from dreams of flying.

Feeling so at home in a strange place lends her an unaccustomed cockiness. She uses her cell phone to write a short e-mail to Patrick, asking about his mother, Norm's wife before Amalia.

She receives his reply an hour later. She reads the first paragraph, gets up, wraps herself in the sleeping bag, and sits outside on the front porch to read the rest.

She knows Patrick's usual writing style—terse and controlled, masterly at condensing major life events into bite-size texts, like his response to Norm's death ("Requiescat"). This mail by contrast seems breathless, as though he had been saving up a long time to say things that now emerge offhand and casual because that's the one tone he can assume without triggering his urge to keep control.

> Hey P., I'm on Mindanao. Great weather, wish you were here. It's weird you should ask that or maybe just that it took you so long and you ask only now that Norm's gone. But I guess he never talked about it, so why would you even be curious.
>
> You know the story how your mother came on the scene, the wild street kid my age, Matt was older (16). Mom was great with her.
>
> How can I describe Mom? Really pretty and sweet. Maiden name Katie Donaldson, from Murray Hill, her family had a little RE empire there (2 bldgs), she was a travel agent and that's how she met Dad. (Look thru his stuff for cute pix!)

> So to make a long story short your mother sexually was a pushover. Like you could say "put this in you (whatever it was) and I'll give you an M&M."

Here Penny briefly doubts Patrick's veracity, but only while she associates the story with her father. As soon as she tries to visualize Norm using M&M's to buy sex from a child, she knows what's coming.

> She's smart now but in 1985 she was diff and a certain 16 year old figured it out fast. I was not into it & Dad was MOST DEFINITELY not. He ended up spending all his covering her ass,

All his what? What exactly did it take to stop Amalia from submitting to Matt for candy? Promises of love? She asked about her father's first wife, and now she's getting the primal scene.

> It was a massive effort and conflict. Mom got stressed out and said she was taking off (from Cartagena, Dad was volunteering with this Drs w/o Borders type thing) to this fishing village to chill out on a houseboat. and that was IT. She got in a taxi and that was IT. GAME OVER. NEVER another trace. No word, no witnesses, no more lives for Mom!!! Like she turned into air and flew away.
>
> Except we both know that isn't how peoples bodies disappear, so it was also like HELL. Even just thinking about it is HELL.

The part about how reluctantly bodies die strikes her intuitively as true. The *HELL* part, she tries to imagine and can't.

She can't put herself in Patrick's shoes, or anybody else's in this story. Patrick and Matt, whose mother vanishes. Norm, searching for a kidnap victim without a ransom note. The starving swineherd turned candy whore. There is no way to parse the emotions of any of them.

Her mother's stories come back to her with hints at how Katie may have ended up. Lucky enough to be raped by the paramilitaries she farms and cooks for, unlucky enough to be dead. She never connected those stories with her mother's life, always assuming Amalia was too young to be talking about herself. Now she still doesn't know if the stories have any relevance, and if so, to what. She only feels grateful that nearly everyone in the house has left for work, so she can keep reading Patrick's letter.

> Dad kept A. and sent her to school. I think he adopted her in Colombia but she had a different ID in America (fake papers) so he could marry her (I heard about the wedding afterward).

That line makes her feel a little dizzy.

> I don't know and (as you can imagine) it's hard for me to think about, because it was her that led indirectly to Mom being gone.
>
> Now maybe you know why I live so far away!!!
>
> I like you a lot, truly I love you, I even love Mats but I love Mom more and it was hard losing her that way. Now after 30 years she's definitely dead and for the probate A. said she will make it official. I have this fantasy A. does due diligence and finds her right away, which is pathetic because Dad already tried everything! He tried so hard. Not gonna happen.
>
> Well, they're together now.
>
> Take care little sister. Your loving brother
>
> Patrick

So Patrick is waiting for news of Norm's death to draw a runaway Katie out of the shadows. A crazy fantasy he cops to—he's not ashamed—knowing it can't happen. Her name will never be besmirched as a mother who abandoned her family (not that it's conceivable, or is it?), and he'll inherit her property free and clear because Norm is finally gone—Norm, traitor to his sons for marrying the interloper who killed Katie. Or not marrying her. She rereads the paragraph. She can't tell. It's confusing.

> P.S. I've got plenty of money and my GF/fiance is loaded (Thai/French), we'll probably get married so please don't sweat the financial stuff, take whatever you need (if A. lets you have it!)

Penny reads the mail many times over.

She pushes it up and down with her index finger, rereading every word—especially "fake papers" and "adopted."

Her anger and resentment crystallize around the postscript. They attract stray emotional metastases that had been wandering her body since her father's death. Why does Patrick combine an offer of money with an attack on her mother? Does he think she loved Norm for his *money*?

She senses that Patrick does not regard Amalia as a member of the family, because she shares none of his genes.

She remembers what Norm said about her ovaries when he was dying—that he could see his grandchildren through her abdominal wall, in effect that he owned something *inside her body*—and in a stress-induced flash she sees, like one of those galactic clouds in outer space, the zillions of spermatozoa he must have created and distributed and discarded every day of his youth.

She experiences a sudden conviction that men are not members of the family. They are corn tassels whose pollen is borne away on the wind. They want their sons to be corn tassels. Their daughters are earth.

Patrick's letter proves it: everyone in her family has always deferred to Matt. Even Norm. Even Katie! Because when your son is fucking the malnourished street whore, you don't practice stress reduction by leasing a houseboat!

The letter shows that she has never really known her brothers, her father, or her mother. Her family is a train wreck. The runaway train of devotion and commitment, reduced to a pile of scrap. No casualties, because no passengers. They bailed on this train long ago.

She feels a dull will to salvage what she can—a little money, maybe?

After nearly an hour she texts back: Did Katie have family? Patrick replies, Not anymore. Parents and older sister w/no kids. Penny: So you guys inheriting apt bldgs in Murray Hill or what? Patrick: Already did, in 2007. Sold just in time! Penny: And the summer place??? Patrick: You can use it whenever. Good night

An eccentric who lives at DJD—a devotee of energy efficiency and solar cells, dressed in a one-piece footed sleeper, a Dartmouth varsity crew letterman known to all as Sunshine—finally pushes the screen door open and asks Penny if she wants some cocoa for breakfast. She looks up at him in silence, eyes red and dry. He grasps her shoulder with his mittened right hand.

"I reacted all wrong," she says. "Somebody nice sent me an intimate personal e-mail, and I wrote back asking for money!"

He says, "That's solicitation."

"I don't mean somebody I'm dating. I mean a family member."

"It doesn't matter. Wherever money gets involved, dignity becomes impossible." He pushes his hood back, possibly to hear her better, possibly to expose his attractive face and hair.

"That's not true," she says. "Money plus dignity is a piece of cake, if it's a lot of money and it's yours."

"Nobody owns money. It's a medium of exchange, with a value assigned by a corrupt system. You have to reject it."

She decides not to ask whether it's possible to own apartment buildings or summer places on the Hudson. She could hit a nerve, given the centrality of real estate in the squatter community. Instead she accepts his offer of cocoa. They sit together on the porch for a while, not saying much.

SHE WALKS HOME TO TRANQUILITY. Slowly, flat-footed, with her hands clasped behind her back, carrying her shoes and socks. Her leggings are scrunched up to her knees. The day is warm.

It seems to her that her way of walking is new. When has she walked like this before? She can't recall an instance. The smooth, bare concrete feels pointy under her feet. Needles of pain shoot up her shins as she walks. She likes being barefoot in the city, filth and all, and she likes that her hands are touching each other where she can't see them. She feels a sense of self-sufficiency. Alone, but not unfortunate. An orphan, but not in danger. Alone with her senses. She feels fine.

She wonders whether some of her recent suffering may have been strategic—calculated to attract Rob's sympathy. Or was she just trying to find a reason to love him less shallow than love?

She shakes her head in mystification. It's right there on her shoulders where it's always been, but she knows too little about it. Right now she suspects it's up to no good.

She mounts the porch, past the bean vines and tomatoes in buckets and the pots of herbs, and says hello to Rufus and Stevie. She continues upstairs to her room, strips, and walks naked to the shower a floor below with nothing on but the thin leather band she wears around her right upper arm and the two thongs with bone amulets around her neck.

The shower tiles have a dark green transparent glaze. The floor is painted glossy white, and the bath mat is an antique—lint-free, long-staple cotton in generous, curling loops. After her shower she stands on the bath mat, rubbing herself with a rough towel. She scrubs her body until it glows pink. Back in her room, she coats her limbs with sandalwood massage oil and cleans her fingers on the ends of her hair. She puts on a smocked top, cutoff booty shorts, and flip-flops, and heads over to Nicotine.

When she arrives, it is four o'clock, and Jazz is sitting in the kitchen with Rob, smoking a homemade cigar. She wears a metallic blue minidress over a footless black lace catsuit.

"You look nice!" Rob says to Penny. "I love your legs."

"And you look like you have a date," Penny says. "Jazz, I have to tell you something. *Do not do this*. I found out from Patrick. He's an abuser. He started having sex with my mom when she was *thirteen*. And that's if she was really thirteen. Maybe she was eleven."

"He's probably your biological father," Jazz says.

"Oh! Oh!" Penny cries, covering her eyes with her hands and leaning forward. "Do *not* be that gross!"

"What? Did you fuck him? They say incest is best—"

"Don't take her seriously," Rob says. "She's just getting in her femme fatale mode. It's an act. It gets her all randy, but for us it's always like yecch."

"Is he coming over here?"

"No," Jazz says. "Some hotel."

"Then why isn't there a For Sale sign in front of the house?"

"Maybe he can't get erections at hotels, and we'll be back here tomorrow."

Penny sits down. "You're amazing. I look up to you. I respect the way you enforce your sexual freedom. I really do. But."

"But what?" Jazz asks.

"But *Matt*!"

"What's it to you, anyway?"

"He's my brother!"

"Skip the clan lore," she says. "Tell me how much time you've spent with this man in your life, and whether you ever liked him."

"He's always been there."

"I mean in the flesh."

"At Christmas, mostly, and a couple times in the summer, plus he got involved after Dad died."

"That's not a brother. That's a stranger."

"Also I dislike him more than anybody I ever met in my life."

"Q.E.D. Rob is way closer to being your brother."

"Then you don't know shit about brothers. We can't all choose our relatives like the Rainbow Family."

"You like your other brother!"

"I barely know him either, but I know he's not *swine*."

Jazz laughs. "Swine," she says. "That's exactly it. The morals of a razorback in the body of an Armenian king. He makes me completely insane. And"—she leans toward Penny, touching her bare knee—"it's not anything you have to worry about. It's outside time and space."

"Wow," Penny says. "That is *so* fucked-up."

"If I didn't know you, I'd say you were asexual," Rob remarks.

Penny hisses, "Having a sexual ethic doesn't make me *frigid*."

"To me, eroticism is transcendent," Jazz says. "It has a will of its own. It's not a sport with rules and referees."

"Having rules doesn't make it a game!"

Into the seething silence of the kitchen wanders Anka. She flings a plastic cereal bowl and tablespoon into the sink. "Hey, Penny!" she says over the clatter. "You look nice! Did you get a haircut?"

Penny shakes her head, and Rob says, "She's having an adrenaline rush."

"It suits you," Anka tells her. "I always think of you as kind of morose and critical, and today you look all perky."

Penny moans. She opens her mouth to explain to Anka about Jazz and Matt and maybe even Rob, then closes it.

"You know I paint sometimes," Anka adds. "I ought to sketch you and capture this moment for eternity. Right now I need to do

Jazz's eye makeup, but when we're done, come upstairs and let me sketch you."

After Jazz leaves—her eyes rimmed in upswept liquid blue—Penny goes upstairs with Anka, who shows her portraits of people she knows: Tony. Rob. Jazz.

Tony is a stolid, homely face like a Rembrandt portrait, knobby nose, knobby background. Rob stands in sunlight, hair almost white, red plaid shirt, hands in pockets. Jazz looks up at the painter like a four-year-old, all innocence and eyelashes. Penny laughs out loud.

"I know," Anka says.

Penny feels a rush of confidence in Anka. Not that she finds her terribly interesting, but her own bitter mix of love, anger, knowledge, and skepticism toward Rob and Jazz—especially Jazz—seems to her right then a mark of intelligence and sensitivity, and Anka seems to share it.

"So tell me about yourself," Anka says. "Just sit in my chair and look out the window, and tell me some story."

She sits in a tattered armchair and says, "A story. I can tell stories."

"What kind?"

She shifts her weight. "Anything you want. There's no better way to manipulate people. Like my parents, shanghaiing me into getting a business degree with tales of the financial and intellectual independence I'd be having. I only learned one thing. How to make things up. Every number tells a story. Probably nothing tells a story better than numbers. Put in some statistics, and people will believe anything."

"Turn back to the right a little bit."

"Why isn't Jazz's nose broken in that picture?"

"That only happened to her year before last. She got drunk and fell down the stairs and crashed into the wall. She said she was tripping on cognac."

Penny tries not to smile, because there is nothing funny about people getting hurt.

"Don't smile," Anka admonishes her. "Concentrate on something. Breathe from the diaphragm. That's what makes your face look nice—when you forget you even have one."

JAZZ SWAYS ON THE HOTEL room's windy balcony, wearing her elaborate outfit, looking across an old quay to the Hudson and smoking. She hears the door latch turn over and turns to look at Matt, who stands immobilized in front of the king-size bed, gazing down at the metal object nestled in the center of the duvet: a semi-automatic pistol.

"What is this for?" he says.

"Anything you want."

He picks up the gun and is suddenly hard. It seems to him that his dick anchors a zone of excitement and heat that encompasses his entire pelvis. It expands to his navel and knees as he lets his index finger touch the trigger. All at once he knows what it's for. "Come and get it," he suggests.

Jazz drops her cigarette and reenters the room. The fetish heels she wears, which would make anyone else walk ponderously, make her unsteady gait appear weightless. She flits like a butterfly. The sensation of weight and heat climbs to his head, making weakness and clumsiness audible in his voice. He does not put aside the gun. "Take that off," he whispers.

"Not unless you give me the gun."

He moves toward her, and she reaches for his belt buckle with both hands. He holds the gun away, over his head. She opens his pants and falls to her knees. When she touches his penis, he convulses and cries out helplessly—he is that hard—inhibited, as he has never felt before, by his fear of lowering the gun to where she might be able to reach it. Groaning, he lets her take off his shoes, socks, and pants. But even while yanking with his clumsy left hand at the thin satin bows that link the two halves of her catsuit, even while fucking her missionary-style on the high bed with the sensation that his balls have become one with his penis and are entering her along with everything else, he never lets go of the gun.

As he comes, she reaches for it. He collapses forward to push it out of her grasp, letting his face crush her face and his tongue fill her mouth and touch the back of her throat, thinking he doesn't know what. That she has unlocked some secret of power. That he ought to join an army and shoot people, because it might be the ultimate high.

"Is this thing loaded?" he asks, rolling onto his back and turning the gun over and over in both hands as his erection subsides.

"Yes," Jazz says. She sits up, two black lace halves joined by a dripping slit, and adds, "Give it here!" He obliges. Without even turning to look, she discharges a round toward the river.

Wincing, he sees the trace of a flash, smells fireworks, sees the curtains flutter between the open sliding glass doors, hears them rattle. "Did you train with the Peshmerga?" he asks.

"Briefly."

"What made you quit?"

"The food."

"I thought Kurds have great food."

"Because the women spend twelve hours a day on it."

He considers her answer and asks, "So where'd you get this gun?"

"Store."

"Why'd you buy it?"

"Because the kick on the shotgun bruised my collarbone."

"That's an answer."

"It's a convenient size."

"That's also an answer."

"Because I used to be alone a lot on the night shift doing twenty-four-hour reprographics. You can print up a lot of flyers, but it gets lonely."

"Now, that breaks my heart," Matt says. "If I had known you

were alone and lonely in an all-night copy shop, I would have had you copy the *Encyclopaedia Britannica* while I cornholed you to Kingdom Come."

"Too late now," she says, turning the gun on him. He laughs, and she lowers it. "It was the PKK, anyway, and they put me on mess detail because of my limp. Not even the PKK wants a ninety-pound girl soldier with a limp."

"They could have trained you as a suicide bomber."

"That's a fascist tactic. The left is too underpopulated to throw anybody under the bus."

"But that's why you need terrorist tactics—because you'll always be outnumbered. Socialism doesn't have that mass appeal. It's a shitload easier to sign people up for a system based on selfishness."

"And easier to talk them into dying for their own benefit than anyone else's. So I guess you're right. We can't win." She puts the gun to her head.

"Hey, hey!" Matt says. "Are you nuts?" He reaches for the gun.

She throws it on the carpet—a quick gesture that he rotates to follow, staring—and declares to no one, arms wide, "My finger's on the trigger, and he's afraid for *me*! I have never in my life felt so loved!"

Matt laughs. He turns back toward her, pushes her down, pins her with his right leg, and reaches under it to thrust two fingers into her ass. "I'll be hard again in a second," he says. "You make me feel like I'm sixteen." With his left hand he toys with her hair and strokes her forehead. He kisses her. She gasps and groans.

AFTER SUPPER, PENNY BRUSHES HER teeth and mounts the stairs to Rob's room. She sees that Jazz is not home yet. She knocks on Rob's door. He says, "Yes?"

Standing in the doorway, she says, "I don't mind if you're asexual. Can I sleep with you?"

"I'd like that," he replies.

"Do I need to keep my clothes on?"

He shakes his head, and she strips to her underwear and crawls into bed.

Her desire is there—she can't get rid of it—but after her night on the DJD, more than anything else she craves security. Rob breathes softly as a child, and he smells like machine oil and borax, except for his hair (natural papaya aroma). He is reading Barry Commoner, and when she snuggles close he rests his hand on her head. He finishes his chapter and blows out the candle. She feels very safe. Too horny to sleep soundly, but the hours pass quickly. She is awakened from a predawn doze by the screeching of jays. Rob is already up, preparing his first nicotine fix of the day.

The skylight lets in a world that looks alive. Brighter. More honest. No more lies to dull her perceptions. Rob is what he is. Wanting him gives her energy. Maybe that's what he's for. It's not a shallow crush. It's existential. She needs a job to stay alive, and a man so she's not the end of the line. What earthly man is more likely to be loyal and faithful to her?

After breakfast, late in the morning, she sits again so Anka can work on the sketch for her portrait. (Anka often works from home because her employer can afford more interns than it can afford office space.) "You look super-perky again today," Anka remarks.

Penny leans back, her eyes half-closed, and says, "Yeah, I'm happy."

More or less simultaneously, Matt texts Jazz from his office in Bayonne. He suggests she come downstairs and let him into Nicotine at one-thirty the next morning, after he gets out of a late dinner meeting.

JAZZ COMES DOWNSTAIRS IN HER dressing gown and slippers and shoves the heavy front door open to a narrow gap. Matt turns and locks his car by remote. It flashes and beeps, and he steps inside. He puts his arms around her and kisses her gently on the mouth. "Yum," she says. Walking behind her, he keeps his right hand on her ass nearly the entire time they ascend the stairs. In her penthouse, he waits for her to drop the robe. Seeing that she is wearing nothing but a necklace of raw opals and thong underwear made of a gold chain tight enough to mark her flesh, he kisses her again. The candles make warm, living light and shadows in the drafty space, on whose many panes of glass their forms are reflected numerous times.

The affectionate act lasts for a good five minutes. Then Matt discovers Jazz's tallboy, a dresser terminating at a height of around six feet in a cornice, the edges of which he can seize for extra leverage as he pins her against it, yanking her chain in time. The drawer handles poke into the spaces between her ribs.

Penny is awakened by thumping, rhythmic yowling, and a swinish grunt so loud and close she thinks at first it might have stemmed from Rob.

"Oh no!" she says, elbowing him. She sticks her fingers in her ears and wiggles them around, standing up to look for her clothes. The yowling continues, sometimes with thumping and grunting.

Rob tugs on her arm, pulling her back down toward the futon. "Don't go out there," he says. "He might see you. Not the outcome you want."

"I swear, she's doing it *deliberately* to drive me *crazy*."

"She might be doing it just to blow your mind. We both know you're not that close to crazy. Like, she wants to mess with you, but not put you over the edge."

"If it were any other guy," she says, sitting down. "But *shit*."

"Take some of my earplugs," he says. "No way I could live next to Jazz without earplugs."

TWO DAYS LATER, WHILE FOLDING Rob's underwear on a table at the Laundromat around six in the evening, Penny looks up and sees Anka.

She feels embarrassed to be caught in the act, and quickly piles her clothes on Rob's. He generates so little laundry in summer—just thin T-shirts and boxers, except on the special occasions when he washes his jeans—that she has decided to do it with hers. Admitting to her love for Rob stimulates her domesticity hormones, and in terms of tact it beats volunteering to clean his room.

She never considers cleaning the kitchen. The gap between the counter and the wall: Is there even caulk under that stuff, or is it merely compacted organic material? What color is the floor, in physical reality? What is reality? She doesn't want to know. The sink is spotless, as are the plates and cutlery, and that seems like enough. Just as a clean body and underclothes are enough. Life at Nicotine reminds her of camping.

"Are you doing Rob's laundry?" Anka asks.

"Just the little things," Penny says.

"I've never seen him in here once, but every time he meets a woman, here she stands. So his clothes are always exactly as clean as they need to be." She feeds quarters into a top-loader and watches it fill before stuffing in her one load of clothing and linens for the week.

"Does he not wash his clothes?"

"He rinses them in a bucket and uses it to water the plants. It's more ecological, and Jazz says it's very nourishing for them."

"Maybe I'll do his sheets and towels."

"Don't hesitate. That would be my tip."

"Has he had a lot of girlfriends since you've known him?"

"A lot of one-night stands that thought they were girlfriends."

Finding this flattering to herself, Penny smiles.

They stand together in front of the bulletin board, commenting on the offerings. Rottweiler pups for four hundred dollars apiece. An industrial sewing machine. Handwritten pleas for living space from childlike (to judge by the nonverbal cues—stars and hearts and smiley faces) adults in chronic financial limbo, with too little money to rent their own places and too much to wise up and leave town. Trapped in the city by jobs that don't allow them, in their own eyes, to grow up.

One sweet, friendly person (loves pets, kids, and everything else) seeks a bedroom with kitchen and bath access near the PATH train for under two thousand dollars a month. Anka rips the flyer down and throws it in the trash. "Imagine a landlord around here seeing that," she comments.

"But the Internet," Penny says. "They see everything anyway."

"I know it's pointless," Anka says. "But I do what I can to keep JC from turning into an SRO like the five boroughs."

Before Penny leaves the Laundromat, Anka tells her that that evening—Friday—is going to be the most interesting session at a free AIDS conference at the New School, and she should come. A famous recipient of the Right Living Award from central Africa will be speaking solo and then in an open forum with American activists. Penny can register on-site, because most attendees will arrive Saturday.

"Do it," Rob says when she brings him his laundry. "You'll be commuting the wrong way."

PENNY DAWDLES AND ARRIVES AT the conference center late. According to her pocket watch/phone, the talk has already started. She jogs up the low front stairs. She sees a sign with an arrow and something about HIV in front of what she thinks must be the registration tables. "Penny!" Anka calls out. She turns.

Anka stands near a seventies-style cast concrete outdoor ashtray—an exposed aggregate hourglass, open at the top, with a bed of sand under a screen of rat wire. She waves and calls out again, "Penny!"

"What about the speech? Isn't it now?"

Anka gestures with a cigarette. "She'll talk for a while."

She introduces Penny to some of the other smokers attending the conference. None of them want to miss the forum, which is why they're all skipping the talk. They say they have heard the African woman's ideas many times over. They criticize her with objections that sound very plausible to Penny. She accepts a Marlboro, thinking that smokers may well be smarter than other people, simply because they take time off to think.

By the time she is done registering for the conference, the speech is over. The lobby and sidewalk flood with activists from all over the world, many in vaguely ethnic costume. Just looking at them makes her feel important and involved. She feels her commitment to AIDS activism grow.

During the podium discussion, she becomes confused. Somehow it all has to do with financing AIDS medicine via some new international fund. She keeps wondering why they need to fund AIDS medicine at all. What kind of creep charges money for AIDS medicine? Or is organized crime involved in making it—all these illicit generics—or the Chinese, or what?

When a panelist says, "There is no financeable cure," she feels spontaneous hostility, like he's raining on their parade by stating a fact. When others mention "opportunities," she resents them for seeking positive angles.

In the end she feels very confused by AIDS, which had seemed like such a cut-and-dried case. She realizes she still has no idea what the African prizewinner thinks. She swears to herself that she will look her ideas up online when she gets home. She hopes she may understand the discussion retroactively. She has her doubts.

When the forum ends, Anka invites her to stay on in Manhattan and learn about gene therapy over beers, but she wants to get back to Nicotine and sleep with Rob—as in sleep, as in sleep poorly, because his presence is like an alarm clock that never stops ringing.

THE NEXT DAY, SATURDAY, PENNY visits Amalia in Morristown. It's a trek involving buses, long walks, and two different train stations in Newark. She arrives hungry. They talk about inconsequential things while she slices tomatoes paper-thin the way they both like. They eat ham sandwiches with tomato.

Penny struggles to work up a confrontational mood, then a confessional mood. She achieves neither. She is too sleepy.

Eventually she says, her tone flat, "You should be patient about selling that house. They might be squatters, but they're making improvements all the time. They're maintaining that house. Enhancing its value while the market picks up. You ought to pay them a bonus."

"No. Peñana, your friends must leave *now*. When you find *ocupas* on your property, the time to evict them is *now*. Because that's why they put up symbols and banners, to start the clock ticking. It's all a big show for the courts. And the judge will award your property to thieves, and read you the law about slumlords and urban blight."

"But the taxes are paid up, no? It's Norm's house, no?"

"Maybe not anymore, unless we expel the squatters. Why don't you understand?"

"We didn't talk about squatting much in school, except in connection with placer mining and fossil fuel extraction. You know, without the mineral wealth, it's not an attractive business model for investors. Too labor intensive. But give me some minerals, I'll lay claim to the fucking *moon*. I'll forcibly resettle my workforce on the moon, like Canada with the Inuit."

"You think no one has the capital to *hire* squatters?" The contempt in Amalia's voice makes Penny respect her for a moment. She proceeds to deliver hard-won South American truths: "What do you think an army is, when it invades and occupies? What is it when a factory, or a farm, or anything else replaces a wilderness? It is *theft*! Property is *theft*!"

"A second ago you're gentrifying JC, and now you're Che Guevara. That was fast."

"I'm telling you that these people are stealing from you. You let this man touch you and he keeps our family home. Oh my god, you're so spacey. You let him do what he wants with you, and for this he gets a big house. You don't want to work—don't tell me you're looking for work, because I won't believe it!—and now when I give you a chance to try some capitalism, what do you do? You give away the store!"

"You want to know the truth?" Penny counters. Briefly she visualizes the truth—grief, asexuality, Matt with Jazz, Matt with thirteen-year-old Amalia, M&M's . . . She puts the truth with all its mystifying uncertainties out of her mind and says, "It's not important. What matters is that we all have places to stay. I've got a house to live in called Tranquility, and it's very nice. And you have this house, which is wonderful, and we all have the summer place. So there's no reason for anybody to take away anybody else's home for any reason. Not even squatters. You've been homeless before, and I just got evicted. It's no fun."

"No one is ever 'homeless.' There is room on this earth for everyone."

"And I'm not doing that guy. I'm really not. He's not like that. He's not *gay,* exactly, but he's not like that."

"You mean he's like Patrick, not Matt."

Penny feels vague dissatisfaction. Something tells her that the earth is not held in common—that some people really are homeless—and that possession of a sex drive does not inevitably turn a man into Matt. "Did you know Patrick has a girlfriend?" she inquires. "I think they're going to get married. He mentioned her in an e-mail, and called her his fiancée."

"He did? That's wonderful!"

"She's French and Thai. I think she might be from the Philippines. She's rich."

Amalia beams. "Is she a Jew?"

"I would guess Muslim, Buddhist, Huguenot—but why the interest in religion all of a sudden? Are you sick?"

"No, no. I was thinking about their marriage ceremony. I think the ceremony makes a big difference."

Penny hesitates, then asks, "What was your wedding like?"

"Hippie wedding! We gathered at the summer place, all our friends. I had a white dress, like a Kogi dress, and we married each other in the presence of God and the community."

"With a rabbi?"

"Norm didn't want anyone official. He followed native ways. There was no person in the world who could have married us. Only God."

"So it was like with a Quaker license."

"It was no license. He had adopted me as his child in Colombia. How can we get a license to marry?"

PENNY LEAVES SOON AFTER THAT. The confirmation of extreme weirdness overwhelms her emotions. It makes her want to talk to a person who can absorb extreme weirdness without a ripple: Jazz.

She runs with the story back to Nicotine—jogs to the station, fidgets on the trains, squirms on the buses, runs to the house, runs up the stairs, flings herself through the door and onto the bed—to declare breathlessly, "My parents never got married. My mom is legally my dad's *daughter*. His child, the same as me and Matt and Patrick! If they did probate, we would be splitting things evenly!"

Jazz sits up to put out her cigar. "Penyushka. Think a second. What does 'legally' even mean? It means sanctioned by the state. It's Napoleonic."

"What?"

"It's statist absolutism. Under common law, the case is obvious. She was his *wife*. You know it. She knows it. Of course, if you want to let the state tell you people are something they're not, go right ahead. If you want to give the government ontological superpowers."

Penny is silent and looks at her hands.

"In business school you learn to read contracts and split hairs," Jazz adds. "It's worse than law school. It makes you the plaything of conflicting interpretations. Reality is clearer. That's why I live in reality. It never stops changing. It's like shadows on smoke. But at least there's only one of it."

"It's strange," Penny says. "You drive me crazy, but I like talking to you so much." She flops down on her side and props her head on her elbow, looking into Jazz's kinetic eyes from a distance of ten inches or so. "You see past my bullshit, and I hate it, but I love it."

Jazz holds up a scarred wrist and says, "Don't overestimate me."

Penny reaches out and touches the scar, running her fingers down it. It seems like a foreign body, not part of anyone. She says, "I don't overestimate you. But you have this clarity."

"I try to see life as it is. I don't understand it any better than anybody else."

"No. You always cut straight to the heart."

"Anything's simple if you cut it to the heart!" She rolls over on her back. "I've cut myself so many times, I don't have an inside and an outside. Simple as a lump of clay. But life's not like that. I wish, I wish, I wish it were like that."

Penny touches the scar again.

"I could cut you right now," Jazz adds. "I could say, 'Bitch, stop pretending you like me. You only talk to me because I'm friends with Rob.' "

"That would hurt!"

"That's what I mean. I know too many things that are only true because I made them that way."

Penny embraces Jazz. They lie still until it is clear they might kiss. Jazz gets up and offers her guest a cup of Darjeeling, and they talk about Kurdistan.

LATER THAT EVENING, PENNY LIES flat on her back in bed with Rob, failing to sleep. Her pose reminds her what sex with Rob might be like, if it were conceivable.

She turns to face him. Her breathing quickens, reminding her of sex. The labored breathing of lovers having sex. Breathing and nothing else, each breath more labored than the one before. Waiting to crest the hill of orgasm. She twitches. She thinks of masturbating, but Rob sleeps so quietly she can never be sure he's not awake. She opens her eyes. She takes a drink from his water glass. She sees herself surrounded by his furniture. She lies flat again and thinks about fucking Rob for two solid hours before she falls asleep.

When she awakens, around eight, she shakes him until he says good morning. She begs him to give up alcohol and nicotine.

What originally inspired his self-medication, she doesn't know, but she feels certain its usefulness has passed. She is equally certain that if his combined BAC and serum nicotine ever fell below artery-constricting, vein-bloating, erectile-tissue-crippling levels, he would awaken every morning a new man, ready to forswear asexuality and pay some erotic attention to the exclusive designer drug by his side, also known as Penny Baker.

"Maybe some other day, when I'm more rested," he says. He gets up to shred a cigarette. She falls back to sleep.

AT NOON SHE GOES TO visit him where he is working that day, at a soup kitchen. She accepts and eats a plate of cauliflower au gratin, but she doesn't see him anywhere.

The parish hall is square. Every surface is white flecked with artificial stains. The shiny linoleum is white with subtle brown streaks. The walls are rough plastic wallpaper with a shadowy moiré pattern. The drop ceiling is thousands of crinkly white panels decorated with an irregular pattern of small holes. The clientele is poor—badly dressed and silent, nervous and loud, fat and thin, but in every case without valuable possessions. Purses are plastic with bursting seams. Shoes are extruded foam clogs, leggings unevenly knit. Men wear incongruous T-shirts and sweat-stained hats. There are easily operable deformities in the room, and open wounds. She looks for Rob and doesn't see him.

Taking her plate to the bus tray, she asks a short-haired woman wearing a gold cross on a chain over her purple turtleneck where Rob might be.

"Showering some guy in the gym." She points.

Penny follows her gesture to a door that opens on a hallway that is part of the attached Catholic school. She opens the double doors to the undersize gym full of foam mattresses and cheap inflatable balls printed with cartoon characters. To her left is the door to the boys' locker room. She opens it a crack and calls out, "Rob?"

"Go away," Rob says.

She walks in, expecting to see something sexual that might bring her peace of mind. She sees him crouched at the feet of an older homeless man whose toenails remind her of Norm's. Down near the floor, Rob is cutting them.

"Scram," he says.

"Let her stay," the man says. "She can clean my foreskin."

"She's been a bad girl," Rob says, without glancing up, "but not that bad."

"She could comb my hair," the man suggests.

"Get out of here," Rob says.

Penny remains transfixed. She has never seen a healthy, mobile human being in such lousy condition—bumps and puckers and discolorations, blood blisters, red patches, blobby joints, bewildering hair patterns, leprous-looking scars, fungi like navigational charts of shallow oceans. She turns to go and leaves slowly.

Back in the gym, she finds and opens the door of the girls' locker room. The air is dense with yeast, a haze of unwashed female. Behind a partition, a shower drizzles. Flip-flops slap the tiles. "Maggots in your armpits," a woman says. She sounds brisk and unfazed, yet surprised, as though expecting maggots elsewhere.

"You're a saint," an aged voice replies weakly.

Penny steps back, not wanting to be heard or seen. She eases the door shut and exits the gym through the crash-bar doors, not returning to the parish hall.

She thinks Rob is amazing. Not merely cute. Truly awesome as a human being. Also that this kind of awesomeness—the capacity to care about a filthy stranger—is something she never consciously wanted from anyone and hopes she will never need.

SHE WALKS HOME TO TRANQUILITY.

She turns on her laptop and writes an e-mail to her former supervisor in the corporate purchasing department where—as the culmination of an unpaid nine-month internship—she oversaw the supply chain for a skin conditioner used in makeup removers and shaving cream.

Anything opening up? she asks.

The supervisor writes back, Wish I could help you. We're down and out—downsizing and outsourcing ☹ Best of luck

She visits a job-search site and sees that the company is seeking a senior procurement manager with regulatory experience for a permanent position in Shenzhen.

She visits her favorite dating site and alters her profile to say she would be open to marriage.

When she rechecks her e-mail before turning off the PC, she has an alert. Twenty-one forty-eight-year-old men want to meet her.

She is tempted to send each of them the same message (that a surrogate mother and nannies would be cheaper). Instead she closes the laptop and removes a pack of cigarettes and a folding umbrella from her bag. She smokes while walking around the block in the beginnings of a thunderstorm.

AMALIA SITS IN AN ARMCHAIR in the master bedroom in Morristown, drinking coffee. She picks up her cordless phone and calls Matt's cell.

He is at work, preparing a tender for six odor-reducing garbage trucks in response to an RFP from Millburn Township.

"What do *you* want?" he says. "Make it quick."

"Hello, Matt. I have a simple request. I want you to do the project of getting those squatters out of Norm's house. Penny will never do this."

"I don't know why you're in such a rush," he says. "It's like having bedbugs that do the dishes. They're not hurting that house. And that neighborhood is on the brink. Those left-wingers are making it safe for democracy. You really want to be first in, first out? The sticker price could double in two years."

"That's what Penny says." She sounds doubtful.

"Penny's a flake, but she knows about finance. You never take her seriously. You don't respect her."

"You sound like an anarchist. Are you in love now, too? Did you also meet someone in that house?"

"Why are you so fucking jealous? Have I *ever* given you a reason to like me? I'm a complete shit to you, Amalia." He enters a number in his spreadsheet, and two other numbers rise disproportionately. He frowns and clicks an icon. "I'm busy. I'll call you."

WHEN PENNY ARRIVES AT NICOTINE in the evening, an impromptu house crisis summit meeting is taking place in the kitchen. Tony wants to use half of the garage where Rob has his bicycle workshop to set up an unlicensed welding business specializing in black-market auto body work for the uninsured.

"You're going to get us beaten up with baseball bats," Anka says.

"She's right," Rob says. "We'll end up like MOVE in Philly. First the neighbors fuck with us, and then the police firebomb the roof."

"That's probably what happened before we moved in," Jazz says.

"And meanwhile I have nowhere to store my bikes."

"It will be loud and dirty," Sorry says. "And it will attract undesirables. Drivers. Since when do we do advocate cars?"

"Are you having a house meeting?" Penny asks.

"An informal one," Tony says firmly.

Anka opines that CHA wouldn't let him go on living at Nicotine, because welding wouldn't be activism. Tony says even nonunion labor is activism, if it helps the poor. She insists that helping the poor drive unsafe vehicles is the totally wrong kind of activism. "The poor need people helping them out with Franciscan salvation-by-works crap like Rob does. The poor are fucking helpless! Don't put them behind the wheel!"

"We have a quorum," Rob says. "Our decisions are binding. Show of hands. All for Tony's muffler and auto body. None in favor. All against. Unanimous. Sorry, Tony."

"Whatever happened to consensus?" Tony says. "I need an income."

"Did you ever think about trying to fund yourself online?" Sorry asks. "You go on some Web site like Kickstarter or Betterplace, and presto, you're Tony the fund-raiser, lobbying for a medical tobacco excise tax exemption or whatever. You brand yourself with a progressive cause, and total strangers fund you."

"Tobacco is way worse than cars," Jazz says.

Everyone looks at her.

"Advocating for tobacco is the opposite of social justice. It's poor, ignorant people who smoke. They aim all the advertising at them, because it's poison—"

"Look who's talking," Tony says.

"Come on, you know me! Would I hesitate to do something because it's poison? For me, nicotine is basically a suicide method. The slowest, most decadent method I know. Slower than slitting my wrists."

"That would be pret-ty god-damn slow," Rob says, dragging the syllables out to maximum length.

"That's a world high mark for sarcasm," Tony observes.

"Smoking is like moving to Fukushima for the privacy," Jazz says. "But at least I'll have lung cancer that spirits me away *quickly,* while you get tumors right in your fucking *face*. How you can eat cigarettes, I'll never understand."

"This is the wrong collective for this debate," Rob says.

"Yeah, I'm confused, too," Sorry says. "Are you planning to quit? You sound almost like you want to quit and move out."

Jazz spreads her hands on the table and looks at her careful manicure. Her pointy nails are dark red. The fingers on her right hand are yellow. She asks, "Is there life after nicotine? That's what I want to know. I've been smoking since I was ten."

"If you quit, I'll quit," Rob says.

"The wager stands," Tony says. "They both quit right now, and this year's tobacco crop is *mine*."

"I'm not quitting," Sorry says. "Even though I could quit anytime I wanted." They all laugh at her good-natured joke. "But it might be hard for them to go on living here if they quit. Just saying. Quitting is not easy. I know that for a fact."

Anka says, "I could give it up for the interim. I'm not a real smoker. More of a social smoker. Like, if I see people smoking."

"So we detox somewhere else," Jazz says. "I got it. We'll go to DJD. Cold turkey on the DJD. Ten days, starting tomorrow."

"I would definitely save money if I quit," Penny says.

"Fifty bucks says Rob can't do it," Tony says.

SURPRISE LATE-NIGHT HOUSE MEETING AT DJD. Its residents acclaim the monitored detox plan by consensus.

The next evening, several linger in the living room after supper to show their support. A lovely and sporty young resident named Kestrel breaks out a guitar and runs through her small repertoire of protest songs. Leaning against the back wall of the DJD, Jazz and Rob warble "Give Peace a Chance." Many photos are posted to Instagram (hashtag: *#bed-in*).

A short time later, Rob begs Sunshine to stop singing the John Lennon song "Imagine," saying his voice sounds like rutting elk. "You suck," he adds gratuitously. Sunshine says his singing perhaps doesn't conform to Rob's commercialist, consumerist standards, and Jazz says perhaps Rob didn't come to DJD to submit to the populist aesthetics of a latter-day Gang of Four. A gentle, well-meaning young woman named Huma confirms that Sunshine never planned to take it on the road. Housemates Feather and Cassidy nod in agreement.

Penny watches Sunshine, drawn to his pretty face, put off by his footed sleeper and terrible singing. Jazz pulls her onto the DJD and whispers that she should rub Rob's back for him. Gently she massages his neck and shoulders. He calms down a little.

Sunshine says, "I have a certificate in shiatsu."

Rob says, "If you touch me, I swear—"

THE NEXT EVENING, AROUND NINE, Rob lies thrashing on the DJD while Penny sits next to him, rubbing his back. Jazz paces the room reading aloud from a stern critique of coal-fired power plants by Naomi Klein. Penny leans forward and kisses Rob's ear, and Rob moans, "Just stop it already!"

"Stop what?"

"Reading aloud!" he says. "Christ, can't you read without moving your lips?" He snorts and shifts his weight. "God, I am bored out of my fucking *mind*. Can't we do this at home?"

The prettiest girl at DJD—Anka's friend Susannah—comes in from the kitchen and offers him some garlic toast.

"Is this with butter?" he says. "That's just what I need. To get fat stealing my food from *veal. V-E-A-L veal.*"

"There's a little butter on it," she admits.

"You want some?" he asks Penny. "Penny will eat it. She'll eat anything."

"It's like he's his own evil twin," she says to no one in particular.

"I love garlic," Jazz says, taking a piece of bread. "Thank you." She returns to reading aloud.

"Is there a working TV here *anywhere*?" Rob asks Susannah. "Because you know what would be a genuine distraction? Watching a game. Aren't the playoffs on?"

"Nobody here has a TV," Susannah says. "We watch series on the Internet sometimes, like *Game of Thrones*."

"I wouldn't mind a little violence right now," Rob says. "It would feel good to see somebody's head get crushed."

THE NEXT AFTERNOON, JAZZ RECEIVES a text from Matt: Hotness, where are you?

On the DJD with P and R, she responds.

Her text is not entirely to Matt's liking. He pulls out to pass another Audi on the Pulaski Skyway, narrowly missing a pylon. To his phone, he says, "Reply. And where is the D space J space D, question mark."

At DJD. Back in a week on a bet. Hang tight J

He looks up DJD: Degenerative Joint Disease and/or Discoveries in the Judean Desert, the Oxford edition of the Dead Sea scrolls. (Online, where strangers can see it, the house remains "Pangaea.") Headlights flash in his rearview mirror. He puts on his hazard flashers and downshifts into fifth.

TWO NIGHTS LATER, FOUR IN the morning.

Penny lies behind Rob, who lies behind Jazz, all asleep on the DJD. The house is quiet. The neighborhood has a barking dog, but no one registers it. It has never stopped barking since it learned to bark.

Dozing half-awake, Penny places her arm more snugly around Rob's waist, and something brushes her sleeve. She lowers her hand.

Unmistakable. Something resembling an erection.

She is so surprised that her first impulse is to nudge Jazz and get confirmation. "Jazz," she whispers. Jazz turns around. She points.

Jazz touches Rob's underwear for one second. He makes a happy sound. Almost inaudibly, she whispers, "What do we do now? Flip a coin?"

"It's *mine*," Penny hisses back.

But she's on the wrong side of him. To fulfill her arguably abusive plan of initiating sex while he sleeps, somehow she has to get in front of him without disturbing him or ending up on the wrong side of the blanket. While trying, she wakes him up.

"Stop flailing!" he says. "Where am I? Jazz?"

Penny kisses him on the cheek from behind.

"Get off me," he says.

He turns over, moves closer until his now inconspicuous hard-on just grazes her shirt, and falls asleep again. She abandons her plan.

IN THE MORNING HE REMEMBERS nothing.

Penny's imagination is inflamed—a throbbing, swollen wound festering with sexual virulence.

Jazz weaves around the house, scanning every surface for anything that might intrigue her, like a foraging raccoon. She chews on caraway seeds and mint leaves. She talks to Kestrel and Huma about solar power. She eats cheap Danish butter cookies with granulated sugar on top—a first. She goes with Feather and Susannah to the co-op and buys two pounds of organic kumquats. She offers Rob kumquats—once. Rob does not want kumquats.

He is immensely irritable. He demands to return home, saying forced inactivity and boredom are the two most wrongheaded nicotine cessation aids conceivable. He finds a novel from the *Master and Commander* series and reads it in silence, ignoring everyone. When Penny asks him how he likes it, he says, "Don't make this more hellish than it needs to be."

With Rob so bitchy, it is easy for her to take a break and go back to Nicotine.

She and Anka clear the house of every trace of tobacco and every ashtray, except for what's in Sorry's room or Tony's. They throw away Rob's special cups and even his baking soda. They search his garage for hidden paraphernalia—anything that might trigger a relapse.

They regard Jazz's plants and the half-cured harvest with perplexity.

Tony says to leave them alone. Rob, he says, can't dip uncured tobacco, and Jazz has willpower.

IN THE AFTERNOON, MATT STOPS by Nicotine. He tells Sorry he just wanted to say hi. Anka and Tony are not at home, and Sorry refuses to tell him where to find Jazz, Penny, or Rob. She suggests he try again next month.

Matt reasons that DJD could be another anarchist house, named perhaps for its address on Don Juan Drive or its political mission (Dealing Junk to Degenerates). He cruises neighboring streets in his car, scanning facades for the squatter lightning bolt symbol. Around three o'clock, he realizes he could call CHA and ask them. But it's Saturday. He finds the CHA office number online, but no one answers the phone.

PENNY, STILL SHARING THE DJD, longs for a change of air and some real sleep. Rob's restlessness, the way he takes all the available blankets and wraps himself up like a burrito: unpleasant. She lies awake, breathing shallowly, thinking hostile, lustful thoughts.

At least that's how it feels—as if she never sleeps—because Jazz at DJD keeps her regular hours. She puts on records and sits in an armchair reading. She drafts poetic manifestos in a leather-bound notebook. The key distinction between 2:00 A.M. and 2:00 P.M. is her light source. At seemingly random hours of the day and night she sleeps, on her front, her face in the crook of her elbow—always in the same position, as though her nose had grown crooked from the pressure of her arm.

Rob keeps similar hours, but he calls his schedule "self-induced sleep deprivation that's going to fucking kill me by destroying my immune system and fucking with my head until I can't even tie my own fucking shoes."

"This is nothing," Jazz says. "Think about people with babies in the house. They never sleep."

"And they're insane. People so strung out they can't tell their ass from their elbow are raising all the kids. No wonder people spend half their time shooting each other."

On Sunday night, Penny returns to Tranquility. While getting organized to take a shower, she falls asleep facedown on the bed. She remains motionless all night with her face in the crook of her elbow.

AROUND SEVEN THE NEXT MORNING, Jazz deliberately brushes Rob's crotch with the back of her hand—gently, casually lets her fingers run across the front of his plaid boxers.

"Mitts off," he says, slapping her arm away.

"No, let me see!" She sits up.

"Get me a pack of cigarettes, and I'll be your sex slave forever."

"They're right outside," she says, indicating the front door of the house a few feet away. "There's nothing keeping you in bed with me. Go for it."

"There's fifty dollars from that fucker Tony."

"Come on. Be a sport."

Rob rolls onto his back and allows his penis to stand upright in his undershorts.

It appears to be roughly the size of a roll of quarters, similar to Bill Clinton's in the testimony of Paula Jones.

"What can I say," Jazz says. "Not my weight class. But Penny's very petite, and she's in love with you."

"Fifty dollars will buy a nice bottle of bourbon," Rob says.

NO ONE ANSWERS THE PHONE at CHA. Matt sends an e-mail.

ON WEDNESDAY, MATT'S E-MAIL HAS not been answered, his calls to CHA go to a voice mail box that is full, and when he goes by the CHA office near Journal Square in the early evening, he discovers that it is a practice space—filthy and unoccupied, but well soundproofed—in a former commercial building called Wherehouse that was founded as a free restaurant and depot for discarded food. The file cabinet with drawers labeled MORTGAGES and LEASES contains a plastic cup encrusted with mold, along with some facial tissues and dead flies.

In his bewilderment, he ironically asks the young woman showing him around where she thinks the money goes when CHA houses pay off their debts to CHA.

"I never thought about that!" she says brightly. "You could ask Island Girl, the guy who founded it."

"Where does he live? Does he live here?"

"He lives at Detonator, but he might be in Portland."

"Where do you send your loan payments?"

"Do we do that? I thought we got grant money from the city!"

Matt retreats. He refrains from driving to Nicotine. He goes to his top-floor duplex in Fort Lee and writes Jazz an e-mail.

> I miss you. Let me pick you up tomorrow at seven and take you to my place? I want you with real wine, real food, real music, and a real brass bed. Disclosure: I also have sort of a wading pool with gilt tile work and art-deco nymphs cast in a marble-resin blend, but I didn't put it in. I bought the place cut-rate from a meatpacker and didn't have the heart to tear out the nymphs. Until now. My nymph. Please say yes. The pool is heated.

JAZZ RESPONDS THAT SHE WOULD be delighted to see Matt's home.

Her enthusiasm is heightened by the entertainment being offered the rehab patients. They sit sweating on the DJD while Kestrel, Huma, and Cassidy perform a dramatic reading of an original, collaborative work of apocalyptic science fiction based on aberrations in the life cycle of the eighteen-year locust. Somehow or other the locusts cause the world economy to be threatened with collapse, but that's not the issue—the economy is a paper tiger anyway. Jazz takes part by making the locust noise whenever Kestrel points at her. Cassidy plays the role of President Hillary Clinton.

Penny shares the love seat with Sunshine. She feels she doesn't know him yet, but she thinks something could develop there. He sits close to her, inside a sleeping bag. His terry cloth shoulders poke out the top. He wears his hood down and appears very comely.

She glances repeatedly from him to Rob. Sunshine seems like

such a sane, uncomplicated person compared with Rob, who is ostentatiously coloring an adult coloring book with a single color (black).

THE FOLLOWING EVENING AT NICOTINE, Tony slaps a fifty-dollar bill into Rob's hand. He waves it in the air and says, "Next stop discount liquors!"

"No, wait!" Penny says.

"Let him go," Jazz says. "He earned it."

"It's his money," Tony adds.

"He'll open a bottle on his way home and get all uninhibited and buy tobacco!"

"Good point," Jazz says. "Go with him." She pushes Penny down the front steps, sees Matt's car coming, turns to Tony and says, "I've got a date." She dashes upstairs.

She comes back down wearing a tailored spring coat in a light pink-and-gray tweed over a stiff yellow Prada dress and fawn-and-white spectator pumps. Her hair is in a bun and her lipstick is very red. She jumps into the waiting car and rolls slowly away.

"Weird," Tony says, reaching down to pet the cat raising kittens in the FREE box.

MATT'S HOME TRASH-COMPACTING SYSTEM FASCINATES Jazz.

"I know what you're thinking," he says. "That you could get rid of anything or anybody with this beast. But don't forget that the human animal is seventy percent water. Trash is about ninety-eight percent air. You can't compact a liquid. It's the most compact thing in the world. Fills every nook and cranny." He puts his arms around her torso and presses against her from behind while she plays with the controls on the trash compactor.

"I bet you can control this with your phone," she says.

Sensing an interest in technology, he leads her to his wraparound black leather sofa landscape and offers her the headset from his 3-D gaming system. He sits down opposite her and opens his paper-thin laptop on the agate coffee table.

The lights come up and she sees him—not in his living room; he is perched on a raft on a particularly romantic bay in Vietnam.

"Wow," she says.

"There's a button on the table," he says. "You can use it to navigate." She zooms closer, close to Matt's face, which turns blurry.

"This is for online sex, right?" she asks.

"That's the idea," he says. "Say I'm some girl at home with my laptop. The program picks up my outline and substitutes a different background. It's the same technology they use to put the ads in sports events on TV. Or in that movie *Wag the Dog,* with the virtual Balkan wars. I see her, but she can't see me."

"Because you don't look real good in this headset."

"She's getting fifty cents, so she doesn't care."

"And she strips for the webcam."

"No, for herself. On the screen she sees herself."

AROUND THE SAME TIME, SITTING on the top step of the Nicotine front porch, facing the street, Rob finishes his fourth bourbon. He pushes the glass of still sharp-edged ice cubes—he is drinking very fast—over to Penny. "You have some," he says.

"I don't want to waste your good bourbon," she says. "You deserve to celebrate."

"I should call my mom," he says, getting to his feet. He lurches forward, catching himself after four steps, not stumbling so far as to put a foot on the front walk. He turns ninety degrees and climbs the stairs sideways. "She'll be proud of me. She always said it was a filthy habit."

"She wasn't lying."

As he passes Penny, he picks up the bottle and the glass.

"Let me stay over," she says.

"I quit using. I don't need to be monitored." He starts away. Then he adds in a kinder tone, "What I mean is, I'm still quitting. Any distraction, and I might quit quitting."

"I don't want to distract you," she says halfheartedly.

"I'm going to be quitting for months," he says. "If it's like alcohol, I'll never be able to stop quitting." He leaves her alone on the porch and carries the whiskey up to his room.

She sits and feels bad. He has a sexuality now, or at least an out masculine gender, and they're both telling him to stop teasing her.

PENNY VISITS DJD THE NEXT night after supper. The weather is warmer, and Sunshine has put aside his footed sleeper for a green T-shirt and Bermuda shorts. The T-shirt reads GREEN in darker green. What a body, she thinks. You can tell he was a rower. He's a good-looking guy, by universal acclaim. Everybody says if he didn't dress like a fool he'd be a ten. And here he is, dressed in a normal way.

She doesn't feel him (as in feel anything in particular when he's around), but she doesn't know the difference between shallow and deep anymore. Are spontaneous feelings elemental, or superficial? Don't feelings mean more if they need time to grow?

They sit outside on the steps, drinking tap water.

"I'm still intrigued by what you said about dignity once," she says.

"I said money makes dignity impossible, or something like that. I was kidding. I think about dignity *way* too much when I'm wearing a onesie."

"I think it's dignified. There's dignity in trying to save energy."

"It's no better than any other form of exhibitionism. I want to make a point by taking a stand. Be conspicuous and different. In the end all I do is make people think conserving energy is weird. I jump off this social cliff, and take the cause with me."

"Well, some of us can't help being conspicuous and different."

"You think that's what you are?" He eyes Penny briefly and looks back at the street. "Maybe in an upscale neighborhood you'd stick out. Around here, you're invisible."

"Wait. Are you trying to be insulting?"

"No. I mean—take Rufus—in the whole CHA system, he's the white whale. We're proud he lives at Tranquility! But not because there's some kind of generalized shortage of middle-aged black men in Jersey City. It's just that most of them would not be open to living in an anarchist squat with a bunch of white kids. So he's invisible anywhere but in the context of CHA. That's the kind of thing I meant."

"This is not a heavily Latin American community. I never see people like me."

"I didn't say they *lived* here. They work night shifts. That's what you look like to me—like the cleaning crew, or a night clerk at a motel. Like somebody who leaves JC at seven o'clock every morning to commute to Edison on a bus."

"That's even more insulting."

"It's just context-dependent! That's how identity works. Say you were in my bed, where usually there's just white girls. The girls who cycle through this house really are beautiful, but they're so close to identical, I forget their names. They sleep with me because I'm good-looking and I went to Dartmouth, but mostly because I live here. They only turn conspicuous when they go out the door into the street. But in my bed, *you're* the one who'd be conspicuous and different."

"Because you're a huge racist sexist." Penny stands up. "I can't believe I came over here to flirt with a guy who wears a bunny suit, because he said something striking about dignity. It's like I'm losing my mind."

"I'm not a racist," Sunshine says. "Maybe if I hit on you because you're a person of color. *That* would be racist."

"You don't even want me to like you," Penny says. "I think you're hoping I'll let Jazz know you're tired of white girls. Except you know what? Even *she* might not fuck a guy in a footed sleeper."

"I wouldn't touch Jazz with a ten-foot pole," he says. "She's too experienced. I like college girls that are all worried whether their bouncy nineteen-year-old tits are good enough."

"I'm going home."

"So go home. You belong there at Tranquility. Come back after you grow up enough to care about an issue that transcends your own skin!"

PENNY FEELS LONELY, GUILTY, JUSTLY accused, and rightfully incriminated—by Sunshine, of all people. Her mood is not good. She looks at herself and sees (her harsh judgment is not entirely fair) the kind of shallow bitch who would weigh her mate choice options like some kind of eugenicist instead of falling in love (she's in love, obviously). The kind of shallow bitch who has so little genuine interest in love that she would neglect her female friends for . . . how many months now? When did Norm get sick?

Her mind is a blank. She remembers that it was cold outside.

She writes two uncharacteristically long e-mails. The first is to her freshman roommate Lucinda, who now lives in Abu Dhabi:

Hey Loose,

sorry I've been totally out of touch. That's what it's like when you're going through stuff you totally can't handle. My father died and he got SO sick first. When he died (hospice) I was there. It was SO sad, I got PTSD, like crying every night. Mom's cool with it, I don't get it but you know she's like 35 years younger than he was and maybe they weren't all that close. I don't know what she's going to get up to next, but it's sure to be a tragicomedy with much OMG. And maybe there's family weirdness coming out and maybe not, but in any case I don't want to get into it because I don't actually know anything. I'll tell you if it gets interesting. Overall there's not a whole lot to say except DAD DYING SUCKED SO HARD, so give your dad a hug!

I'm living in a group house (Grove St/Journal Sq) looking for work. Nothing promising yet.

Give my love to Abby!

Penny

The second is to her best friend from high school in Morristown, Fontaine:

Hey Fon! Don't ask—it's all sad. Dad's dead, I'm unemployed, living in a squat (!), Mom's nuts, Matt's a shit, Patrick's damaged goods. So I haven't been in touch, sorry about that. Thank the good Lord PM [pachamama] Dad paid for my school! If I had debts coming due I would have to go underground.

So how's business? How's Terre Haute? I'm in JC with a SERIOUS crush on this dude who lives in the house where my dad grew up, which is creepy, but come on, where else would I meet men? Just share in my joy that he didn't squat somebody else's house! Why he seems so perfect, I don't know. We've kissed but we haven't really made out really. I'm talking about a GROWN MAN here, living in an anarchist free love group house. I know you'll say go online and broaden your horizons, and I promise I'll do that just as soon as I attain medium height/build with medium hair/eyes so somebody even fucking READS my profile before he offers me children and the maid's quarters based on my photos. I'm not bitter. Anyway, this crush distracts me from all the death-related PTSD, so I'm behind it all the way. That's the latest, fill me in on life in Indiana—love, p

LUCINDA WRITES PENNY BACK FROM a polytechnic university under development around a small artificial lake lined with PVC in a rocky portion of the interior of the United Arab Emirates.

> I'm sorry about your dad, I hope you're feeling better. I have bad news too—my father-in-law Hamad doesn't want us in contact because of your relatives in the (let me clear my throat) Zionist Entity. I know it's insane, but he says Abdullah could lose his job over it and it's such a big deal for him getting to build up a new department from scratch. We'll be out of here in five years max. Abs says his career is riding on it. I will tell you one thing (top secret): I'm pg. I haven't even told Abs (too early), but this might be my last mail for a while, so if I want to tell you it's now or never. I won't be naming it after you or raising it in this—greetings noble censors, think I'll skip the descriptions of dust. Our servants (I'm pretty sure somebody pays them and they're not really slaves) are great, they get that dust out so fast every morning, you'd never know it was ever there.
>
> See you soon. Don't write me any secrets! I'll call you if I get anywhere near NYC.
>
> Love you
>
> Lucie

FONTAINE WRITES BACK FROM TERRE Haute.

> Come visit me. The bar around the corner has the best karaoke, all these fat guys dedicating metal ballads to their wives (home taking care of the kids but they make it sound like they're off fighting in Iraq—probably makes more sense than you wish it did). Though you

might have better luck here with your new medium height/build and medium hair/eyes . . . forget I said anything . . . You know you picked a hard row to hoe with that trashy Anglo-ass name! It makes you look so *adopted*. Your dad's gone now (I was saddened to hear that, he was such an inspiring person and helped so many people, I'd be so proud if my dad were anything like him), so you could finally start calling yourself something that fits, like "Paloma Gellis." Otherwise Terre Haute is pretty meh. Work is great. Respectable colleagues, responsible job, house I might buy, the usual: paradise on earth, once you drown your memories of NYC. I'm working on it.

Stay cute

Fon

PENNY GOES DOWN TO THE Tranquility kitchen to make raw ginger tea. She feels slightly sick to her stomach. She envies Fon for having a job. She feels certain that if she can discover Rob in her grandparents' attic—a very small sample of men indeed—Fon can discover her own perfect man in bustling, cosmopolitan Terre Haute.

She imagines Fon's perfect man as being sexually rather user-friendly when compared with Rob. She imagines him young enough to be slim in Terre Haute, but somehow already graduated from high school. She thinks of Rob's body. She takes a sip of her tangy tea and remembers kissing him. The concentration in his kiss, how it lingered on her mouth, his indifference to both their tongues and her entire body. It dawns on her that he may not be the perfect man after all. She singsongs to Tranquility's nameless gray cat in a baby-talk voice: "The perfect man for me wouldn't be *asexual*. No he *wouldn't*!"

The cat, curled up on the seat cushion of a straight-backed chair, spreads and flattens without changing its pose, as though the earth's gravitational pull had increased. Rufus enters the kitchen. "You like that cat," he says.

"I like a lot of things."

"You know whose cat that is? Girl who moved away. She just moved away and left her cat."

"Cat seems happy."

"Somebody should adopt that cat. It's got nobody."

"That's not true. It's better off than any of us. People come and go, but the cat can stay. Nobody's going to pressure it to take a job in Terre Haute."

"Lazy-ass anarchist cat," Rufus says, taking a beer from the refrigerator.

The cat balls one front paw into a fist as it stretches. It turns slightly on its axis and raises its chin. "It's not the cat's fault you feed it valerian," Penny says, patting its belly.

ON SUNDAY MORNING, ANKA KNEELS on the kitchen floor, painting the hashtag *#climbit* on twenty sheets of blue poster board.

"I'm searching for that hashtag, but there's nothing there," Penny remarks, thumbing her phone.

"There will be," Anka says. "You know that douche bag over at DJD who calls himself Sunshine?"

"Yeah, I know him."

"Well, he has these friends in Greenpeace. You know how Greenpeace guys are all super-macho bros, and really into tech, and they're all on like WhatsApp and Snapchat and everything else like that, so the cops know where they spend every waking moment and what all their friends look like before they even turn on the Stingray."

"At least they don't tattoo their faces," Sorry comments from her place at the table. “My favorite kind of revolutionary. Like wearing a fucking license plate.”

“But these guys are worse. They go around with Bluetooth headsets, so the cops even know who they ran into and stood near and exactly when and where, because their phones register it—but anyway, they can’t do direct actions anymore, because the cops are all over them. So where do they turn? To *Sunshine*! To the man who doesn’t have any electronics because they might use electricity! He told me once he wrote his college term papers by hand with a pencil and natural light. Did you see him in wintertime?” She turns to Penny. “I guess not. You haven’t been around that long.”

Penny says, “I saw him in this weird bunny suit—”

“That’s his spring and fall outfit. When it’s cold out, he has this like bag thing he wears with reflective foil inside, and this *hat*. So *anyway,* for whatever reason, Sunshine always knows these athletic women, like snowboarders and climbers and stuff, so he singlehandedly organized this action for Greenpeace, where Greenpeace is going to rally against climate change uptown as a distraction while these women climb the base of One World Trade Center with suction cups. That’s why the hashtag. Nobody’s going to know what it means until it’s already happening. None of you guys is an informant, right?”

“We’ll know it when they raid DJD in ten minutes,” Rob says.

Penny sets her phone on the table. “I had a line open to the FBI all this time, but I never imagined you guys would say anything interesting!”

“Isn’t a phone a spy microphone even when it’s turned off?” Sorry says. “I read about that with Snowden. You’re supposed to put your phone in the refrigerator, with the battery taken out.”

“They’re climbing the Freedom Tower,” Rob says. “It doesn’t matter whether anybody’s listening in. They’re not going to arrest us for talking about a peaceful public protest. They’ll wait until a suction cup touches glass. It's more serious charges. They *might* intervene to stop us making a bomb."

"Or not," Sorry says. "Depending on who we're planning to blow up."

Anka finishes her last *#climbit* and Rob fetches the tack hammer from the silverware drawer.

"So is this a Blue Bloc protest?" Penny asks him. "Because we're not really the Blue Bloc anymore."

"Maybe you're not, but I still value my pariah status," Sorry says.

"I was just asking because I think it might be fun to go downtown and check out the climbers, instead of hanging around the smoking section of a climate rally."

"It's an idea," Sorry says. "The rally draws police away from the climbers, and the climbers draw police away from the smokers."

"Who draw police away from people who don't clean up after their dogs," Rob adds. "That's smokers' role in this universe."

"Nobody walks dogs that far downtown," Anka says. "But who's smoking today?"

"Just me, I think," Sorry says.

"Where's Jazz?"

"I know she's around, but I haven't really talked to her in days."

HALF AN HOUR LATER, THE Nicotine residents depart for the rally. Rob suggests taking the Holland Tunnel, and Penny, Sorry, Anka, and Tony agree. They are glad for the change of plans: instead of waving signs toward the rear of a flash mob at Columbus Circle—a rally that will be generously spiked with male volunteers in black balaclavas, to lend an air of urgent danger—they will loiter near the bay, enjoying the view. Perhaps then a beer on the waterfront.

Rob parks in a semilegal spot just south of Canal, and they walk. The day is lovely, with a warm breeze and white clouds. The tower bends against passing clouds and changes shape like an illusion. They walk in circles, looking for Sunshine and his crew. The tower has four sides, and they don't know where the action is planned.

They find it by the commotion—or rather, by the one climber who has not yet fled. A young woman in green polypropylene clings to the West Street facade of the tower, her head perhaps fifteen feet above the sidewalk. While security guards look on, a policeman pokes her ankle with his nightstick. Leaping, he swats her calf. He aims carefully, to avoid damaging the valuable imported glass.

"Shit!" she cries out. "Shit!" She turns toward the Nicotine inhabitants. They know her; it's Susannah—daughter of a poet and an essayist in Boulder, Colorado, ecology major at Reed, six-month veteran of life on the East Coast. "Stop hurting me!" she screeches. But she doesn't climb down. She begins a difficult traverse toward the marquee. The policeman hits her shin hard enough to make a cracking sound audible above the shouting. She climbs farther aloft, instinctively trying to protect her hips, her torso, and her head from cracking sounds. She slips and catches herself by her suction cups.

Anka screams, "Stop it! Stop it! Susannah, get down here!"

Sorry says, "She's going to fall."

Penny stands with her mouth open and her palms on her cheeks.

Sorry raises her phone and begins to make a video. From behind, a policewoman seizes both her hands and ties them together with a cable binder ("zip-cuffs"). Her phone skitters across the pavement as she loses her balance and lets her weight fall, landing on her knees with a gasp. Penny picks it up.

"Give me that," the policewoman says to Penny, indicating Sorry's phone.

Penny turns and runs. She hears a scream. She glances over her shoulder and sees a crowd of police. Anka and Tony are running as well—scattering, behind her and to her left. She sprints. Her messenger bag on a long strap thumps on her hip. Sorry's phone is still in her hand.

She tears through a row of bushes and runs across traffic, down Vesey Street, and into a bagel place. She walks hurriedly to the rear. The restroom is locked, so she squeezes into a space reserved for cleaning supplies. Then a seat comes free at a booth, and she sits down. She looks up and sees Tony. He approaches her without looking at her. "Take it, take it, take it," she whispers in a rush, putting the phone on the table. He slips it into his back pocket and leaves the deli.

As he exits, two police officers enter. They do not recognize him as being connected with the case. He is older and nondescript.

Penny might as well be wearing a license plate. They ask her to come along.

They wait to put zip-cuffs on her until just before they load her into their big, high-walled van. In the van, she meets Sorry. "It's cool," she whispers. "I mean, I found a cool place for the thing."

"Cool," Sorry says.

"Where's Susannah?"

"Hospital. She has a compound ankle fracture, and she passed out and hit her head. Her mouth was bleeding."

"Oh shit. Fuck."

"It's no big deal. She'll spend the rest of her life as a cauldron of seething rage, and no mainstream citizen will ever take her seriously again as long as she lives. But she'll bounce back, unless she ends up with slurred speech and a limp. Then her media career can really take off."

"Shit. And for what? The fucking *climate*?"

"Most important challenge facing humanity today," Sorry says. "But she was a foot soldier, a follower. She *knew* they were going to fuck her up. And that's what I'll *never* understand. College-girl cannon fodder. You'd think they'd save that shit for the provocateurs.

But if you saw her ankle, you'd know she was not in it for the money. She got what she wanted. It makes me so sad."

"Fuck." Penny is greenish, thinking about the ankle. There is silence as the police van trundles on worn-out shocks. It rocks like a cradle, forward and backward. "Where are we headed?" she asks Sorry.

"Probably the Tombs."

"Is that like Rikers Island?"

"It's like a crusty squat without the rats. But you're from the slums of Brazil. You'll be fine."

"Our house had a wall and armed guards."

"Then you're going to feel right at home."

"That's it. If you liked the White House, you'll just love the Tombs!"

"I keep forgetting you're a rich kid," Sorry says. "It's not the way you look. Maybe it's that you're careful? Or insecure? The other rich kids are out there laying their privilege on the altar of justice and burning it alive, and you just keep on creeping on, watching your back."

"That doesn't sound too good."

"They're not privileged. Susannah just found it out the hard way. She had a hard landing in reality. She's going to be pissed when she wakes up and realizes Mommy and Daddy lied. She'll be like, 'But I'm entitled to do whatever I want, wherever I want, and the police can't touch me!' I don't get the feeling you have that problem."

"Yeah, I have other problems," Penny says. "Like the feeling that I'm getting my period, and I don't have any ibuprofen."

"They wouldn't book a woman with cramps," Sorry says. "There's no cramps in the CIA torture memos. Cramps would way exceed their mandate."

"Do they even torture women?" It's a serious question. Penny can't remember reading about any torture charges against the CIA involving a woman victim. "I mean like at Guantánamo." She becomes pensive. "Were any of the fighters—wait, is this space miked?"

"Yeah, maybe you should shut up about Al Qaeda," Sorry says.

AMALIA PULLS UP SLOWLY IN front of Nicotine, peering up from behind the steering wheel of her white Taurus sedan. To her it is her in-laws' house, the house where she was never welcome. A house that filled with cinders and standing water—only fair after the way its inhabitants treated her.

As she approaches, her heart sinks. But not because the house is intact. Her point of contention is Matt's car. The black Audi stands in front of the garage where Rob's minivan usually stands.

She pulls up behind it and parks. She reads the license plate to make sure. She kills her engine and sits silently. She sets the parking brake, picks up her white purse, and walks to the front door. She wears a knee-length electric blue zebra-print dress. Her purse is a long, narrow "baguette," significantly out of style.

Her doorbell options: JAZZ, TONY, ANKA, ROB, SORRY. She hammers on the door with her fist. Nothing happens. She sets the switch to JAZZ, because it is the first name on the list, and pushes the button.

"All my instincts," Peter Gabriel sings. "The grand facade." She hammers on the door. She cries.

On the roof, Jazz disengages herself from Matt and walks out the open door of her conservatory to look down at the street. "You're parked in," she says. "There's some guy's car behind you." She returns to bed.

Matt gets up naked as a jaybird (a cliché that makes no sense until the jaybird has been plucked for eating) and looks down. "That's my stepmother's car." The song keeps wafting up the stairwell. "Oh Jesus."

"She won't make it inside," Jazz says. "Come back to bed."

"You don't know her," Matt says. "She's scrappy."

"I've heard a little bit about her from Penny. Like that she's younger than you are."

"She's passionately in love with me."

"Since your father died?"

"Since I was sixteen."

They hear a window break.

"Fuck," Matt says.

"Call the police."

"She owns the house."

Amalia seizes the bars on the front kitchen window—cheap telescoping bars, the kind you might install to keep a child from falling out of an upper floor—and shakes them like an ape protesting its cage. She is light and not strong. They don't break.

All the windows have similar bars. No number of broken windows can help her. She sits down by the FREE box of kittens. She calls Matt on the phone.

"Take the call," Jazz says.

"No fucking way."

"This is going to get boring if she doesn't leave soon. How passionately?"

Matt exhales and rolls his eyes.

"Did you fuck her?"

"Not in a *long* time."

Jazz rocks from side to side on her knees on the bed, grinning. "I knew it, I knew it! I *knew* you were Penny's father!"

"Aw, *ugh*!" Matt returns to her and whacks her on the arm with a throw pillow. "Get your mind out of the fucking *gutter*!" He whacks her again. One more whack, and he is hard enough to forget Amalia, who writes a note on the back of a lengthy Best Buy receipt she finds in her purse, using a pen she also finds there:

Dear Matt, you are breaking my heart. You don't love me, that is my problem, but you are not honest, that is your problem. It is unworthy of the honor of a MAN. Tell me what is occurring. All my life, all your life, I was sure you are lonely. But maybe the life of a single man in New York is not so lonely. ~~I am the stupid one~~, maybe your love turned to nothing many years ago. But at the least I never lied to you. Be honest with me Matt. I love you.

She tucks the note under a windshield wiper on the Audi and walks to the bodega—she had noticed it as she drove past the school to the house—to buy beer. She intends to drink it on the porch and wait.

ROB PARKS ON THE STREET because there are two cars in his driveway. Anka notices the broken kitchen window, and Tony reads the note attached to Matt's car.

"Uh-oh," Tony says. "You are not going to believe this. It's a love letter from Penny's mother to her *brother*." He looks around, wondering where Amalia might be. "Do you think that's her car?"

He peeks through the front passenger-side window of the Taurus and sees bone amulets hanging from the rearview mirror on leather thongs.

Rob walks through the house, saying softly, "Amalia? Amalia?" He opens doors, including that of the bucket monster. But she is not there. As he enters his room he perceives that Jazz and Matt believe they are alone.

Amalia returns from the bodega, carrying a four-pack in a paper bag clutched to her hip, and sees Tony holding her note to Matt. Her grief is instant, utter, and uncontrollable.

"You bastard!" she yells. "How can you do that! It's a private letter! Bastard! Bastard!"

"We've never met," he says. "So you don't know that. Here's your note back. I didn't read it. I thought they might have ticketed you for parking on the sidewalk. See how your car is partly on the sidewalk?"

Amalia hovers, uncertain, because Tony's claim makes no sense (the "ticket" was on Matt's car). But she puts her receipt in her purse and says, "Thank you."

"You remind me of my friend Penny," Tony says. "Are you her sister?"

She looks down. "Mother. I'm her mother. But I'm not very many years older."

"You must be Amalia. You got an extra beer in there? I had a rough day."

"You! Ha."

"No, mine really *was* rough. A demo went south. A girl from DJD got hurt bad, and Penny and Sorry got arrested."

"Penny under arrest? Oh my god. Who cares. She will never find a job anyway. Why she studied business, I don't know. She'll never pass a criminal background check. My stupid baby." She wipes her eyes. Holding her skirt with her hand in a ladylike fashion, she climbs the front stairs, sits on the top step, sets her purse down, and removes a beer from her paper bag.

Tony smiles and says, "Don't worry. Half the jobs out there, they *want* a criminal record, so they can pay you less than minimum wage. Gut rehab. Cook. Social worker in a halfway house. I did all that shit."

She rests her elbows on her knees as she opens her beer and takes a sip. Tony takes a beer out of the bag for himself. He opens it and drinks half in one gulp.

"I'm a human resources professional," she says. "I know what I'm saying. I know Penny will never find work. Just look at her, oh my god. But I was a bad example, always bitching about my job. Now she wants to be unemployed forever. I was a bad mother."

"'Never work' is classic anarchist tradition. She fits right in. Where's the problem?"

"Work can be so valuable. Her father had meaningful work, helping the sick. And all the time I was making money, as much money as I could. Why did I do it? Money can't buy happiness!"

"It's a symbol. Like having a nice car." He glances disapprovingly at the Audi, hoping to score points.

"What I need now is dialectics. To overcome and break the false ideas."

"The ideologies?" Tony suggests.

"Out with the ideologies! Time for revolution." Knees primly together, she turns toward Tony and raises her beer. He raises his beer, and they drink a toast to revolution.

"But that's an individual decision we make for ourselves," Tony says. "It's too risky, dragging other people into it."

"One revolution is all I need. Revolution in *my* life. A return to meaningful work that brings happiness. Did you ever hear the saying 'labor is value'? What I want—can I trust you?"

"I'm a bastard, I really am. You got that right. But you can trust me."

"I want to work in my garden."

"I love gardening," Tony says, finishing his first beer.

Amalia and Tony continue talking on the porch while Anka adds titles to Sorry's cell phone video and uploads it to YouTube. She writes that Sorry was an independent "legal observer," and that the anonymous climber in the video suffered incapacitating injuries from police brutality.

Amalia stays for dinner. Matt stays upstairs.

Around eleven, Amalia drives home to Morristown with her emotions in a whirl. All sorts of interesting things she had thought dead jump upright and advance toward her en masse, like a dust devil with arms and a face, inside her head while she drives.

At home she lies down wide-eyed. She thinks of Matt and doesn't—to her relief—give a damn. She feels desexualized. All the dumb horniness drains from her body, and her unburdened soul rises curiously to check out this alluring inner demon of romance.

She falls asleep while the demon and her soul hover over her, still whirling.

ROB AND ANKA TEASE TONY.

He defends himself. "She's suffering from unrequited love. She's so lonely she wants to *garden*."

"I thought you liked Penny," Anka says.

"She's the mature, knowing version of Penny, with a past."

"And a mansion in Morristown," Rob says. "And maybe a big house in Jersey City. Somebody needs to rescue this damsel in distress! And better you than me."

Jazz comes downstairs to fetch food and wine for Matt. He stays the night, forgotten by Amalia.

OVER THE NEXT SEVERAL HOURS, the *#climbit* video receives a few viewings and a number of negative ratings. Sorry's wobbly footage lasts only six seconds. Anka's titles speak of her own shuddering at the sound of bone hitting concrete, but the clip ends before Susannah falls.

THE TOMBS CELL PENNY AND Sorry share with two Chinese shoplifters is cold and uncomfortable. There is a toilet with toilet paper, a sink with no soap, nothing to eat (no appetite), no sanitary supplies, no medications, and no offer of phone calls, because they are supposed to be held for a maximum of twenty-four hours. The painted plaster walls are slimy with condensation.

"This place reminds me of the first time I saw Nicotine," Sorry says. "This was the kitchen."

Penny is bleeding, but not too badly. She tucks some toilet paper into her underwear and changes it every hour or so. She lies with her head on Sorry's lap and concentrates on the pain. She knows that if she can descend into it with her mind and inhabit it, it will change into a feeling of pressure that's not nearly as bad. She hasn't experienced menstrual cramps in a long time.

Sorry doesn't pat or stroke her head. They both feel it's better not to touch anything in the Tombs, especially anyone's eyes or nose. She merely serves as a pillow.

In pain, Penny recalls Norm's death. But her mind skirts the usual chasms. Her surroundings tug her back toward problems that admit of political solutions: women without access to analgesics, women in countries where you can't even get alcohol! Their pointless suffering—especially pointless because it might so easily be stopped. As if unstoppable pain automatically had a point. As if the agonies of strangulated hernia and cancer and appendicitis worked to deter people from getting them. She feels the logic of the hospice as never before. If death is inevitable—the logic says—it needs to mean something, like what happened to Job.

As for her own pain, she doesn't look for a point. She knows if she can inhabit it fully, it will eventually go away. And after ten or eleven hours, it does. It goes away.

RIGHT AROUND THE TWENTY-THREE-HOUR MARK, Sorry and Penny are let go.

Their valuables are returned to them, including Sorry's cigarettes and Penny's phone. "I am so fucking happy to hear from you,"

Rob says when she calls. "You would not believe what's been going on here. How's Sorry?"

"Defiant. Unbowed."

"She should be. I'll tell you later."

Sorry appears elated enough to skip. "I'm so fucking relieved," she says, inhaling deeply from her first cigarette on the sidewalk outside the facility. "They never even ran my driver's license!"

Penny, too, is pretty darn cheerful to be out of the Tombs. She uses her phone to summon an Uber (gypsy cab), remarking that she will probably start receiving advertising aimed at petty criminals, based on her location alone—and it's true. Ads on Google mail spontaneously offer her bail bond and mail-order weapons with no background check.

"Are you sure you want to take a car all the way to JC?" Sorry asks. "I have enough cash for the train."

Penny says she's allowed to use her mom's accounts in emergencies. She orders the driver to drop her off at the nearest Duane Reade and circle the block. Getting back in the car, she sings "ibuprofen" to the tune of the "Hallelujah Chorus." She washes one down with cola, even though the pain is gone. She offers Sorry an ethanol-drenched disinfectant wipe, and they scrub their hands, cheeks, foreheads, noses, necks, and ears.

The driver steers toward the tunnel entrance. She searches for *#climbit*. She sees Sorry's video. She feels surprised that there is no call to action from DJD.

She texts Sunshine, wondering if the DJD residents plan to do anything in response to the events at the Freedom Tower. He replies that Susannah's parents interrupted a strategy meeting with urgent requests that all actions be halted, and that the DJD residents are complying, despite their rage. He is reliant on Susannah's parents—who are staying at a hotel in Manhattan and not eager to talk to him—for information on Susannah's condition, so he can say only that she has regained consciousness.

THEY ARRIVE AT NICOTINE TO find Rob in the kitchen making macaroni and cheese with spelt rotini and Gruyère (soup kitchen donations nobody wanted). Sorry calls dibs on the shower, so he tells Penny the story of Amalia's visit.

He makes it brief, dry, and factual: Amalia came to Nicotine, stalking Matt. Tony led her aside, calmed her, persuaded her to reveal a set of values more indicative of a Maoist guerrilla than an HR manager at a bank . . . "Your family is full of surprises," he concludes.

During the story, Penny squirms in embarrassment and says "oh my god" many times. Repeatedly she glances at her phone, but she does not call her mother.

She waits until after eating, and for the boiler to reheat completely following Sorry's long shower, to take an extra-long shower herself.

She falls asleep in Rob's bed. Her own suffering is forgotten, but as she dozes off her body jerks awake with images of Susannah's fall.

Rob watches her and strokes her hair. When she is asleep, before nine o'clock, he grabs the bottle containing the last of his expensive bourbon and goes downstairs to chat with Sorry.

AROUND 11:30 P.M., ROUGHLY TWENTY-FOUR hours after their parting, Amalia texts Tony, inviting him to visit her sometime in Morristown.

Already in his sleepwear (too-large T-shirt, nothing on the bottom), in bed with his tablet computer, Tony volunteers to visit the very next day. He looks up the Kogi on Wikipedia and reads about them. He looks up Norm and finds him on Amazon and Google Books. He reads a few excerpts and decides that even alive, he would have been no competition, because he was a huge bore, obsessed with illness and purging.

Long after midnight, he tries the search term "Kogi" on the

environmentalist pornography service he subscribes to ("Fuck for Forest"). It offers no Kogi-themed videos.

He watches an Italian teenager play with a dildo free of charge on YouPorn.

THE NEXT MORNING, ROB MAKES boysenberry pancakes for Penny. He sees her off for her walk home to Tranquility in light rain with an umbrella from the FREE box. He returns upstairs and knocks on Jazz's many-paned glass door. "Come in," she says.

"Hey, J. How's the climate?"

"Supreme."

"How's the landlord?"

"Hot. I'm reading this great book, the memoirs of Jean Cocteau."

"I heard he was good."

"He's got that breezy, casual sophistication I'm always aiming for and never hitting. Like fucking a garbage truck designer who drives an Audi. He's not really a princely prize. His art collection is the latest in porn tech. But he's hot."

With a sigh, Rob sits down on the bed so that Jazz can read his mind.

"You're too paranoid," she says all of a sudden, leaning toward him to rest her hands on his forearm. "It's like you got your entire sex education from Houellebecq novels. Now you think it's a heterosexual market economy and you're overleveraged—like any woman who sees your dick is going to run out and write a blog post about the emperor's new clothes. Well, guess what? It's *not* a heterosexual market economy. Heterosexuality is *over.* Who even wants intercourse anymore? Me and the landlord, maybe! Every other woman I know wants head, not to mention every other man."

Reaching up tenderly to fix a stray bobby pin in her hair, he says, "But I always wanted to be a heavy-hung stud and impale women on my prong until they're helpless, quivering protoplasm."

She frowns.

"I mean, when I go down on a woman, it kind of makes me want to fuck."

"Happens to me all the time," Jazz says. "It's the heteronormative paradigm in action. But"—she holds up a slender fist—"I can go right up most girls with my arm."

Rob looks down at his large hands and says, "It wouldn't be the same for me. I have options."

"So use your dick!"

"Jazz. That's what I'm saying. Nobody wants it. Fucking happens in a woman's mind. You can't fuck alone. You know what I mean. You do the exact same thing, and depending on whether she wants it, it's rape or the highlight of her life. Well, girls take one look at my dick and say, 'Ooh, baby, I love it when you make me come with your mouth.' "

Jazz laughs.

"But God forbid I should ask anybody to do so much as jerk me off. Even the virgins in high school were like, 'Excuse me? This is not what I ordered.' And you know women compare notes. If I get naked once, it's over. My body image is fucked. I'm traumatized by rejection like a fat chick—like a *hairy* fat chick, with boils on her butt she drains with a shunt. I seriously cannot imagine getting naked with somebody who wasn't in love with me—but you know what? I am not interested in that person. The woman who loves me no matter what, like she's my fucking mom. I'd rather be a monk. There's generations of religious in my family. It works for me. Sort of. Not really. I have problems. I'm not happy right now. I want to get bombed off my ass and dip tobacco until everything goes back to normal."

Jazz leans back to reflect. She says, "You ever done bondage?"

"Nope."

"That's what you need. Tie a person up, and it's all relative. Just look at her. After a while, she'll come if you touch her *nipple*. If it's protoplasm you're after."

"Sounds like fun, for her—"

"Then blindfold her before you take off your pants, if you're so worried about the visuals! Keep your hand on her to confuse her. Don't use rope or belts. Use scarves. And don't say 'impale.' It's gross."

He picks up a conch shell lying on a bookcase. He turns it this way and that, holds it to his ear, stretches his arms and back, and says, "I love you, Jazz."

"I love you, too, Robby."

"Anybody else might feel sorry for me for like *one second*. But you're always like, 'try my obvious solution, you whiner.' I can't talk to you without feeling better. And I didn't even *want* to feel better."

"Did you hear the ocean?"

"Yup. It's right in there where you left it." He returns the shell to its place on the bookcase.

TONY COLLAPSES HIS FOLDING BIKE to take it on the bus. As a hostess gift, he packs one of Jazz's tobacco plants into a garbage bag, tying it shut with a green ribbon liberated from Anka. (The ribbon has been lying on the kitchen floor for several days, so he feels it is fair game.)

He rolls up to the house in Morristown, guided by the maps app on his phone. When he arrives, he sees that the black and maroon blobs on the green background around the black H are large hemlocks and copper beeches. He presses the solitary BAKER button on a black panel with room for several more buttons, and Amalia buzzes him in.

"So much space and no garden," he says. "With acreage like this, you could keep a flock of pygmy sheep." He hands over the tobacco plant.

She sets it down on the brick front porch and laughs, flattered. “Yes, it’s big, no? Norm was a smart investor.”

“I’m sorry about him,” Tony says. “I mean, that he died. Though I might not be standing here if he were alive—”

“He was old and sick. I was his second wife, you know? A lot younger.” She smiles. She wears black leggings and a white T-shirt—a look inspired by Penny, or rather a look directly borrowed from Penny, some of whose clothes are upstairs in a drawer. “Coffee?” she asks.

When the conversation flags, she takes him around the yard. He plants the tobacco in a shallow pit, adding neither water nor fertilizer. She warms up lunch. They eat, speaking at intervals with long gaps.

After lunch Amalia drives Tony to the botanical garden, saying it might give her some ideas.

She is very conscientious, reading the labels on roses and camellias. She stands transfixed by a potted palm and remarks, “How can it live in winter?” She touches the leaves to see if they are plastic. In the herb garden, she points out oregano with delight, saying she has eaten it with spaghetti sauce.

“You don’t know jack shit about gardens, do you?” Tony asks, deep in the arboretum.

“No! I told you, I work in HR.” Scampering, she grasps a young pine tree bole with one hand as she passes and swings around it like a teenager displaying herself. Her long hair sways. Tony feels an indistinct pleasure.

“I thought you were from some primitive hill tribe. Subsistence agriculture or what-have-you.”

“I learned to gather foodstuffs in the forest. That’s how I survived when I ran away.”

“That’s amazing, that you ran away and survived.”

“Ha. For girls, it’s always easier if you run away. You don’t have to share anymore! Ha, that sounds bad. But it's a different life when you have nothing. Now I like to share."

Tony grabs her free hand. She stands still, looking up expectantly, and he kisses her.

ON SUNDAY, PENNY VISITS HER mother in Morristown.

"You're not going to believe it," Amalia says. "I have a lover."

"Oh god, Mom! Stop!"

"Why?"

"I already know. I *know* him. It's Tony."

"I never thought I would experience passion again. But passion is a part of me. It was there inside me all the time, and now I can express it. I am so happy. Be happy for me."

"Matt must be relieved. I heard you met Tony because you were stalking *Matt*. That asshole! You treat me like a *stepchild,* and you're in love with that *asshole*." Penny wipes her eyes and blows her nose on a napkin.

Heavy sigh. Long silence. "Tony was in love with you," Amalia says. "You know that, right? But everyone can make a mistake. The love is there inside you, and you meet the wrong person. Human beings are filled with love. That's how it was with me. I loved the wrong man all my life—"

"Dad was the wrong man?"

"No. He saved me."

"From what? Matt? Patrick told me about how Matt used to abuse you. Remember when he tried to rape me? Matt's an *asshole*."

"Why do you listen to Patrick? He hates me. Why do you think he lives so far away?"

Penny is silent.

"Patrick was a child. He thought love is holding hands."

"You were his same age!"

"I had no family in Cartagena. I was a big girl, alone. Matt was a young boy. You say he abused me. What if it's the other way around? What if I abused him? Think, my baby."

Penny thinks.

She imagines Norm striving to make up for Amalia's deficient upbringing. He and Katie serving her rich meals, giving her pretty clothes and a safe place to sleep, waiting for the light to dawn that children are fed and housed and clothed for free, simply because they are children. Meanwhile, back at the ranch . . . Penny knows pictures of Matt from when he was young. Soulful, hunky teen heartthrob for Amalia's first innocent schoolgirl crush. The ideal object—the perfect victim—for a girl struggling to act out how she was manipulated. Because that's also love. Maybe no love is needier or more intense.

One reality, mutable as shadows on smoke.

She sees Norm rejecting Amalia's advances because he was a good man, and Matt accepting them because he was neither good, nor a man. The paradox that makes her want men who reject her. The eternal conundrum of dating. She covers her face with her hands and says, "No. Yes."

"In the end I married Norm because he loved me. You remember how he loved me."

"That's true," Penny says. "He loved you."

"I believed in him. He gave me a good life, and such a wonderful daughter. And it was him who saved me. I will never reveal from what he saved me."

Penny leans back and shakes her head, as though shaking might make the fluff fall out. "Come on, Mom," she says. "Tell me something I don't know. I enjoy finding out what things were really like."

"The past is gone," Amalia says. "Norm taught me that all is one."

"The facts are not all one!"

"Yes, they are. Even the facts are interconnected. There is

conservation of energy. When they beat you and they rape you, they become bad and you become good. As long as there is life, the balance will not change."

Penny has trouble following what Amalia is saying. She wants it to make sense. It sounds to her like straight-up prevarication, masked as mysticism, as though Amalia is talking around something big and solid. She suspects Norm and Jazz of having masked similar prevarications as rationality, but at least—she thinks—*at least they made sense*. She wants to hear things equally persuasive from her mother. That sense of insight she felt just now, when Amalia pointed to teenage Matt's sexual inexperience: she wants it back.

"Life is like water," her mother is explaining gently, "flowing to the ocean and up to the clouds to rain upon the hills. It can only consume itself. A river eats water. If it gets enough water, the river is a true river. Then it can carry many heavy things without pain."

Casting about for facts to cling to, Penny's mind flashes to an image of Norm's body. Bloated and waterlogged, purple arm raised, it rocks back and forth in the shallows at the mouth of a seasonal river in western Peru. It's not the image she wants. It's extremely counterfactual, among other things.

Seeing her unhappy look, Amalia adds, "Do you see now? The river is life. That is the meaning of the cosmic snake."

"What? The river is a snake?"

Amalia nods, and Penny shakes her head. She takes a deep breath and says, "Patrick told me about Katie."

Amalia's fuzzy solemnity gives way to bald annoyance. "Not that," she says. "Katie was my true mother. Don't mention her." She stands up to take a tissue from a dispenser, and blows her nose.

"Did it happen the way Patrick said? She just disappeared?"

"What did he tell you?"

"I want your version first."

"She took a taxicab. She waved good-bye. That's all."

"That's all?"

"We had been fighting. Norm said she needed peace and quiet. Oh my god, he looked for her everyplace. And from the beginning we know that she is kidnapped or dead, because she loved us so much. The police didn't help us. Colombia was very bad in those days."

Amalia's eyes are wet now, and Penny says, "I'm sorry."

"We left Colombia right away, me and the boys."

Penny takes another deep breath and casts her line out for another possible truth. "Some people say Matt is my father."

"Ha-ha," Amalia says, with studied sarcasm. "We never touched after I married Norm. I was a good wife. I loved him as a mother until Norm died. I never touched him for thirty years. But who cares about that garbage man? Let me show you something."

She scrounges in her purse and finds the note to Matt on the back of the Best Buy receipt.

"Here, read this. My first love letter to Matt in all my life, on one subject only—how much I hate him. And you know why I hate him? Because I love him, but it's impossible to love an asshole. An asshole like Matt you can only hate, unless you're a worm."

Penny reads the note. "Yeah, you pretty much hate him!"

"Compared to Norm, he's a worm."

"He's a worm compared to most worms," Penny says, giving her back the note. "When you said beating and raping—"

"Stop it! He was my lover, not a *para*! You think he's bad for fucking stupid sluts from the Internet? It makes me angry, too. But it's not evil. Does he kidnap and torture them? Does he kill their families? No. He's not a bad man. He is *normal*. He cannot love anyone, and that is normal. Norm was a special man."

Penny tries hard to think. Her mother's words seem to lower the bar an awful lot, calling Matt normal because war criminals are bad. She wonders if this is an insight into anything but her own mind. "But you did love Matt, when you were young," she insists.

"I was horny like a worm!"

The words carry an echo of a blanket condemnation of sex—though this resonance, too, might not be in the words at all, but only in her mind—and she goes on the defensive: "What's so wrong with that?"

"You want to sleep with a worm? A squirmy worm, squirming around? Or a man who loves you?"

Penny frowns. She shakes her head. She opens the refrigerator and changes the subject to the immediate desirability of BLTs.

She slices some tomatoes, very thin.

JAZZ STANDS ON THE TERRACE of Matt's apartment in the early evening, wearing her fetish heels and a garter belt. A breeze from the Hudson wafts her hair up and down and into her eyes and mouth (it is on the nineteenth floor, and the wind tends to hit the building and swirl) as she smokes. "Hey, Jazz, I want to try something," Matt says.

She looks inside. He is lying on his back on the couch wearing a blue morph suit, the 3-D headset, and a blue condom. His laptop, open on the coffee table, faces his crotch.

"You look ultra-pervy," Jazz says.

"I took a Viagra to match my outfit. Sit on my dick."

"And what will you see?"

"You, on my dick."

"With what background?"

"Secret."

She sits on his dick and transfers—she doesn't hesitate, and Matt doesn't resist—the headset from his head to her own. She sees herself sitting astride a black, scaly monster. The odd perspective makes her lose her balance. She dismounts briefly, exposing the cruelly barbed end of its outsize penis. "What *are* you?" she says. "Priapus the pangolin?"

"You don't like scales?" Sitting upright, he turns the laptop so that she sees the monster's head—roughly that of a wolverine—while he makes some adjustments. The scales vanish.

"Give yourself better fur," she suggests. "Glossy, like a mink."

"Why not," he says. "I like you in that mask."

"Is there a camera on the headset?"

"Not on this model. Should I get the one with a camera?"

"I don't know," she says, fucking him. "It strikes me as sort of—a novelty—item—unh." The giant weasel's arm enters the frame. Matt adjusts something, and it turns into the black, scaly monster. His hands press on her ears. She sees its jagged penis tearing her skin and its pelvis drenched in her blood. She closes her eyes, and Matt turns on the sound—piercing screams. She pushes upward on his forearms. She rips at his fingers. She can't take off the earphones. Opening her eyes, she tries to slap the monster in the face and misses, blinded by the headset, her equilibrium gone.

She fumbles with one hand on the coffee table and slams the laptop shut.

Matt pulls the headset off her and drops it on the carpet. She shakes her hair loose and looks down. Though obscured by the morph suit, entirely blue, he appears relaxed. Amused.

In her mind, she senses absolute self-control. In her body, she tries to exhale and can't. Her lungs quiver like they need a defibrillator. She feels palsied.

To him, she looks harrowed. It's a good look, he thinks. Suits her. The look of impaled protoplasm, and he's not even close to done. "Need a break?" he says.

He lets her stand up and walk to the balcony. Her eyes are wide. She grasps the railing in both hands and puts one foot up on a planter.

He sees what she's up to and makes a lightning three-point landing. Before she can jump, he is inside her again, his dick pushing her into his arms. She fights and struggles to get away, over the railing, but he won't let her go.

She'd rather die? Fine, let her try. He knows that would be the wrong choice, and he won't let her make it. His body and his conscience are one person. It's a kind of sex he has never known. Sex as a life-giving act—the higher, spiritual sexuality priests and rabbis are always talking about. The kind he never believed existed. He thinks back on the scene with the gun, when he thought there might be nothing hotter than killing, and he feels like Saul on the road to Damascus. He was so wrong. Life is hot. Death is not. He saves her life because he needs her alive so he can save her again. The rescue operation is as circular as breathing air so he can live to breathe more air. Pure, self-motivated ethical action. The categorical imperative. Virtue as its own reward. Love that gives life that gives love. The cosmic snake, nourished by its own tail.

By the time two minutes have passed, he can't imagine life without it. He pulls her back inside the apartment where she is safe.

As they cross the threshold she relaxes suddenly, falling against him with a high moan, and the sound and the motion combined are too much for him. He comes so much the condom is awash in fluid. It caresses him like a soft-lipped mouth, high inside her body.

He imagines what it might feel like to get her pregnant. He holds that power. He could give her a life beyond her own. Or even several. He could give her descendants like the sands of the seashore.

"I'm breaking up with you," she says after her shower.

"No, you're not!" he says. "Are you crazy?"

MATT DROPS JAZZ OFF IN front of Nicotine. She runs up the stairs, opens her door, throws herself facedown on the bed, and sobs. It is 10:00 P.M.

Rob hears her crying. He puts down Jean Cocteau and peeks out the storm door. He puts on his striped summer bathrobe and crosses to her room. "Jazz," he says.

"I'm such a moron. Why am I a moron?"

"You need to ask me a question that means something."

"Why was I fucking Matt?"

"Did I just hear past tense?" He sits down and puts his hand on her back. "Did something happen?"

She turns over and says, "Please stay here for a minute. Lie next to me, like you did at DJD. Stay with me." He lies down, and she stares into his eyes. "Rob," she says, holding his head between her hands. She lowers her hands, turns her face downward into the pillow, and cries.

"What the fuck happened?"

"It's hard to explain. But it was *wrong*. It was just *wrong*. The kind of thing, when somebody does it, you know he's not right."

Rob puts his arms around her and hugs her tight. "It's okay. It's over, and you'll forget it soon."

"I thought I was so hard-core."

"No way! Not you. You're the sweetest girl I ever knew."

"And I'm turning you on."

"Yeah," he says, backing away.

"Don't go. Stay. Make love to me, Robby."

He backs farther away and sits upright. "That's not a very nice thing to say! I'm too small to 'fuck' you like everybody else, but I can still 'make love'? Should I blindfold you first?"

Hiding her face, Jazz returns to crying.

"Don't cry!"

"Then don't hurt me that way," she says. "Don't turn me into an evil creature that can only fuck. That fucks people and doesn't love them."

"I didn't do that. Nobody could ever do that."

He lies down again and embraces her. He is immediately hard, in his small way. She smiles, nuzzling her crooked nose into his bathrobe. They kiss each other. He looks around. "Where do you keep condoms?" he asks. "I don't have any—"

"Don't use one. Make love to me. I'm too skinny to ovulate, and you've never had sex before in your life, so who cares? I want to feel you, your skin and warmth, you know? Not to be poked with a medical device. I am sick to death of being poked with safety equipment—using lube so I can pretend I'm turned on enough to want to be poked with safety equipment—doing scenes and fantasies and role-playing to distract myself from the reality that I'm being poked with safety equipment!"

"You're outraged," he says. He hugs her again. He embraces her shoulders, her ass, her waist. He kisses her hesitantly and is soon short of breath. He trembles, and his heart races. She makes herself small, cuddling into his arms. They peel the underwear from each other's rear ends, pull it to knee-level with their hands, and push it the rest of the way down with their feet.

Saying, "I can't believe this is happening," he kisses her and touches his bare penis to her vagina.

"Are you inside?" she asks.

He laughs and goes inside.

THAT NIGHT, MATT SUFFERS FROM insomnia—the sort of insomnia that saves a man's life.

He is worrying intensely about a woman who wants nothing to do with him, and the more he worries, the more he feels he has a right to worry. That's how love works. It grabs and takes and snowballs, an emotional ambition, and it's nowhere more at home than in hell. He calls her over and over, but her phone is turned off, and of course it is, because she made him promise never to contact her again. But that doesn't mean she won't contact him, right? He thinks about having an Ambien and a nightcap, but he doesn't want to sleep. He wants his phone to make a sound that will be Jazz, saying she needs him.

It's so quiet. The city that never sleeps makes its accustomed whooshing sound on the other side of the Hudson. Fort Lee hangs suspended above it, a concrete hammock filled with sweaty snorers. No sound but predawn traffic on the bridge and tunnel approaches, crows cawing, little babies. He gets up and dressed and behind the wheel of his car, where falling asleep would be life-threatening. So it's a good thing he has insomnia.

He wants the city. He crosses the George Washington Bridge and drives down the West Side toward a strip club where he knows a hostess. He used to think she was wild. He breezes past it and makes a left on Twenty-Third, toward his estranged girlfriend's dorm at NYU. He thinks of fucking her dull face while she fingers the pink vibrator in her rump and turns south again to take the Holland Tunnel to Bayonne. Why not just go to work? It's four. The sky is getting light. The birds will be singing.

When he gets out of the tunnel, he finds he still has options. He keeps making choices. Negative ones. He says no to everything. No coffee, no diner, no impulse trip to Vermont. The car wheels in great arcs, like a hawk marking its territory. Then it lands.

MATT KICKS IN THE FRONT door of Nicotine.

He knows the quiet click the latch makes when it closes, so he is unsurprised to find that it breaks easily. The only sound is the splintering of the doorframe to a distance of about two feet above and below the latch.

Sorry wakes up. She hears footsteps charging up the stairs and shouts, "Hey! There's somebody in the house!" Anka yawns, turns over, opens her eyes, and dials 911. Holding an empty wine bottle in one hand, Tony peers into the hallway. But Matt is faster, already sprinting up the last flight.

He strides across the roof and opens Jazz's door. Rob stands up to face him, naked. A downy golden body, a mass of fluffy pubic hair like a hippie girl. That's not what he expected to see. He opens his mouth to say something, bends his knees, and punches Rob hard in the stomach.

Rob falls down. Matt kicks him once near the groin. He picks up Jazz's armchair, places it with one leg near Rob's navel, and kneels on it.

Rob is too weakened to scream. He can barely breathe. The chair leg does not perforate his abdominal wall, instead sliding along it as he turns. At waist level next to his torso, it tugs the skin of his front down to meet the skin of his back. It looks as though it might punch a hole.

Matt kneels and bounces. It's as though he were righteously killing a vicious animal with no feelings, but it's Rob.

Finally Jazz, on her knees in front of her bookshelf, finds the handgun on the floor where it fell down last time she hid it behind the books. "Matt," she says to get his attention. "Matt."

He looks up and sees her. She is not cowering anymore. She is naked and barefoot, just like Rob. He has never seen her naked. This realization really, really, seriously pisses him off.

He stands up, kicks Rob once in the ribs, and moves toward her. She wiggles the gun to make him notice it.

Tony, standing behind Matt with the wine bottle, also notices the gun. Jazz gives him this look like maybe he's in her way, and he turns and runs down the stairs. Matt follows him. Jazz, too. A breathless scuffling and running down the slippery wooden staircase ensues, with no shots fired. Past Anka, now barricaded in her room (because Tony screamed, "She's got a gun!") on hold with 911, and down to the second floor where Sorry stands in the hallway with her hand on her doorknob, unsure what to do. Tony pushes her inside her room, joins her, and locks the double doors on them both.

With no one left in front of him, Matt turns to face Jazz.

He knows that look. He saw it earlier, when she was about to jump. Except now she is pointing a gun at his nose.

"Let's get out of here and fuck," he says. "I want you every day for the rest of my life. Marry me."

She takes a step toward him, closing her eyes instinctively to protect them from the spray of meat and bone.

He sees two alternatives. He can turn and run down the stairs while she is free to take aim at his back. Or he can test the obvious assumption that the door next to him opens on a space with at least one window to the roof of the porch.

He pushes open the door opposite Sorry's and ducks into the bucket monster's room.

Jazz is close behind him. He misses his chance to close the door. She stands in the doorway. He turns and crouches the way he did before he punched Rob. He believes he is going to charge her and knock her down. He believes she will not pull the trigger.

She picks a low bucket on an outside row and fires. The bullet scars the rubber and digs a small hole in the plaster.

He looks down and palpates the front of his body. He seems uncertain.

She steps into the hallway and closes the door. She lowers the gun.

Shut inside the room with Matt, the monster sways. The ricochet has set it in motion. One bucket is weakened, no longer symmetrical. The monster cannot return to its stable condition.

He approaches to grasp the top board and stop it from moving. In response, its opposite end sways toward him. It sways away. The second board from the bottom slides a quarter-inch on a waxy film of fermented excrement, and two buckets near the top wobble and slosh. The monster undulates. It shimmies. It bounces against the wall. The stalemate between architecture and the force of gravity is over.

The monster blocks access to the windows, and Tony (because he has the strongest hands; Sorry grabs him around the waist to add traction) is holding the room's only door shut from the other side. Matt kicks at the latch before seeing that it opens inward. He pulls on the slick glass doorknob until his fingernails hurt. He kicks the door's solid chestnut panels hard, but he cannot break them.

With the suggestion of a circular, backhanded motion, with the grace of a sower strewing grain, the wall of buckets throws itself down.

Matt slips and falls. He howls as though being eviscerated. On his knees in years-old shit and piss, he tries to use his phone. He can't see the screen. The indescribable substance fills the room to a depth of one inch and creeps under the door into the hallway. Under Matt it finds gaps in the floorboards and seeps to a new dark spot on the kitchen ceiling. A broad, viscous droplet forms above the kitchen table like a stalactite.

Matt stops making noise. It is worrisome. What is he doing in there?

He is facing the window, expecting to be shot at any moment, wondering how to get past the heap of buckets in leather-soled shoes on a floor like a sheet of ice. He is sticky with indescribable filth, and the dirtiest part of him is his hands. There's a hair or an eyelash or something in his eye and nothing he can do about it. He is freaking out, but without moving, because he doesn't want to slip and fall again.

Anka creeps down the stairs and whispers, "Did he get hit?"

"Not even close," Jazz says.

"Rob looks bad."

"You should all leave. Just get out."

Anka runs back up the stairs.

Sorry, Tony, and Jazz notice the substance that is beginning to ooze from the room. Sorry lets go of Tony, and he lets go of the doorknob. Jazz says to the door, "Matt! I'm ready!"

Sorry and Tony hasten up to where Rob is lying on the roof, half inside Jazz's room. The pool of blood under him is only about two feet in diameter—maybe a pint and a half? "I'm okay," he insists. Anka is applying direct pressure with a towel to the ragged wound in his side. The towel is very red. Her phone lies faceup beside her, the line to 911 no longer open. (When they finally answered, she was distracted.)

"Let's all go to the hospital with Rob," Sorry suggests. She picks up a pillow from the bed, pulls off the pillowcase, and starts stuffing it with random clothing and the contents of Jazz's desk and dresser drawers: money, electronics, ID.

Anka comprehends. "Do mine, too," she says. She stares down at Rob. Both of them are colorless. "Do everybody's. Come on, Rob. Let's get out of here."

Sorry packs fast—maybe four minutes. In Rob's room she grabs his wallet and the clothes on the chair. She owns a military surplus duffel bag, and so does Tony, both full of linens, and she empties them to run from room to room, stuffing in recently worn clothes, valuables from bedside tables, and random paper from in and on top of desks.

Anka gives up on ambulances, because she and Tony are able to get Rob down the stairs. Rob's vehicle will be faster. By the time they reach the minivan, Sorry is in the driver's seat, feeling very anxious, yet happy Matt didn't park them in. The Audi stands in the street at an odd angle, two feet from the curb.

Jazz occasionally taps the door with the barrel of the gun to make sure Matt knows she hasn't budged. She is stationary, but shivering.

Only after everyone has left the house does she dash down the stairs. Quietly she closes the broken front door. The minivan is idling, waiting for her. She swings herself in through the side door, slides it shut behind her, and says, "Fuck!" Sorry revs the engine and honks the horn twice as she lurches into reverse—a friendly beep-beep—to signal their departure. The response is a howl of anguish like nothing they have ever heard.

Sitting on the bench seat, Jazz turns to look at Rob, who is lying in the cargo space, wrapped in a blanket he uses to protect the carpeting from muddy bikes. "The landlord's going to trash the house," she says.

"So call the police," he replies.

They know they might never set foot in Nicotine again.

MATT SLINKS OUT OF THE monster's room. A flood of the substance follows him and flows down the stairs. He finds the shower in the corner of the kitchen. He strips and stands under it, holding his car keys and credit cards in his hands. He soaps up over and over, and scrubs over and over, with special attention to nooks and crannies such as the ears. He vomits into the toilet and drain several times each. He keeps going after the hot water is gone. When he emerges, the substance is dripping from the kitchen ceiling and two inches deep on the hallway floor. He locates a plastic bucket and a salad bowl and wades to the porch. He walks naked to his car.

Beep! it says, unlocking its doors to his command. He imagines trashing the house, destroying, stealing—but the stairs are coated with the substance. He imagines trying to climb them. The substance is so greasy. Of all its horrors, grease is most salient. Surprising how greasy. Slippery and sticky at the same time, like pork or ice cream, substances he may never touch again.

No one sees him. The neighborhood has gone back to sleep. There is no sound but a dog barking somewhere.

He drives home shuddering. Sometimes he pulls over against the median to vomit—a dangerous maneuver, but he is lucid and sober and burning with hate, and that makes him invisible to the police. An all-white man in an all-black car, like a grub in a rotten pecan.

WHEN ROB IS DONE CIRCULATING through the ER, it is dawn. Sparrows chirp in the Japanese maples and juniper ground cover around the hospital. Trucks deliver perishables.

Sorry stands outside with the orderlies, smoking. Anka dozes on a row of chairs by the reception desk with her head on Tony's lap. Jazz holds Rob's hand as he emerges from an examination room with a prescription for antibiotics, a thick bandage around his middle, and a fresh tetanus shot still stinging under an adhesive bandage. She leads him to the row of chairs. Tony wakes Anka and she sits up.

"What now?" Jazz says.

"We hit the road," Rob says. "Far away. Gas up the van and go."

"You sound scared," Anka says, "but you are currently holding the hand of the only person I ever saw hold a gun on anybody, so I have no option but to conclude that you're insane."

"She saved my life."

Jazz squeezes his hand.

Tony says, "Obviously you want to lay low if that fucker's after you. But in my opinion there's no need to leave Jersey. May I offer a beneficial suggestion? I personally happen to be dating the one person in the world who hates Matt more than you do, and she lives in a defensible compound."

"My solution is nonviolence," Rob says.

"Her estate in Morristown has a commanding view to the four points of the compass," Tony continues. "Big trees, no underbrush, and the perimeter is fenced and gated. High, narrow windows, and a half-basement with slot ventilation. It's like a fucking crusader castle. We should drive there now and establish our war room."

"Stop it, Tony. You're not funny," Jazz says.

"I think it's funny," Anka says. "But I'm moving into Susannah's room at DJD. I'm sure she's never coming back. Her parents would kill her."

"I'm serious, though," Tony says.

"So move to Morristown!" Jazz says. "The landlord has nothing against you. It sounds like a great house."

Sorry returns from her cigarette break outdoors. She hugs Rob gingerly and asks, "What's our strategy?"

“Tony’s moving in with Amalia, and Anka’s going to DJD. Me and Jazz are driving as far as we can get the hell away from here, and you, I don’t know.”

“What about Penny?”

“Penny,” he says. “Penny is Matt’s half-sister, and right now, anything to do with that motherfucker—pardon the expression—”

“Penny is Penny.”

“She lives at Tranquility. None of this affects her at all.”

“Of course not.”

“I’ll talk to her,” Jazz volunteers.

“That is *so* not your job,” Anka says.

“I’ll talk to her,” Rob says.

“And what about me?” Sorry says. “I’m not going back to Nicotine. We need to squat a new house.”

Rob sighs. “In Greater New York in 2016? That’s why I was thinking maybe Detroit.”

“I heard about a house that’s empty,” Anka says. “It just needs some rehab in the kitchen.”

“It needs to *burn down*,” Sorry says. “They will never find anyone to clean it up, ever. I don’t care what country you ran away from, I don’t care what you’ve been through, you are not going to take that job. Nobody is that desperate. You’d need soldiers or prisoners, or slaves. Controlled burn. It’s the only way.”

“But not our job,” Rob says. “I can make a living anywhere there’s bikes. I just need to pick up my tools.”

“I second the motion,” Jazz says.

Cautiously, he stands upright. He wobbles on his feet.

“First stop Morristown,” Tony announces. “So we can reconnoiter.”

“Not with me,” Rob says. “No way. That’s your gig. And it’s my van. We’re going to Nicotine to get my tools.”

“Drop me off at DJD,” Anka says.

“Can I have your gun?” Tony asks Jazz. “I presume you don’t

have a concealed weapons permit, but I can use it legally to defend a home."

"And shoot Matt with the same bullets they're going to find in the wall at Nicotine. Whatever. Buy your own damn gun. They're cheap."

"Amalia probably already has an arsenal in the basement," Rob says.

ANKA SQUATS SUSANNAH'S ROOM AT DJD.

That is, someone answers the front door and lets her in, and rather than applying for house membership through the usual channels, she goes up to Susannah's room, puts on one of Susannah's flannel nightgowns, crawls between Susannah's Liberty of London sheets, and passes out.

"DETROIT," AMALIA TELLS TONY, "WILL be very hot this time of year. They should go to Colorado. Snowbird areas. Vail, Crested Butte. All of those are empty now."

She sits at an antique dining table made of kauri wood, drinking coffee from a stoneware cup with matching saucer. A plate of Fig Newtons occupies the center of the table, under the halogen light fixture.

Tony fidgets in the kitchen. He glances frequently at the closed-circuit TV that shows the front gate—a small, fuzzy CRT, like an old baby monitor. The tonic water is flat, so he mixes vodka with orange soda.

"I don't know what they're doing and I don't care," he says, returning to the table. "I'm thrilled to be here with you. It's like fate." He sits down and pulls over a coaster for his dripping old-fashioned glass.

"We'll see how long it lasts." Amalia sighs. "This is not my house."

"Huh? Whose house is it?"

"It belongs to my husband, Norm."

"The dead guy. So it belongs to the estate. Aren't you the sole heir? Or at least the executor?" Amalia looks away. "The person carrying out his last will and testament—is that you?"

"That process will start when it starts. I haven't yet told everyone. Not the authorities."

Tony flashes a grin. "Are you still depositing his Social Security check?"

Amalia smiles, a bit hesitantly, not sure she should be smiling.

"A government pension, maybe? Lifetime annuities? Is the body still in the house, or did you bury it in the yard?"

All at once, she trusts him. His expectations are so terrifically low. Surely he will not sit in judgment on anything short of violence or other genuine evils. She says, "Stop it, Tony! It's not funny! When he died, I went through all the papers and the safe-deposit box at the bank, and I don't find any kind of will. And what else is not there? No adoption papers. No life insurance. Only his name on the title to the house. Legally, I am *nothing*. I bought this house partly myself! I gave all my paychecks to Norm, always. But we were never father and daughter. I know that now."

"Ooh," Tony says. "That sounds hairy."

"Yes." She nods.

"I mean seriously hairy, like one of those thirty-pound hairballs they find in cows. Wasn't he your husband?"

"I came to this country with no identity. First I was his child, afterward the mother of his child. We were married in the eyes of God."

"I understand," Tony says. Then he adds, "What I mean is, I don't understand. But it's so lawless that as a card-carrying libertarian, I'm absolutely blown away."

She snorts. "I told Penny and the boys that New Jersey is a community property state, and they bought it. Everybody but Matt. But you know who the courts will appoint as executor of the estate? Matt! I was so in love with him, you know? But now I know he will take everything from me, if I get death certificates for Norm."

"That guy is a *bad seed*."

"Oh my god, yes. His father was an angel, his mother was an angel. Why is he so *bad*?"

"His father was no angel, and I bet his mother wasn't either. If you turn out to be an angel, I'm going to be very disappointed."

Soon they are making out in her bed.

PENNY RIDES HER BICYCLE FROM Tranquility to Nicotine. She sees from a hundred yards away that the front door is open. Drawing closer, she sees that the downstairs windows are broken. She smells a pestilential smell.

She leans her bike on a shrub and climbs up to look over the porch railing at a safe distance from the front door.

A plastic bucket and salad bowl stand in the substance on the welcome mat. Round prints betray that someone used them to walk through it—one foot in each, presumably holding the rim of the bowl and the handle of the bucket. The trail of prints leads to the kitchen door. The house is silent. She feels sure it is empty. She recognizes the work of the monster. She calls out, "Hello!" to be sure. No answer.

She calls Rob on the phone. "Where are you?" she says.

"Pennsylvania Turnpike. Long story. I'm with Sorry and Jazz."

"Hi, Penny!" Sorry calls out.

"Where are you going?"

Silence. "Portland? We don't really know. We had to get out of town in a hurry. Did you hear what happened?"

"Fuck, no! Nobody tells me anything. You're in Pennsylvania? You didn't even say good-bye?"

"Don't get upset. You think you have a right to be upset? You know who tried to murder me? Your fucking brother."

"Why?"

"Why," Rob says. "I guess that's what anybody would ask."

"To get the house? It's trashed, so it's kind of a Pyrrhic victory."

"Why are you asking *why*? As if anything could justify what he did!"

"I was just wondering."

"Good-bye, Penny. You want to talk to Jazz or Sorry?"

"I'd rather talk to you."

"Hey, Penny," Jazz says.

"Is this one of those 'don't call us, we'll call you' things? Fuck you, Rob! You too, Jazz!" Penny wipes her nose. On the sidewalk, she walks the edge of the yard until she is standing where the cracked, foot-high retaining wall rounds the corner. "I see a police car," she adds, raising her eyes to see a police car.

"Where are you?"

"In front of the house. I came over on my bike."

"Ride away," Jazz suggests.

She rides away. Two blocks later, she halts and calls Rob again. Jazz answers, and she asks where Anka and Tony are. Anka: DJD. Tony: Morristown. She wipes her nose some more, and Jazz sings, "It's only castles burning."

Penny interrupts her by asking, "So what happened? Who knocked over the buckets?"

"Didn't you hear Rob? We're all still totally in shock, especially him. I don't want to talk about it while I'm driving. We'll call you when we get where we're going. Hang in there. We love you, right?"

"We love you, Penny!" Sorry calls out.

Penny rides home to Tranquility.

THE MINIVAN STRUGGLES ON THE ascents, but it makes up for lost time with its worn-out brake shoes on the downhills, and it is soon deep in the Appalachians.

It starts to rain. Sorry is driving, with Rob on her right and Jazz asleep on the bench seat. Squinting, she says, "I wonder if I need glasses, or if everything is really this blurry."

"Let's find a place to crash," Rob says.

"The next exit has three motels. One's a Motel Six. They're cheap if you book online a couple weeks in advance."

"I thought we'd sleep in the van."

"How?"

"I put the tools up here, we leave Jazz where she is, and you and me bed down in the back. How about it?"

"But where?"

"Truck stop."

Sorry shakes her head. "Where is there a truck stop?"

"In eighty miles. Pull off and we'll get some coffee."

They get coffee from the drive-through at a Jack in the Box and return to the highway.

Eighty miles takes about an hour and a half. Over sixty miles an hour, the road starts to feel bumpy no matter how smooth it is. Rob comments that his suspension is his reason to stay with the turnpike—the smooth ride. Sorry sticks to the white line at the right-hand side of the road while immense trucks heave past them in gales of spray. The windshield wipers scrape one way and slap the other. And still Jazz sleeps.

She wakes up to the clanking of tools hitting the floor in front of her. "We're turning in," Rob says. He kisses her on the forehead. She glances out and sees towering semitrailers. Out on the highway overtaxed haulers pass with a furious choppy whine, tensing and releasing the air around the minivan. When the back is empty enough to fit Rob and Sorry—assuming they don't move around much—they climb in and lie down.

"I'm glad I'm exhausted and in shock," Rob says. He swallows a painkiller. He closes his eyes. He falls asleep. The windows begin to fog.

A feeling of chilly dampness strikes Sorry in the kidneys. After one attempt to turn over without waking Rob, she creeps forward to her duffel bag. She pulls out her tablet computer. She nudges it into life and looks for cheap motels located near exits in western Ohio.

The lights dancing on the ceiling awaken Jazz. She asks Sorry what she is doing.

"Booking a motel for tomorrow," she replies. "It's on me."

"You have a credit card? Is it stolen?" She looks closer. "Visa Platinum. My word, aren't we bourgeois."

"It's a relic from my secret past. I think Platinum might be the lowest level now, but they never cut you off. It's enough for a motel. I'm too tall to sleep in this cargo space. It's worth it. My gift to you."

Jazz smiles her radiant smile and says, "I love you, Mama Sorry." She stretches her arms, closes her eyes, and turns over.

"Sleep tight, little Jazzy J."

Sorry crawls back to her overcoat, tablet tucked under her arm. She holds it above her head and reads a long feature in the *Times* magazine about a Parisian couturier until her arms fall and she loses consciousness.

THE NEXT EVENING, PENNY VISITS Anka at DJD.

Anka tells the story: Matt's jealous rage, the death of the bucket monster, Rob's injuries, their night at the hospital, the fugitive trio petrified of Matt.

"Matt's always been pathologically jealous," Penny replies. "Sex is the only way he's ever been close to anybody, so if he sees two people in bed, he automatically assumes they're having sex." This is bullshit straight from outer space. She has no evidence to base this on, other than her desire to assert that Rob and Jazz would never, ever have sex.

Anka pauses. Briefly she wonders how Penny can be simultaneously in love with Rob and concerned about justifying Matt's behavior. But maybe denial is inevitable at first when your brother tries to murder the man you love? Delicately, she agrees it's likely the case that Matt is a jealous person who jumps to conclusions. Soon she gets into the spirit of denial, laughing off the others' fears, even appending a slightly exaggerated account of Tony's scheme to turn the Morristown house into a survivalist fortress.

In the end, Penny says she's almost sorry she didn't see the bucket monster fall. She would have liked to join them on the road. "I missed all the fun," she says. "I can't wait until they get back. We can found a new house."

"Matt is mental," Anka replies, "but it's Jazz who owns a nine-millimeter. I wouldn't live with her ever again, anywhere. I just hope I can stay here at DJD."

"What will you do when you want a cigarette?"

"Don't let anybody know, but I bought this thing." She opens the drawer in Susannah's cherry bedside table and pulls out a tin cigarette with a pink filter. The label identifies it as a V2. "It's a digital e-cigarette."

"What's digital about it?"

"You hold it in your fingers, like this."

"I'm serious. Is it part of the Internet of things? Do they know when you're smoking it?"

"I don't think so. I think they just mean it works on electricity." Anka leans her head back and puffs a cloud of sweet-smelling vapor that quickly disperses. "It was either this or that gum that tastes like snuff. It averages out to cheaper than analog cigarettes, if you do it enough. And you become a nonsmoker. Nobody here knows I own it, so you better not tell them. I even smoked today at *work,* because there's no smell."

"You're going to end up addicted to nicotine, if you're not careful."

"I know! But it's a small price to pay for a room in a nonsmoking house."

THEY PLAN A FORAY TO recapture Anka's paintings and whatever else they can grab that means anything to anybody—hard-to-replace things, like people's winter boots and the sacred BVM dildo.

Anka asks Sunshine whether the DJD community, with all its protest acumen, happens to own any gas masks (no).

So the plan is to run in and loot the house as best they can, as fast as they can, and either nail down the broken doorframe and lock the place, or board the doorway shut somehow using tools and scrap wood from the garage. The entire procedure will be conducted, insofar as they are able, without either of them taking a breath.

As darkness falls, they approach the house. Anka gets close to the entrance. She quails. She twitches and covers her mouth. She says, "Fuck it, who cares," and turns back, saying she cannot imagine taking anything porous or permeable out of that reeking hell—not art, not shoes, not curtains, not anything. She will start over.

PENNY FEELS THE SAME WAY. Time to go to zero for a reboot.

She doesn't hear from Matt. That surprises her. He ought to be calling to complain—to say mean things and ream her out verbally. But he doesn't. Not a peep.

It feels like a sign that maybe he is backing away from her life. One more emotional male Baker who can't turn it off, falling away. Female Bakers are different. Merchants of patience. To indulge passionate impulses in her current situation would make her crazy. Even remembered emotions would make her crazy. She doesn't know where Rob is. Even *he* doesn't know where he is. She needs to watch and wait and hoard her feelings for future reference.

THE NEXT AFTERNOON, SHE VISITS her mother in Morristown. They watch Tony mow the lawn.

"Such a nice man," Amalia says.

"Yes, very nice."

"And so funny. Now he is staying here because Norm's old house is a big mess, like I always said. Now you see, I was psychic!"

Penny asks whether she has heard from Matt.

"No," Amalia says. "But Tony tells me how your lover and Matt's lover ran away together—that's so funny—"

"I wouldn't put it like that, but whatever."

"Do you still want to fix up that house? Tony says it is completely filled from top to bottom with shit." She laughs. "No matter. That house takes four corner lots zoned for mixed use, you know? It's worth much more without the house. We could put in a gas station, or a church!"

"Oh god, leave me out of it. I've had just about enough of that house. What I need to do is get my job search moving. I can stay in the house where I'm living for now. I just need a job and money, so I can travel and be independent and do what I want. You know. Start living my life!"

She is sincere. She wants to get a grip, her act together, her ducks in a row, and offer Rob a place to stay, which he will surely accept—once he calms down—now that he's homeless. But before she starts some stressful new job with zero vacation days, she needs to figure out where he is, and go see him. So she needs a way to pay for a trip to see Rob, plus a big apartment to put him in. Also she needs a distraction until it all works out, and a new job would certainly be distracting.

"Well, as for job searching, I have been thinking about your career potential," her mother says.

"I always wished you would," she lies.

"You specialized in purchasing, so you always consider working in consumer products. But it's not a growth area."

"I know. Globalization is stalled out. Everybody sees through that BRICS nations stuff now. The emerging markets are tanking."

"But *tech,* Peñana. Now the bank is going into sourcing raw materials for tech companies. Tech commodities! At a bank, can you believe it?"

"Like pork bellies and corn futures, but tech."

"Rare earths and lithium. There is so much tech growth in the mature markets. Developing nations are on the ropes. It's a fire sale! But we have to do monitoring and oversight, because the investors and the governments—oh my god, what liars they are! They say they're mining with energy from a wind farm, and we visit and look on the satellite, and there's no mine and no wind farm. They bluff like poker players."

"Or nations at war," Penny says.

"Exactly. You would have travel and responsibility. Your languages would be so valuable. If you write a résumé like this, I will bring it to the bank and they will *jump* on you." Amalia touches her arm. "Commodities analyst! You will make top dollar. Excellent compensation. You *really* can do this. I know it."

"It actually sounds interesting. I'd be like a spy."

"The bank is becoming an empire with colonies. But you know who will do it if we don't do it? Organized crime."

"So I'd be doing well by doing good," Penny says, joking without smiling.

"I want you to have money, Peñana. Nothing in the world is more expensive than your anarchist revolution."

Amalia smiles, but Penny knows she isn't joking—especially not about the price of revolution. She promises to put together a commodities-enabled résumé as fast as she can.

When Tony comes in from the yard, she can't stop herself from congratulating him, as though he had won an award. He does seem to be in an enviable position as lord of the manor. Having lost several pounds, he is dressed in natty new clothes. A barbershop has restored a kind of dignity to his head.

The three of them go out to a fern bar on a picturesque square in central Morristown and eat Cajun salmon with glazed turnip risotto (Tony), mozzarella sticks (Amalia), and a Cobb salad (Penny). Tony remarks that he has died and gone to outlaw heaven, and that it shouldn't surprise him that all it takes is money. Penny doesn't feel the need to ask him what he means. Amalia toasts her new love and pays the bill.

IN HIS CAR IN FRONT of Nicotine, Matt glowers. His windows are rolled up. He tries calling Jazz. The call won't go through. He gets out and stands up, creaking from the unaccustomed exertions of recent days. He wears navy blue sweats labeled YALE in white.

He comes close enough to see that no one has made any new tracks in the substance. It is drying to a potentially malleable sludge. The house stands open, an invitation to looters, pranksters, arsonists . . .

Imagining his ancestral home in flames, he limps to the garage. Two claw hammers still hang on random nails in wall studs, and there is a stack of old shelving on the floor.

Balanced with one foot in the plastic bucket and one in the salad bowl, he boards up the doorway.

He goes back to the garage and finds something else he wants—spray paint—in an ancient, rusting can encased in loose, illegible paper. The can is nearly empty, but it contains enough black paint to cover the squatter lightning bolt and the letters *i c o t i n e*. For spite, he drenches the doorbell as well. Paint drips down and pools on the greasy sludge. He turns and sees a neighbor watching him.

"You taking over the house?" the man asks. He is about thirty-five, in a jogging suit, walking a mastiff—a white ethnic Guido-type working-class greaser, Matt thinks.

"The squatters left, so yeah," he says.

"You going to clean that up? You going to hire some poor asshole to clean that up, you with your fucking Audi and your fucking Yale sweatshirt? You better do it today. That stink is all in our house. It's in my daughter's hair. Our whole fucking neighborhood smells like your *shit*."

Matt struggles to leap gracefully from the bucket and bowl to the bare wooden section of the porch. He succeeds, and says, "Well, I don't like your fucking huge dog shitting everywhere either, but do I say anything to you about it? This is my property."

"Fuck you, asshole," the man says. Without missing a beat, he turns toward Matt's car, lowers his fly, and begins to urinate on the passenger-side door handle.

Frowning, Matt approaches the man and the dog. The man pees luxuriantly, as though he's been saving up. He relies on the dog to protect him.

And in fact the dog does protect him. It is the dog that loses an eye and spends the rest of its life wheezing. It lunges toward Matt, and he spray paints it—the entire head and neck region, inside and out.

He gets in the Audi and drives away. A few blocks later, he stops to check the finish for possible fine droplets from the mist of paint, but it appears that the breeze was in his favor. Except for the salty pee, his car is immaculate. He drives home and tips the guard in the parking garage to wash it.

ROB SAYS HE'D LIKE TO pick the next motel for the night. He abandons the interstate for a fifties-era U.S. highway bypass with too many stoplights.

The motor lodge he selects is home to migrant workers, homeless families, couples in love—cash only, off the grid. The room key, made of brass, hangs from a plastic square that asks the finder to drop it in any mailbox. Its only Web presence is an urgent TripAdvisor warning about the showers.

Sorry calls Penny from the room after dinner (cornflakes) to say they're near St. Louis, headed for Oklahoma City. Final destination: Santa Fe.

Jazz says firmly, "Taos."

Sorry repeats that they'll talk about where they're going after they get to Santa Fe.

Rob and Jazz make love under mustard-colored blankets on a lopsided queen-size bed. Because she is watching a violent TV series on a tablet computer in the other bed with earphones, Sorry is mostly oblivious to their humping, nuzzling, and coo-cooing. But as they approach simultaneous orgasm with sounds she would—if called upon to speak—categorize as cheerleading, she says, "Hey, you biohazards! Keep it down!"

"You were right," Jazz says loudly. "We should have invited Penny."

"Then tell her to fly to Santa Fe!"

Sorry takes her tablet into the bathroom for a smoke so they can finish in private.

MATT SITS ON HIS OFFICE couch, considering his options. He calls a friend who is a building contractor. The contractor calls a friend who works in demolition.

The demolition subcontractor doesn't call anyone. At six o'clock the next morning, he swings by Home Depot in his pickup. From the crowd of migrant day laborers on the curb, he selects four Guatemalans who seem to be acquainted with one another. Two clamber into the cab with him and two into the back under his camper shell.

"Es un trabajo corto con un gran montón de mierda," he explains.

"Eso es normal," the man next to him replies. *"Estamos acostumbrados a mucha mierda."*

At the house, each man receives a snow shovel and two heavy garbage bags to tie around his legs. Each raises his tan bandanna to cover his mouth and nose. The substance has dried somewhat. The demolition subcontractor calculates that it will fit easily into the buckets whence it came, give or take the extra plastic bucket he found on the porch.

The four men shovel the substance—still slippery, not like something dry—maybe things that oily never really dry—into the buckets. Full buckets are toted to the curb.

To forestall new extremes of neighborly hostility, Matt has commandeered a state-of-the-art prototype, currently beta testing in Saddle River, to visit Jersey City that evening. Around seven, the gracefully streamlined garbage truck in iridescent blue-green approaches the house. It hovers, compressed natural gas engine running near silence, then cuts the power with a sigh. Batteries drive the powerful motors that swallow, compact, and encapsulate the substance. All fifty-two buckets are soon on board, along with plastic buckets, pots and pans, trash bags, shoes, throw rugs, welcome mats, linoleum, ruined plaster, and many unidentified globs.

Observers (the event draws a high-turnover crowd in constant rotation) speculate that once the last item leaves the curb, the smell will improve.

When the curb is empty, a soft breeze carries the smell away, but it returns immediately. "Smells like pig manure," one observer remarks. "Like living out in the country."

The day laborers accept one hundred dollars each and a tacit invitation to ransack the house. They discover a stash of clean clothing in Tony's room. They wash in the kitchen, scrubbing their nails with dish soap and toothbrushes (the subcontractor forgot gloves), and put on the clothes Tony abandoned when he embarked on his new life. They agree to be picked up the next morning, same place, same time. They will continue cleaning the house the next day, at a new lower rate minus hazard pay.

The subcontractor drives them to the bodega, where they stand leaning on his truck, drinking beer, in the gentle yellow light of a Meadowlands summer afternoon.

JAZZ CALLS PENNY FROM THE road in Oklahoma the next morning.

"It's beautiful!" she says. "We're in a landscape of total abstraction. Planet Earth re-imagined as a primitive computer graphic. We're driving a black line bordered with green in the interstice between a gray plane and a yellow plane, with no landmarks except the bugs on the windshield."

Penny tells her that she's very sorry, but she can't fly to Santa Fe. She has a job interview.

"Bummer," Jazz says.

"No, I think it's a good thing. I need to be self-supporting. Everybody's self-supporting in their own way, even if it's just by getting somebody else to support them, like Tony. I don't want to do that, not right now. I need a job. And this really might work out. It's at my mom's bank. They like her a lot. So maybe they'll like me."

"They might even think you're related, assuming you don't open your mouth and speak."

"Believe me, letting my personality run free is not my first priority at job interviews. You wouldn't even know it was me. I get all corporate."

"Sounds like a really meaningful use of your time."

"Don't be a snob. Do you even work? I have no idea what you do for a living."

"Whatever it is, I haven't done it since you met me. The money I have now, I got waitressing on a cruise ship last winter. Sometimes I lead these bus tours for retirees, to places like Atlantic City."

"And turn tricks with the old guys?"

"Now you're the snob," Jazz says. "So get a corporate job, make some money, and chill out. You want to talk to Rob?"

"Maybe."

"Hey, Penny," Rob says. "I'm sorry I blamed your brother on you. I'm still scared of him, but you should come see us when we get to Santa Cruz."

"Taos," Jazz says.

"I'll tell you which it is," Rob says to Penny.

"What's in Santa Cruz?"

"I mean Santa Fe. I don't know. Sorry wants to go to Cuba."

"Cuba is where the action is!" Sorry says. "The bicycle scene there is legendary! They use modified bikes to climb coconut palms!"

"I don't have a passport," Rob says. "I've never been out of the country."

After the call ends, he says, "I can't just go places, with no passport."

"You'll love Taos," Jazz says. "It's full of hippie yuppie tourists who would buy a bike as a souvenir. Even if they never use it, it costs money and might turn out to be useful. Like owning a tent or an ice-cream maker. You never know when you might need it."

"The problem is raw materials. I need bikes. In JC I was scoring at least two free bike frames a week. I'm a scavenger. I can't live in a place without trash."

"But won't tourists pay more for your stuff than people in JC?"

"Like hippie yuppies really buy recycled shit."

"So get a passport and come to Cuba!" Sorry says.

"And get paid in—what do they have in Cuba?"

"Free health care."

"That would be a sad ending to my story. Liberating poor people's bikes, in exchange for the health care I'm going to need when they beat the shit out of me. Anyway, I already have free health care." He turns and indicates his bandage.

"Medicaid's an instrument of oppression. We'd have had a revolution a long time ago if the poor were dying in the streets like they're supposed to."

"You been downtown lately?"

"Those people aren't poor!" Sorry says. "They're crazy, or drunks, or drug addicts, or subverting the dominant paradigm."

Jazz says, "You won't see any of that bourgeois decadence in Cuba. They don't even have artists or homosexuals."

"Okay, okay," Sorry says. "Maybe I'll go to Venezuela, or Bolivia. One of those places where the revolution's working out, because they have crude oil instead of sugarcane."

"Oil is the key to autonomy," Jazz says. "I say that in my capacity as an ethnic Kurd."

"Oil is death," Rob says.

"That's right. Valuable enough to be worth fighting for."

"*Nothing* is that valuable. People need warmth and transportation, not oil."

"The IS and Boko Haram are fighting for God and virgins. Tell me how bikes and solar power are going to replace *those,* you anarchist peacenik."

Looking out the window at the featureless plains, Rob hums like Winnie-the-Pooh.

Following a lengthy discussion, the three select a new destination: Oakland.

None of them knows anything about Oakland, except that it is near rich places (San Francisco, Palo Alto), yet itself poor as Jersey City. They hope for Jersey City–like conditions.

"I heard the squatter scene there is kind of embattled," Sorry says.

Rob says the market for bicycles rises and falls with mass transit, and that obviously squats aren't going to be welcomed in a place with decent mass transit. You don't get those same dead zones. But that's life on the edge.

"Also it's way north. It's in *Northern* California. We should be going via, like, Denver."

Rob pats the dashboard and speaks to the minivan. "Don't be scared," he says. "She doesn't mean it." Turning to Sorry, he adds,

"We're going south no matter what, because the Rockies are high. Really tall. It means we have to drive up the coast, but I've done worse things."

"I hate beaches," Sorry says. "But it doesn't matter. As long as we get there. We can go via Albuquerque and take I-5."

"Did you used to live out there?"

She holds up her tablet computer. "I have this brain."

AFTER WORK, MATT DRIVES FROM his office to Nicotine to meet his contractor friend and survey the team's progress. He pulls up around the corner, parking at a safe distance from the large green container into which workers with leather gloves are throwing handfuls of broken glass from a mortar pan.

The work is going well and quickly. The four Guatemalans hired to do the demolition have been joined by a carpenter and a plumber with crews from Fiji and Ukraine. The house is empty of furniture and possessions such as Anka's paintings (who knows where they went). Every floorboard, baseboard, and piece of plaster that was touched by the substance has been ripped out. An odor wafts from the container in the driveway, but the house smells unremarkable. The demolition crew works on the roof, knocking down Jazz's room with hammers. By the time Matt and his friend the contractor arrive upstairs, it is a heap of wood and broken glass interspersed with leafless tobacco plants, textiles, and books.

They enter Rob's attic space and examine the chimney. It has one porthole for a Franklin stove, sealed up with a pie plate.

"I could open this out into a fireplace," the contractor says. "I'd just have to reinforce the stack below and cantilever it here."

"It's too small," Matt says. "I might want to build an extra chimney on the end of the house. A little bit of self-indulgence after I insulate this place and put in a heat pump."

They walk downstairs. "You could fit more than one unit on each floor," the contractor advises Matt. "Make these apartments too big, and you're going to get families in here. Never trust a tenant to stay single. You have to put the squeeze on them from the start."

"It's not apartments. It's a community center. The first floor is an anarchist café bookstore. Above that we have our yoga classes, baby massage, all that shit. And I live on top. One apartment. The showers are for the yoga studio."

The contractor is silent. Finally he says, "That could work out pretty nice for you."

"It's called the Norman Baker Center, after my father. He was born in this house. It's a 501(c)(4) charitable institution."

"It's going to revitalize this neighborhood right up, you old horn-dog."

That's Matt's plan. The name might attract donations or other support from his father's cult, reducing his time to break even while freeing up cash for real estate speculation. Ultimately some neighbors may face rent hikes, but one anarchist in particular, if all goes well, will dwell rent-free in more comfortable surroundings than she has ever known. His own generosity moves him to tears, as he knows from hearing the Bread song "It Don't Matter to Me" on the radio on the way over.

PENNY CATCHES THE PATH TRAIN to midtown Manhattan for her job interviews at the bank. She feels sullen and rebellious, as well as tired. Those emotions keep her face still, her gait steady, her handshake firm, and her answers straightforward. She leaves with an appointment at an assessment center in Piscataway. She will spend the following Thursday and Friday taking IQ tests and vying with coapplicants for imaginary leadership roles.

She arrives home fatigued. She dumps her briefcase by the door and heads straight to the kitchen. She longs for cigarettes and beer. She compromises on beer.

Barry tells her the news. (Later she hears it from Maureen, Rufus, and Stevie.) "Did you hear Nicotine is being turned into an anarchist community center?"

"What? Are they back?" Her mind flashes to the condition of the house when she last saw it, and she adds, "That's impossible."

"No, it's some guy we don't know doing it. It's going to be called the Norman Baker Center."

"The *what*?"

"Don't freak out, it's just some local anarchist who happened to have the same last name as you, probably a hundred years ago. Anyway, there's going to be a bookstore, and a bar, and meeting rooms. The Nicotine guys split, and nobody knows where they went, so it was up for grabs. I think it's great somebody's doing something for the community instead of just looking after their own interests by grabbing free real estate to live in it. You know what I mean? Squatting should be a means to an end, like with CHA, not just a way of saving on rent."

"Some people *need* to save on rent," Penny says firmly.

"Those people will always need help, until the revolution makes a clean slate. Giving activists a space to share strategies for effective resistance—that's what will help us in the end. I worked at a bookstore in Arcata for a while. I'm going to talk to that guy. Maybe I can work at the store."

"If he's putting money into fixing up the house," Penny says, "maybe it's not going to be a free store."

PENNY TEXTS ANKA, AND ANKA invites her to DJD to eat vegan pupusas.

In the kitchen, Sunshine is singing Matt's praises, sight unseen. He already has plans to co-opt the Center for educational events and films that celebrate energy efficiency—the climate change strategy that will finally make electricity too cheap to meter. (The feedback loop works by depressing demand so that coal-fired power becomes producers' only economically viable option* [*under free market capitalism].)

After dinner, Penny and Anka continue their talk upstairs, sitting on Susannah's bed. Anka says, "Go back to the beginning, as if Sunshine hadn't been in the kitchen. Tell me again."

"Matt is renovating—"

"*No! No! Bad! Wrong! Not happening!*" They both laugh.

"I'm sorry," Penny says, "but if you had any idea what kind of thing Matt is capable of—"

"He tried to kill Rob! Does he need to be capable of anything else? And now he's taking over the house. He's the scariest violent lunatic I ever saw, even including Jazz, and he's rich, and good-looking, and obviously well connected in local government, if he can get a building permit that fast. We should go to the *police*." They both laugh again. "I bet he has powder burns on his suit," she adds. "Jazz would be so fucked."

" 'Norman Baker Center,' " Penny says. "You know what's going to happen. All the jam-band kids that think my dad was a psychedelic drug wizard are going to show up and be tripping out and sleeping in the yard."

"Well, as long as they're white," Anka says. "They won't mar Matt's excellent investment."

"We should get a loan and buy DJD from CHA before the market takes off."

"Like CHA even has title. I mean, it's *possible*. But I think they just do classic microfinance. Like three thousand bucks for two years at twenty-five percent, because everybody defaults. That kind of thing. It's not on the scale of—where are you working again?"

"Don't make me say the name of Mom's bank. It's so embarrassing they might give me this job."

JAZZ RUNS DOWNHILL THROUGH GRAY badlands. Rob pulls on belts, checks oil, refills coolant. Sorry smokes a cigarette, sitting in the open side door of the minivan. The sun, behind a mountain, leaves the valley in shadow. A coyote crosses between the car and the low wall that divides the Petrified Forest parking lot from the surrounding expanse of talcum-powder-like dust.

Rob follows Jazz down one of the many paths scofflaw tourists have worn into the landscape. It twists and turns. He enters a cool wash with a flat floor made of sand. He looks around in the stillness. A bird pipes thinly. Uphill from him, she lies on the sand. Her arms are stretched out, scars showing pale against tan skin.

"I don't want to go to Oakland," she says. "I want this. The desert. Crisp, subtle colors and animals that are shy. With this huge, high sky. Not noise and chaos and junk."

"I can relate."

"Young people go to cities to show off."

"Do you know anybody in Taos?"

"I have an old friend who moved there years ago."

Rob is silent for a long time. With a stick, smooth as driftwood, he scrapes a *J* into the hard sand. "I'm guessing it's a man, and you want to make love to him."

Still lying motionless on her back, she says, "Yes."

AT 9:00 P.M., WHEN SHE assumes no one will be working, Penny breezes past Nicotine on her bike. The house is sheathed in scaffolding. Romanians are replacing the windows with modern double-glazing. Hondurans are painting the newly installed window frames dark green. As she walks up the front steps, she can see that their foreman is drinking iced coffee. He wipes his sweaty forehead and addresses her in Spanish. Without answering, she reads a brass plaque on the freshly sandblasted brick of the facade: NORMAN BAKER CENTER. The plaque is about two feet square and very shiny. She takes a quick picture of it with her phone. She peers into the former dining room and sees tall built-in bookshelves mounting to the ceiling. The kitchen has acquired a long, curving display case for baked goods. She returns to her bike and rides away fast.

At DJD she finds Anka watching *Homeland* with Sunshine (her program, so not his CO_2 footprint) on a laptop in the kitchen. “Hey,” she says. “I’ve got an idea.”

Anka follows her out to the living room and asks, “What’s your idea?”

She shows her the plaque. “We go tonight and write ‘Nicotine’ on it, and take another picture, and send it to Sorry. Because I haven’t told her about this, and I don’t know how.”

“What about telling Rob?”

“Fuck Rob.”

Anka regards her gravely and says, “Rob and Jazz didn’t do anything wrong. I think you’re getting confused.”

“I’m not confused,” Penny says. “I know exactly how I feel. I don’t miss Sorry or Jazz, but I miss Rob so bad I could fucking kill him.”

“That’s not childish.”

“It’s how I feel. It’s not my job to tell the story in a way that makes me look good.”

“You might feel better if you did.”

Penny acquires a stark and tragic look, with tears. “So I should cut my losses, and take a write-down, and find another guy where I can get in on the ground floor? No way! Rob was my idea. I’m not ready to settle. I want my day in court!”

“He’s your intellectual property,” Anka says, laughing.

AFTER DARK, THEY RIDE OVER to Nicotine with a thick black marker.

“Whoa,” Anka says when she sees the scaffolding. She creeps toward the porch, marker in hand.

Penny says, "Stop."

"Why?"

"Look up. Look at the light fixtures."

Anka looks up. Surveillance cameras.

In the ceiling of the porch, where lightbulbs ought to be, transparent bowls studded with (fake) cameras. Anka retreats. They ride away.

Up in Susannah's old room, Penny sends Sorry the earlier picture of the plaque by daylight, headed "NICOTINE. Not a joke."

SORRY SEES IT A BIT later. Feeling bored, she is reviewing recent messages, sitting on the white molded plastic chair outside a motel room in eastern New Mexico, smoking a cigarette. She calls Penny and says, "What the fuck? Hey, Penny. We're in New Mexico. Explain."

"There's not a lot to say. Nicotine has been squatted by Matt and a bunch of construction workers."

"It really looks *real*. You're not putting me on, right? Is there a Norman Baker Center somewhere else? Shit. You mean *Matt* Matt? We have to fight this."

"Good luck. Everybody loves it. It's going to be an anarchist community center with a café bookstore and meeting rooms and a yoga studio. It's going to anchor political empowerment and economic development in the whole neighborhood. Anka and I are already discussing our real estate investments."

"Seriously, what does it mean?"

"It means Matt's into power. He gets a big kick out of power. Ask Jazz. Power excites him."

"I can't believe he got it cleaned up so fast."

"You'd be amazed the things people will do for money. I, for instance, just accepted a job offer from my mom's bank."

"So are we safe if we come back? Matt's going to be the fucking king of anarchy!"

"Of course you'll be safe. What could give him more pleasure than watching you sip latte in his café? Maybe he'll let Rob bus tables."

"Jersey City is dead to me now," Sorry says. "That was it. Did anybody tell you where we're headed? Oakland."

"What's in Oakland?"

"Bicycles."

"I'm not going to ask whose idea that was."

"From there I might go to Venezuela."

"Go there with dollars. You can sell them for incredible amounts on the black market."

"Tell me all about it. But not on the phone."

"Deal. Are Rob and Jazz around?"

"They're in the room, doing that thing they always do way too long. I'm like, cut to the chase, people! But Jazz wants us to drop her off in Taos."

"Wait—what thing they do?"

"You didn't know?"

"Anka said, but I didn't believe—I mean, she said Matt flipped out because he saw them in bed, and I thought it was just Matt."

"It was not Matt. It was the love weasels."

Penny has been working very hard at emptying her brain. She does not want this new information filling it up again.

"How come he didn't tell me?" she cries. "I never knew!"

"They're joined at the hip. They're driving me crazy."

She turns off the phone. Her eyes drip cold tears on her hot face.

INSIDE THE MOTEL ROOM, ROB is saying to Jazz, "You are aware that if you go all the way to Taos to 'make love' to a guy you haven't seen in forever, you're actually 'fucking' him."

"I'm not going there to fuck him. I'm going to see how I feel about him."

"And when you land on his doorstep, he's going to know exactly what method you plan to use. Nobody travels that distance to talk. They have these things called telephones now. You're laying yourself open to get hurt. Can't I worry about you sometimes?"

"Why?"

"What are you going to do if he cooperates? I mean, after he makes love to you and says, 'Have a nice life'? Walk out in the desert with the gun? You're making it way too easy for him. All he has to do is let you have your way, and you're turning it into a love story before you even see him. Do you have any idea what a fox you are? He's not going to say no. It used to be at least you had some anatomical standards. So yeah, I worry."

"I really loved this guy, and he was a nonsmoker with a nonhuge dick—a nonstarter."

"How many of those do you know? Do you have a list you're working off?"

"I'm in a different state of mind now."

"*Totally* different head. That's why you just 'made love' to me while you were planning how to get to Taos and ditch me."

"I thought you were familiar with nonmonogamy."

"At least make him do something. Like, tell him you're coming to Santa Fe, and see if he volunteers to drive down."

"I don't think he'd do that."

"So what makes you think he still loves you, for fuck's sake?"

"He doesn't love me! I left him for having a small dick and not letting me smoke! He probably *hates* me. Forget it. I'm going to go get a cigarette from Sorry."

"You quit."

"But if I started again, it would give me such a good excuse not to visit a doctrinaire nonsmoker."

"Stay in bed with me, and I'll take you to Taos."

Jazz gets up, opens the door, and steps outside. Without a word,

Sorry shows her Penny's photo of the brass plaque. Jazz pulls her into the room. They show Rob.

AROUND ELEVEN THE NEXT DAY, they drive into Santa Fe. They window-shop, carrying large coffees from 7-Eleven. "Norman Baker Center," Rob says out of nowhere.

"You're like a Furby," Sorry says. "Remember that toy that says random shit like it's tripping?"

"Eight years I worked on that house. Eight years."

"Spare us your lamentations." Jazz points at a Zuni necklace in a window. "What's that stone? It's really beautiful."

"It's from a mine. You have no right to wear that stuff unless you work in a mine."

"Look at that painting."

"Where is that?"

"That's Taos pueblo, man."

Rob looks closer. "We could go to Taos."

Sorry enters Jazz's friend's address in Google Earth. Her phone shows them the precise route from where they are standing, in front of an antique shop in downtown Santa Fe, to what appears to be the summit of a mountain. They microwave burritos at the 7-Eleven for lunch and depart.

The phone directs them to a dirt track opposite a youth hostel on bluffs above the Rio Grande. The minivan slips and slides as it climbs the hill. It stumbles down the other side over largish rocks. It slips up the next hill and down another one. Wireless LANs are out of reach. Even the cell signal is weak. The road courses along the bottom of a valley, in the streambed. They reach a potential turnoff, and Sorry says, "This phone has no clue where we are. But we need to bear right."

Rob turns right. The minivan lurches over the lip of the creek bank and lands on a broad gravel road. "This must be new," he says.

He turns left (he is entering the road at a right angle, so he has to go left to bear right) and bounces, now at a healthy pace of ten to fifteen miles an hour, over washboard-like waves of crushed blue granite.

On a hilltop, the phone gets a cell signal. "Only six more miles," Sorry announces.

"He better be cute," Rob says.

"More to the point, he better be home," Sorry says.

"People out here don't lock their doors," Jazz says. "It's just a way to guarantee they'll get broken."

"You squatter *slag*," Sorry says.

Rob slows the minivan for a blind curve. "Any neighbors?"

"Not on Google Earth."

Rob sees wapiti. He stops to watch them browse in the streambed. He puts his hand on the ignition key, but he doesn't turn it off. He shifts back into drive and rolls again, and the wapiti raise their heads. "This is beautiful. What do people eat when they're stuck out here for weeks?"

"Survivalist apocalypse chow, like wheat berries and mandarin oranges in cans. But don't get your hopes up! He might be home."

Half an hour later, the driveway ends in a tight loop. They examine the bluff in front of them, confused. Finally Sorry says, "I see it!" She jumps out of the minivan and runs toward the front door, which stands almost parallel to the visitors' line of sight. The house lies partially embedded in the mountainside, tucked halfway under the rock face like a cliff dwelling. Its facade is rock with lichens and saxifrage. The copper roof is painted dull brown. The outlines of the house are hard to see, even from close up.

"It's weird he built a camouflaged house like this with a driveway visible from space," Rob says.

"He's not a survivalist," Jazz says. She rings the doorbell. She knocks. She yells, "Anybody home?"

Sorry walks back to Rob. Facing the front door, she says to him conspiratorially, "There's no car."

"And no garage," Rob says. "The road looks brand-new. He must have built this place with mules."

"The house is open," Jazz says. She goes inside.

The furniture is improvised from planks resting on stacks of hardback books still in their dust jackets and shrink-wrap, mostly in foreign languages. All are by the same author: Barrett Cartwright.

"I take it this is Barrett Cartwright's house," Rob says.

"It's his writing studio," Jazz says. "He's never here. He told me he keeps it stocked with food in case he ever feels like writing."

"You make no sense to me at all. *None*. I thought you wanted to see him."

"I did. But it's not my life's dream."

Sorry stands in the humming glow at the open door of the fridge and says, "There's at least four cases of cider in here."

"He must have put in the road when he put in electricity," Jazz says, distributing bottles to herself and her friends.

Intending to wash her hands, Sorry opens the tap over the kitchen sink, but nothing comes out. "Did you ever see *Avanti Popolo*?" she asks. "Israeli film about this Egyptian Shakespearean actor who survives in the desert by drinking vodka he gets from these dead Swedish blue helmets. Actually I can't remember whether he survives—"

"No."

"I hope your boy Barrett has water here somewhere."

"Relax," Rob says. "We're a day's walk from Taos."

He explores the house. After he turns on the main water supply in the pantry, the tap spurts clear and cold. He turns on the boiler.

SORRY TAKES A WALK THE next morning before breakfast. Over steel-cut oatmeal with molasses, she proposes they found a farming commune and stay at Cartwright's house forever. She removes the sixteenth cigarette from her second-to-last pack of American Spirits, taps it on the table, and goes outside to smoke.

Rob suggests one week. Jazz agrees, saying that the water (tank on the roof) and food (pantry) supply are not infinite. Even the four-plus cases of cider suggest a single man-month. Three guests for a week leaves her friend a week's grace before he has to go shopping. Sorry comes back inside and proposes they stay five days, explaining that in emergencies she can get by on five cigarettes a day.

AT THAT VERY MOMENT, AN online gaming buddy of Matt's who works in the NYPD's "Real Time Crime Center" data-mining and crime anticipation unit (cf. *Minority Report*) agrees to locate Jazz's cell phone.

His first attempt fails. On World of Warcraft's internal chat software, he writes, No dice. Prob burner phone.

PKK pond scum, Matt replies, but hella hot, if I catch up she will be so raped.

THAT DAY, SORRY SMOKES FIVE cigarettes.

She intuits that using up her cigarettes is going to make her unhappy. She doesn't want to leave Cartwright's house.

On the second day, she smokes four, and two on day three, leaving her with fifteen.

Day five: three. Day six: three. Day seven: three. Day eight: none.

Day nine, she feels the return of her mania. She wonders whether it might be a reverse placebo effect, but the colors seem so vivid, the sky so vast and blue; Cartwright's work so gripping, her own unwritten poetry so *good*.

She walks the hills on the hottest days alone. One day she climbs a small but steep and jagged peak, and standing on the top, she takes off her shirt and says to the sun, "Sunlight. Fill my heart." Thereupon sunlight fills her heart (inexplicable process defying prose description). On her return she gives the six remaining cigarettes to Rob. "Keep these for me," she says. "If Cartwright materializes, I'm really going to want them."

He rolls one between two fingers and says, "I don't know how you can smoke these anyway. They're way past stale."

"It's the dry heat. It's like they're always burning. I can sniff them and get a rush."

He sniffs one. "I could have one right now without getting addicted. There's nowhere to buy more."

"That's not how it works. You're addicted forever. You'd just go back into withdrawal."

He sighs.

UPHILL FROM THE HOUSE LIES a sort of roofless cistern, a steep-sided reservoir about twenty feet by thirty, of unknown depth. "That's our backup drinking water," Rob protests when Jazz suggests going swimming. She points out the little fishes and the turtle. In the shimmering heat of the afternoons they all swim, pawing away mats of algae.

At the full moon, Jazz goes out alone, naked, to swim at night in the cold. She sees two wide-set eyes on the bank, watching her, shining bloodred, and in the morning she finds mountain lion tracks. Each is as big as her fist, like a dog track without claws.

"Let's get the fuck out of here," she tells the others the next morning. "I was almost eaten alive by a mountain lion."

At the news, Sorry lights American Spirit number negative six.

THAT VERY SAME SECOND, MATT'S friend in the NYPD concludes his series of attempts to find Jazz. Sorry dude she's underground, he messages Matt. Clear blue sky.

"NOTE, OR NO NOTE?" JAZZ says, regarding the dining table.

"Don't leave him a note," Sorry says. "Let him wonder."

They bump nine miles down the new gravel driveway. At the bottom, where it hits the main road, there is a fence, a ditch, and a new, high, solid gate, very much locked. The security system involves a camera pointing outward and, on the uphill side, a post with a keypad. They turn around, drive back two miles, and use Google to find the shortest route to Taos. It directs them back the way they came in.

Rob says there's something symbolic about benefiting from the time lag between information and reality.

Jazz says Google is a palimpsest—not a menacing medium that never forgets, but a return to the days when parchment was precious, before paper became common and disposable. It is a library that maintains all of human knowledge, eternally safe from fire and decay. "Got to have our Internet pieties down cold if we want to survive in the Bay Area," she adds, putting her feet out the window.

Dusty wind swirls in the minivan as it creeps downward through dry valleys to Taos, where they stop for sodas.

THE FIRST MEETING OF THE Committee to Retake Nicotine is well attended. On a Tuesday night at eight, thirty people crowd into the DJD living room, with eight on the DJD itself.

Anka describes the night Jazz shot the bucket monster. She carefully avoids prejudicial labels such as "asshole," relating the events as accurately as she can.

"I'm confused," a young man says. "Isn't Matt Baker the guy who cleaned up Nicotine to open it to the community?"

"Let her finish what she's saying," a woman says. "I saw about this house on Facebook, and I'd definitely be interested in living there."

Anka keeps her speech short, around three minutes. She closes with a plea for solidarity. No one, she says, should be allowed to drive residents from CHA homes.

When she is done speaking, Sunshine raises his hand. He presents arguments for eminent domain.

(1) The Center will attract visitors and new community members, growing the community and raising its profile. (2) Nicotine was the largest house in the CHA community, with the largest rooms—a natural community center—yet it was entirely in private hands, although it lacked a coherent activist agenda. (3) Rob may have brought it on himself. (4) Trashed by its residents, Nicotine is being restored by the Center's donor free of charge. (5) Sunshine's own increasingly popular climate change events have outgrown DJD's facilities—particularly the DJD itself, which is showing significant wear and tear—and for several years he has [resented] (he uses a different word) Nicotine's having a very large living room that goes unused because it smells like an ashtray. (6) Once that room is aired out, there will be space for an indoor day care center with yard access on the ground floor—unless the bookstore is planned to be really huge, which Sunshine doubts. (7) On social media, there have been rumors that the second-floor yoga studio will have a changing room and showers.

Because the community's few toddlers currently gather in a Children's Garden consisting of picnic tables in a vacant lot that has broken bottles and rusty scrap poking up out of the ground, several women stand up to applaud. A Stayfree resident proposes that Stayfree spearhead the cooperative day care center at the Baker Center. Another suggests teaching the children to bake so they can pay their rent in kind—in cake pops for the café!

There is happy laughter, along with a murmuring groundswell of approval for the yoga initiative.

Penny sits passively on the floor. She imagines telling the room about her relationship with Norman Baker. She imagines warning them against trusting Matt, as though Anka had not said enough. She imagines inspiring them to retake Nicotine the way she wants it retaken. Each time her hand begins to creep into the air, an adrenaline rush raises her heart rate, and she lowers it. Her interest in the topic is too strong. It's crippling.

She is tired out from doing the recommended preliminary reading for her upcoming assignment as a global commodities market analyst trainee. She is already in regular contact with her supervisor. Her mother receives glowing reports. She brings intense concentration to the books and PDFs, with the continual sensation that if she didn't, she would be staring at her phone for eighteen hours a day, ritually conjuring thoughts of Rob while ritually banning thoughts of Matt.

It can't be done. The two men are linked now by irreversible violence.

In fact her daily time investment in ritual phone staring is a mere two hours. She feels done for and double-crossed, and she has seldom been more productive. Still, when the topic is Nicotine, her default mode is vacancy. She concentrates on her new job. Her feelings are down deep inside her head where they started out.

OVER THE NEXT WEEK, SUNSHINE conducts what he calls an "open mouth strike" against the Nicotine residents and Penny. He impugns their motives. To maintain plausible deniability, he avoids social media. In person, he intimates to friends that the Blue Bloc's intervention in the *#climbit* action may have led to Susannah's injuries. He insinuates that the Blue Bloc may include police informants. "Why were no charges filed against Penny and Sorry? Why wasn't Jazz at the Freedom Tower?" he asks, rhetorically.

Susannah's friends fume. When they see Anka or Penny, they don't say hi.

Susannah's circle includes all the youngest and prettiest women in the CHA community. Their clout is massive.

Sunshine doesn't bad-mouth Nicotine to anyone who lives at Tranquility. His strict honor code tells him it would be wrong to render Penny homeless. As for rendering Anka homeless, he figures it's only a matter of time anyway, since she's living at DJD provisionally, on Susannah's furniture, and no one is talking to her. She's going to get lonely and move out. Her work on HIV doesn't fit the house's profile anyway.

THE SECOND MEETING AT DJD is sparsely attended: Anka, Penny, Rufus, Maureen, Stevie, and Barry—that is, Anka and all the Tranquility residents except Jacob. The DJD residents go about their business, upstairs or in the kitchen.

"This is the perfect issue for Tranquility," Anka says. "We have native people being driven from their homes by an entrepreneur. This isn't like normal gentrification, where it's just renters being priced out. Rob and Jazz built that house. They own it. It was a ruin before Rob moved in."

"But it was in that guy's family," Maureen says. "So he's naturally more attuned to the spirit of the house. The genius loci, you know, the sense of place? That's where his roots are. It's part of his childhood."

"He let it fall down, and now he's tearing it up. He doesn't care about that house! He's putting in new flooring and wallpaper, and repainting everything! It's going to be *unrecognizable*. How is that like having roots? To him, that house is just one more investment. He's probably getting primed to sell it."

Stevie says, "Anybody who would sell his own heritage doesn't deserve to inherit it."

Penny doesn't say anything, but she feels proud of her housemates.

The committee reaches consensus that Rob and Jazz are indigenous to Nicotine and that Matt's financial commitment cancels out his hereditary claims.

But no one has a practicable suggestion for what to do about it. Sabotage plans keep running up against the (dummy) surveillance cameras, while plans to betray Matt to various authorities founder on the uncertain legal status of the CHA houses and/or Jazz's gun. The committee agrees to reconvene.

THE THIRD MEETING IS HELD at Tranquility. Penny finds herself alone with Jacob. Having skipped the first two meetings, he is now curious about the movement. He asks Penny to fill him in. She tells him everything she knows about Matt's plans.

In response he lauds Matt's work on the house, which frankly was a dump, with the toilet in the kitchen and a room full of buckets of you-know-what, come on, admit it, that's so weird it's almost sick. He never met Rob but you have to admit—

Penny says she doesn't have to admit anything, and breaks the meeting off.

SHE SITS AT THE KITCHEN table on Saturday morning with her chin in her hand, spinning a nickel on its edge. She does her best not to think about anything but commodities, because her competing thoughts, when she has them, tell her she is sad and stupid.

Her campaign against Jazz's thing with Matt, for instance—that was real bright. She got what she was after. They broke up! Nice work, Penny! What happened then was so obviously bound to happen, she feels like she did it herself. Drove Rob and Jazz into each other's arms. Scared them into leaving town together. Why the big blind spot? What made her think Matt would ever submit calmly to frustration?

She recalls her not-so-long-ago insight that even her father deferred to him. At the time she thought it meant Norm was weak. Now she feels—like a stomachache—how presumptuous she was to think Matt might be thwarted and threatened and placated and rendered harmless in due order like a normal person.

When she thinks of him now, she imagines a stone idol that must be propitiated by regular sacrifice. She sees herself throwing marigold petals on the Matt statue and rubbing its feet with ghee. Nothing can hurt it. No knife can penetrate its stony power. "I hate you," she says aloud.

She opens her laptop and writes to her friend Fon in Terre Haute.

> Hey Fon, how's it hanging? So much for a life of crime! I got a JOB. At Mom's bank. FUCK! And that man I'm IN LOVE WITH is in WHERE THE FUCK, I DON'T KNOW. He had no reason to leave town or stop talking to me, unless you count my fucking brother trying to kill him. West Coast? With two of his housemates. One's fat as a tick, not an issue, the other is this armed and dangerous love goddess

She regards the draft e-mail. She realizes she may not be doing anyone a favor by sending it over the Internet. "Armed and dangerous." Not good.

She considers G-chatting with Fon, or calling her. She remembers the dictation software in her phone that understands her every word.

She deletes what she has written and starts again.

> Hey Fon. Things here are crazy. But I got a job! Mom's bank. I'll come see you in paradise after I get vacation days. My new Anglo name is Gypsy Lee Baker. Like it? Love, GLB

She sends the e-mail and doesn't get an answer.

Her phone rings. It is Rob. Without the sadness lifting, she has an out-of-body experience, wound up so tight she can barely breathe.

"We'll be in Oakland soon," he says. "You want to come out?"

"I got a job."

"Already? You already working?"

"No. I took an offer with a starting date next month."

"So come to Oakland."

"Where are you now?"

"Albuquerque. Lot of bikes, but no subway. It's hot as fuck. I'm looking forward to the coast. Come join us."

"No. Bye, Rob." She hangs up.

She stares at her phone and feels her stress evaporate—the stress of being in love. It's as if she ordered herself to cut it in half with scissors. She isn't just one person anymore.

Barry enters the kitchen. "Hey, Penny. Why you crying? I hear you got your reasons."

She wipes her nose and says, "What are you talking about?"

"You were standing with the Blue Bloc at the Freedom Tower."

"Yeah, and I got arrested and spent twenty-four hours in the Tombs!"

He snickers.

She closes her laptop and goes up to her room. She goes online and shops for studio apartments.

She hates her housemates now, and nearly everyone in CHA, with a hate that is conscious and rational. Given the choice between her and Matt, they have chosen Matt.

Her hate for them flows parallel to her hate for Matt, so the two might reasonably be expected to unite into a single, stronger hate. Instead she broods about how much she hates anarchists. How much she would pay to get away from them. What a shitty apartment she would rent in Queens just to be sure she never sees them again.

That is, she can't consciously hate Matt without thinking of Rob and Jazz, so she hates anarchists instead.

But she barely hates them at all, really. They're such ineffectual live-and-let-live pseudo-revolutionaries, she has to laugh.

She goes back to hating Matt, imagining him with Jazz. For a moment she forgets the issue of apartments.

Seeing an opportunity, her mind jumps on the idle computing power and devotes it to the long-neglected task of remembering Rob. He flashes on her like a forgotten dose of LSD. She goes from staring at a listing for a studio in Inwood to feeling hot and cold and a little sick and like he's right in front of her, so close they overlap. There's a dull ache in her vagina, and her soul is banging on her breastbone from the inside.

She calls him back and reaches him in the passenger seat of the minivan. Sorry is driving, and Jazz is sprawled out on the bench seat.

"Tell me," she says without saying hello. "Are you *really* moving to Oakland?"

"I don't know. Right now I'm afraid to come home. If I even had a home! It's that simple."

"I love you and I want to be with you."

"Then come visit us in Oakland."

"Why are you saying that? *Why*? To hurt me? So I can come out there and hang with you and Jazz?"

"We're not a couple."

"*They're not a couple!*" Sorry yells, so loud Penny can hear her clearly. "*They have fucking wretched sex! When they fuck you can hear a pin drop!*"

"Tell Sorry thanks," Penny says.

"*It's you he loves!*"

"We can't be described as a couple," Rob reiterates. "We're non-monogamous."

"Let me talk to Sorry," Penny says, and Rob gives her the phone. "Hey, Sorry. Do *not* fucking torture me. Don't say that shit if it's not true." Penny hears a harrumph of confirmation. "I know Jazz is there. Hey, Jazz. Jas-mine!" Sorry hands the phone to Jazz. "Jazz, dude, tell me the truth. Do you and Rob have hot sex?"

"I can't stop thinking about Matt."

"God almighty!" Rob cries.

"Cut me some slack," Jazz says. "He's a very intense experience."

"That's all I want to hear," Penny says. "I think I might come out and visit before I start my job."

SPRAWLED OUT ON THE BENCH seat, Jazz is texting. *Out skinny-dipping I saw a panther,* she writes. *It reminded me of you. It had its claws in my heart and its teeth in my throat. It was unforgettable. Not in a good way. I don't want to see you again in this life, but I'd be happy if you were the last thing I saw.* She composes absent-mindedly, like a teenager drafting a diary entry he plans to delete—deep feelings, too worthless to matter much. She adds another *Not good* and makes the text go away by sending it to Matt.

It is not a style of rhetoric calculated to calm him down. His wish to fuck her seems to take in not only his genitals but also his entire body, his office, several feet of the topsoil of Bayonne, and the sky. He wipes away a tear, feeling that unsatisfied lust such as his has never been known by any man.

Guess you're west of the Rockies, he types. Thanks to his friend on the police force, he knows roughly where she is and can find out her exact coordinates on short notice. But he assumes that simply knowing where she is won't be much help, since it generally equates to knowing where Rob and Sorry are. What he wants is to make a date, and for that he needs the name of a city, so he can look up a highly recommended restaurant with a nice hotel upstairs.

It doesn't matter where we are, she writes. *I don't want what you want. It's over.*

We need to talk before you know what I want. We never talked.

Jazz can't deny it. She taps out, I don't want to talk. It's too late. Think about what we did to each other. Make yourself THINK about it. You hurt my best friend so bad. I love Rob. You made me fuck up our house. I loved that house.

He replies, You would have been within your rights to kill me, as an intruder in your home. It would have been self-defense. But you didn't kill me. You didn't even hurt me. You can't. And I would never hurt you. I'm so sorry about your friend and your house. So sorry. Because I lost the best thing I ever had. Something I didn't know existed until I met you. Love for a woman, of all things. I love you, Jasmine.

Reading that gives her a strange sensation, as if her eyes had gained weight. She squeezes them shut, wanting to dive in. The memory of holding a gun on him is traced into the gesture of scrunching up her eyes. The hesitation before diving into blood. The same sense of power and mercy floods her mind, making her feel weightless. She squirms. Sorry turns and looks at her.

We might make the suburbs of SF soon, she taps. You name the vegan lesbian coffee shop, I'll give you a date and time.

Never be scared of me again, he replies. I cannot make myself want to hurt you anymore. Tried. Can't do it. Mea culpa!

Nothing ever terrifies me but myself, she replies.

A moment later she adds, And you're the next best thing.

Another moment later: Also mountain lions.

In his office in Bayonne, Matt feels his balls tighten and flatten against his perineum. He shifts his weight and opens his fly just to give his dick some space. He touches himself with his index finger and thumb and rummages in his takeout bag for a napkin. He does not feel happy.

LATE THE NEXT MORNING, WHILE Penny is drinking coffee in bed, Amalia calls her to say an old family friend is visiting from Baltimore, and can she come over.

"Now?" she asks.

"The day after tomorrow."

"I'm flying out Thursday to see some friends—some Jersey City friends who just moved to Oakland. I'm going to their housewarming party, to help them get set up. I'll need to pack."

"What about Lorraine? She hasn't seen you in so long."

"I'll see her next time. You'll have fun together. She'll meet Tony. But, Mom, there's something I have to tell you. You know Dad's house that filled up knee-deep with shit? You know what Matt did? He kicked my friends out and squatted it, and cleaned it up, and he's turning it into a community center called the *Norman Baker Center.*"

"That is so nice! What a happy ending! Now you both have productive work!"

"No. This is *Matt,* Mom. He kicked my friends out by trying to kill one of them, and they had to fight him off with a gun, and he trashed the place, and they went on a road trip because they were so scared of him, and now they're hiding from him in California."

"That sounds like crazy psychodrama, and finally Matt is doing something worthwhile. He was always so selfish, working with garbage. Who needs garbage? But a community center for that terrible ghetto! Maybe he will grow up to be a man we can respect."

Penny pauses with a sense of reaching up into her brain and flipping a switch to turn her principles off. She has met her mother, after all. She knows the reality of Amalia—adaptability and pragmatism. Like Jazz, her mother dwells in the monadic real world, where the truth is just another way of manipulating people. The best way.

And what's even stronger than the truth? Warm bodies to defend it. Facts on the ground. She sees a way to tip the balance of power away from Matt, if only for one day.

She says, "You know, Mom, I was thinking—I don't know exactly when the Center's opening—but you should spread the word in

Norm's network. All those people who came to the memorial service. They're going to be just thrilled about the Center."

"Oh yes, I'll do that."

"I bet Matt will do a really nice grand opening party."

After the phone call, Penny lies back. To clear her mind of thoughts of Matt and her mother, she entertains sexual fantasies of Rob. The landscape of San Francisco plays a central role. Rob does not come to her bed; he stands wreathed in fog on a grassy promontory, behind him a huge red suspension bridge. She floats toward him, disembodied. The bridge remains visible out of the corner of her eye, whatever the imaginary Rob does to her with his mind.

THE SIGN GOES UP: BAKER BOOKS. The relevant permits have been expedited. The remodeling of Nicotine has taken less than six weeks. The grand opening is scheduled for a Sunday afternoon in September.

The sign is pale green, with pink lettering. Between BAKER and BOOKS stands a variant of the circle-A emblem of anarcho-syndicalism—a capital *A* in a heart.

ROB, JAZZ, AND SORRY APPROACH Oakland from the south, via Alameda, and as the first highway signs begin to point the way to the airport, Sorry says, "Take me there. The airport. My shit is packed, I have the cash, and I'm going to Venezuela. I'll fly standby. Take a right."

Rob puts on the turn signal and says, "This is sudden."

Jazz asks, "Don't Jordanians need a visa for Venezuela?" She takes her phone out of her bag.

The minivan slows into a curve. Rob says, "I wish you wouldn't do this so suddenly. You know how many years we lived together? And now you're blowing us off, just like that. It's upsetting."

"Your heart's on the left, and you're clutching the middle," Sorry says. "That's not your heart. It's your Rob sappiness, which I treasure more than any bodily organ in the world. You're a great guy, and I'm going to miss you. But I'll be back! It would be stupid to insist on having input on where we're staying and all that, when all I want to do is leave. And this is San Francisco. I could end up broke before we even get settled."

As they approach the terminal for international departures, Jazz finishes reading the relevant information from the Venezuelan consular Web site. "You need to apply for a visa in advance," she says, "and provide evidence of regular income in your country of residence."

"Shit! What about Cuba and Bolivia?"

"Isn't North Korea Communist?" Rob asks. "What about Turkmenistan?" Jazz titters. Sorry frowns. He glides past the stopped cars and the people unloading baggage without slowing down. "I swear," he says to Sorry, "Oakland is not going to cost you a dime. And you know why? Because you're with us. And we're broke."

"We don't even know where you hide your cash," Jazz adds.

She goes on Twitter to ask Oakland anarchists about a place to stay. Not having signed on in weeks, she is surprised by the tenor of tweets addressed to her, many with the hashtag *#climbit*. "That's weird," she says.

"What's weird?" Sorry asks.

"Look at your Twitter."

Sorry reads a bit and says, "Fuck." She calls Anka and puts her on the speaker.

"Where have you been?" Anka almost screeches. "You've been off the grid for weeks! Do you have *any idea* what's been going on? People are saying we set up Susannah! They think Rob's a snitch. You know who they *love*? Penny's brother Matt! I have to get out of here."

"Who says that?"

"Everybody. It's common knowledge."

"Who started tweeting it?"

"Barry at Tranquility. But I think it can be traced back to Sunshine, who's *my* fucking housemate."

"Pack your bags," Rob says. "We're almost in Oakland. You should come to Oakland! Penny's coming."

"You've never been to Oakland. It's like West Philly. It's gangland, with Crips and Bloods and Mara Salvatrucha. I mean the *real* West Philly, not the part near Penn they've been buying up. I mean like Sixty-Fifth Street! Promise me you will *not* go into any empty houses in Oakland. Swear it to me, right now."

"She's making me nervous," Sorry says.

"So where are we supposed to go?"

"I'll read some feeds," Anka says, "and tell you if there's some squat in Oakland that's on your side."

A few exits later, Rob sees a Wal-Mart sign and pulls off the highway. He buys a cheap Coleman four-person tent, four summer-weight Coleman sleeping bags, a large air mattress, Sunny Delight, Wonder, and Jif.

Jazz scans maps for an obscure park with a dull name. (To find a vacant campsite in summer in California, it helps to stay away from beckoning words like *national* and *beach* and *tree*.) She selects Anthony Chabot Regional Park and reserves a narrow space under pines with a concrete pad for the minivan. They camp.

LATE THE NEXT MORNING, ROB drives alone back to the airport to pick up Penny. He walks to the arrivals gate and waits for her. She arrives weary.

She throws her arms around him while he holds the handle of her carry-on. She has almost nothing to say. Several times in a row, she says "Rob."

After a while he pries her loose and starts her walking back to the minivan. "Talk to me," he says. "I don't understand what's going on. They're all like, 'You're with Penny now. Deal with it.' Like it's this fait accompli. So I thought you'd at least be happy. But you look about ready to cry."

"I'm worn-out. Let me pay for the parking. I got a job."

He feeds her money into the machine and tucks the card into his breast pocket. "This way," he says.

She stumbles along behind him toward the parking spot, dragging her little suitcase. "They're not stupid. It's a fact that you should be with me. It's so obvious."

"That's what I hear," he says. He opens the side door of the minivan, puts her luggage inside, and places his arm around her waist.

"Just stop it!"

He squeezes her. She gasps, and he asks, "Does that hurt? Do you have a bruised rib or something?"

"No," she says weakly. "It's just that when you touch me, I can't breathe. Let me sit down. I feel dizzy."

She sits down in the open side door of the minivan, breathing slowly. When he touches her shoulder, she shudders. She takes his arm and draws it toward her until he sits down next to her. She buries her head in his armpit and starts to sob.

"You've been under a lot of stress," he says.

To which she says, "Rob!"

He kisses her gently, opening his mouth just a little, and she shakes like a patient in a fever ward.

So this is bondage, he thinks. A woman hog-tied by the fear I might not want her. Quivering protoplasm before she even got off the plane! He regards her helpless body, sees her eyes overflow with damp, unabashed sorrow (a touching spectacle framed in perfect skin and thick, glossy hair), hears her shameless crying, and the whole thing begins to take on a very definite shape in his mind. It's a shape he knows not from experience but from instinct: the shape of something that wants to get fucked, like, *right now*.

It's not Penny exactly. It's her body. Penny was made for higher purposes. That's why she fights it. She's forced into the position of being the sufficient and necessary condition for the fuckable thing.

"Listen up," he says. "You know I want your body."

The announcement makes her inhale sharply and stiffen like a possum playing dead. Then she vibrates like a scared bat, as if her heart is beating three hundred times a minute. "Scooch over," he says, compelled to take the initiative. He scoots backward on his butt, pushes the luggage aside, pulls her onto his lap, and leans forward to slide the door shut. After a glance around the cluttered floor of the vehicle, he wedges them both into the narrow space between the front seats and the bench seat. He sits back on the hard, uneven vinyl, wishing he had a mat or a sleeping bag. He pulls her toward him and kisses her mouth, which has never seemed so defenseless and soft. He yanks down her leggings with both hands, peels them off her with his toes, and realizes he has hit a wall.

He whispers, "I think there might be condoms in the glove compartment."

She chirps, "Okay!"

As he unbuttons his jeans, she turns and crawls into the passenger seat to extract a roll of brightly colored lubricated condoms—the kind AIDS activists give away—from among the parking tickets. Without a word, she unrolls one over him and proceeds to have sex with him as though he were a perfectly normal guy. Clearly she is neither perturbed by his size nor hankering to pronounce some awful verdict. Instead she moans with strange joy. She makes animal sounds.

He whispers, "I wish Sorry could hear you." Instead of laughing, she shakes her head so that her hair hides her face. She cries out. She comes. He can feel it distinctly, even through the condom, and as he takes a more active role (she gets clumsier and clumsier, ceding ever more control, so he has no choice) he feels a kind of pressure and resistance he has never felt before. With a moment's effort he flips their configuration over. He attains physical incoherence and bangs his head against the interior paneling and the back of the driver's seat. He puts his mouth on hers for orientation and to quiet them both down. He grabs her ass with both hands. He comes.

"My God, what was that," he says, panting wide-eyed.

"I love you so much," she says, hugging him with her arms and legs and kissing his face all over. "I've been so totally crazy about you for so long!"

"I mean the sex. I figured Jazz was—I shouldn't say this. It's different with you."

"Didn't you ever read the Kama Sutra? You're a hare man, and the hare man is supposed to be with the deer woman. That's all."

"How did you know?"

"Matt's my brother. I've seen him naked, and I did the math. Like, if Jazz can even sleep with him, then, you know. She's above average."

"I see," Rob says. He slips off the condom and ties a knot in it. "Should I save this as a souvenir? I'm thirty, but I guess there's a first time for everything." He puts on his pants, walks barefoot through the parking garage to the trash can next to the elevators, and throws it away.

"What were you talking about just now?" Penny asks on his return.

"I never had sex with a condom before."

"You *what*? With *Jazz*?!"

"Hey, hey. Calm down! She'd never had sex without one, so it evens out. Trust me. I'm clean as a whistle."

"Right. Glad I got the HPV vaccine."

"Your virgin act is not cutting it. And Jazz would not lie to me about being disease-free. You slept with her yourself."

"Okay, okay, sorry."

"She's going to say let's have a threesome, so you better start thinking about your answer."

"What's yours?"

"My polymorphous perversity just hit an all-time low. But if you want her kissing you or whatever—I mean, if she stays out of the way—"

"No, thanks."

"I don't need anything or anybody but you," he says. "Your body is all that and more." He tucks a hand under her knee and kisses her inner thigh. "Maybe if your family was Latino, you'd know how beautiful you are? Maybe it warped you growing up with a bunch of white dudes calling you 'koala-face'?"

She points out that the alleged likeness involves her having inherited her father's wide-bridged nose.

THAT AFTERNOON THEY BED DOWN in the tent, leaving the minivan to Jazz and Sorry. But five acts of intercourse in four hours seem like enough, and around six Penny gives in to the urge to converse—as a way of keeping the intimacy going, not breaking the spell, not taking a nap. She starts by requesting immunity from prosecution. "Can I tell you something?"

"Sure," Rob says.

She tells him how Norm died.

She shares a few narrative highlights—cerebral stuff, bitter ironies, cruel contradictions—but mostly it's images and feelings. Images of suffering, feelings of failure. She says, "Adolf Hitler didn't deserve to die that way. Dad was so good and smart. I was such a coward not to help him."

"There was nothing you could have done legally, and *The People versus Penny Baker* is not a fair fight. Nobody can ask you to lay down your life. Especially not your dad."

She sniffles.

"Maybe it had a happy ending anyway," he adds. "You know how when you're really sick and get better, you get this ecstasy? People looking at you can't see it. All they see is damage, and you're in the eye of the hurricane."

She blinks. "Maybe," she says. The image of death as a hurricane works a little too well with the image of the soul as a small bird.

"What are you thinking?"

"I saw his soul."

"What do you mean?"

"I didn't really *see* it. I just knew it was there. He died, and then—don't laugh at me—his soul flew out the window."

"Souls are nomads. They see that hurricane coming, they hit the road."

"I know you're kidding, but I watched his life leave the room. Life can't die, so it must go *somewhere*. It all follows. It can't squat a new body unless you believe in reincarnation, so where does it go? The great refugee camp in the sky, where they'll let you in even though you have nothing left, not even a body. I don't believe in it any more than you do."

"I wish you'd told me this stuff a long time ago."

"I didn't want your understanding and sympathy. I wanted what we have now."

"Well, maybe we would have gotten closer faster, if I'd had any clue what was going on."

She shakes her head. "I think it's an interesting coincidence that you fell in love with me *while we were fucking*."

"True," he says. "I feel this incredible inner peace since that happened. And now we're having this conversation. It's so stupid. Not you. Me."

SORRY IS NOT SURPRISED WHEN Jazz declares her intention of going out that night. It must be difficult, Sorry feels, to see the love of your life usurped by a rival claimant—especially if you're Jazz, used to getting exactly what you want from men (perhaps because you consistently want the thing they most want to give you), and your rival is Penny, who wants so much from men that it's astounding they give her the time of day.

Jazz calls a yellow cab from the entrance to the campground. It's a long way into San Francisco, but Matt says he'll wait in front of the restaurant to pay off the driver.

And there he is. Standing at the curb, in close-fitting chinos and a white shirt, looking very well. He opens the door and Jazz steps out, in a sort of long T-shirt made of sheer turquoise rayon tricot over a crocheted bikini that's the closest thing she owns to a bra and granny panties. "Skip dinner?" he suggests as the cab drives off. "I got a suite."

"I'm here for the food," she says. "That's why I wore this roomy dress. I want prime rib, like a twelve-ounce steak. We've been living on Grape-Nuts."

"You'll need to earn that kind of treatment," he says. They walk in, straight to the elevator, ignoring the reception desk and the restaurant.

To Jazz, his voice alone has a certain momentum. She feels light as a meringue and slippery between her legs with that sweet-tasting transparent stuff, and when he goes to press against her in the elevator she says, "Careful of my dress." He pulls the hemline up to her waist and caresses the bones of her hips. "Is that a camera?" she asks, looking up. He drops the dress. When the elevator door dings, he leads her down a long hallway to his corner suite. "I'm starting to realize we should have talked on the phone," she says. "This is looking an awful lot like sex."

"What about?"

"You're the one who wanted to talk."

"About how much I want to fuck you, probably."

"Be a big boy," she says. "There was something you wanted to say. Out with it."

"I think I told you I love you."

"Not that."

"You've put on weight."

"I've been eating with Rob and Sorry."

"No talking," he says. He pulls her dress off over her head and lets it fall on the floor. He cradles her shoulders in his hands, fingertips pulling softly on the straps of her bathing suit. "I have missed you. I have missed you so much."

"I thought this was our good-bye dinner. So I brought my gun, but no condoms."

"I don't have any either. I don't care. I want you. It's all I can think about. Being inside you. Just you and me. And maybe somebody new, somebody who's both of us. You know what I mean."

"That's it," she says. She stoops to retrieve her dress from the floor. "You're out of your cotton-picking mind."

"Come on," he says, seizing her around the waist. "Let's be happy."

"Don't do this to me," she says. "I love you. Of course I want your baby. I want to be happy like that. But I was not cut out to be happy like that. I will *never* be happy like that. I wanted to fuck you more than anything in the universe, after we talked and had dinner and whatever, and now I can't."

"I'll pull out and come in your ass—your mouth? Anywhere you want?"

"Can I get your permission to enforce that with the gun?" She puts on the dress, pulling it all the way down to her knees. She shakes out her hair, combing it with her fingers. "Forget it. This is love. It's the closest thing to love between a man and a woman the world has ever seen, and any baby who survived it would be a pretty fucking lucky baby."

"I swear, I'll pull out."

"Listen. You're my bête noire. My destiny. But I'm not ready to meet my fate, not yet. I don't want to lose myself and live for you or anybody else. Not in this lifetime. Maybe when I'm so old I don't mind. When I'm a wisp of a little old lady, all alone and poor, I'll go there. That's the deal I've made with myself. I will *not* give myself up. I fought too hard to get this far alone!"

"What?" He squints as his head wobbles in bewilderment. "What are you saying? Do you need me to force you?"

"No. No! If it were just me, sure, but a baby? I'd be mixing up somebody else in this sick thing. Somebody who has a right to be happy. I'm not a happy person, but I'm under no obligation to give a fuck. It's just me!"

Matt's emotions are very exasperated—exasperated desire and exasperated fear, linked by exasperation into incoherent helplessness. "I don't have to see either of you," he insists. "I'll pay for everything, and you can live by yourself, on top of your old house. You know I'm making a really nice apartment up there, on the roof where you used to live, but with fireplaces and climate control. You'll be so happy, with all your friends. I would help you. It would be easy." He pauses, then adds, "I'm so sorry about what I did to your friends. But you couldn't really expect me to get along with Rob, under the circumstances. I'll make it up to you."

"How would that help anything? I want to fuck you, but you don't want to fuck me." He makes a gesture of protest, but she goes on. "If you wanted that, you wouldn't want me *pregnant* and a *mom*. Right now you don't even know it. It's hormones, because you've never been a father, and you're getting old. It's your biological clock. I'm twenty-four, Matt."

He goes motionless and quiet.

"We can fuck," she says firmly, "with birth control. We'll get condoms from the concierge."

He sits down on the bed. All his strongest desires conflict with his desire to be liked by Jazz. He could grab her right now and fuck a baby into her, and if she didn't abort it, she would love it very much whether she liked it or not, and it would love him the way he loved his parents, from a respectful distance. But she still would not be the love he wants, because (as he knows) it wasn't him she was talking about. It was herself. They are too similar. He knows what he would say to a woman who offered him a baby to raise. He would say, "Tell it to your biological clock."

He feels the helpless, unpleasant sensation of being trapped in a conversation with an equal. Sex never makes him feel helpless. Love appears to consist of helplessness and nothing else.

Maybe she's right, he thinks. Maybe love is a bad idea. He tries to imagine casual sex with her, and can't.

Eyes shut, he hears the door close. She is gone.

He jumps up to run after her. Then he sits down again.

"I SAW MATT LAST NIGHT," Jazz tells Rob as he stands at the campground deep sink to do some hand laundry. "We didn't fuck."

"What do you mean, 'saw'?"

"Got together. You were busy."

"I wasn't *that* busy. I would have found the time to throw your phone on the fire and tie you to a tree." She is silent. "Let's be friends. Talk to me." He lathers up his socks for the second time, paying extra attention to the grubby heels.

"He's in love, and he thinks it's forever. It's like he's seventeen. He wants my baby."

"And what are you going to do?"

"Leave the country with no forwarding address."

"That's a little harsh," Rob says. "I mean on me."

"Nothing is forever, except babies."

"Let me see your phone a second." She hands it over. He bangs it against the stucco wall of the restroom building, cracking the glass of the display. He drops it in the water. It lies forlornly at the bottom of the sink, emitting bubbles.

"Breaking my phone won't make my accounts go away," Jazz says. "He can still get in touch with me."

"I miss modern life," Rob says. "Remember when you could leave Dodge after high noon and the sheriff wasn't in your fucking *pocket*? You're going to be fielding booty calls from that fucker forever!"

"Rob. Rob. I left him sitting crying in a hotel room. I didn't fuck him. You're the last man I ever fucked. I love you. I don't want to be anybody's baby-mama. Rob!" Down in the water, the phone lights up for a fraction of a second, then dies. They both glance at it, and Jazz says, "It's still *working*?" She picks it up and shakes it, and water flies out. She taps the display a few times. "Oh well. I guess it's really broken."

"Maybe hang it out to dry. I'm sorry."

"I wanted a new phone anyway. I want a burner clamshell phone like you and the other celebrities have."

"You're crazy," he says. He touches her face tenderly. "I really think you should have a baby, just so you get a chance to love somebody who deserves it. You're such a loving person, and the guys you love are such fucking jokes."

"Rob the romantic," she says. "One night with Penny, and you're a breeder."

"I love her. She's as tormented as you or anybody, but when she's in trouble, it's through no fault of her own. I spent so much of my life around self-defeating fuckups, I forgot that was even possible!"

She looks down, unhappy. Her phone's display is black and blank. I'm not going to chase you, Matt writes to her. I know what campground you're in. I also know you can't want me as much as you do and not come back to me. You're not that strong. That's what you always say, and I'm starting to believe it. But she can't see it, not right now.

BACK AT THE CAMPSITE, ROB proposes they all spend the day doing some sightseeing together.

He drives into San Francisco, intending to cross the Golden Gate Bridge. But the toll situation is vague and intimidating, requiring or not requiring an RFID sticker that might or might not require a credit card, and in the end he parks near Fort Point and they walk the entire way up to cross the bridge on foot.

In the middle of the bridge, Jazz makes a joke about suicide hotlines. Rob offers her his phone. Sorry says she's so light, she'd waft down like a leaf and not get hurt. Penny grabs her arm and doesn't let go again until they're in Marin County.

They leave the road and hike down to the first beach on the left. Past the scarred pines and ruined amenities, below the empty campground, Sorry sits down on the tar-blackened sand. The others wade into tiny waves that make the smooth stones go clack-clack. A dark wall approaches over the ocean, low and sinister, and eats the bridge. "Fog," Rob says knowingly, but there is reverence in his voice.

They return to the minivan exhausted, after a long march through blank, boring whiteness.

After a few wrong turns, they find Golden Gate Park, nowhere near the Golden Gate, and park. They can't find uninhabited benches, so they sit on the grass.

Penny's euphoria is fading. She hasn't had sex with Rob in nearly seven hours.

She feels irritable and needy, seeking his attention and ashamed of herself for doing so. She doesn't so much mind the idea of flying to California every weekend—she's small enough to curl up in economy, and she'll have the money to pay for it if she keeps living at Tranquility—but she will miss him so much. She knows it already. All week, every week, she'll be his lonely girlfriend, his lover in name only, pouring her erotic creativity into dumb texts, kissing his distorted face on frustrating video calls, staring stupidly at her phone.

She will bridge the weeks between their encounters by implementing the new life skills she learned in his absence—skepticism, apathy, how to run on empty—while the pleasure she would take in seeing him every morning and every night will lie there like a five-hundred-dollar bill on the sidewalk, with no one to pick it up, until it blows away.

She doesn't feel she has a choice. She's not going to find anything better than what she has. For jobs and men, it's a seller's market. There are no other fish in the sea. If she throws these ones back, she'll be empty-handed.

She sniffles and interweaves her fingers with his fingers. She tries hard to entertain the notion that she might be jumping the gun. You can't sleep with a guy for one day—no matter how hard you've worked to get him—and go straight to long-term future plans, right? After his career as CHA's leading tease, he might be raring to try out Californication. He's a man, after all. That's why she loves him. She leans on him and says, "I love you." He puts his arm around her and nods hello to a stranger who's staring at him as she walks by looking like a younger version of Kestrel in wrestling booties and a black silk romper. Penny adds, "I'm getting a headache. I need coffee."

"I second the motion," Sorry says, and Jazz agrees.

Penny and Rob walk into a nearby business district to look for takeout. She pays thirteen dollars for four paper cups of drip coffee. They take small, hot sips as they walk back to the park, still not seeing a bench anywhere. They deliver the coffee to Jazz and Sorry and sit down near them on the grass, and Penny says, "Rob."

"Yeah?"

"Do you really plan to stay here?"

"I don't know."

She is silent. Then she says, "That doesn't give me much to work with."

"I truly don't know. I have absolute freedom."

"I don't. I have a job that starts in two and a half weeks, and I want to start it. I need to make money, and I need to learn more. It's an interesting job, and I know I'll learn a lot. But I'm in love with you, so it makes me feel like shit."

"Isn't love supposed to make you happy?"

"I can't go back there." She leans on him and clutches his arm. "I want to be with you. I *need* to be with you. If I have to go home—I can't imagine it. I'll *die*."

"That's an easy one," he says. "Since it doesn't matter to me, and you want to be in New York, we'll go back to Tranquility. If we start tomorrow, we can take it slow, like two hundred miles a day, which is nothing. But do you have gas money? That's the main thing holding me in Oakland. I spent everything I had on a tent and sleeping bags. It was still cheaper than the motels in this place."

Penny sobs.

"Don't cry!" he says, embracing her. "I love you!"

"I'm not crying," she says. Immediately she stops. She shakes her head, aware that it is chock full of fluff.

"Oh good," he says.

They walk a few feet and sketch their plans to Sorry and Jazz.

"Me, I'm going to Hawaii," Sorry says. "California squared!"

"Hawaii!" Jazz says. She hits Sorry on the arm. "Shit, what a great idea! Why didn't you say that before? It's a tropical island *in America*. You don't even need a passport!"

"And you know it has a *major* tourist trade. Maybe I never told you guys this, but I can make these baskets—really professional-looking baskets. I learned it in the hospital. I could sell them on consignment at gift shops. I mean, nobody in New York is going to buy native crafts, because there are no natives, but in Hawaii—"

"You look kind of Hawaiian. Doesn't she?" Jazz says.

Penny and Rob regard Sorry in this new light.

"Yes," Penny says. "Definitely. She totally has the hair, and in Hawaii being heavy is a sign of belonging to the hereditary ruling class."

"We can squat on public land," Sorry says. "Can I have your tent? If there's just the two of you, you can sleep in the van."

"It's so basic, I don't know if it's really waterproof. Hawaii probably has monsoon rains."

"I think it's one of those places where it rains on one side of the island and not on the other. We'll go to the dry side."

"Okay, you can have my tent."

Several minutes later, as Sorry and Jazz are booking last-minute one-way tickets to Honolulu on Sorry's tablet, Penny says to Rob, "I can't believe it. I was all tortured deciding whether to throw my life away for love and move to Oakland. Now it's like, Oakland who? Where am I? What am I even doing?"

"You're on vacation." He kisses her.

"Seriously! Every time I think I know what's happening, the cards get reshuffled."

"You could get a job in Hawaii," Rob says.

Penny laughs, frowns, and says, "I'm going to miss them."

"They'll be back. Jazz is like a comet. Try to slow her down, and you'll get your hands ripped off. But wait it out, and she always comes back."

"That's like this seventies saying my dad used to quote—'If you love something, set it free'—except it's like, 'Set it free or it will rip your hands off.' "

"I think you might be missing something about that saying." He croons in a hippie voice, " 'I promise you, baby, I'll never set you free.' "

"Oh right," Penny says.

"My dad is like that. He tells women he loves them but they're free to go, and he lives in a thirty-foot trailer with no electric. Now, when I'm in love, there are nicer things I can think of to say, like"—he affects a girlish falsetto—" 'I'd *die* if I had to be separated from you for even *one day.*' "

"Stop it!"

He lets his hands drop from her body.

She picks them up and puts them back. "I didn't mean *that*. I meant stop gloating."

TWO DAYS LATER, ROB DRIVES his friends to San Francisco International, on the other side of the bay. Traffic is bad, and they arrive rushed. Sorry leans forward to stub out her cigarette in the dashboard ashtray. Simultaneously, she presses five hundred dollars in cash into Rob's hand.

"I can't accept this," he says. "I've never known where you get your money, but I know you need it more than I do."

"I got a divorce settlement. If I'm ever so down and out I need five hundred dollars, I'll know who to call."

They all disembark and set their luggage on the sidewalk. Sorry wears a long, stretchy black gown and a bone amulet on a leather thong (gift from Penny). Jazz looks smashing, in red sandals and a new white dress patterned with big red flowers.

"Well, no need for good-byes," Rob says, "since you'll be back in two months."

Standing at attention, Jazz says, "Or maybe this is good-bye. Because there's something I should tell you."

At that he looks worried, because the possibilities are virtually endless.

"It's about when I shot the monster. You probably think I was acting in self-defense and missed. But I made a conscious decision to trash the house. I was going to execute the landlord for what he did to you, and I choked. But something had to happen. Something extreme. I couldn't do it, because he saved my life once. But I'm a killer. You should know that."

"Merciful Jesus," Rob says. "Please tell me you know how to make sense."

"You're not a killer," Penny objects. "It's like the personal injury lawyers say. 'Give me damages, I'll find liability.' Something stopped you. There's no body."

"She's right," Rob says. "You stopped him torturing me to death. I'll never forget it. But you don't want to be a good person. That's too boring for you. And don't even think about telling me how he saved your life. Your death wish is proof positive that our culture is totally fucked and needs to be reinvented from the ground up."

"I'm leaving the gun behind," Jazz says. "It's under the spare tire."

Rob cries out in frustration and anger.

Frowning at Rob, Sorry says to Jazz, "You're a wonderful person. Just stressed out. You need to get off this dog-eat-dog continent and breathe some South Sea air."

Jazz whispers, "Rob. Really. I'll be okay."

"You'd better be." He says to Sorry, "Do *not* let her out of your sight. No new phones. Monitor her communications. Make her go cold turkey on that son of a bitch."

Jazz says, "You're too sane to understand me. My life doesn't fit in your head."

"What's there to understand? You're not honest with me."

"Every time I try to be, you get upset. It's only since you started caring about me. It makes it impossible to be friends."

Now Rob looks sad.

"Not impossible! I didn't mean that. But stop caring about me. I'll break your heart."

"You've got it backward," he says. "I always loved you enough to be your fucking doormat, and you started needing me the day you met him. In all the time I've known you, I've never seen you outside your comfort zone. Until now."

"Yeah, I guess you could say I've met my match."

In the conversational impasse, Penny hugs Jazz, saying she is pleased that Matt lives on, because they would all be in such deep shit otherwise. Jazz hugs Rob until he says he will always love her no matter what and that she'd better fucking take care of herself and come back from Hawaii in one piece. Sorry kisses Rob on the cheek and says that all animals have a right to live and be free. Embracing Penny, she thanks her for bringing some anarchy into their humdrum lives.

"Bye!" they all call out at last.

The travelers hike their duffel bags onto their shoulders and depart. Rob and Penny stand by the side door of the minivan, waving. They watch the duffels weave through the terminal—one high, green, and majestic, the other blue and bobbing like a cork. "Divorce settlement," Rob remarks. He closes and locks the doors, checking for forgotten personal items. "Divorce settlement," he says again.

"You sound like a Furby," Penny says.

"I thought Sorry was a lesbian."

"Lesbians can get divorced! Now they can even divorce women they used to be in love with, instead of chumps they married for the settlement."

"The world is going to hell in a handbasket," he agrees. He starts the engine. "Next stop Surf City."

"Where's that?"

"Somewhere west of here. The place where we're going to rent a paddleboat and drop that gun way out in the ocean." He pulls out past the double-parked cars into traffic.

"What do you think will happen to Jazz?"

"Definitely something. Sorry might find a comfortable holding pattern, but Jazz—no way. Like she says, something has to happen."

"I bet she meets somebody new on the plane. Like some Japanese businessman, and the next time we hear from her she's in Nagasaki."

"I don't think so. I think Matt's her Mount Everest, and she's not going to come down until she's been on top."

AMALIA LIKES™ THE NORMAN BAKER Center (aka Sunshine—the Center can't really interact socially) on Facebook and declares it her friend™. She encourages all her friends™ to attend its grand opening on the second Sunday in September.

Patrick direct messages her and Penny and Matt: Nice work. Didn't know you had anything planned for the house! I'll be on Mindanao but thoughts with you. Great job. Looks terrific. Dad would be proud. Baker Books! YES! Hugs P

Penny texts her: In Big Sur. So gr8. Be back in time. Love you.

SUNDAY MORNING, SEPTEMBER 11, 2016.

In Fort Lee, Matt kicks off his duvet. He picks up his phone, checks his mail and social media, and selects an old Funkadelic MP3 to pipe to the speakers in the kitchen. He picks his way downstairs. There are wineglasses on the open wooden staircase, and dust bunnies, some resting on the remains of wine. He is thinner, with dark circles under his eyes.

He dresses carefully, in indigo Levi's, a long-sleeved T-shirt, light fleece jacket, Timberlands, and a solar-powered Timex. It reads nine-thirty-three.

AT TEN-THIRTY, ROB AND PENNY awaken in Tranquility. "Let me make coffee," Penny says, crawling out of bed.

In the kitchen her mood is placid and sunny. As much as she abhors Matt, she is pleased his vengeance takes the form of a memorial to her father. Of course his motives are the worst and he's a domineering lunatic, but the benefit to her is clear: the Norman Baker Center makes her feel that Norm will soon cease haunting her. Instead he will enter into a denatured existence as an icon in a niche—the patron saint of JC anarchism—with Matt, of all people, as his priest. She reflects that she could move all his nasty furniture over to the Center and buy some decent Scandinavian stuff from her salary at the bank.

She muses and hums as she arranges two cappuccinos, toast, and mango preserves on a tray. Unbeknownst to her, her thoughts represent a state of unconditional love. She asks nothing of Matt but Mattness, and grants his right to exist. She even grants Norm the right to be dead and forgotten, his legacy erased.

"Today's the day," she says, handing Rob a red Zoloft cup of milky coffee. "The Norman Baker drug cult meets the Norman Baker shopping center. It's like matter and antimatter."

"I can't believe you want to go there at all."

"It's going to be great. Dad's friends love me. You will be so weirded out when you see how they treat me."

She dresses carefully, selecting particular amulets she feels will be appropriate for no particular reason. Over them she arranges her white cotton shift and a red crocheted shoulder bag with her phone. Rob remarks on her lack of underwear and shoes. "They're not part of this outfit," she explains.

"Well, I won't worry about you, if you don't worry about me."

"Deal," she says. "We're all grown-ups here."

BEFORE NOON, MATT IS DOWN at the Baker Center. His staff—manager Kestrel, baristas Feather and Huma, booksellers Sunshine and Cassidy—stand erect at their stations as he enters. "Looking great! I'm psyched! I love this book display. Did you do this, Sunshine? This is great work. You guys are set to do some serious business today."

Feather says, "Would you like a latte? I'm still practicing."

"Well, then, make me a latte!"

Cassidy says, "Matt, I wanted to say, because we were talking about it, and we wanted you to know how much it means to us that you did this. I worked in so many stores, and this is the *first* time I got paid. And the inventory is, like, amazing. We have so many books!"

"Thank you, Cassidy! Now I have to do some last-minute stuff in my office"—he is already ascending the stairs—"so if you need me, come get me."

Matt reaches roof level, holds the banister, and sighs heavily. He steps out into the angled light of early fall, which is creating colorful geometric patterns on the fawn-colored carpet via prismatic glass in the Glasgow-style transoms of the French doors facing west. He plunks down in an arts-and-crafts armchair with camel hair cushions and puts his feet up on the white-tiled hearth.

He hears drumming and struggles to his feet. He looks over the edge of the roof and sees an older man he hasn't seen since Norm's funeral, sitting on a rattan stool in the street, playing a conga. A teenage boy next to him keeps time with a shell-and-gourd rattle.

Matt sits down. He leans back hard, drowning out the sound with his thoughts. Because of the nature of his thoughts, he soon switches to drowning them out with the sound. He notices a second drummer joining in, playing tabla. He hears ululation and a rhythmic clattering of wood on asphalt.

He gets up to look down again. A troupe of women in sarongs with palmetto leaves in their hair, looking vaguely Polynesian except that they are white and African American, is performing a dance with broomsticks. Four crouch, raising and lowering parallel broomsticks in a cross shape, and four others dance among them. The attitude of the dancers' hands unmistakably suggests a Scottish sword dance.

"I did *not* order this," Matt says aloud. He calls the landline downstairs to ask Kestrel what's up.

"It's a community celebration," Kestrel says.

"I've met this community. It sicced its dog on me. Ask those people where they're from."

She lays the receiver on the counter without putting Matt on hold. He can hear his staff clapping in time with the music. He hears voices and laughter, and she returns. "Followers of Norman Baker!" she says. "They came all the way from Cincinnati!"

"Thanks," Matt says.

At around 1:00 P.M., he starts hearing complex polyrhythms. He looks down again. There are so many people dancing and drinking in the street that he can't make out individuals.

In particular, there are so many small, dark-haired women that he can identify no one relevant to his mood. He sees Jazz and Penny many times—mostly Penny—but it's never the real Jazz or the real Penny. Interspersed among the many doppelgängers are poor locals, gangs of wild-looking little kids, a wide array of anarchist youth of many genders, and the guy whose dog he painted. He blanches. He rehearses his speech about creating community.

PENNY APPROACHES A GROUP OF her father's friends to exchange congratulations and condolences. They embrace her and tell her how lovely she is looking. They are thrilled about the Baker Center, and sad that Norm can't be on hand.

"I was surprised to hear it was Matt's idea," one woman says. Her husband looks at her critically. He takes Penny aside.

He is old, but vigorous and animated. Young for his age, the way Norm was before he got sick. Penny's known him all her life. Not well, but from the time she was a baby in Manaus. Like a relative. His name is Ed, and she trusts him. He says, "Penny. Let's go sit down somewhere quiet and talk. I have something to tell you."

They walk to his old VW camper parked around the corner, climb inside, and sit at the dining table. It's humid and stuffy. Penny picks her hair up off her neck and tries to tie it in a knot the way Anka does, but her hair is too flexible and slippery. He smiles when she gives up.

"Hot day," he says, offering her the joint he's smoking.

She takes it and inhales deeply. "Whoa," she says.

"Penny, I believe your father wanted you to know the truth about where you came from. He told me you're his spiritual heir."

Modesty leaves her no option but to laugh. "You know he didn't leave me anything nonspiritual, right? No money, no possessions. Not even facts. I know he wanted to tell me stuff, but he lost the ability to talk. He was going to dictate it and hide it in a time capsule for fifty years. I ended up with nothing but this spiritual—burden—I don't know, it's hard to describe. That's what I got when he died. He flew away like a bird, and I got something so heavy I couldn't carry it."

"That spiritual freight is also a gift," Ed says. "I hope you found somebody to help take the weight."

"In fact I did," she says. "My friend Rob! He's the best. But this weed is knocking me on my ass. I don't know anybody who smokes weed this strong."

"I don't smoke dope for its own sake. It's a road, not a destination. Sometimes I just need a little nudge to get me moving down the road. Now I want to tell you about Katie, because you need to know."

She is not surprised that the secret about Katie is her father's legacy. People with secrets may consist of little else. "I know all about it. I asked Patrick."

"I always say, 'You can't always know what you need, but if you try sometimes, you get what you want.'"

"What do you mean?"

"What I said. Be careful what you wish for. You asked him what he knew, and he told you."

"Mom said the exact same thing."

"That was Norm, lying to protect them. That's why I'm telling you now."

"Oh."

"What happened was this. He and Katie had been together twenty years, and it wasn't always easy. He was seeing this"—he pauses—"backpacker, this biology student named Penelope." Penny sucks hard on the joint, pondering her own given name (Penhana). "When Katie got wind of it, they broke it off, obviously. But he was a romantic. He went back to the dump in Cartagena where she'd taken him to see the wildlife, and instead he saw this little girl in need of help, and he put two and two together. He thought it was a sign. So that was your mother. Katie goes overnight from almost losing him to chasing after this uncontrollable wild child. She snapped. She took a machete—" He pauses.

"She what?"

"She cut up her legs and went in the Pacific. Like she thought a shark would come and get it over with. The current took her out and she swam all night, because who wants to die? And a fishing boat found her with hypothermia and bacteria from raw sewage just eating her up. They were not doctors. They put raw meat on her wounds to draw out the poison."

"Holy shit. God. But why? I mean, what a weird—that's, like, mentally ill—"

"She was a schizophrenic."

Penny tries to empty her brain to make room for this. She goes around inside it, sweeping with tendrils of the pot smoke, which forms a shadowy cloud in the bus, and finally responds, "Did she go off her meds?"

"Meds don't always work like they're supposed to."

She nods.

"The first thing Norm did when they found her was put me and the kids on a plane to Jersey City. So they never found out."

"But how come they still don't know?"

"The boys aren't strong like you. They're like Katie."

"They're grown-ups. They have a right to know."

"Look me in the eye and say it again: 'Matthew Baker, mature adult.' You really want to hand him a precedent for an insanity defense? I think I like him better when he's trying to measure up to Norm. And Patrick's a sensitive guy. I wouldn't want to know my mother died that way. It wasn't a slow death or a hard death—not if you're used to cancer—but still."

"Maybe Matt stayed sixteen forever because he was frozen by the shock. And I know Patrick wants to know. He told me not knowing is *hell*."

"Then why in *hell* doesn't he ask me, pardon my French?"

Penny can find no plausible answer.

"That was something your dad used to say, about how it's the stories we tell ourselves that cause all the problems. If you look reality straight in the eye, you end up a lot less confused. It's a matter of signal-to-noise ratio. Any story you tell has to be all signal. Any distraction is noise. Anything extraneous is noise. Now try to define *extraneous*. In life, nothing's extraneous. There's no noise. It's all signal. That's Freud. The early Freud."

"He tried to teach me that, but I'm so bad at it. Like just now with Patrick. You're right. I *try* to see past people's narratives. Sometimes I do it right. Like with Rob, my boyfriend. Basically we ended up getting together because I didn't believe a word he said."

"About what?"

"The workings of his body. But I never told him anything either. We were all reality, all the time. As in total lying phonies. We had to take our clothes off to even communicate."

Ed nods and says, "Been there, done that. Right above the level of the physical world, that's where the signals are strongest. Like the colors of the rainbow or the pentatonic scale. You don't need a narrative when you're making love."

"But the second you stop, life gets complicated."

"So you take some time to agree on a beautiful narrative of why and how you met each other. Now, I never managed to make one of those stories work for me more than about six months, but maybe you're more romantic. I'm not a big storyteller. I have to make a conscious decision every time to trust my gut. All my actions feel arbitrary, because I'm not persuasive even to myself. That's how lousy a salesman I am. Makes it hard to live with your own decisions."

"I know," Penny says. "What I usually do is live with them for a while and hope I notice if they suck."

He laughs. "So like I said, I'm not enough of a storyteller to convince myself Matt's a normal guy with some interference and static. I have to assume everything he does is part of the signal. And the signal is on red alert. The Norman Baker Center, proprietor the garbage truck designer who thought Norman Baker was a fraud and a quack. What the heck is that?"

"It's a café bookstore with a yoga studio."

"If he hasn't turned gay on us, there's something bogus going on. What happened to his arrogance? It's almost masochistic."

It occurs to Penny that Ed doesn't know about Jazz. She suspects Jazz of being silent partner to Matt's machinations whether she knows it or not. But she can't tell Ed—the narrative would violate her own privacy—so she reverts to the topic of the past. "Hey," she says. "What do you know about Matt and Mom in Colombia?"

"That, you'd have to ask them. Whatever it was, they were sneaky. I know it upset Katie, but she was easy to upset, and Norm was never sure." After a pause, he adds, "I know he had to take your mother to a gynecologist a couple times, but there's a million reasons for that. I don't want to speculate."

Penny looks down at her hands and says, "You know what? Forget it."

He nods. "The past is gone."

"It's never gone," she says. "It's as real as the present. It's shadows on smoke. And we figure where there's smoke there's fire, and where there's shadows there's light, so there we are, all trying to get to the fire and the light, because of some story we saw in the shadows on the smoke. We're all crazy."

He bows toward her, palms together, thumbs to his forehead, and says, "Bodhisattva." In response to her skeptical look he offers her a cold bottled pilsner from the fridge. She turns it down, saying she's buzzed enough already. He opens the twist-top with a church key (he has arthritis) and toasts her health as she opens the side door and steps cautiously down to the pavement.

She hears drums, loud and fast, coming from under her feet. "I am so fucked-up right now," she says.

AT THREE MINUTES TO TWO, Matt goes downstairs for the grand opening. The odor of ganja intensifies with each downward step. Like a dollop of foam on the quadruple espresso of his anxiety now is the question of how a visit from the police might affect his personal safety and property rights.

Dancing on the porch, where he couldn't see him from the roof, is someone he did not expect to encounter again in this lifetime. Rob.

Nope, no way. Not expecting to see the dickless wonder ever again. Especially not here. Not doing the pogo to Beninese voodoo like it's Black Flag. Not standing foursquare and seeking eye contact like some kind of faggot, holding out a big, calloused, working-class hand to shake. "Hey!" Rob says with a friendly smile.

Matt gives him a swift fake hug—left hand around shoulder, right fist punching car key into wound from previous fight—and says, "Get off my porch."

Listing to the left, in significant pain, Rob says, "I hear Jazz didn't want your baby."

Matt says, "That's it, cocksucker. Prepare to die."

Frowning, Kestrel taps Matt on the shoulder. She glances at the car key in his hand and looks up hurriedly. "Excuse me, Matt. Did you just say 'Prepare to die'?"

"It's a figure of speech."

"That kind of language is *not* in accordance with principles of nonviolence, and I'm going to have to ask you to leave."

"It's my grand opening in two minutes. If anybody has to leave, it's this shithead."

"The Baker Center is part of our movement for social justice and peace. Violence, whether physical or verbal, is *always* inappropriate. We can discuss this at the next collective gathering, but right now you have to take a time-out."

"You're my employee, Kestrel."

"That doesn't exempt you from observing nonviolence! Go upstairs and come back in an hour. If you don't, I'll tell everyone to go home. Violence has no place—"

"Go fuck yourself," Matt says. He pushes her against the door as he reenters the house. "Fucking *fuck* you," he adds to Cassidy as he passes her. He climbs the stairs to his apartment, eager to wash Rob's bodily fluids off his hand.

Kestrel asks Rob, "What on *earth* did you do to him to get him so pissed off?"

He raises his T-shirt, now sporting a pink stain of blood and lymph, to show her his left-hand waistline. "He put me in the hospital because he caught me in bed with Jazz. That's why we left town."

"He must be *so* possessive."

It is two o'clock. Kestrel turns to face the crowd.

She has to yell a bit before the drummers quiet down. At last she is able to bid hello and welcome to everyone.

In response, the Norman Baker fans chant, "We want Penny! We want Penny!"

"Penny?" Kestrel says, looking around. "Does she want to say something to open the Center? Somebody definitely should. Is she here?"

Penny is in the street, swaying ecstatically at the center of a mob. Her admirers interrupt her and direct her toward the front steps of the house.

She mounts them unsteadily, like a child dizzy from spinning around. At the top she turns this way and that to get her bearings. Kestrel arrests her rotation so that she faces front.

Seeing the crowd in front of her, she begins to speak.

"Welcome to the Norman Baker Center," she says, as loudly as she can. She's not sure how loud that is, but she gets the impression she's audible. "My friends. I love you all. I'm so happy!"

Briefly drowned out by applause, she considers stopping right there. Hands folded in front of her mouth, she adds in a near-whisper, "I need to talk to my dad." Her tone is pleading and trusting, like that of a three-year-old saying it needs its sippy cup.

"Speak up," Kestrel says.

"He taught me so much, but I was too young to get what he was getting at, most of the time." Speaking seems more difficult than usual. A potential rest stop appears before her like a flashing highway sign, and she raises her voice to call out, "Hey, Mom! Why don't you get up here and tell them about Dad!"

"No!" Amalia shouts. "I'm not Norm's woman!"

Penny says, "Say what?"

She searches the audience, shading her eyes. Amalia is swallowed up by the mass of people around her. She is too short for anyone on the porch to see where she might be standing. Tony waves his ball cap helpfully. She can see that they are quite far away. Young people in the crowd begin to relay Amalia's statement to the front with the human microphone, à la Occupy, but the effort peters out due to the Norman Baker fans' unfamiliarity with Occupy procedure and their unwillingness to shout that they aren't Norm's woman.

Penny's phone rings—Amalia. She takes the call.

"I can't be Norm's voice," Amalia says. "You are still your father's child, but I'm with Tony now."

"Wow," Penny says, impressed and dismayed. "You forgot about him already?" As a response she can almost see—in fact she does see, due to all the THC—Amalia rolling her eyes. "What should I say?"

"His ideas."

"Which ones?"

"The river?" Amalia prompts her. "The cosmic snake?"

Kestrel taps Penny's arm. "You're in the middle of a speech," she advises her.

Penny puts her arm around Kestrel's waist and drops the phone on the floor. While Kestrel stoops to pick it up, she raises her eyes to the restless crowd and calls out, "Life is alive! All is one!"

This time the human microphone works. The Norman Baker people, having gotten the idea, adopt it as their own. "Life is alive!" the crowd echoes. "All is one!" Applause, in the form of brief outbursts of dancing and drumming, spreads down the street with the two phrases.

"Life is a river made of life!" Penny shouts.

She pauses to let the microphone do its work, her claim resounding four or five times as it makes its way through the crowd.

"Life flows downhill, but it rises again like the water cycle! Or a snake? I am way too stoned to be doing this."

The human microphone develops some technical difficulties. She has to admit that her pronouncements lack the note of celestial wisdom she is aiming for. Feeling thirsty, she releases Kestrel and says, "Sorry about that. I'm usually a better public speaker."

Kestrel leads a final round of cheering and applause and announces that Baker Books is now formally open. In response, several people come inside to drink tap water and use the bathroom.

ROB FINDS PENNY AT THE side of the house, examining a bed of lavender. She appears to be deep in thought. He whispers her name so as not to startle her.

"Rob!" she says. "Boy, am I glad to see you. We need to talk. I found out some really crazy stuff."

"I need to head out," he says. "I played a scene from *Hamlet*. I should get home before Matt remembers what happened to Hamlet."

"First promise me you'll always be nice to him."

He strokes her hair and says, "Baby, have you lost your mind?"

"Swear!" she insists. "Swear you'll always go easy on Matt."

"All right, I swear. I have to go. We'll talk later. Call me when you're done. I'll come pick you up."

In front of the house, he unlocks his bike from the signpost it shares with Penny's. On further reflection, he uses his own lock to lock her bike down twice.

It is Tony who finds her after she gets stuck in the backyard. She wants to swim in the pool—a crumpled sheet of blue vinyl, spiked with rusting struts—and the branches are scratching her, plus doing something confusing when they touch each other, making this noise. She has numerous mosquito bites, which itch like crazy, some on her body, some (somehow) on or under her dress. She is quite delighted to see Tony. He summons Amalia by phone to help put her back together. They load her into the Taurus and deliver her to Rob at Tranquility. He cleans her up and puts her to bed.

She is happy. She looks it, and she feels it. She drifts into sleep, breathing fresh, noisy air. She feels how strength and life flow into her with every breath. "Life is also air," she proclaims.

"It's totally air," Rob agrees, not looking up from his book.

LATE IN THE AFTERNOON, MATT comes down to the café to accept the congratulations of his father's old friends. His mood can be described as very, very bad.

He feels bad. Also angry, which is less unpleasant but more of a spur to action. Still he stays calm. What else can he do? In the last analysis, everything is fine. He has supplanted Rob. Commerce can begin. Even his father's old friends are paying for their tea. Jazz isn't there, but as the Bread song says, it don't matter to him.

IN THE MORNING PENNY GETS up at half past six, feeling groggy. She puts on panty hose, a tight blue suit, and platform pumps. She teases her hair with a viscous product and pins it into a chignon. She sneaks downstairs to make coffee and call a cab to the PATH station.

No one else is awake—except Rob, who comes into the kitchen in his sleepwear and says, "Who are you, and what have you done with Penny?"

"I'm her earthbound other self, 'money-Penny.' Get it?"

"Well, I hope you have a very good day, because it's a very hot look. I might be interested in taking it off you when you get home." He pours himself a cup of coffee to take back to bed. "God, I remind myself of Tony."

"As long as you don't remind *me* of Tony."

"It's those shoes," he says. "They make your skirt twitch around when you walk." He grabs her around the hips and gives her a damp and elaborate kiss. "Who needs money? Let's go upstairs."

"No chance," she says. "Especially not now that I know what turns you on. The management consultant look. This outfit cost seven hundred dollars, so if you don't mind, I have to go occupy Wall Street now."

"We don't have to take long."

"I am *way* too tired to have sex."

"You're not too tired to go to work!"

"It's not like I'm a waitress, or operating a jackhammer or something. All I have to do is get to Manhattan and sit down."

"Looking at you, the financial crisis makes a lot more sense to me," Rob says.

HER FIRST DAY OF PRESENTATIONS in darkened rooms with her fellow global commodities market analyst trainees in the investment banking division of Big Bad Bank is grave, dignified, and uneventful. She goes out with her classmates after work, for just one drink. She heads home to Tranquility bleary-minded and happy.

And there's Rob, waiting for her in bed, reading a magazine! She couldn't be happier. She can't think of anything that has happened lately without just feeling happy as all get-out. She fucks him in a trance state and falls asleep, rising the next morning at six-thirty to shower.

Rob isn't as passive as he looks. He feels an avid longing to move to a house with a space where he might set up his tools and work on bikes. He even knows which house he wants. He just can't see how to get it yet.

THE NEXT MEETING OF THE Baker Books Collective (they refuse to call themselves employees) takes place without Matt. They can hear him upstairs moving around. They ring his doorbell. They text him. He stays upstairs.

There is consensus that his behavior must be censured. Kestrel is charged with speaking to him.

It takes her two days, but she catches him coming home from work and asks for a word in the hallway. About twenty seconds into her formulaic and pompous explanation of anarchist collective protocol, he fires her.

"You can't do that."

"Yes, I can. Take your shit, leave my bookstore, and never come back."

The other employees walk out with her. He has to lock the door himself.

THE DOOR STAYS LOCKED FOR two weeks while Matt hires experienced booksellers from Brooklyn. The store reopens discreetly. No customers come.

None. Zero. Hashtag: *#boycottbakerbooks*. The movement's Facebook page demands collectivization of the store and removal of the violent profiteer Matt.

The meeting rooms and yoga studios are bustling centers of community activity, but no one orders a coffee in the bookstore. No one eats a cake pop. No one buys a novel. In their spare time (they have nothing but spare time), the Brooklynites try to launch a mail-order business. They ask Matt for a capital injection.

Matt announces on Facebook that he is firing the Brooklynites and closing the store. Unceremoniously, the store closes.

THE NEXT DAY, IT REOPENS. Matt comes by after work to find Kestrel manning the register. Feather is in the act of selling a large latte with three shots of espresso to Jacob in exchange for one dollar in tips.

Matt turns back toward the door and sees that the lock is broken. A heavy new padlock—not his—dangles from a hasp. He walks up the stairs to his anarcho-pied-à-terre, ignoring the Center staff and patrons to the best of his ability.

Soon DJD takes over staffing the café in rotation. Within a month, the store is consistently filled with people. In addition to books, magazines, and vinyl, it sells T-shirts, tattooing pigments, condoms, one-hitters, vibrators, and unusual shades of hair color in large bottles. When it rains, the Children's Garden shelters in the children's section—a carpeted corner filled with toys and dirty, dog-eared books that will remain forever unsold.

IN NOVEMBER, MATT STOPS COMING around.

He stops coming around because his Real Time Crime friend discovers Jazz back on the grid. Her pattern of communication with Rob and Sorry emerges on a throwaway phone in a woodland shantytown on Oahu. Immediately he adds her to the no-fly list.

Now say thnx, it wasn't easy, he texts Matt. No surveil on Kurds, we're arming them now WTF?!

Sorry, he adds, is never far away, except when Jazz goes down to Waikiki Beach, which she does at such regular intervals that he has to assume she has a job there.

Matt takes a break from his new hobby of buying up houses near the Baker Center to go in search of Jazz.

Her phone lacks GPS. Finding her is a matter of triangulation. It's imprecise. He stakes out the waterfront for two fruitless days in heavy rain.

Aware that he's making a tactical error, he drives into the hills and hikes to the squatter encampment where she lives. He chooses early morning, hoping she'll be at home and asleep. It's a forest of plywood shacks and moldering portable homes, half a mile up a logging road popular with mountain bikers. There's a café with one table and two chairs to raise money selling the bikers lattes and hash. The usual psychedelic barber poles, mandalas, and towers of junk. It reminds him of Pippi Longstocking's place, if she and her friends had been flabby nudists.

There he sees Sorry emerging from a composting toilet—an outhouse high in the air, perched on a rotating drum of sawdust—only after she sees him. They don't converse. Immediately, she starts yelling. She calls him bad names. A crowd gathers. The one question she answers, she answers with, "In your dreams, asshole." Then she returns to cursing him.

"Jazz!" he shouts. "I know you're there! Jazz!"

In an old narrow-gauge caboose at the edge of the settlement, a woman Jazz is about to massage says to her, "You hear that? Somebody's looking for you."

Jazz warms ylang-ylang oil by rubbing her hands together. Placing them motionless on the woman's back, she says, "That's my fiancé. We're getting married the day I turn fifty."

"Congratulations," the woman says.

Matt slogs away through mud that reminds him unpleasantly of his last encounter with Sorry. He sits in his rental car next to the trailhead for the rest of the day, but he doesn't see Jazz. She takes a different path to catch her bus to where she works late, washing dishes at a dinner theater. She turns off her phone. The next day, using Sorry's Social Security card and driver's license (it's an old picture), she lands a twenty-eight-day gig standing in the galley of a fishing vessel. A day later she is on the ocean, learning Tagalog.

HE FINDS HER, JUST ONCE. Passing outside a massage parlor between the convention center and the boardwalk, he is accosted by a Romanian girl who looks like her. She pleads with him, saying, "I want you all night long." She holds out one hand to him, pressing the other against her abdomen, as if to prepare or protect it—a pitiful wisp of a girl, too hungry, too young. Motives the same as any woman's. The human condition gives her no choice but to make love or die.

The gesture makes him think of whirling dervishes dancing with one hand pointed at the sky and the other at the ground. Power flows through them. A gesture of the purest femininity. He almost blows the sixty bucks. Then he thinks, Hell, I can't fuck this girl. She's too weak. Transmitting my power would destroy her. He imagines coming inside her and watching her die—with sadness. The image strikes him as inexpressibly sad.

It also strikes him as completely crazy. He's sober enough to know that much. He breaks into a sweat and runs all the way to the beach. There he sits down on a bench on the boardwalk, breathing heavily.

He rises again to get a drink from a bar below him on the sand. Maybe it's the bar where Jazz works. He always imagines her tending bar.

He recalls her off-kilter walk, her off-center nose, her frizzy curls, her jagged scars, her stubborn, frail body. Her eyes like portholes into space. Say you want her, and she names her price: her life, yours, the loss of everything she owns. She doesn't hesitate. She acts. He thinks, When the world was empty and void, her drama and grace called me into being, and now there are two of us in the whole world.

These philosophical reflections make his balls hurt. As the bartender hands him a double Scotch, he can barely suppress a cry of pain.

"I know," the bartender says. "I wouldn't call it a double either."

Collapsed in a lounger, he views the steady stream of foot traffic along the water's edge. Self-confident women draw past in bikini tops and fluttering sarongs. They turn dark, blank eyes on him—big bug-eye sunglasses, some mirrored, some brown. Their bodies remind him of thoroughbreds before a race. Pure brainless restlessness, restrained by the calculations of jockeys. No worries wrinkle their brows. They are sex-mongers carrying their wares to market. Their femininity is pure sham.

He reflects that while his emotions will surely fail to be satisfied in any way by sex with one of these women, his body may calm down quite a lot. He invites a woman of about thirty-five to his hotel room, buys her liquor from the minibar, and takes her to bed.

It's a relief. She seems to value their tryst for its quickness alone, for the opportunity it affords her to appear blasé. Briefly, when he first slips a finger into her cunt, she plays coy—*what a sickening parody of innocence, what a distasteful travesty of feminine weakness,* he thinks as she turns her head away—saying, "What am I even doing here? I was just taking a walk! I need to get back!"

He resists the urge to slap her. He pushes her away and says, "Oh brother. Now you're going to say this wasn't consensual." She responds by reaching for her purse and extracting four strawberry-flavored condoms. Four! Each no doubt traceable to her credit card and preferred customer program at her drugstore chain of choice. To Matt they look like little certificates of indemnity or papal indulgences. She puts one on him with her mouth.

Fondling her brittle hair, he resolves never to buy a condom again. Servicing men is her art form, the challenge she has set herself in life—as a feminist, most likely. He laughs aloud, and she looks up. He gives her a gracious smile, and she goes back to work.

He doesn't know her last name or anything about her, except that she lives in Texas, comes to Hawaii every year around this time, and (presumably) likes strawberries. Does she have a husband or kids? He has no clue. He guesses she has a husband, and that this husband's erotic ideal is the flat-rate Thai body massage. In New York, he tells himself, she would be single (marriage there is how people retire from sex, not how they start), rifling through his pockets for his wedding ring while he takes a piss, extracting sixty dollars from his wallet for a taxi to Bedford-Stuyvesant. Furthermore, she would wish to do this again tomorrow, and within a week she'd be getting creative—as in competitive—trotting out her bag of tricks (ceramic strap-on, opera tickets her boss gave her) in hopes of holding his interest. No such thing as safe sex in New York. And let's not even talk about Vegas—

The woman interrupts his reverie by pushing him down on the bed to fuck what she apparently thinks is a full erection. Her lube: strawberry. When he corrects her position to be more to his taste, she thanks him. When he's done, she jumps up like a sheep after shearing, saying she needs to get back.

So get back, he thinks.

He in turn goes back to the beach, where he scores again. Back to the room, where the minibar has been restocked. He's starting to like Hawaii. His return flight gets back in two weeks.

MATT TAKES THE TIME TO look around, using the same proud, blank gaze the adulteresses use on him. Not a look trying to do the impossible—see through walls, or through women's eyes into their brains. Just to catch all the signals. The "What's in It for Me" gaze of the mature adult.

What he sees are high prices, low wages, a well-funded public sector reliant on tourism, heat, humidity, and strong seasonal fluctuations in garbage volume, all working together to create optimum conditions for profitable importation and maintenance of the world's most discreet, silent, odor-reducing, micro-compacting, ultrapremium garbage truck.

He can sense it. Hawaii wants his truck. He can't walk the streets without seeing its streamlined, iridescent blue-green form glide by—in his mind's eye and nose—spreading an odor of putrescence and decay, but only barely.

He goes to see some people and drops some business cards. Immediately he gets Hawaiian traffic on his Web site. He plumbs some bureaucrats by phone and hears the jangle of low-hanging contracts.

He has an urge to slap himself in the face and say, "What were you doing!" Some people were born to live out their lives in Jersey—people like Amalia. He hereby grants those people leave to live and die in situ and play Billy Joel at their funerals. Others have the sense to move up and out.

Ever judicious, Matt blames his mistake on sibling rivalry. If only Patrick hadn't moved to the South Pacific first.

But that doesn't matter now. He's past all that. He's on a move.

But of course his assembly plant is in Bayonne, and his employees (judging by what he knows of them) were born to live and die in Jersey.

It's a logistical challenge. It's daunting. He doesn't want to break in new contractors. And he doesn't relish moving his whole shop to Honolulu. Real estate there is out of sight.

But shipping is cheap. Shipping is in the basement.

He thinks day and night. The women he picks up think he must be very creative and important, because he jumps out of bed to write in a spiral notebook he keeps locked in the hotel room safe. He keeps his phone turned off, happy that industrial espionage hasn't yet mastered the remote monitoring of pencil points.

He doesn't go looking for Jazz. He thinks of her only tangentially, as a medium-term goal, like his new company. He defers gratification as never before. He has never wanted anything so much, and he has never been so methodical about waiting. It's a brand-new skill for him, though most children are said to develop it by the age of five.

When he gets back to New Jersey, he begins exploratory negotiations. He hopes to liaise with a certain publicly traded waste management company and site his new plant in a special economic zone near the Korean DMZ. His two senior engineers express interest in signing on. Matt is poised to become seriously rich and Hawaiian.

AT THE BAKER CENTER, THREE weeks pass without a Matt sighting. Then, on a Wednesday night at eight, he is seen departing through the café, carrying a large cardboard box and a laptop case.

It's the talk of DJD. In general they don't pay much attention to Matt. When he passes through the café, he creates a faint ripple of bad vibes. What he does up in the apartment, nobody knows or cares. He doesn't seem to spend much time there. Just marking his territory, they guess.

But now he has departed the premises with a big box of stuff and his home computer. That can only mean one thing: he means to rent his place out furnished.

A low sibilance is heard in Jersey City as anarchists begin to consider how much they would pay for a location that ideal and enviable, and who might work as a share. Strangers sidle up to bookstore staff and find roundabout ways of asking for Matt's contact information. They say it's confidential. Kestrel is designated to text him and ask about his plans.

He doesn't answer.

Four days pass before Anka hears about it from Sunshine. Evidently he is the only person she ever speaks with who doesn't hope to take over the apartment himself. Immediately, she calls Rob.

LATE THE NEXT MORNING, ROB goes to the café.

He doesn't much like it there, since it used to be his kitchen and bathroom. To the DJD residents staffing it, he's still Rob the rat fink who put Susannah out of commission—that's Anka's theory on what they think, at least, and he has no reason to disagree with her. They don't look at him or talk to him.

All those sporty young women who used to be so nice! They treat him with disdain now. They ignore him. So he doesn't know whether his plan for the retaking of Nicotine can work.

Kestrel is their leading personality, and when he gets there she has a shift, just as Anka said she would. He asks her straight-out what she thinks of him. She responds by asking how things are going with Penny.

"Great," he says. "Why?"

Kestrel looks sad.

"I said great. She's wonderful. We're perfect together. What's wrong?"

"I don't know."

"Come on. What is it?"

"I'm sorry." She turns back to the espresso machine and wipes her eyes.

"Please tell me. I came here to find out what my rating is with you guys."

"I believed that you were asexual," she says. "I guess it took a new kid on the block to see the obvious truth."

"Kestrel."

"I was so *blind*. And now you're a *couple*. You blew off Jazz for her. I mean, Jazz! You must be so in *love*." Her tone is tragic. She turns away to clean dried froth off the milk steamer attachment with a rag, rather too vigorously.

"We're not a couple," he assures her. "I was always polyamorous, and I still am. I'm just picky, and slow on the uptake. I never notice when women have crushes on me. It really helps to tell me flat out. Seriously. I'm grateful."

She turns, and her look brightens. "You want some Cake Zero?" she asks. "It's free." (The name is by analogy to Coke Zero, because when a recipe is free of that many allergens, it's easier just to say what's in it.)

He points at the millet-butternut-safflower variety and says, "This one looks good. You know, Kestrel, there's one kind of sexual freedom, which is doing whatever you want with whoever wants to. But there's also another kind, which is feeling relaxed enough to do anything at all. Sometimes I think I don't need a lot of—you know—housemates looking over my shoulder?"

She cuts him an extra-large piece and lets it fall on a plate with trembling hands. She takes a deep breath and says, "There's something I've been wanting to tell you."

"What?"

"Matt moved out. He took his shit and left like five days ago."

"That's interesting."

"I'd see a lot more of you if you lived here like you used to. Everybody knows you built this house. You should occupy it."

"Hmm," he says. "And you don't think I sold out the climate march?"

She lowers her voice. "You know why the climate march was such a massive fail? The fucking Freedom Tower, that's why. And that was Sunshine's idea."

"He's a dork," he says through a mouthful of cake.

"I think he's a *cop*."

He nods, busy eating.

He gathers his strength. He walks upstairs—past the steamy yoga studio full of women high on the placebo effects of folic acid, past the legal aid office, where Rufus is revealing his identity to a law student who thinks he qualifies for the GI Bill, past the Internet radio station dispensing nutrition advice from an MP3 recorded in Tulsa in 1999, past the workshop full of puppeteers in various stages of blissful self-delusion. In their midst stands Stevie, dressed as a jubilant gray prophylactic. It's a dolphin costume that's not quite working yet, but there's still time until the oceans summit.

He kicks in the door of the elegant apartment on the roof, and he and Penny move in.

PENNY DOESN'T KNOW ABOUT IT for several hours, because she has meetings. As soon as she hears Rob's message, she calls him back.

"Yay!" she says. "I never thought I'd get to move into Nicotine!"

"I wouldn't call this Nicotine exactly," he says. "It's so pretty and sparkly. The furniture is all beech and birch and white suede and cashmere on random-width pine flooring, and this rug I'm lying on, it's so soft, I can't even describe it. You know I fucking hate Matt, but the first thing I did when I got in here was take off my shoes."

"It's not surprising. He's a designer."

"Well, my work is done. There's nothing I need to do on this apartment except try not to get it dirty."

"How are the appliances?"

"You're the expert. I don't know what half of them are."

"That's so great. You know what you could do? Landscape the backyard and open up the back door. The kids could play back there instead of spending all their time in the store. It would have access to the garage. You could teach them to fix bikes!"

"Like a sheltered workshop, but with toddlers."

"Okay, maybe not. I was just thinking you could expand and employ somebody. The unemployed or whoever. Maybe you could get it subsidized?"

"There's a reason anarchist work is unpaid. Wages are for getting people to do stuff they don't like doing. That's why the minute a guy becomes your employee, he starts hating you. You know the IWW slogan? 'The working class and the employing class have nothing in common.' If somebody wants to fix bikes, they can borrow my tools and I'll show them stuff. I work with those people all the time. But I'm not going to bribe anybody to pretend to like doing what I do."

"I'm sensing that your economic ideal is long-term sustainability rather than growth."

"Yard work is unskilled. I'll go home and get our stuff, and tomorrow I'll found a collective to clean up the backyard so we can sit out there."

WHEN PENNY IS DONE TALKING to Rob, she calls Matt (on his cell, in what she assumes is Bayonne) to say she's taking her quarter of the Baker Center. "Because it's my fair share," she explains.

"Like I need that kind of penny-ante distraction in my life," he says. He is sitting in the lobby of an office building in Honolulu, waiting to be escorted upstairs. "Take the whole house. See if I give a rat's ass."

"All right! I will!" she says.

"You're welcome!"

Matt puts the phone in his pocket and types an e-mail on his laptop:

> Hotness. Hope you're well. I just gifted your house to Penny and her boyfriend He-Man. Even Steven? Question: Spear fishing on East Asian partner's humble oceangoing yacht, weekend after next. Skill in harpooning sea turtles in the eye from 4-5 feet away de rigueur in these circles but not a strict requirement. We'll talk. The pros he hires are not brilliant conversationalists. Birth control is on the house.

THE NEXT AFTERNOON, JAZZ REPLIES to him.

> I wrote some poems about ex-lovers like I sometimes do. Meaning you and Rob. I'm reading them Friday at 9 in that pinkish yurt you may have noticed when you came to visit. Sorry will be there. If you can sit still through that, we're cool. P.S. You'll need a real flashlight. It's the new moon. No phone is bright enough.

MATT WRITES BACK,

> I'll be there. I won't be bored. Thank you. I'm already less bored. You know I was crazy about you. Literally insane. I might put some serious effort into making it tolerable for you to be around me. I'm not sure how yet, but I believe in my heart it can be done.

ABOUT THE AUTHOR

Nell Zink grew up in rural Virginia. She has worked in a variety of trades, including masonry and technical writing. In the early 1990s, she edited an indie rock fanzine. Her books include *The Wallcreeper, Mislaid,* and *Private Novelist,* and her writing has appeared in *n+1*. She lives near Berlin, Germany.